A DATE WITH THE DEVIL

The rain intensified. The sound of it, drumming on the car, unnerved Alison; her heart was pounding . . . pounding . . .

Too late she realized the sound wasn't coming from within. Something was speeding toward her car. Something big, black . . . Impossible. A horse-drawn coach, coal-black as sin. For one heart-stopping moment she looked up and saw large hooves, a wild mane, a thick neck—

Alison screamed and hit the brake. The car slued around; she fought to control the wheel.

They have no heads.

Both driver and beast. Headless. Just thick stumps oozing blood.

The car skidded into the trunk of a massive oak, and Alison was thrown violently to the side, her head cracking against the window.

After a moment, she heard a scratching sound. She turned her head . . . and screamed. Blackness took her then, but not before she had seen it: red eyes; a mouth full of long, sharp teeth; a frothing muzzle dripping gore, agape and grinning. Evil.

DEVIL'S GATE

ELIZABETH ERGAS

PINNACLE BOOKS
WINDSOR PUBLISHING CORP.

To Bosworth Hannibal Bear and his Dad

PINNACLE BOOKS

are published by

Windsor Publishing Corp.
475 Park Avenue South
New York, NY 10016

First printing: April, 1991

Printed in the United States of America

The Beginning

I

Eleazar Fortune

The rain started at midday and fell steadily, inexorably, throughout the afternoon. In the curve of the notch, back where the land was fertile enough for farming, the fields quickly reached the saturation point. The farmers, helpless, could only stand and watch as crops on the point of harvest drowned in a matter of hours.

Still the rain fell.

By early evening the river that ran behind the fledgling town had risen alarmingly, and still there was no sign the rain would stop.

By six o'clock the call for help went out.

The mill.

By nine that night they feared it was doomed. Nevertheless they worked. Covered in mud, with clothing plastered to bodies aching from exhaustion, they stuffed burlap sacks with the clay of the land and piled them on the riverbanks.

Still the water rose. Every man and boy and woman and child lent a hand, for if the mill went, so would the town. It was that simple.

For a time they kept pace. Hope, so necessary a part of the human condition, infused their will. They bent their backs and worked even harder. The rain poured down.

By midnight they started to fear for themselves. Now only a small knot of men still worked, the hardiest and those in

5

such despair they didn't know enough to drop where they stood. The women and children were long since gone, sent home to salvage what they could, to pack for what would likely be a hasty retreat. Flood was on their minds.

Samuel Pate, drunk with exhaustion, was the first to hear it. "What's that?" he shouted. John Peacham, eyes wild and staring, lurched up over the makeshift levee to stand beside him. Samuel grabbed his arm, leaned in close to his ear to be heard above the roar of the river and the rain. Always the rain. "What's that?" he screamed again.

Zenas Hutchins let out a yell, recognizing the sound for what it was. Like one already dead he turned toward the mountain from whence it came.

"Slip! The mountain's coming down!" William Hale, never the bravest, turned to run.

"Where do you think you're going?" A big, mud-grimed hand clamped down hard on William's shoulder. "We're all dead men unless we do something."

William stared unbelievingly into the stone-hard face of Eleazar Fortune. "Are you crazy, man? Run, run whilst you've got the chance." He tried to brush the hand from his shoulder, but the grip only tightened.

"No one's running."

Amos Gilman, his pale red-rimmed blue eyes the only thing not smeared in mud, intervened. "Let 'im go. He's right. There's no saving the mill. Let 'im go. I say. It's ev'ry man fer hisself now. Any fool c'n see it."

"It's not impossible."

"You're a fool, Eleazar Fortune," John Peacham cried. "The mill is doomed. Good God, man, look about you. We'll die if we stand."

"We're dead either way. We might as well die trying."

"Y'er a fool and ye'll be twice damned," Amos Gilman yelled. "Think of yer family. Yer sons."

Eleazar turned his back on them and started for the mountain. The rain was icy cold, washing the mud from his head and face, plastering his dark curls down. They all knew he would do what he had to do, if need be, wedge his broad

6

shoulders into the earth, if only to buy a few moments more.

"Fool!" Amos Gilman spat.

They all stood and watched him walk away. The rain continued to pelt the earth. The swollen river roared with swift-moving destruction past the temporary banks.

Zenas Hutchins took several steps after Eleazar. Samuel Pate put a warning hand on the younger man's chest. "Don't throw your life away, son."

"But, perhaps—"

"No! It's over. There's nothing to be done." Sadly Samuel shook his head.

The others took it for a signal. They picked up their shovels and turned to leave.

Suddenly a stranger materialized out of the dark wet night. It took several moments for weary brains to register that there was one among them who wasn't covered from head to foot in odorous black ooze. Tall and broad, the stranger commanded attention without a word. They formed a rough semicircle before him. He smiled. "I can save the mill."

"Who are you?" Abel Crandell asked.

The stranger smiled again and they all knew it didn't matter who he was, only that he was there. He waited silently, imperturbably, as if the ice-cold rain were nothing more than a spring-kissed breeze upon the land.

"How?" It was Eleazar, summoned back by Zenas Hutchins. He strode up to the stranger, through a path hastily made by the silent men. They stood face-to-face, two tall men, both dark of hair with strongly chiseled features as unreadable as stone.

The air turned even colder; ice pellets struck painfully against exposed skin.

The stranger fixed Eleazar with a piercing stare. "The how is not important if you trust me with the task."

Neither the stranger nor Eleazar moved. They stood with gazes locked: the stranger with a sardonic gleam in eyes as black as night, Eleazar with the beginnings of a terrible

7

knowledge seeping into his soul.

Behind them, Josiah Treadwell shifted his feet. "Let's get going. By the looks of things we ain't got much time."

Wearing a curious expression, Eleazar faced his friends. The men of New Hope, covered in mud, looked like the dead resurrected from unquiet graves. "We need to know —" he began, when Josiah rudely cut him off.

"What's to know? A neighbor helps a neighbor. Ain't that right, friend?" Neither the stranger nor Eleazar said a word. "Ain't that right?" Josiah asked again.

The men began to mumble.

Wild-eyed, Amos Gilman beseeched them. "If he c'n do it, let 'im."

"It's impossible," Samuel Pate said, and spit right at the stranger's feet.

"I can do anything you want. All you have to do is ask." The voice was deep and sure and filled with a dark meaning.

They all started to speak at once, raising their voices to be heard above the rain. Perhaps it was a trick of the dim light, but the stranger seemed to grow in size until he towered over them. The smile that never left his face taunted them from his new, great height as they questioned and argued and struggled to accept that they really had no choice. Finally they fell silent. The stranger searched their faces, each in turn. "Well," he asked, "do you understand? Are you agreed?"

"Yes," they said, but it didn't satisfy him. One by one he made each answer, all twenty-three. "Aye," they said, some loud, some soft, some angry, some afraid. When the last one had pledged, they turned to the mountain. Even from this distance they could all see it now, the water, sluicing down, taking the land, the trees, the rocks as it came. As they stood, watching, the ground began to shake. A roaring sound, wrenched from the bowels of the earth, filled the air.

"Landslide!" Ezra Leavitt cried.

Doomed. The communal thought snaked through their minds. Shoulders slumped in defeat. Despair tainted the air. They had hoped, for one brief moment . . . But now, with catastrophe seconds away, even the staunchest believer among them abandoned faith.

Before them the stranger stood, of normal size, no more now than any of them. Nothing but a man. The cold, dark smile twisted his lips without reaching his eyes. Then he was gone, swallowed up by the night as if he had never been.

The earth beneath their feet began to move as huge chunks of the mountain tore away. Some fell to their knees and began to pray. The more perceptive ones among them suspected it was useless, that by their actions this night they were now beyond the pale.

2

The Present — Monday, December 3
Draconia, NH, 1990

Richard Fortune

Weathered wood, seasoned gray by wind and water; crumbling brick; broken windows; inside, rotting floorboards; nests of mice: certainly not something to stand looking at like a rube at a sideshow. Certainly not with a chill wind whistling down from the mountains, through the skeletal trees, trying with prying little gusts to penetrate the layers of clothing to the warm flesh beneath.

The old mill.

Derelict. Forlorn.

Richard Fortune shoved his hands deep into the pockets of his ski parka; even with the gloves they were cold. He hunched his shoulders against the wind, wondered for perhaps the thousandth time why he felt this compulsion, this *need* to come to this deserted place. It belonged to the birds and bats and rodents and insects, had for many decades.

The landscape appeared desolate under winter's cloak, but he knew it was not. A swift-moving shadow on the snow drew his gaze upward. A red-tailed hawk cruised the leaden sky. All around him were the tracks of its prey, the small mammals and birds that wintered in the notch despite the severe weather. "You're crazy to be here," he shouted to a varying hare. It sat back on its haunches and stared.

He began to laugh. The sound of it filled the silence, rolled outward over the river, still running despite the thick ice padding its banks, and flowed into the hills.

Not for the first time he wondered if he were losing his mind. *Alison*. She couldn't hear; wouldn't listen. Not anymore. He knew now he had driven her away.

He shivered. The icy wind had penetrated to his skin. Miserable, intent on thoughts that tormented him, heedless of the outside world, he turned to leave. A shadow fell across the snow. Man-size. It began to stretch, slowly lengthened into caricature.

Richard stood stock-still, a sudden, unreasoning fear drying his mouth, accelerating his heart, tightening his body into primal readiness. He shaded his eyes against the glare of low sun on ice. A man stepped out from a stand of spruce and began to walk toward him. The stranger's shadow shortened with each step he took. Quickly, almost furtively, Richard looked around. No sign of a car or any other vehicle.

The stranger stopped at the point where their shadows merged. He smiled.

Richard shivered at a sudden blast of icy air.

The stranger's thick black hair remained unruffled by the gusting wind. His attention shifted from Richard to the mill.

Richard turned around. He never knew how long they stood, silent, staring, engrossed by the spectacle of decay. He only knew that at some time he ceased to feel the cold, to be bothered by the biting, icy wind. They talked then, of the mill, of what it could be.

"I can do anything you want," the stranger said.

Richard's thoughts were a jumble of ideas, of plans, schemes so far beyond his means that he had never before dared give them room in his mind. Mixed in with them was the image of Alison, forever lost to him.

"I can do anything you want," the stranger said again, softly, beguilingly, understandingly.

"Yes," Richard replied, understanding. He held out his hand, a gesture instinctive, ingrained.

There was no one there.

3

Friday, December 21
New York City

Alison Crandell Fortune

Manhattan sulked under a leaden sky. A brisk wind, raw
with moisture, swept through the brick-and-glass canyons,
scouring and abrading. It carried papers and dust and parti-
cles of ice, sheared off mounds of frozen snow left from an
earlier storm. Its voice sang a lonely, soulless song.

Alison Crandell Fortune gasped when she stepped from
the revolving door of her office building onto the street. Immediately she hunched her shoulders and turned up the collar of her wool coat until it covered her neck. Her legs were
cold; any other day she would have been wearing boots.

The next figure through the door was tall and lanky and
so swathed in clothing that its sex was not readily apparent.
Winda Green, with a face that belonged on the cover of *Eb-
ony* and a disposition that rivaled the toughest drill sergeant, made a pungent comment about a certain portion of
a witch's anatomy.

Alison smiled despite her discomfort. Hopping from foot
to foot, she tried to peer behind Winda. The wind captured
her shoulder-length dark hair and blew it across her face.
She had to remove several gleaming strands from her mouth
before she could speak. Bulky wool mittens made the maneuver awkward. "Where's Gina?"

"Eckert caught her at the elevator."

"Poor Gina."

"Better her than us." Winda flashed a smile the Cheshire cat would have envied and hooked her arm through Alison's. "Let's go, girl. There's a party waiting."

Laughing, made breathless by the wind, they hurried the few blocks up Fifth Avenue to Rockefeller Center. The restaurant where Neumann, Fox, Greenbaum, Deutsch, Metzger, and Simonson held their annual office party was adjacent to the famous ice-skating rink guarded by the gilded statue of Prometheus. They took a brass-trimmed glass elevator that descended from street level to the concourse below.

"Well, hel-lo," Winda breathed when they stepped out into the restaurant. Once unraveled from scarf and coat, she pointed with practiced accuracy. "The bar is thataway."

Alison ordered sherry on the rocks and took a ladylike sip. Winda had no such reservations. Drinking thirstily from her vodka and tonic, she surveyed the scene. Ice cubes tinkled, people laughed, and little fairy lights entwined in white wreaths winked on and off with a mesmerizing regularity. "Uh, oh, time to go." Before Alison could react, Winda was away in a swirl of camel-colored suede, leaving behind only the heavy fragrance of Opium.

"Give us a kiss, Mrs. Fortune." Alison whirled to confront a grinning Alan Eckert. Over his shoulder Winda pantomimed a close escape. "See, mistletoe." He held the evidence aloft with one hand while the other snaked about her waist, pinning her arm to her side.

"Are you certain?" With her free hand Alison plucked it from his grasp. "It sure looks like bearberry." A passing waiter presented her with the perfect opportunity. Quickly she substituted the bit of greenery for a canapé of rolled smoked salmon and cream cheese on a round of rye bread. She placed the offering in Alan's hand and smiled sweetly.

"Naughty, naughty." He leaned down close to her ear, the arm around her waist preventing retreat. The affable playfulness had all but disappeared.

A chill suddenly feathered down Alison's spine. Her body quivered ever so slightly in reaction. The hand at her waist tightened, pinching her flesh through the thin layer of silk. "We're both adults, baby, and I've got what you need."

Alison stiffened at the crude words and instinctively pushed at his restraining arm. He subjected her to a practiced leer. "Later." He popped the food into his mouth and swaggered away.

Alone, Alison deposited her drink on the nearest table and then rubbed her hands up and down her arms, but the chill that had invaded her bones did not abate. Vulgar as Alan was, he had never before elicited such a response.

"Never mind him. Every firm has one or two like that."

Alison smiled into the concerned hazel eyes of Gina Ricci, one of the other two paralegals employed by Neumann, et al. She shrugged slim shoulders. "He doesn't bother me." Once the words were spoken she realized they were true.

Gina sighed and shook her head of frizzy honey-colored curls. "You've got to give the creep credit. He never stops trying." She nudged Alison. "Look." Across the room Alan approached a woman dressed in a severely styled gray business suit. Gina made a little clicking sound with her tongue. "I guess position doesn't matter. Lois is senior to him, but if you're female you're fair game to his kind. Just look at those moves," she said, her voice filled with reluctant admiration as Alan crowded the woman against a table, using his large frame to intimidate. "I don't know where that man hides his antennae. I only heard about Lois this morning."

"Heard what? Oh!" Alison gasped when another cold chill gripped her. Her spine tingled, as if probed by unfriendly eyes. She whirled about and searched the noisy groups directly behind her. No one seemed interested in her.

"Alison? What's the matter? You're shaking." Gina anxiously tugged on the sleeve of Alison's dress until she regained her attention. "Do you think you have a fever? The flu's going around, you know. Mike told me three people were out from our floor alone this week, and last Tuesday I had to cancel a closing because the attorney on the other side was sick."

"It's nothing." Instinctively Alison hugged herself. "Just a

14

goose walking over my grave." She took another quick peek over her shoulder. The people directly behind her were all laughing. Mike, the boy from the mail room and the source of well over ninety percent of the office gossip, caught her eye and winked.

Reassured, Alison offered Gina a shaky smile. "Sorry," she apologized, but Gina wasn't listening. Something else had caught her interest.

"Look, there's Metzger's new client. The orders on him are strictly VIP treatment all the way." She giggled, an oddly endearing mannerism in a street-wise woman raising a seven-year-old son alone. "Clare says he's as handsome as sin."

Intrigued, Alison followed Gina's discreet nod to a group in a corner of the intimate restaurant. If Clare Bauer, Irwin Metzger's rotund, motherly secretary, made such a comment, the man must be something quite out of the ordinary. Unfortunately, his back was to the room. She had a view of a tall, well-built man with broad shoulders in an expensive tailored suit. Dark hair curled around the collar of his white dress shirt. "The rear view is certainly attractive." She narrowed her eyes assessingly. "He looks young."

"Fortyish, I'd guess."

"You've met him?"

"No, not really. I was picking up a file when he came to see Metzger the other day. I just got a peek." She stopped a waiter and took two glasses of champagne off his tray and handed one to Alison. "Drink. This is the good stuff from France." Alison obediently took a sip. "I wonder if he's married?"

The champagne was very dry and very easy to swallow. "Don't you know?"

"Mmmnn?"

"If he's married?"

"You know I don't gossip." Gina tried to assume an affronted air but failed miserably.

Alison laughed. "That means you couldn't find out."

A sheepish grin flitted across Gina's face. "Clare's a tough nut to crack, but I'm working on it. I do know that he must be filthy rich. You've got to be if you're planning on practically rebuilding an entire town, even if it *is* out in Podunk. Darn," she said, holding up her glass, "this is empty."

Alison discovered her glass was empty, too. They immediately exchanged them. "Podunk was originally a place in Massachusetts, somewhere in the central part of the state, I believe," she said with the careful precision of one whose tongue feels thick.

"No shit?" Gina said, and giggled. "This place is in New Hampshire. Draco something."

"Draconia?"

"Yeah, that's it." She took a healthy swallow of champagne and frowned. "Hey, I thought you didn't know anything about him."

Alison made a wry face. "I don't, but I'm from Draconia."

"No shit?" Gina said again and hiccupped, then looked away when a disturbance across the room distracted her. "Say, look," she pointed, a wide grin stretching her face, "Lois is really giving it to Eckert."

She wasn't the only one to notice. People nearest to the couple turned to stare, most quickly looking the other way as soon as they realized that the nature of the confrontation was not friendly.

"God, who would have thought she had it in her?" Gina smiled with satisfaction as the plainly dressed woman finished whatever she had been saying so heatedly and stalked off, leaving the wolfish Eckert with a dull red stain climbing his neck.

Alison finally made the connection. If God's gift to women was interested, it could only mean one thing. "Then Lois is—"

"Separated. I thought I told you." Gina snorted derisively. "Another target for any creep wearing trousers." Bitterness laced her tone.

Sympathy for Lois Shuman shuddered through Alison. Four years had not dimmed her own experience with the

16

agonies of separation and, ultimately, divorce. "Too bad. Perhaps they'll get back together soon. They have so much going for them."

Gina turned exasperated hazel eyes on her. "This is the real world. Would you be so quick to take back a man who walks out on you and two children under the age of five because he doesn't want responsibility? Could you ever trust him again?"

Hard questions with no real answers, or different answers, depending upon the people. After four years of searching her soul, Alison now knew that she might never have answers to her own particular questions. That in itself was a victory, a difficult lesson learned. She shrugged her shoulders helplessly.

The younger woman shook her frizzy head negatively. "Neither one of us is qualified to answer."

Alison thought about that as she filled a plate with big pink shrimps and little Swedish meatballs swimming in gravy. The caviar looked like black pearls. Neumann, Fox, Greenbaum, Deutsch, Metzger and Simonson always went first class. The cynical thought that they could afford to, since they weren't shy when it came to fee building, flitted through her mind.

She found a place at one of the tables crowded with the younger employees and their spouses. Eliot Weber, a quiet young associate who did mostly corporate work, went to the bar to get his wife a glass of wine and returned with one for Alison also. She thanked him, but couldn't remember if she had requested it or if he had played the gallant. The wine tasted the same either way.

Bonnie Weber, Eliot's wife of six years, was one of those women with only one topic of conversation. In the third month of her second pregnancy, she could converse knowledgeably about formulas and leak-proof diapers and little else. Her disappointment in Alison's lack of interest in her favorite subject was short-lived once she learned Alison was divorced and had no children. Then she became so sympathetic that, without her usual grace, Alison made a hasty

17

excuse and left.

She needed a few moments to herself. The control she usually exercised over any thoughts of her marriage had been battered first by the mention of Draconia and then by young Mrs. Weber. She had thought she had put it all behind her, but the twin assaults only proved how fragile was the protective barrier she had built. And the phone calls . . .

Alison quivered as memories engulfed her. A waiter offered champagne, she accepted, and bolted down half the contents of the glass in one swallow. She was becoming numb; everything except her mind. She didn't want to remember. Hadn't she spent the better part of the past four years trying to forget? Making something of herself? Trying to build a new life?

Holidays were dangerous; they belonged to happy people; they belonged to families. Four years ago . . .

No! It was gone. All of it. The dream had gone sour. Six years of marriage—how many of them good? Two? Three? Four?

She was a different person now. The woman who had lived in New Hampshire had been weak. The new Alison had gone back to school, trained for a career in the legal profession, and become a strong, self-sufficient person. So what if the new Alison was lonely? Was that such a high price to pay for self-esteem?

Alison drained the last of the champagne, and using slightly more force than required, placed the glass on the nearest flat surface.

"Hey, who are you angry with? Did Eckert get fresh?" Winda appeared beside Alison, an audacious grin brightening her dark face. "Want me to go teach him some manners? It would, without a doubt, make my day." She was at her most outrageous as she drew out each word for maximum effect.

Alison offered her only a ghost of a smile. Winda sobered at once. "Got the blues, huh?"

"Don't mind me, Winda. This, too, shall pass."

"Help it along, girl. Now, what I'd do, is hie myself over to Saks, just as soon as I could duck out of here, and buy something sinfully expensive. Then I'd get a creamy cheese-cake and a bottle of wine and go on home for a good cry. Nothing like it, girl, to cleanse the soul."

At that moment someone called to Winda. She left Alison with a farewell bit of advice. "Have an affair," she said. "It's better than cheesecake."

If anything, the well-meant advice left Alison feeling more forlorn. The new Alison was afraid. She wouldn't — couldn't — risk another relationship.

Feeling alone and vulnerable, hemmed in by the noisy, carefree crowd, she sought a quiet place. With a few exceptions, most of the people were congregated in the middle of the room. That left the periphery. One wall of the restaurant was all window. A man in white tie and tails played senti-mental old favorites on a white baby grand piano in front of it. The space behind him was unoccupied.

With a nod for the musician, Alison squeezed past the piano. Outside, skaters whirled around the famous oval where the gilded Titan's magnificent body stretched across one side of the rink. Their breath produced little frosty plumes as they circled. Above everything towered the gigan-tic Christmas tree. She had heard that the Norway spruce stood seventy-five feet tall and sparkled with eighteen thou-sand lights.

She was hot and tired and she should never have had so much to drink, certainly not in such a short space of time. Trying to calm her tumultuous thoughts, she pressed her face to the window and concentrated on one of New York's most fabled scenes.

The cool glass felt good against the heat of her forehead. Round and round the skaters went, twirling and dipping, until to her fevered brain they were all a blur of flashing skates and blending, bleeding colors. She closed her eyes against the gaiety before her and immediately the sensation of eyes probing into her back assailed her again. Her body jerked in response, her eyes flying wide open. She stared, straight ahead, afraid, as an icy-cold finger tapped her spine.

The skaters faded as the window silvered into a mirror. She trembled as a darkly handsome face appeared, grew large, drawing her spirit into deep, all-seeing eyes.

Richard!

Alison forgot to breathe as a panicky feeling lodged in her chest. *He's not real. I've had too much to drink.* She blinked. Richard didn't go away.

She wouldn't turn around. She wouldn't.

To her left a woman laughed, the sound throaty and full of promise. Behind her the piano tinkled.

Alison forced herself to take a breath. She tried to think what would be worse—only to imagine her ex-husband, haunting her, or to actually have him back in her life. The thought of either was insupportable.

His image taunted her. He looked so presentable, so normal, his expression one of cool understanding.

Fraud, she thought, determined to ignore him. She lost the mental struggle and whirled about.

No one. Nothing.

She turned her back on the room for the second time and clamped her eyes tightly closed. Her body was so tense it vibrated. She should leave. Go home to Queens. Take the F train and travel beneath the river, praying the moisture she glimpsed on the tunnel walls as the train flashed past was not the start of the great flood.

The media would love it. XMAS TRAGEDY would blacken the front page. EAST RIVER SWALLOWS COMMUTERS, story, pix, p.3. Probably a centerfold. The print media would be augmented by the evening news. Such a splashy—no pun intended—story would engender a special report. "We interrupt this program . . ."

A hand touched her arm; her muscles jerked in surprised alarm. *Please, please don't let it be Richard.*

"Alison, Mr. Metzger would like you to join him for a moment."

Alison opened her eyes to Clare Bauer's image superim-

20

posed on Prometheus's groin. Dizzy with relief that she didn't have to deal with Richard when she wasn't quite in control, she frowned at the reflection and unwisely said the first words that popped into her head. "Didn't an eagle or a vulture peck out his liver?"

"Alison!"

Clare's affronted squeak wrenched Alison back to cold sobriety. "Oh, not Mr. Metzger!" Shocked that her self-imposed restraints could so easily be upset, she struggled to regain her equilibrium while offering Clare a hasty explanation. "Golden boy, out there." She inclined her head toward the statue. *"Prometheus Unbound.* Shelley, I think. Or Aeschylus. *Prometheus Bound.* They each wrote one, but I can't remember which is which."

Clare's lips twitched ever so slightly. "Either/or, it sounds painful."

Alison smoothed the silk paisley over her hips and nervously flipped her hair over her shoulder. Irwin Metzger was big league. "Uh, Mr. Metzger . . . did he say why?"

Clare shrugged, again the compleat confidential secretary. "I'm only the messenger."

Irwin Metzger, tall, spare, aloof behind old-fashioned wire-rimmed eyeglasses, did not inspire feelings of bonhomie in his employees. Alison was none too pleased when Clare immediately murmured her excuses and left. The senior law partner cleared his throat, for a moment looked as uncomfortable as Alison felt. "Ah, here you are, Mrs. Fortune. I want you to meet someone. Adrian, this is the woman from Draconia."

Alison had been so anxious about being summoned into Irwin Metzger's rarefied circle that she had failed to notice the man standing by his side. Now, as she looked up into eyes as dark as a moonless night, she wondered how she ever could have been so blind. Clare hadn't lied. *As handsome as sin.* She frowned. He looked familiar. The teasing memory vanished as he took possession of her hand in a movement so smooth she didn't realize he held it until she felt the pressure of his fingers on hers. Her world narrowed down to a

21

pair of devouring eyes and the tactile sensation of skin against skin.

"I'm Adrian Blaise," he said in a voice of smoky silkiness as he bent low over her hand.

Alison thought at first that he meant to brush his lips to the air, in the continental gesture so beloved of romantics, but at the last possible moment he turned her hand over. He held her eyes with a compelling gaze for long moments, moments in which the room, indeed, the world, ceased to exist. There were dark promises in those eyes. Erotic promises. She watched with a feeling of unreality, spellbound, as he lowered his dark head and pressed his lips to her palm. She went rigid as his tongue tasted her sensitive flesh.

It was a delicate touch, but it sent fire racing through her veins. Her mind filled with a mélange of disjointed images. So real were they that they transported her out of time and place. Dark, steamy thoughts twined like lovers through her head. Secret delights, forbidden pleasures beckoned. Her body softened, flushed with a painful, wildly escalating passion. She trembled as desire shivered through her like a hot, licking flame. Unbearable ecstasy melted her bones, quivered down her length. *Skin on skin. Flesh sliding on flesh. Hair-roughened legs glided between her smooth ones, parting them.*

Trembling with arousal, she moaned . . . and was back in the restaurant as the senior law partner of one of the most conservative law firms in the United States talked about her hometown of Draconia, about condominiums and renovating the old mill and building a mall with outlet stores and a theater and restaurants.

The anchor to the fantasy was gone. Adrian Blaise no longer held her hand. Feeling disoriented, Alison tilted up her face until her eyes locked with his. From his great height Adrian Blaise regarded her with a faintly amused expression on his handsome face.

Uneasy, Alison frowned, trying to understand why he looked so teasingly familiar.

Mr. Metzger droned on, apparently content with a monologue, not pausing even when Alison suddenly gasped. Her hands clenched into tight fists and her eyes narrowed as she stared at Adrian Blaise, finally realizing that it was his face, not Richard's, she had seen reflected in the window.

Adrian Blaise still smiled at her. *Paranoia!* whispered through her mind, for the resemblance was superficial at best. Shaken, Alison forced herself to relax. Slowly she unclenched her fists until both her hands hung naturally at her sides. The right one had an itchy, burning sensation in the center of the palm. She resisted the urge to examine it.

4

Thursday, January 24

It started to sleet an hour before closing time. Alison heard it from Mike when he whizzed through for the last mail pickup of the day. She had come to depend upon Mike for all weather bulletins in the two years she had been working for Neumann, et al. Her office, a partitioned cubicle, did not have a window. The nearest one was half a city block away.

Today he exuded cheerfulness, despite the gloomy weather. "Anything?" He looked toward her empty out basket. "No? Well, hope ya gotcha boots, beautiful."

Alison looked down at her new leather pumps and sighed. "The weather report on the radio this morning didn't mention rain."

"Whadda dey know?"

Alison smiled and shrugged. She listened to Mike's lighthearted progress down the hall for several minutes before picking up an environmental report on a warehouse in Long Island City. Her eyes skimmed over the padding and went to the important paragraph. There was no trace of asbestos. This removed the last impediment to the bank's granting the owner a mortgage.

When she first became a paralegal, more than three years ago, hardly anyone had heard of such a report, much less demanded one as part of doing business. Now, everyone was going crazy over toxic materials. It had turned into a very lucrative commercial enterprise: first a costly survey and report; then, if you were an unlucky bastard and something turned up, the price of fixing the problem could be astronomical. The legacy of the Industrial Revolution manifesting itself with a vengeance.

She made a note on her calendar to call the bank's legal department for a closing date and returned the report to the proper file. Gina rapped on the partition just as she started to read the riders to a lease for a sublet in a building on Sixty-seventh Street. Their client was in a rush, with good reason. Decent apartments were scarce.

"God, did Mike give you the good news?"

Alison looked up and smiled. Gina had a pencil stuck in her frizzy mop of hair. "About the sleet?"

"Yep. I'm wearing suede shoes, and of course I forgot my sneakers today. How about—" she began when Alison's phone rang.

Alison made a face. "Damn. I hope it's not Mrs. Lowicki. That woman's near impossible." She reached for the telephone, murmured, "Hello, please hold a moment," and covered the receiver with her hand. "How about what?"

"Pizza?"

Alison hesitated, not liking to get home too late, especially now when it got dark early. But eating at home meant a frozen low-calorie dinner heated in the microwave. "Sure."

Gina grinned. "Atta girl." She waved and disappeared around the partition.

Alison took her hand from the receiver. "Hello. I'm sorry I kept you waiting." The line was open but no one spoke. "Hello. Hello?"

No answer.

One more time. "Hello . . . ?" Static crackled loudly. She jerked the receiver away from her ear. That did it. Whoever wanted her could damn well call back.

The receiver was inches from the cradle when she heard her name. ". . . Allliii—son." Very slowly she brought the receiver up to her ear again. It couldn't be. Not here. Not in the office.

Please. God, no. "Hello," she whispered, intuitively knowing the silent prayer was too late. Her muscles tensed, painfully contracting as fear engulfed her.

"Alison."

Just her name. Just her name, yet the voice had the power to hold her, paralyzed, though every instinct she possessed screamed for her to break free. Impossible. Hypnotized, she listened as the voice evoked thoughts and images so carnal, so lewd—so *real*—that her body reacted on some elemental level while her mind recoiled in horror.

Finally, it released her. She slammed down the receiver. Her right palm itched. Slowly she brought her hand up until it was directly in front of her face. A small spot in the center of her palm burned fiery red.

Three of them went out that night. At the last moment Winda Green caught Alison and Gina at the elevators. "Did I hear mention of pizza?" she asked.

Gina groaned. Winda was famous for her exotic tastes. "No anchovies."

Alison, at five feet seven and one-half inches, still had to look up at the lanky office manager. "No olives."

"Done and done." Winda linked arms with the other two. "Now be nice, ladies, and I'll tell you all about the new word-processing software we ordered today."

The restaurant was crowded and noisy and filled with smoke, despite the strict New York City No Smoking Law. They found a table in the back and ordered pizza with mushrooms, sausage, extra cheese, and onions and decided on wine instead of beer. Gina and Winda started a serious discussion on why Gina couldn't lose weight and why Winda's current significant other had changed his cologne.

As the level of wine in the bottle moved downward the possible explanations became very risqué and more and more outlandish. Alison sat tense and quiet. Winda finally rounded on her. "What's shaking, girl? You've been kinda draggin' ass lately."

Gina hiccupped and reached for the last piece of pizza. "Beautifully and succinctly put, Green."

Winda ignored her. "You've hardly said more than three words, not counting 'Pass the wine,' and you had next to nothing to eat. No slur intended, but you're looking mighty white tonight, especially around the gills. Now give, girl."

Alison took a deep breath and then let it out in a whoosh. Why keep it secret? Perhaps talking about it would help. "I've been getting . . . um, *calls* . . ."

"A breather or a talker?" Winda could be merciless in search of information. She leaned forward, her face alive with interest, and snorted cynically at the surprise on Alison's face. "You're still a hick, kid, it sticks out all over you. I bet that back in Monrovia, or wherever you come from, you don't get that sort of thing, but here in the Big Apple, why, it's an ev-er-y day occurrence."

Alison shuddered. Gina reached over and poured more wine into her glass. "Drink." She rounded on Winda. "Can it. It may happen every day, but not to someone we know."

"Well," Winda asked unrepentantly, "which is he?" To her chagrin, Alison began to cry. Winda's big dark eyes filled with concern. She placed a hand on Alison's arm. Even in the restaurant's hazy light the nail tips gleamed blood-red. "There, there, baby," she crooned, "let it out, let it all out."

"I'm sorry," Alison said, and fishing a crumpled tissue from her purse, blew her nose.

"*You* haven't done anything wrong," Gina pointed out indignantly.

"I know. That's what the police said. But, I . . . I feel so . . . so violated. And now, it's happening in the office, too . . . No place is safe anymore." Unshed tears pooled in her eyes, magnifying the large dark-brown irises into twin lakes of misery. She gulped in air, then let it out raggedly. "He . . . he knows my . . . my name. He says *Alison,* draws it out, suggestively. It's like . . . like, he's hypnotized me. I can't hang up. And all the while, in my mind . . . images . . . sexual . . . *lewd.*" She grasped Winda's hand, which still rested consolingly on her arm.

27

Winda squeezed it reassuringly. "How long has this been going on?"

Alison hunched her shoulders disconsolately. "Quite a while—weeks. The first one came at the beginning of January. I changed my number at home. It's unlisted, but I *still* get the calls. And now he's calling *here*."

Gina and Winda exchanged a significant look. It was Gina who spoke. "Uh, Alison, who has your new number?"

"The office. My aunt."

"The one in New Hampshire?"

"Yes."

"Anyone else?"

Alison shook her head. Her hair swung forward, obscuring part of her face. "No."

"What about Dave?" Winda asked. "Isn't he the guy you've been going out with?"

"Dave Franklin? We're not going out in the sense you mean." She frowned, thinking. "Besides, I don't think he ever called me at home. It's more of a casual thing. You know, a call at the office for lunch, or for dinner and a movie the same evening."

Winda looked at Gina, gave a slight nod. Gina gentled her voice. "Anyone else, maybe in Draconia?"

Alison's head snapped up. "You can't mean—" Even now she found it difficult to say his name. It still had power over her. She could still revert to the person she had been four years ago.

"Peculiar name, Draconia," Winda said, trying to ease the escalating tension.

Alison gratefully grabbed for the distraction. "Draco is Latin for dragon. Draconia is named for the Dragon."

Winda's red-painted lips twisted in feigned incredulity. "You have a dragon in New Hampshire?"

Alison took another sip of wine, hoping the slightly rough-tasting liquid could ease the parched tightness of her throat. "That's Dragon with a capital D, another name for Satan."

"As in Lucifer? They actually named a town after him?"

"Uh huh." Winda looked so astounded that Alison found she still knew how to smile. "Draconia started out as New Hope, but legend has it that one dark and stormy night the Devil saved the mill from being washed away. He wedged a huge boulder between the walls of a gorge in the mountain behind the town. Water had started a landslide, and the rock damned it. It's called the Devil's Dam and is Draconia's biggest tourist attraction."

Gina leaned across the table. "That must be the same mill the Mountain Venture group is renovating. Metzger's big client, Adrian Blaise," she explained to Winda. "He's so good-looking he's almost beautiful. The girls on the twentieth floor swoon every time he steps off the elevator. It's gotten so bad that Clare hides Metzger's appointment book."

"Be sure to call me next time he's due in," Winda said. "I could surely use a little titillation in my life." She pronounced it tit-tillation.

Gina laughed. "You have a fat chance. Clare's very protective of him."

"Who? Metzger? That's old news, girl."

Gina blotted oil from her lips with a paper napkin, then wadded it into a ball. "Not him. Blaise. I hear he has pull at a school that specializes in helping kids with Nicky's problem."

"Oh." Winda's flat comment said it all. They all knew how anxious Clare was to get her autistic grandson Nicky into the proper school.

Alison sighed. Her problems paled next to Clare's. "It's late. I'd better be getting home."

"Good idea." Gina began to rummage in her purse for her lipstick.

Alison picked up the check and automatically added the figures. She was preoccupied with doubling the tax to get the tip when Winda quietly asked another question.

"Does your husband have the new number? Would your aunt give it to him?"

"*Ex*-husband," she said automatically and then nodded. "Yes. It's quite possible Aunt Lucy gave him the number. I should have thought about that, but, no, it's not him. He's not making the calls. It's not his style."

Winda shook her head consideringly. "You can't be sure. For my money he's probably the best bet. Besides, from what you've told me, and even more to the point, from what you haven't told me, I'd guess that he's just the kind of creep who would like to lay a bit of misery on you. He sounds like the type to enjoy a nasty little mind game."

Alison sighed. "But—"

"No buts, girl. Call the bastard and tell him you're wise to him. That ought to spoil his fun."

Alison shook her head stubbornly. "Ordinarily I'd agree with you. Richard might indulge in some telephone torture, but not now. The timing's all wrong."

Winda's expressive face twisted into disbelief. "How so?"

"The mill. Richard and his brother Daniel are the major shareholders. It's complicated, but they stand to benefit the most from the real-estate deal in Draconia. In addition to the mill they own much of the land around it. The money that comes in from whatever deal they have made with the Mountain Venture people should go a long way toward giving Richard what he has always wanted. He's probably very happy right now and doesn't need to take out his frustrations on anyone." Impatiently she combed her fingers through her hair, then shrugged. "Besides all that, I'd surely recognize his voice."

"Not necessarily. He could disguise it, you know, run it through a synthesizer or something. I saw a show on—"

"Spare us, Gina. This is real life." Winda rolled her eyes disbelievingly.

"You know . . ." Alison said slowly, then shook her head.

"What? You can tell us. We'll help if we can. Come on, girl, you've thought of something."

"It's nothing," Alison murmured, and rubbed her itching palm up and down against the rough wool of her skirt.

5

**Tuesday, February 12
Draconia, NH**

Lucy Crandell

Lucy Crandell stepped out the front door of the inn she had owned for over fifty years and took a deep breath of the pure, invigoratingly cold mountain air. The night enfolded her—dark and mysterious and somehow oddly comforting. If you lived your life in the mountains you knew your place in the universe.

She shook her head of carefully coiffed silver curls and sighed, her breath escaping into a thin white veil that hovered before her in the still clear air. She had been entertaining too many similar thoughts of late. Overhead, stars glimmered in the black dome of sky, winked and blinked, were born and died. Just like people, only on a far grander scale. Birth and death; she was far from one and close to the other. She experienced no fear at the thought. That is what the mountains taught you, if you heeded them.

A strange, mournful cry suddenly shattered the night's peace. Lucy tilted her head, listening. It sounded again, high-pitched, wild, evoking in her mind a picture of a coyote howling at the moon, but this was the East and that couldn't be. Here, in the heavily forested mountains of Draconia Notch, the closest animal to a coyote was a bobcat, and she doubted that any cat could produce that plaintive gnarl.

Lucy remained close to the door, reluctant to leave the safety of shelter. Because of the configuration of the notch it was difficult to judge where the sound came from, whether whatever made it was near or far. Sounds carried very well in the thin mountain air.

Several minutes passed with nothing to disturb the silence. Lucy crossed the wide front porch and slowly descended the three broad steps to the graveled drive, now hard with packed snow. She walked until she could see the entire building without straining her neck. Dragon View Inn had been owned and operated by Crandells for over one hundred fifty years. It had weathered those years like the Crandells themselves; solid, dependable, like a dowager who had never been attractive so had cultivated character and charm to lure and entice.

Behind the inn loomed the bulk of Dragon Mountain. Lucy shivered and drew the soft blue cashmere scarf, her niece Alison's Christmas present, more tightly about her neck. The trees, the rocks, the solid earth of the mountain had long endured, would be there long after she claimed her own piece of earth.

Although she loved mountains, their grandeur and their changing seasonal faces, she had never liked this one. It stood alone, a monadnock, not connected to the other mountains by high-altitude ridges. She knew it intimately, had hiked its trails, sipped cold water from its streams, bathed in a hidden pool on many a hot summer's day. Once, long ago, she had made love to a fine young man on a bed of fragrant pine needles on its western slope. The man was long dead, his name on a brass plaque gone to green on the war monument in the center of town. Despite the memories, she looked coldly upon the mountain, her spirit straining toward it, trying to ascertain her reasons for such dislike.

Wild, chilling, another eerie howl pierced the frigid dark. Silky. Seductive. Lucy shuddered, gripped by an overwhelming, primitive fear. A second voice joined the first, this one much closer, louder, its uncanny wailing making her skin pucker into goose bumps and the fine hairs on her body stand erect. This time she knew the direction, turned toward the eastern arm of the notch.

It was as if she looked back into time, into the shrouded past. No houses, no lights, no trappings of civilization marred the virgin land. Nothing but the dead lay in that direction, for only the old cemetery was in the eastern curve of the notch.

And the old mill.

Both places of death and decay.

Closer yet, the unearthly baying sliced through the night. Lucy began to shiver, seized by a chill seeping from her soul. A grave, her own, yawned wide. Deep. Black. Waiting. Soon. Sooooon. She almost howled herself, held in thrall by the frightful music.

Twin beams of light pierced the dark as a car turned up the drive toward the inn. By the time the ten-year-old Buick huffed to a stop, Lucy was standing at the foot of the stairs.

"Whatever could you be thinking of, to be waiting outdoors on a night like this?" Bertha Rice remonstrated the moment Lucy slid her body inside with an agility belying her seventy-nine years.

"Death," Lucy replied, "and hello to you, too."

"Old fool," Bertha muttered as she yanked the car into gear. The Buick's transmission screeched, as if reminding the two old ladies that it as well felt the press of years and required a gentler touch.

They drove in silence past the inn, Lucy twisting to view it from the changing perspective. She didn't stir until they swept around the drive. The building with its familiar outline, its windows spilling squares of warmly glowing yellow light on the frigid landscape of snow, the lazy curl of smoke from the great fireplace in the lounge, disappeared from view. Then she faced front, but not before taking a last glimpse of the mountain, darkly mysterious, brooding, immutable. Her eye caught movement in a stand of birch trees sitting in the mountain's shadow, thin white ghosts with naked, knotty limbs. Shadows slithered into shadows. Black into black. Twin points of red gleamed briefly in the headlights. She shivered.

"More heat?" Bertha asked and reached for the controls.

"We're almost there," Lucy replied. The coldness she felt came from her mind.

Bertha concentrated on driving. Although the county people had plowed the road, there were still many icy patches. She risked a quick peek at her lifelong friend. "Feeling poorly, Lucy?" The casual mention of death had scared her.

"Nothing wrong with me."

The tart response brought a smile to Bertha's lined face. "We needn't go tonight, you know. Bert's got this whole thing tied up with a red ribbon. We're just window dressing, is all. Way I heard it, it's got to be put before the voters to make it legal. That's the only reason he's called the meeting. The councilmen are going to vote the zoning changes whatever's said and done this evening. We have to face it, the complex is going to be built whether or not we approve. After tonight Dragon Meadow is going to be a reality."

Lucy sniffed, but didn't say anything. They circled the snow-laden common and found a parking spot near the town hall.

With the engine off, the silence begged to be filled. "Are you sure you're all right?" Bertha's tone was sharp. In the harsh glare of the streetlight she could see something new, something frightening, in Lucy's face. When did all the flesh disappear? How could she have failed to notice that frail, translucent look when she saw her almost every day? Suddenly very fearful, Bertha managed only to squeeze her friend's name past a throat closed tight with dread. "Lucy?"

"Why, whatever's the matter with you tonight, Bertha? You've been carrying on like an old lady ever since you picked me up."

"I *am* an old lady, and so are you." Indignant, her fear temporarily forgotten, Bertha pulled the keys from the ignition.

Lucy laughed, a dry crackling sound that shattered the frozen air. "Chinky chose," she said in the lilting accents of childhood.

Bertha softened her spine. Lucy again looked as she always had. "You had me worried. That talk of death . . ."

"I've lived too long," Lucy said, snapping all Bertha's concerns on to full alert again. "I don't like this world and what it's come to, and I certainly don't like what's going on here."

"Progress—" Bertha began.

Lucy rudely cut her off. "I know what progress is, and this sure as shooting isn't it. This is an abomination. It's rape. Rape of a way of life."

Bertha shook her head sadly. "I know it is, but what can we do?"

"Nothing. We can't do a thing, except tell them how we feel, and that's exactly what I'm going to do tonight. Bert and the rest of the council may push this through, but not before they hear what's on my mind. Besides, they're fooling with things better left alone."

Lucy's vehement statement made Bertha feel uneasy. "What things?" she whispered, loath to ask, but knowing she must.

Lucy ignored the question and opened the door; admitting the biting air. "Let's go. We don't want to have to sit in the back."

Using her cane for leverage, Bertha carefully climbed over the snow mounded at the curb and joined Lucy on the sidewalk. Her friend was staring broodingly back into the notch, toward the mountain. Bertha's uneasiness intensified. "Lucy? What things are better left alone?"

The Lucy who answered was the woman she had known for almost all her adult life. But the words she spoke took her out of the twentieth century and placed her in a time when life was simpler and people were closer to nature; a time when the unseen forces that govern the earth were explained by superstition and fear. "Things that decent folks shouldn't meddle with. I grew up here, Bertha. I know this place. There are some things that should be left to lie undisturbed."

"I know it, too. I've lived here sixty-seven years. Pa got a job at the mill when I was sixteen. You ought to know that, unless your memory's gone begging."

Lucy shook her head. "It's not the same. You didn't grow up with it."

"Lucy! You're not talking about that business with the mill, are you? Why—"

"I am, and I'm not ashamed to. They're about the Devil's work tonight. You'll see."

Amos Hubbard saw them coming and waited at the top of the steps. "Evenin', Lucy, Bertha," he said, and gallantly held the door. "Big turnout."

Lucy sailed past him with a regal nod. Bertha was slower, hampered by the need to use her cane. "Amos. Thank you." She waited as he carefully closed the door. "How's the arthritis?"

"Lousy. But I ain't ready fer the final cure." He cackled loudly at his wit.

Bertha shuddered. There was nothing funny about death. She opened her coat with fingers that suddenly trembled. It was too hot in the hall. Above the hubbub of voices spilling out of the meeting room she could hear the hiss of steam clanking through the old pipes and radiators. She hurried inside, happy to see Lucy had found two seats quite near the front. Amos, considering himself J. Norbert Edgehill's personal watchdog, took a seat in the first row.

Slowly the room filled, the residents of Draconia leaving the warmth of hearth and home on a cold winter's night to exercise the privileges of a free society. Part of the bedrock of democracy, the New England town meeting guaranteed every citizen a voice in community affairs.

The proceedings got under way thirty-seven minutes late. As she waited, Lucy observed her friends and neighbors with only part of her mind; the other part couldn't detach itself from the disquieting thoughts that plagued her.

A high, provocative laugh pierced her introspection. Seventeen-year-old Vera Alderbrook, as usual wearing too much makeup, dressed in the loose, layered look so popular

36

with the young, was flirting outrageously with a tall, broad-shouldered, dark-haired man. Lucy's heart lurched within her thin chest. Richard! She squirmed on the uncomfortable metal folding chair, pressing her spine more firmly against the back. The sight of him still hurt her. She had had such hopes, but Alison was happy now, and that was all that mattered.

"Such a handsome man," Bertha said, noticing the direction of Lucy's gaze.

"All the Fortunes are handsome," Lucy snapped. It was true. Richard and his older brother Daniel, both with tall, leanly muscled bodies, dark hair, and clear-cut features, could be called classically handsome. By the looks of Daniel's two boys, the genes also were present in the newest generation of Fortunes. "Handsome is as handsome does," she said primly, the words spilling out before she thought to contain them.

J. Norbert banged the gavel, calling the meeting to order. Vera Alderbrook's high, thin girlish laugh floated into the sudden silence. Lucy, with almost ninety-five percent of the others present, turned to look at her. The other five percent were latecomers, busy finding seats, removing gloves and scarves and hats and bulky outerwear.

Richard was bending over Vera's hand. Lucy's lips thinned into a tight, straight line. The silly girl was almost swooning with delight, while Richard . . . But it wasn't Richard. This man was taller, broader, slightly older. Vera giggled. Lucy noted Vera's father, John Alderbrook, grimace with distaste. A councilman, he had a perfect view of the scene from his place of honor on the raised platform in the front of the room.

Another giggle brought her attention back to Vera . . . and Adrian Blaise. How could she have thought him Richard? The resemblance was superficial. She should have recognized him since he and the other members of the Mountain Venture group had stayed at the inn several times during the past months. Rumor had it they were going to buy or lease the old Justice place as soon as plans were finalized and the renovation and construction began. That suited her just fine; she preferred a relaxed, vacationing clientele to a group of harried, stressed businesspeople.

She studied Adrian Blaise with assessing eyes. The man was indecently handsome. Now, in full view of her parents and neighbors, he turned Vera's hand over and pressed his lips to her palm.

Bertha sniffed. Someone in the back of the room tittered. John Alderbrook's expression went from frosty disapproval to down-right outrage. Two spots of red colored the high planes of his cheekbones, rouging his usually pale complexion. Lucy enjoyed it. Despite knowing her all his life, the coldhearted bastard always treated her like a stranger every time she had dealings with the bank.

J. Norbert applied his gavel with more authority and the little tableau broke up. The Mountain Venture people went to the podium one by one, delivering report after report, analyzing, hypothesizing, doing everything to sell the people of Draconia the idea that brick and mortar and macadam were preferable to trees and rocks and quiet glades with trout-filled streams meandering through them.

You had to give them credit, these men and women of Mountain Venture, for they sought to dazzle, and with charts and maps and surveys and slides and scaled-down mockups of every inch of Draconia, the *new* Draconia, they certainly did their job.

A polite smattering of applause heralded the last speaker. Tall, redheaded, possessed of trim ankles and taut calves, Ms. Monica Stevens gracefully arose and made her way to the platform. J. Norbert, Bert to the voters and Bertie to his wife Milly, leaned forward to get a good view. John Alderbrook, seated next to him, spoke into one of those strange silences that pop up in large gatherings. "Sit back, you fool," he hissed, "before you land on your ass." He pronounced it "arse."

The mayor turned such a murderous glare on him that the air fairly sizzled between them. Alderbrook stared straight ahead, wearing his deadpan banker's face. There were a few snickers from the audience and one outright guffaw from old Amos Hubbard, who disliked them both.

Ms. Stevens coughed delicately to gain the audience's attention, then spoke for ten minutes on land conservation and wildlife preservation. To hear her tell it, the renovation of the old mill and the tearing down of trees to build condominiums and malls wouldn't perceptibly alter nature. The influx of cars and buses with their noxious fumes and their need for large spaces for parking would only minimally affect the environment. Minimalize this and maximize that—Draconia heard a lot of that these days.

The redheaded Ms. Stevens finished her report, smiled prettily, intimately, at the audience, then took her seat with the grace of a trained dancer. As J. Norbert struggled his plump body out of his seat there came a shuffling of feet, a clearing of throats, a nervous twittering that spread like a wave at a football game. The real business of the evening was about to begin.

"Now," Mayor Edgehill said in his most pompous manner, "you have all heard the proposal the people from Mountain Venture have put before the council. Before we vote on whether to grant them the variance they need to begin renovation of the old mill and construction on the condominium and mall sites, we will open the floor to questions. Each speaker is, ah, limited to two minutes."

"Does that include you?" called a male voice from the rear of the room.

Laughter greeted this sally. J. Norbert glared at the crowd until he caught his wife's eye. Milly smiled serenely up at him, her pleasant face, its prettiness fast fading into the blurred lines of middle age, transmitting a silent message.

Bertha made a small sound of impatience deep in her throat. "Right boring," she said, not bothering to lower her voice. "When're they going to talk turkey?" Lucy smothered a smile as the mayor scowled down at them. Bertha calmly ignored him, transferring her cane from her left hand to her right, thumping the old wooden floor loudly in the process.

J. Norbert hastily opened the meeting to questions.

The questions came, one after the other, some practical, concerned with sewers and water supply and service personnel, such as police and fire fighters. Draconia, too small to warrant a law-enforcement unit of its own, depended on larger towns and ultimately on the state whenever a problem arose. One rarely did, as almost three-quarters of the people were related and crime virtually did not exist. You didn't prey on your family.

Lucy sighed, wondered when this orchestrated farce of a meeting would come to its predictable end. Didn't these people realize that with the condominiums came strangers, strangers who knew or cared nothing about Draconia? It wouldn't affect her. Her intuition told her that. She turned her head toward the window and stared out at the dark. Soon. Soon she would lie out there, under the rich dark earth, nourishing it. She could feel it in her bones, this death of hers, and felt no fear. Not even at night did she despair when sometimes she lay in bed and wondered where it all had gone, her hopes and dreams, and even the flesh with which she faced the world.

Her attention snapped back to the proceedings when she realized Everett Hale was on his feet, yelling at J. Norbert about one of his pet peeves.

The mayor was yelling back, his round face wet with perspiration, patches of it spreading under his arms. "Now's not the time, Ev, you know that. This meeting's for the vote on the Dragon Meadow complex, not for your gripes. Next meeting we'll all be more'n glad to discuss the sanitation issue, but not now."

"Sanitation's part of it." Red-faced, Everett windmilled his arms, causing the people on either side of him to duck. "The more people you have, the more shit—"

"Everett!" His face purpling until he resembled an eggplant wearing a fringe of hair, J. Norbert strove to be heard above a rising murmur of voices. A young male voice shouted vulgar encouragement to Everett. Again laughter rumbled through the hall.

"Let me, please." Monica Stevens didn't have to raise her

40

voice to be heard, she merely waited and the stirrings died down. Then the tall redhead spoke about waste, solid and liquid, and about dump sites and containerization and all manner of unpleasant things in such a pleasant way that before long almost everyone but the still-bellicose Everett subsided back into acquiescence.

"Ain't nothin' these people haven't figured out to their advantage," Amos observed loudly.

J. Norbert worked his gavel vigorously.

But Amos had sat quiet too long. "Damned meddlin' city folks. Always pokin' their noses inta things. Should stay in Boston where they belong."

Looking innocent, Ms. Stevens announced in a pretty voice that she hailed from Boston. "And I must admit I do enjoy getting away from the noisy, crowded city," she purred, nothing but a harmless kitten.

"Tits and ass," eighty-three-year-old Bertha observed tartly to Lucy, "these people don't miss a trick."

Amos had lived too long to be fooled. "That's a'right, honey," he bellowed, "you c'n make it in Massachusetts, as long's you spend it in N'Hampsha."

Amid the general hilarity this popular sentiment elicited, Lucy got to her feet. J. Norbert didn't notice her at first, busy giving his gavel another workout. When he finally recognized her erect, thin figure, he pounded the gavel one last time and directed Amos to resume his seat. "Miss Crandell has the floor," he said formally.

All the strange feelings, the inner stirrings of disquiet, the perception of *wrongness,* crowded Lucy's mind. She had meant to argue in favor of status quo, to plead with her friends and neighbors to abandon greed and stay with the quiet way of life she had cherished all her days. But as she looked at them, the young, the old, the newborn in Gretchen Mitchell's arms, she knew that there was only one question to be asked. "Why here? Why Draconia?"

The room grew quiet. All movement stilled. The simple question opened something dark, hidden, hitherto ignored. Lucy glanced down at Bertha, who sat with lips pursed tightly together, then transferred her gaze elsewhere. John Alderbrook stared fixedly at her, a frosty expression congealing his face. Jerry Treadwell coughed nervously, avoided her eyes when she turned toward the sound. Behind him sat Richard Fortune, a strange, almost helpless look on his handsome face. His eyes slid past hers. They looked haunted.

At the side of the room a tall, black-haired man slowly arose. He turned toward Lucy, held her immobile with the force of his compelling dark gaze. She blinked as the edges of the room began to blur. For her there was only Adrian Blaise; only the reality of eyes as deep and black as the night sky. He smiled sardonically, a mere lifting of his lips. She waited, suddenly breathless, for what he would say. When he spoke his voice moved through the air like smoke sifting through sand. "I made a promise," he said. "Long ago."

His eyes held her for long moments, then he let her go. Lucy sensed her body relax. "Yes," she breathed, and thought she knew.

A collective sigh rippled through the room. All the small noises connected with a large crowd filled the air. The world returned to normal.

"Lucy. Lucy!" Bertha tugged anxiously at her hand. "Sit down."

"What?" She felt strangely unsteady without the support of the dark gaze. "Oh, Bertha," she said, her eyes focusing again, "I think I'll step outside for a minute. It's very close in here."

Bertha anchored her cane and prepared to rise. "I'll go with you."

Lucy's hand stayed her. "No."

In the front row Amos was on his feet again. "I want t'know about the money," he trumpeted. "So far no one's said one thing about it. Where'd it come from? It ain't A-rab, is it?"

Lucy finally reached the hall. There were people milling about. She needed privacy, and above all, air. She thought she might faint.

42

Without even a second's hesitancy she tugged the front door open and stepped out into the cold night. The first breath of frigid air cut through her lungs with the sharpness of a blade. Her thin frame shuddered. Behind her the door opened and then quietly closed.

She took another breath, drawing the ice-cold air deep inside, conscious of the reflexive action. She turned toward the notch, to the inn and beyond it, the mountain. Her vision blurred as a sudden dizziness assailed her. Her head began to ache. She lurched to the side as another wave of dizziness speared through her.

She knew what was happening, knew it in her heart, her mind and in every cell of her body. Knew it and also knew, with a sudden clarity that came late, much too late, that she wasn't ready. Not yet. Death held no attraction.

With an effort that took all her remaining strength she turned until she could see the man who had followed her outside. Dark eyes regarded her gravely from a great height. "Help. Please . . ." The words were slurred, almost indistinct.

From the back of the notch, faint but clear, borne on the cold winter air, came a wild, feral cry.

He smiled.

Part I

6

September 1823
New Hope

Eleazar Fortune

Alive.

They were alive.

The earth shook and shifted. Sounds filled the air, the fierce, violent, rumbling sounds of primal upheaval; as it did when the earth was young.

Whatever cataclysm occurred passed them by. The storm continued to rage, feeding the river. Swollen and angry, cheated of its prey, it roared in defiance; white-foamed, mud-laced green death boiling frenziedly through its confining channel; challenging, teasing, relentless.

All through the night the men worked to save the mill. Like zombies they slaved, bodies beyond the clench of pain, minds numbed by exhaustion, aware only of the imperative to build a barrier high enough and strong enough to protect against the river.

With the first pale, watery streaks of sunlight the drenching rain let up. Steam rose from the mud, transforming the familiar landscape into a scene from hell.

Abel Crandell leaned wearily on his shovel and raised his face toward the sky. "It's over."

"Over."

"Over."

"Over."

"Over."

45

"Over."

"Over."

Like a breeze fluting through full-leafed trees the message passed down the chain of men. It transfixed them. They stood stock-still, grotesque living statues covered in mud. Realization took time.

The storm was over. They had come through the night.

Eleazar Fortune broke the spell. He threw down his shovel and climbed up over the levee. Like one bewitched he turned toward the mountain. All through the dark hours it had taunted him, the need to see, to know. In the still, quiet air of early morning the night before seemed unreal. A waking nightmare.

Abel also turned to stare. "Let's go see."

The words released the men. One by one they dropped their shovels; threw the burlap sacks aside. Before many minutes they formed an oddly silent crowd. They looked to Eleazar, suddenly unsure, remembering. Remembering another man, born of the storm. Had he been real, the tall dark stranger with the voice as smooth and dense as sin? Had he promised the impossible? Had they given him their pledge?

As if he heard their thoughts, Eleazar shrugged. The mountain beckoned; he heeded its call.

The others fell into step behind him. Storm-tossed debris impeded them. They picked their way carefully, in silence, following the easiest path back into the notch. In the distance they could see smoke rise, knew the women were stirring, had wood dry enough for fire. The thought of hot coffee and porridge was a powerful lure, but so was the need to know. To discover what dark miracle had befallen them.

When they reached the road they stopped and stared. The only way in and out of the notch was blocked by a mountain-high mound of dirt and trees and stone. Zenas Hutchins let out a loud whoop that shattered the quiet air. Ducks rose squawking from a new-formed pond.

"Landslide," Samuel Pate said tersely. " 'Tis a wonder it

stopped where it did. Why, we could have lost the town as well as the mill."

Thomas Spooner pulled his sodden cap from his head and knelt in the mud. Seeing this, Daniel Sayward, his face as gray as the thin hair on his head, gave a great shout. "Stop!" he cried in a voice of frantic thunder.

Thomas jerked his head up. Shocked. Confused. "We must give thanks to the Lord, for seeing us through the night."

Shoulders stooped by fatigue, Daniel shuddered as if with ague. "Which Lord is that, my friend?"

"Blasphemy!" Noah Alderbrook bellowed. He pushed his way through the men until he and Daniel stood toe to toe. His face was dark with the blood of outrage. "You speak sacrilege when you should be giving thanks like our brother here. Where is your faith, man?" His eyes were wild, desperate for denial.

Daniel wouldn't budge an inch. "I gave it away, same as you. Don't you remember?"

Noah seemed to shrink into himself. "It was a dream."

Eleazar walked away. He knew it had been no dream, knew it in his bones, in his aching soul. Still, he needed to see. The mountain called to him with a siren's song. He didn't need to look to know he was not alone.

Their route took them past the inn. It was battered but whole. Trees were uprooted in the yard, limbs like skeletal arms reaching toward the sky. The storm shutters hung drunkenly from the windows, ripped off by a capricious wind. A thin trickle of smoke escaped the kitchen chimney. "Sarah's about her business," Abel said. The others noted the relief which laced his voice.

Soon they came into the shadow of the mountain. Like a cloak its shade lay over the land. Deep within it, hidden, waited the answer.

There was a winding, much-used path, but as one they veered off to cross through the Justice farm, taking the most direct route. They entered the fields without a qualm, following the mud-clogged paths between the neatly planted rows. No more than ten paces inside the field Eleazar stopped. Slowly he turned a complete circle, then hunkered down.

"What is it?" William Hale asked. "Snake?"

Eleazar arose to his full height. His brow creased. He stared about him, turned completely once again. "Jedediah . . .?"

Jedediah Justice didn't answer. He was on his knees, hands scrabbling through the waterlogged earth. In hushed silence the men watched, gripped by apprehension, unsure of why this should be so.

"Look at the fields. What do you see?" Eleazar asked, his voice soft, gentle, although he wanted to scream, to rage, to roar, to bellow his fear in the clear light of day.

"My crops!" Jedediah cried. "They're whole! They were drowned. Yesterday I was ruined."

Dawning understanding colored the faces of the men. "Well, I'll be—" Noah started, then broke off. Once again his face darkened with hot blood.

Damned.

The word wavered in the air, played through their minds, chilled their souls. It accompanied them deep into the woods, up a steep trail. Everywhere they looked they saw the damage the storm had wreaked. The going was rough; not a single man complained.

The sound of rushing water grew loud. They followed it, weaving through the obstacles created by wind and rain. But long before they reached its source they suspected what they would see. Overnight the earth had rearranged itself, had reshaped from raw clay during the cataclysm that changed their world. Only something beyond their ken could have stopped the river of water and earth and stone that had roared toward the town.

At last they came to the wellspring. Far above them water poured from the earth, down between a sleek-sided gorge. Its voice was thunder; its power untold.

It had been stopped.

Wedged between the walls, a giant boulder interrupted the flow. The water, robbed of its velocity, tumbled over, pooled in a basin below.

In awe, they stood and stared.

"The Devil's dammed it," Eleazar said, and knew then that the price would have to be paid.

They worked for two days to carve a path through the mountain of earth across the road. In the middle of the second day they heard voices from the other side, knew that others worked as they did to force an opening.

The dread and fear that had accompanied them down from the mountain had abated somewhat. After all, nothing had happened. Nothing but that they were saved. Dark thoughts, late-night musings, were largely ignored. The secret of the dam was held closely to their hearts.

With dawn of the third day came a discovery. Overnight a gate had appeared. Just beyond the boundary of the cemetery, it stood at the farthest tip of the mountain's shadow.

A gate. Nothing else. No fence. No wall. Iron bars painted black; the arrow-shaped tops, wicked-looking, sparkled with the gleam of gold in the rising sun.

Questions flew like the leaves of autumn in a briskly blowing wind. No one knew who had put it there.

By noon they broke through to the outside. Friends and relatives from neighboring towns poured in, expressed relief to find them well. Whole.

That night was the first to find every man in his own home, in his own bed. They slept that night deeply. Exhausted. Afraid.

In the morning they knew they had been right to fear. Twenty-year-old Patience Breed was missing. Gone from her home, her bed, without a trace.

It didn't take long to find her. Dead, her long golden hair

49

spread out around her in artless abandon, she lay sprawled beneath the new gate.

Where before there had been only bars of black and gold, there now were letters, twisted bars of iron etched against the cold blue sky: intricate, Gothic, chilling.

DRACONIA

7

The Present — Thursday, June 13
New York City

Alison stopped by the police station even though it would make her late for work. The 112th Precinct in Forest Hills was a hive of activity. As central booking for Queens, it was the first stop for all arresting officers and their detainees. Its dull-green walls and worn linoleum-tiled floors were enough to depress even the most innocent of souls.

Alison gave her complaint number to the desk sergeant and waited to see an officer. The visit was probably futile, but she felt she had to do something. The obscene calls were driving her crazy.

The police officer who waved her into a stark room sparsely furnished with metal furniture was not one she had seen before. He flipped through her file and then looked at her with kind brown eyes that had seen too much. "You're still getting these calls?"

"Yes."

He turned back to the first page, frowned. "The first call came, uh—"

"January." January to June; it sounded like a romantic song.

"Look, these creeps just wait for a reaction. Don't give it. Hang up as soon as you know it's one of those calls."

Alison took several moments to study the officer. McMahon, his I.D. read. What did he know about fear? What did he know about being a single woman afraid of her only means of communication with the outside world? She took a deep breath; no use getting angry.

"He calls at all hours. I've got an answering machine now. It's on day and night." Her eyes looked haunted.

"Look, miss, er . . ." he glanced down at the complaint form, "Mrs. Fortune, the fact that this has gone on so long, without, er, without anything else occurring is a good sign. This creep appears to be strictly a caller."

"That's just terrific. Look, Officer, I'm a divorced woman living alone. Every time the phone rings I get sick, physically sick, just knowing it could be him."

"I'm sorry," he said, "but we can't do anything . . ." He paused, uncomfortable, and they both knew the end of the sentence.

Until he *does* something.

"Right," the policeman said, as if the thought had been spoken. "You changed the locks on your door?" She nodded. "One's a dead bolt?" Another nod. "How about at the office? I see here the calls come there also."

"My secretary screens all my calls. I don't pick up at all anymore."

It was his turn to nod. "I'm afraid . . ." he began, but Alison also knew the end of this sentence and couldn't bear to hear it again.

"*I* am the one who is afraid." Despite her resolve to be strong, a sob caught in her throat. "Isn't there something you can do. Anything?"

He steepled his hands and regarded her gravely. "A long chance. We could put a mechanical tracer on your telephone."

"You mean like a tap?"

He shrugged. "It would monitor all your calls. Perhaps we'd get lucky and find out where they're coming from." His tone told her how little he thought it would work. Creeps like the caller didn't make calls from only one telephone.

The obscene calls were bad enough; having the police

privy to every conversation would make her feel too much like a victim of theirs also. She rubbed her itching palm against the skirt of her linen suit. "I'll think about it."

The call came a little after eleven-thirty. Alison looked at the red light blinking on the phone and threw down her pencil in disgust. Angrily she punched the intercom button. "Kathy, I thought I told you to hold all calls?" God, she sounded like a bitch. She bit her lower lip, angry with herself for the gruff edge to her voice. "Sorry. What's so important?"

The voice of the secretary she shared with the other two paralegals came huffily out of the phone. "There's a Mrs. Rice on line three. Long distance. Says it's personal and urgent."

"Mrs. Rice?" Her mind still on the Levine closing statement, she couldn't quite place the name.

"Yeah. D'you want her?"

Alison forced a humbleness she didn't really feel, hoping her tone would help to mollify the secretary. "Yes, thank you." When you shared personnel in a big firm you learned very fast to keep in that person's good graces. Either that or get your work done last. Line three winked at her. Pushing her calculator away, she depressed the button. "Hello." The voice she heard grabbed her attention immediately.

"Alison? Dear, it's Bertha." The precise New England voice allowed no interruptions. "I'm sorry to call you at work, dear, I know how important you are, but Richard—"

Richard. Alison closed her eyes, willing herself not to tense at the mere mention of her husband's name. Ex-husband, she automatically reminded herself.

"—said it was all right, so I just took the liberty. I hope you don't mind. Actually, he was the one who gave me your number. I don't know why I didn't have it myself, in case of an emergency, you know."

Alison firmly pushed all thought of Richard to the back

53

of her mind. With a ruthlessness born of practice she smoothly interrupted Bertha's monologue. "I'm glad you called, Bertha. Is there a problem? Is Lucy all right?"

Bertha's voice was dry, yet compassionate. Alison listened with her eyes closed, her hand gripping the receiver so hard her knuckles showed whitely through her skin. Lucy, Alison's aunt, the person she loved most on the face of the earth, had had a stroke in February and another one more than six weeks ago.

"How is she?" Time later to go into details, to wonder exactly what Lucy was thinking of not to let her know.

"Up to her old tricks, that's what she is," Bertha replied tartly. "That's why I'm calling. You know I come by the inn most days for lunch, sometimes just to read the paper and have a glass of Chablis. And now, since the strokes, I try to get there at least once a day so's—"

Alison couldn't stand not knowing another second. "Is she going to be all right?"

Forced to pause, Bertha took the opportunity to take a breath. Alison suffered through it. "No reason for her not to be, if only she'd do like she's told."

"And that is?" Alison asked, knowing Bertha had arrived at the reason for the call.

"The inn . . ." Bertha coughed dryly. "She's got to rest, but you know Lucy, she says there'll be plenty of time to do that when they lay her in her grave."

Alison knew her aunt very well. "I take it she's giving everyone a hard time."

Bertha snorted. "Home five days from the hospital and already acting up. Kicked the nurse out first thing this morning. I found out about it from Dottie Cutter when I went down to Leavitt's to buy some milk and eggs. She said Henry doesn't know what to do."

Alison silently digested this information. Having lived twenty-eight of her thirty-two years in a small town, the message was clear. She looked at the pile of manila folders on her desk, then down at the open file in front of her.

"Are you still there, dear? I truly didn't want to bother you, but . . ."

"You know it's not a bother. Actually, I'm angry that you didn't call when she first got sick. I could have been there with her. She *is* my only living relative."

"You know Lucy, dear. She's so independent. She wouldn't let me call. She's—"

"Impossible. I know. Well, I'll just call and tell that impossibly dear, stubborn aunt of mine to look for me sometime tonight. I have a few things to clear up before I can start—"

"Oh, no! You can't possibly do that."

"Bertha—"

"Don't call. You know Lucy. Just come, Alison. It's the only way."

Bertha was right. Alison knew she was, yet the desire to pick up the telephone and call her aunt grew with each passing moment. Just to hear her voice, the tart, gruff no-nonsense New England accent, would make her feel better. Instead, Alison punched out Winda Green's extension.

"I need some time off," she said tersely to the office manager. Within two minutes Winda had the whole story.

Alison spent another hour putting the finishing touches to the Levine closing statement and dictating a memo on the other matters she had pending. The intercom buzzed while she was stuffing everything into a red-rope folder.

"You're cleared," Winda said. "Not to worry. Gina's cut some slack and Eckert said he'll take the contract matters."

"You're terrific."

"I know," Winda said modestly. Alison laughed. "What'd you do, girl, to make that Eckert so ahhh-menable? Could there be something you'd like to tell your old friend?"

"Good-bye, old friend," Alison said dryly. "And . . . Winda?"

"Yeah, girl?"

"You really are terrific."

Alison picked up her purse and the bulky folder, checked to see the tape was inside, then took it out to her secretary's desk.

Kathy accepted it with a sympathetic smile. The office tom-toms had been busy. "Call if you need anything."

Moved, Alison smiled her thanks. "I'll keep in touch."

Normally slow, today the elevators seemed to crawl. By the time the red down indicator finally pinged on, Alison had paced the length of the elevator bank several times. The doors opened and Clare Bauer rushed out. "Oh! Thank goodness I caught you." Alison watched the elevator doors close. Clare touched her arm. "I'm sorry. This won't take a moment. Mr. Metzger wanted you to know that there is absolutely no reason to rush back. Take your time, do what you have to for your aunt. Your job will be waiting."

Alison inclined her head slightly, wondering why Neumann, et al. would bother to reassure a low-level employee. The answer came immediately.

Suddenly ill at ease, Clare avoided Alison's eyes as she got down to business. "Mr. Metzger wondered, if possible, you could say hello to Mountain Venture's local counsel while you're up there. Just let them know you're in the neighborhood. See if they need anything." She handed Alison a piece of paper with a name and address. "Liaison," Clare mumbled. "Mr. Metzger said Mr. Blaise would appreciate it."

Without even bothering to look at the paper, Alison folded it and stuffed it in her purse. Clare reached out and jabbed the down button. The elevator came in no time at all. "Good-bye," Clare said. "Good luck."

"Good-bye," Alison managed as the doors closed. Her damned hand was itching again.

Once home in her small basement apartment in a private house on a quiet, tree-lined street in Forest Hills, Alison showered, changed into jeans and a cotton sweater, and packed in record time. Draconia lay eight hours to the north, if she didn't stop along the way. Her best time so far had been ten hours. That would put her in the White Mountains around midnight.

It took an hour and a half to reach the Connecticut Turnpike. An eighteen wheeler had jackknifed and overturned on the New York State Thruway near the northern perimeter of the Bronx. Alison sat and fidgeted in the surreal shadow cast by the massive bulk of Co-op City. The delay meant she would hit rush-hour traffic.

The crawl up Connecticut's industrial coast to New Haven, where she stopped for gas and coffee, took twice the usual time. The congestion didn't ease when she turned north on Interstate 91, heading toward Hartford.

Traffic thinned fifteen miles into Interstate 84. Alison relaxed her rigid posture, kneaded the back of her neck in an effort to work out some of the tension-caused kinks. People were hurrying home to dinner; soon she would own the road.

Disaster struck in a sparsely populated section of northern Connecticut. It started as the merest wisp of smoke, curling lazily, whitely into the backdrop of gently rolling dark-green hills. The wisp took on body, became billows. Alison barely made it over to the right shoulder before a new problem announced its presence with a menacing mechanical thwang thwang thwang.

Two teens in a rusted relic of a Beetle helped her get the hood up. Steam hissed and crackled out in alarming volume.

"Overheated," one teen said.

"Handkerchief?" the other asked. Alison handed him a wad of tissues. He opened the radiator cap and jumped back.

"I wait for it to cool down and add water, right?" Too anxious to be fearful of the unlikely-appearing knights of the road, Alison hoped she had the correct prescription.

"Yup," the first teen said. He wore jeans with more holes

than material and a T-shirt that announced SHIT HAP-PENS. "Distilled is best."

"Distilled?"

"Doesn't matter," the second teen said in a muffled voice. Alison felt relief. He straightened from poking about inside her Mustang. "Belt is busted."

Alison tried not to be distracted by the diamond stud in his ear. "That's bad?"

"Lady," Diamond Earring said, "you ain't goin' no-where."

8

Draconia

Sam Chandler

Sam Chandler finished entering his notes into the daily log he always kept while on a job and stretched, his fingers laced above his head. God, he felt stiff, and no wonder, tramping the damp woods for half the day and then climbing all over the construction site like a man five years younger. *Ten* years younger, he amended, wincing as sore muscles protested the movements. Bending hunched over paperwork for a couple of hours hadn't helped, either.

His stomach rumbled. Surprised, he checked his watch, tapped the crystal in a meaningless gesture, but it read the same. It couldn't be after nine. He rubbed his tired eyes and contemplated the big electric clock above the drafting table wedged into a corner of the trailer. Twelve minutes after nine.

His stomach rumbled again; an imperative. Among its amenities, the trailer boasted a noisy little refrigerator. Sam approached it with more resignation than hope. He wasn't surprised. Beer, in bottles and in cans, filled the space. A potpourri of brands. He helped himself to a Sam Adams and poked about halfheartedly. His investigation yielded a lone container of apricot yogurt, pushed to the rear. *Yogurt?* He thought of the construction crew, then remembered pretty little blond Jennifer Cutter, recently hired to help with the mound of paperwork a project of Dragon

Meadow's size engendered.

He polished off the beer in three long swigs, then tossed the empty across the room into the wastepaper basket next to his desk. A three-pointer. He must be losing it to forget sweet Jennifer for even a moment. Either losing it or over the hill.

Not a thought to entertain on an empty stomach. He locked all his papers in the desk and went outside. The soft breath of spring assailed his senses as he walked the few steps to his car. The rich smell of earth permeated the night.

In the few months he had been in Draconia Notch he had come to love the land. The old arguments began to rage in his head. He had come to change the land; to build. To change the land, yes, one part of him replied, but carefully, gently. Preservation, conservation: those were his watchwords. He had had this argument before: one part of him always won; one part of him always lost.

He drove toward the inn, disgusted that tiredness had tricked him into internal strife. He needed a hot shower and a hot meal. *And a woman.* How long had it been? A disquieting thought. He hit the steering wheel with the flat of his palm. The small pain helped distract him.

He would think of food. Too late for the inn, they stopped serving at eight. That left Sonny's Tavern. But first a hot shower and a change of clothes. Even Sonny's clientele wouldn't welcome him as he was.

The headlights picked out a figure walking toward him on the other side of the road, heading back into the notch. Young. Female. Runaway? Sam thought of Mandy, and immediately his insides knotted in pain. Was his sixteen-year-old daughter out tonight, walking a dark, lonely road? Would some stranger stop? To help? To hurt?

The pain of that thought bit into his gut, followed swiftly by another, more familiar feeling. Anger. Anger at Denise, his ex-wife. Anger at himself; his inability to do something, anything. But what could he do, three thousand miles away? Three thousand miles and fourteen years, to be precise. He only got to see Mandy once a year since Denise took her to

California, and that only grudgingly after she remarried when Mandy was six. He had accepted it, made the best of it, for what else could he do?

But then, three years ago, the trouble had started. Mandy, like so many of her peers, had become dissatisfied, had run from home and problems she found too difficult to bear.

She had come home after six weeks, that first time. After ten weeks the second time. There had been a third time and then a fourth. She had been home now for almost six months, though, and everyone, her doctors and therapists included, had hope. A marvelous word.

He knew he would have to try to help this girl. For Mandy and all the others like her.

Sam followed his impulse and made a U-turn and drove back, slowing the car to a halt when he came abreast of her. He touched the control, and the right window slid silently down. "Need a lift?"

The girl took several steps backward, hastily shook her head no.

Sam was disgusted with himself. What did he expect? He could be anybody, out here late at night in God's country. "Look," he said, running a hand through the thick reddish-blond hair that curled too long over his shirt collar, "my name's Sam Chandler and I'm the project manager for Dragon Meadow. I—"

"Oh, Mr. Chandler." The girl came closer to the side of the Lincoln. "I didn't recognize the car."

Sam frowned, and then his brow cleared. "The bank, right?"

The voice that had been light and pleasant moments before turned sullen. "Yeah. My father says I've got to work there this summer."

Sam mentally groped for a name. "Vera, isn't it? Vera Alderbrook."

"Yeah."

He had lost her. Mention of the bank had conjured her displeasure with parental authority. Knowing it was hopeless, he still had to try. "Look, Vera, it's late and it's very dark here. Can't I drop you somewhere?"

She stepped back, shaking her head, her face almost instantly becoming a pale blur in the dark. "No. No thanks. I'm fine. Really." She started to walk away, then stopped and turned and waved.

He had to be content with that, but he didn't have to like it. There was nothing back that way except the old cemetery and the parking lot for the Devil's Dam.

When he got to the inn the front door was slightly ajar, spilling light and sound out into the dark night. He pulled up a little past the steps and got out. Too much trouble to park in the small lot in the rear for the few minutes he" needed to shower and shave. Gravel crunched as he walked around the two-year-old Lincoln. He climbed the steps and then halted on the wide porch. So peaceful.

Smiling, he emerged scant seconds later from the short entryway into the inn's front hall. The inn was filled with fishermen. Loud laughter, the deep rumbling of male merriment, and the clink of china and cutlery came from the rear of the building, from the cozy dining rooms beyond the spacious parlor on the right. He sniffed appreciatively at the rich cooking odors; Luke had made something that smelled wonderful. His stomach growled loudly.

"New England pot roast dinner. You're too late, we ran out more'n an hour ago. Shut the door behind you, the night's turning chilly."

Sam did as bid, biting back a smile. He had his amusement under control when he approached the front desk. "Good evening, Miss Lucy. Didn't anyone ever teach you manners? A 'please' wouldn't have gone amiss."

Lucy Crandell snorted and made a small to-do out of settling her cardigan more snugly against her neck. Her shoulder blades poked sharply against the thin cotton sweater.

Sam frowned. She had a disturbing pallor. "Why are you working this late? Where's Jessie?"

"Helping serve. Adele didn't show tonight." Anger brightened her eyes and brought a semblance of color to her cheeks. "She didn't even bother to call in. Can you imagine?" A shake of the head set silvery curls dancing. "*I* had to call *her.*"

"You didn't fire her?" Sam had been living at the inn on and off for more than two months now. He knew how difficult it was to find and keep help.

Lucy snorted again in a very ladylike way. "I'm not addled yet, you know."

"How should I know that? It seems to me that anyone just home from the hospital should be tucked up in bed by now. You, Miss Lucy, need a keeper." He kept his tone light, to take the sting out of the words.

But Lucy Crandell hadn't lived almost eighty years to let someone less than half her age have the last word. "And you, Samson Chandler, need a wife. Working till all hours without a bite to eat."

"Is this the principle that the best offense is a good defense?" he inquired silkily.

Lucy came out from behind the desk and marched up to him. He towered over her, but that didn't faze her in the least. She sniffed delicately, then poked him right in the middle of his belly. "Beer doesn't count. I'm going to bed," she announced, and left him with amusement crinkling the corners of his eyes.

Sam didn't move until Lucy had made her slow way through the parlor and disappeared from his view into the first dining room. She almost always took the shortcut through the kitchen entrance at the rear to the small house behind the inn where she lived. Briefly he wondered if he should have offered to escort her, then knew that she would have spurned his help. Miss Lucy Crandell came from hardy New England stock. She prided her independence. It was clear to everyone just how touchy she had become on that very issue since her most recent stroke.

The second floor of the inn was quiet. Sam took a quick shower and pulled on a pair of slacks and a shirt, then splashed some cologne on his face, almost dropping the bottle, startled by the wild, reedy call of an animal. The sound spilled out of the notch, piercing the dark. Savage.

Frightening.

He rushed to the window and yanked the sheer curtains aside. Lucy stood in a path of light pouring out of her front door, listening, facing back into the notch. When the night continued quiet, she turned and looked up to Sam's window, then went inside, cutting off the light.

Now only a pale moon rode the sky, concealing more than it revealed. Sam watched for a while, but nothing stirred. He made a mental note to speak to Lucy in the morning. Perhaps she knew what kind of animal had such a haunting cry.

Vera Alderbrook

The moon bathed the old cemetery in pale white light, a gentle wash that softened the realities of sunken, lichen-encrusted stones. Vera Alderbrook hesitated at the entrance, then quickly stepped from the road into the burial ground, instinctively seeking the shadows. A shiver rippled through her firm young body, although it was warm for a June night in the mountains. She wished he had asked her to meet him someplace else.

The cemetery was small and crowded with stones and bushes and trees, a jumble of headstones and footstones and monuments with no pattern to them. Carefully picking her way, Vera moved deeper into the graveyard. A rustling sound came from behind her. She whirled around, her heart thumping heavily against her ribs. "Hello? Are you there?" she called.

No answer. Only the rustling again, from down low. The fine hairs on her nape and the backs of her arms stood up, like tiny antennae searching the dark. Vera preferred not to think about what would make such a sound.

She was early. Eager. Who would have thought he would be interested in her, little Vera Alderbrook, just eighteen years old last month; when he could probably have any girl he wanted? Any *woman* he wanted. Another shiver rippled through her body, this one delicious, anticipatory. She hadn't hesitated when he said to meet him here. It had seemed romantic, something illicit lovers would do. She knew, without asking, that her parents wouldn't approve. He was too old for her, too experienced, which, of course, was part of his allure, along with the tall, broad build, the thick, dark hair, the strongly chiseled features. He was handsome, almost beautiful.

Aimlessly she wandered, full of restless energy. It was spooky here at night; familiar shapes, landmarks well known from childhood, shifted and altered by shadows, were suddenly unfriendly. Threatening. Unconsciously she scratched her itching palm.

Five minutes. She'd give him that much more. The thrill of the forbidden was still a strong lure.

Suddenly a loud, tearing sound, a harsh rasping screech, ripped through the air. Again it sounded, an unholy screaming that swallowed reason as it shattered the night. Before her heart beat again, Vera succumbed to an all-encompassing fear. Her body acted instinctively. She ran, blindly, her only purpose to distance herself from the mind-numbing unearthly sound. Panic clogged her throat, seized her brain, disorienting her. A cloud raced across the moon. Momentarily blinded, she tripped, went sprawling flat, then lay still, panting, fear throbbing through her veins. The smell of earth filled her nostrils. Quiet descended, unnerving.

The cloud deserted the moon; light again bathed the land. She turned her head; her eye filled with the sight of a golden rosette, the letters GAR imprinted on it. Grand Army of the Republic. Beneath it a faded flag hung limply in the still air. Now she knew where she was. She was lying on a young man's grave. One of three. Three young men lost to war, a large number in a town as small as Draconia.

Stunned, afraid to move, she embraced the earth. They were long dead, these men lying beneath her, butchered by their brothers in gray. A picture rose in her mind of long bony fingers, reaching upward, seeking, sensing her warmth, wanting it. An hysterical mewling cry escaped her lips. These men couldn't hurt her. Surely they were no more than dust.

The heart-stopping sound shrieked again, filling the air. Vera sobbed, pressed herself harder against the unyielding earth. Was that a sound she heard beneath her? Impossible.

Another loud screech. She stifled a scream and rolled over, coming to her knees. All at once she knew.

The gate!

Slowly she arose, turned toward it, where it stood in mysterious isolation on the edge of the sacred ground, dwarfed by the rugged bulk of Dragon Mountain rising behind it. The glossy black iron bars, the spokes trimmed in bright gold, the twisted letters that spelled Draconia, shimmered in the moonlight. No one knew why it was there. No one alive. At one time it must have had a fence, or so it was assumed, for why else bother to put it up? Good Yankee logic supported this supposition. There were no facts. The gate simply *was*.

All Draconia's children, at one time or another, played around it, tried to open it, dared each other to climb it. During the day, of course, because at night, when the land reverted to dark, when the predators of the shadows emerged to stalk their prey, ground fog swelled around its base. Then it seemed to float in phantasmal mist, and although only a thing of bars and space, become a portal to a place better left alone.

Like now.

Again the ear-piercing screech tore through the night. Run, she screamed inside her head, but her feet didn't respond. She was as firmly rooted to the soil as was the gate. Rooted in dread. Whimpering, she couldn't tear her eyes away.

The gate swung open . . . one inch . . . two inches . . . then stopped. Where before there had been a clear visibility, a view of trees and bushes running up the foothills into the mountain, there was now a wedge of lightlessness, a *blackness* complete. The ever-present fog curled upward, sinuously, winding about the spokes, seeking a way into the stygian darkness. From out of it a hot wind blew, like air escaping an ancient tomb. The flags of the Civil War dead danced, snapping loudly against their wooden stakes. A frantic rustling in the grasses signaled the hasty retreat of small mammals. Then, abruptly, the wind stopped. The gate opened wider. Something came out, emerged from the pitch-black obscurity of a world hidden, unknown, into murky shadow. It surged over the wall onto the hallowed ground of the cemetery, stood motionless for a moment, then moved off. The gate closed.

She couldn't see what it was, didn't *want* to see it, but for the second time that night Vera *knew*. Whatever had come through the gate had come for her. The human urge to survive rose within her breast, sure and strong. Without waiting to see what pursued, she turned and fled.

A high-pitched, excited howling rent the air.

Vera moaned, felt her muscles tighten in superstitious dread. *Wolf?* she wondered, and pictured yellow eyes, long, pointed teeth. Panicked, on the edge of hysteria, she ran as fast as she was able over the treacherous ground.

The chase ended almost before it began. Hysterical, sobbing, Vera stood with her back jammed close against the cold marble of a tomb. Before her crouched a preternatural beast, a large black nightmare come true. Her voice, a little girl's voice, pleaded in vain. "No. No. Please. No." She moved to the left. Another waited. She turned her head to the right. There were many more. Crouching. Waiting.

The sound of a shoe scraping stone penetrated her fear. She dragged her head around, looked up, saw with relief that he had finally come. "Help," she said, a sad little whisper on the wind.

He smiled, and for the last time Vera knew. "Damn you to hell," she screamed, then made one final, desperate, doomed dash.

It was as if they herded her, these phantoms from the mist. Death waited beneath a time-warped root. Her foot snagged, she fell, the back of her skull crashing down onto a sharp edge of polished granite. He found her easily, where she lay, under the time-smoothed stone with the letters ALD RBOK still apparent. She sprawled in obscene abandonment, shed of mortality's modesty. His shadow covered her, like a lover, then moved off, taking the now silent beasts away.

The cemetery again lay peaceful under the moon.

As if in mourning, the moon soon was veiled in gray as pewter clouds streamed across the sky like shredded shrouds. The celestial light dimmed, then disappeared. The night grew cold.

The wind that doused the light brought rain. At first it fell softly, gently, onto the earth. The springtime loam, dark, fecund, welcomed it greedily, drinking it down, deep, this necessary flow of life. After a time the tempo of the rain increased; harder, faster, it fell; soaking, saturating; punishing in its intensity. It became a silvery curtain, a deluging wall of water. Concealing. Dangerous.

9

It began to rain lightly just as Sam pulled into Sonny's parking lot. All the spaces near the entrance were filled, mostly with four-wheel-drive vehicles and pickup trucks, forcing him to park some distance away. By the time he entered the dim, haze-filled room, moisture sparkled in his hair and across the shoulders of the windbreaker he had put on at the last moment. He was glad for its warmth; the night had turned chill.

As usual on any given weeknight, there was quite a crowd. At a glance, Sam figured at least half of the construction crew was present. He found a table as far from the jukebox as he could get. Angie, the prototypical world-weary waitress, swiped it halfheartedly and then tossed the rag onto a tray crowded with empties. She treated him to her version of a pleasant smile. "Yeah?"

"A draft and a couple of burgers."

Angie pivoted her pelvis toward the bar. "Kitchen still open?"

Her voice was high and harsh and too close to his ear. Sam had to make a concerted effort not to wince. Sonny himself leaned out from behind the bar to see who was hungry. He gave Angie the go-ahead nod and Sam relaxed. There were too many miles between Sonny's and the next eatery. Briefly he thought of New York with its choice of cuisines at every hour. Chinese food would taste good now.

"Okay," Angie said, already moving away.

"Make the burgers deluxe, with plenty of fries. Oh, and if you've still got onion rings I'd like an order of those, too." He had almost told her to give him an order of barbecued spareribs.

Angie regarded him with an assessing eye. "My, you must be hungry tonight."

Her tone told it all. Sam remembered his earlier thoughts, but Angie didn't even tempt him. "I missed dinner, is all," he replied mildly, letting her figure out if it was a brushoff or if he was just dense.

After his meal he moved to the bar, seeking the easy conversation of the regulars. Sports, specifically baseball, particularly the Boston Red Sox, was the topic. They were busy losing to the New York Yankees, five to three in the bottom of the seventh at Yankee Stadium, much to the loud disbelief of the fans in Sonny's. At a commercial break Amos Hubbard swiveled his ancient neck around and regarded Sam from suspiciously bright eyes. "You're a city fella, ain'tcha?"

As subtle as one of the huge earth-moving machines back at the site. Sam nodded, guessing where the nosy old man was headed.

"Boston?"

Sam shook his head no.

Amos licked his lips. "New York?"

Sam shook his head yes.

Amos leaned past Sam and hollered down the bar. "Sonny. Hey, Sonny. You know what we've got us here? Why, we've got us a Yankee fan, I'll betcha."

Heads swiveled. Sam smiled blandly. "There's more than one team in New York."

"Yeah, but I'll betcha you're one o' them damn Yankee fans." Amos nearly cackled with excitement.

Sam shrugged, and then signaled Sonny, indicating the people at the bar. "The next round's on me." Amos poked him in the ribs with a sharp elbow, in lieu of a thank-you, he supposed. Attention returned to the television as the Red Sox took the field for the top of the eighth.

"Hey, boss!"

Sam swiveled around to find his foreman standing close behind his barstool. "How's it going, Rufe? Just get here?"

"Nope. Been here a coupla hours. In the back." He jerked his head toward the pool table.

"I see," Sam said, but he didn't see at all. Rufus McClain looked uneasy, like a man with something to say and no idea of how to say it. There were deep furrows across his broad forehead, emphasized by the lack of hair above it. His gray eyes, usually cool and penetrating, held a hint of wariness. "Join me?" Sam asked, already signaling Sonny. Rufus would say what he had to say in his own sweet time.

The foreman slid onto the stool next to him, maintaining silence until Sonny had been and gone and was occupied at the other end of the bar. Half of the golden liquid in his glass disappeared before he cleared his throat.

His interest now more than piqued, Sam nevertheless acted as if this were only a friendly after-hours drink. Rufus was a dependable foreman, liked and respected by the men he worked for and the men who worked for him. Sam knew he would take whatever Rufus had to tell him very seriously.

"Smooth job," Rufus finally said.

"So far." Sam was careful to keep his voice neutral, to act unconcerned, but the deliberate way McClain was *not* saying anything had him worried. Small talk wasn't his way.

"On schedule?"

"Near as can be."

Rufus nodded, took a long swig, emptying his glass.

Sam started to raise his hand for Sonny, but Rufus forestalled him by sliding off the barstool. Sam wondered if he was going to just walk away, leaving him with questions and tension and nothing else. A sharp, stabbing pain nibbled at his gut. He rubbed his stomach, wondering if the problems and stresses of his job had finally resulted in an ulcer.

"Thanks for the brew."

Sam knew he couldn't let him go. Not without trying. "Anytime. McClain—"

A roaring noise from the television followed by loud exclamations from some of the customers indicated that the action on the field had heated up. To the left and slightly behind him, Amos was busy thumping his glass on the bar and mumbling encouragement to the Red Sox.

Sam automatically looked up at the set, then swiveled around, putting out his hand to stop Rufus from leaving. Under cover of the excitement he pitched his voice so that only the foreman could hear. "McClain?"

Rufus shrugged his broad shoulders noncommittally, but the wariness in his eyes was still there. "Some of the boys're a little spooked. You know the way they get sometimes."

If anything, Sam was more confused. The men of the crew were practical, down-to-earth types. They put in a good day's work for a good wage. No frills. Rufus looked as if he would bolt any second. Knowing he was running out of time, Sam chose the direct way.

"No, I don't think I know. Why don't you tell me how they get?"

McClain took a deep breath and then carefully let it out. "Do you know who we're working for?"

Surprised, Sam slowly got down off the barstool. Even though the foreman was an inch over six feet, Sam topped him. "It's no secret. You know Mountain Venture is developing Dragon Meadow. So what of it?"

"So nothing, I guess. Just some of the boys, well . . . they got spooked by some old story. I've seen this sort of thing once or twice. It can queer a job."

Alarmed, Sam knew he had to get answers. That was the second time the pragmatic McClain had used the word "spooked." He leveled a hard stare at the foreman, ignoring another twinge of pain in his gut. "Just what am I dealing with here?"

"Probably nothing, boss, nothing more than the name

72

of this burg. There's talk that this is the Devil's town and that he owns everything and everyone in it." Again his broad shoulders rose and fell. "Some of the men . . . well, let's just say I'd like us to finish and get out."

Hoots and catcalls erupted around them. McClain took advantage of the distraction and quietly walked away. Sam turned back to the bar. Old Amos grinned widely at him, lifted his glass, as if in salute. Uneasily, Sam wondered why.

Last call came and went. Sam had his final beer with the single men from the crew. The married ones were either on the dime-size dance floor working off calories or paired off by couples at the tables nearest the juke. Sam wondered how they could take the noise.

To his surprise, Sam was one of the last to leave. He stood in the dark, under the questionable protection of the awning over the front door and watched the rain come down. In the last couple of hours it had changed from a gentle fall to a deluge. It was difficult to see; driving was going to be a bitch.

Suddenly the night got even darker. Startled, he swung around. Angie grinned at him and pulled the front door closed behind her. Sam relaxed, realizing she had just turned off the outside lights. "Some night," he said. "Need a lift?"

"No. I'm right over there."

Sam watched her dash through the downpour toward a beat-up old Chevy, pondering the thought that it was his second turndown of the night. This one didn't bother him at all. He felt relief.

Without looking at his watch he knew it was very late. He should get going. Work started early. Still he stood, just watching and listening to the rain. A truck rumbled around from the back, the red brake lights going on when the driver saw the Lincoln. Sonny poked his head out of the cab window and looked around, withdrawing it as soon as he spotted Sam. He tooted farewell as he pulled out onto the road.

Time to go. Sam didn't even bother running; he was already soaked through to the skin within three steps from the building. Wet and clammy, he turned the heat on, then had to use the defroster when the windows fogged up. Finally he could see enough to get going.

Driving was even harder than he had imagined. Visibility was next to nothing; the headlights illuminated a silvery cascade; beautiful but potentially deadly. The radio produced nothing but static. He pushed a cassette into the slot. Bach. Now all he needed was a roaring fire and a warm, willing woman. He banished the thought immediately. Driving required his entire concentration.

Alison pushed the Mustang as hard as she dared. Tired, scared, she knew a serious accident could be only a blink away. Stupid not to stay at a motel. Stupid, but the desire to get to Draconia was a raging need within her. She didn't question it. Lucy needed her; she wouldn't let her down.

Almost there. She should have had them change the wiper blades when they replaced the fan belt, but since they had been surly enough about doing that, she hadn't wanted to push her luck. She should have, though, should have demanded they throw new wiper blades in for what they had charged her. *Goniffs,* as her landlady, Mrs. Seligson, would say. But thieves or not, they had fixed the Mustang. For that she was grateful.

If she got there. The night seemed darker in the mountains. The rain was almost solid now, sluicing in sheets against the windshield. She narrowed her eyes, trying to see as much as she could in the instant after the blades swiped across the windshield. They were virtually useless. A glow up ahead signaled a town. She let out her breath in a great gusting sigh of relief as the familiar sign of Treadwell's garage materialized out of the gloom. She had reached Draconia.

Down the main street she drove, slowly, carefully, mentally cautioning against haste now that she was so near.

The ungainly bulk of the war monument on the southern end of the common alerted her she had to turn off soon. She squinted, afraid to breathe, to fog the window and miss the only road that led back into the notch to the inn.

The headlights caught a gleam of white. Alison aimed for the marker stones that pointed the way. The rain intensified. The sound of it, drumming on the car, unnerved her so, that unconsciously her foot pressed down; the car surged forward.

Almost there. She drove on her last reserve of adrenaline, her heart pounding in her ears and head. Loud. It was very loud.

Pounding . . . pounding . . . pounding . . . pounding.

Too late she realized the sound didn't come from within. Something was coming down the road, toward the car.

Time slowed; stood still.

Something big, black . . .

Impossible.

Nightmare! *Please, God, let me be asleep.*

Impossible. A horse-drawn coach, coal-black as sin. It rapidly drew closer. She saw big hooves, lifting high; a massive chest, sleek with rain and sweat; a long, wild mane, streaming out behind the powerful neck . . .

Alison screamed, a long, loud ululation; hit the brake. The car slued around; she fought the wheel; sobbed. *I WANT TO WAKE UP WAKE UP WAKE UP WAKE UP WAKE UP WAKE UP. PLEEEASSSSSE GOD-DDDDDDDD. LET ME WAKE UP.*

The car swerved into the side of the coach, bounced off, spun around. For one heart-stopping moment Alison looked up. The broad shoulders of the coachman dipped. The raw stump of his neck bobbed courteously down to her.

Alison's hands left the wheel and clapped over her eyes, the fingers pressed tightly into her forehead, the palms grinding painfully into her cheeks. Her mouth was open but no sound came out. She couldn't get her lungs to work. *OH GOD OH GOD OH GOD OH GOD OH GOD OH*

GOD OH GOD OH GOD OH GOD OH GOD.
 THEY HAVE NO HEADS.

Both man and beast. Headless. Just thick stumps oozing blood.

The car skidded into the trunk of a massive oak. The sound of breaking glass filled the air. Alison was thrown violently to the side. Her head cracked smartly against the side window and her knee met the steering post with a sharp rap. Pain lanced through her; hot, red, pulsating. A long bony finger of a tree branch traced a line across her right cheek.

Her eyes popped open, against her volition. She was looking at the ceiling; her head canted against the side window. Slowly she levered herself upright. The tree was in the car, allowing rain to sheet in, drenching her in moments. Dripping leaves brought a moldy smell. She sneezed; wished she hadn't as her head exploded with fiery shards of pain. A scratching sound came from her left. With infinite care she turned her head—

. . . and screamed and screamed and screamed again, tearing the sound from a throat already raw and bruised. Blackness took her then, mercifully, but not before she had seen it all: red eyes; a mouth full of long, sharp, pointed teeth; a frothing muzzle dripping gore—agape, grinning. Evil.

10

Friday, June 14

Sam carefully inched his way through town, almost missing the turnoff to the inn. *Easy does it, only a couple of miles to go,* he silently cautioned himself. The rain concealed, then revealed. In the next moment his hands tightened on the wheel, his foot left the gas and eased down on the brake as he automatically executed the procedure to slow the car from a crawl to a stop. Then he sat helplessly watching a skidding car crash into one of the giant trees guarding the perimeter of the road.

The sound of it was a shock that vibrated through the night.

Cursing silently, steadily, inventively, Sam maneuvered his car across the road, bringing it to a stop directly behind the other car. Something big and dark and silent moved away from the wreck. He squinted, but it was raining too hard to make out details.

The rain beat against him punishingly the second he stepped out of the car. He swiped it out of his eyes with a hand that trembled. It looked like part of the tree had smashed through the front windshield. Glass crunched under his shoes. He found himself praying he would find whoever was inside alive.

* * *

A woman; skin as white as chalk; eyes closed; un-moving.

Sam tried the door. Locked. He moved to the shattered windshield, leaned in close to get a better look. "Oh, shit," he mumbled. She was held in place by the seat belt, her head thrown back against the headrest. The entire lower right side of her face was masked by blood.

"Shit," he said again, loudly, forcefully, while his brain raced, assessing, analyzing, concluding. It would take too long to get to a phone. She could die while he was away. Police, he thought, and knew it was a sure-fire lead-pipe cinch that a county or state patrol car wouldn't come cruising this way. He'd never seen one, so surely not on a night like this.

But what if by moving her he aggravated whatever injuries she had sustained? No choice. She needed help, fast, and he was it—the only game in town.

The passenger door was also locked, smart for a woman traveling alone, now potentially lethal. There was no way in past the hole in the windshield. He was afraid to move the branch for fear more glass would shower on the woman. He would have to break in another way.

The trunk of the Lincoln yielded a tire iron. He hefted it, feeling its balance, while he went to take another look. He figured the best way to get inside was to break the left rear window and then reach inside and unlock the driver's door.

The rain had intensified, making the grass on the verge slick. He lost his balance and grabbed the Mustang's rear panel to keep himself from going down. Through the rain-streaked window he thought he saw her head roll. Hoping it was not just a reaction to the jarring of the car, he leaned down to wipe some of the moisture from the window. Big dark eyes stared out blankly at him.

Sam felt something tight inside him ease. "Thank God. Don't worry, I'm going to get you out." Brilliant. He was babbling instead of doing something, but relief momentarily overwhelmed him. "Unlock the door so I can get to you." He smiled, reassuringly, he hoped, beginning to worry that she showed no signs of reaction.

In the next few seconds he got more reaction than he wished. Her eyes focused, her mouth opened, and she screamed. Loudly. Very loudly. Over and over and over again.

"Please. Don't. Miss, you'll hurt yourself. Please don't scream. Hold on, just hold on, I'm coming to get you." Frightened, he thought she was in shock and he had to get to her. In a hurry. Get to her and get her warm. That about summed up what he knew about treating someone in shock.

He stepped back and swung the tire iron against the rear window. She screamed louder and began to twist and turn. "Almost there," he shouted above her screams and the noise of the engine and the rain. "I've almost got you." He swung again, putting everything he had behind it. It did the job. The safety glass sagged inward. He took off his jacket and wrapped it around his hand, began punching the glass inward.

"I've almost got you," he said, over and over again, a promise of rescue. The screams had degenerated into a thin wailing sound. Her hands were fumbling ineffectually with the locking mechanism of the seat belt. "Don't move," he said rather sharply, afraid she might further injure herself. Finally he had a hole big enough to get his hand through. Hastily, he ripped the jacket off it and reached inside to unlock the button. She turned her head and bit his hand. Hard.

Sam howled. "Let go," he roared, and to his surprise, she did. He promptly withdrew the injured member from the field, cursing under his breath when he saw she had drawn blood. Pierced to the quick, he thought disgustedly. Some knight in shining armor. Gingerly holding his throbbing hand, he moved to the front of the car where she could see him. "Look, lady," he said, his tone harsher than he wished, "my name is Sam Chandler and I'm trying to rescue you. I don't know how badly you're injured. Now stop obstructing me, goddamnit, and let me get on with it."

She stared at him. Without the screaming he was more aware of the rain, by now almost a solid sheet of water, pouring down with a hurting force. "I'm cold and I'm wet and you are, too. Believe me, lady, I only want to help. Okay?" She nodded, and then, to his immense relief, unlocked the door.

Sam understood just how much courage that simple act had required. He opened the door and leaned in, switching off the lights and the engine before turning to the woman. Without the mechanical noise the rain seemed even louder. He felt her breath on his neck; smelled a light, flowery scent. His senses tingled into heightened awareness. His body tightened. His timing was terrific.

"Is it gone?"

He felt each word as a puff of breath against his cheek. Had there been another car? "What? Was there a collision?" he asked as he fought the jammed seat belt release. She twisted her body, making it difficult for him to maneuver in the cramped space.

"Please look. Make sure it's gone."

Sam responded to the urgency in her voice. The memory of a large dark shape slinking away from the car surfaced. Surely it had been nothing but a trick of the rain and the shadow of the tree in his headlights.

"Please."

Her eyes were full of fear. Something had to have triggered it. Feeling rather foolish, but being a sucker for a damsel in distress, he backed out of the car and revolved a complete circle. Nothing. Nothing that he could see . . . but the rain prevented visibility for more than a few feet. A sound from behind the tree drew his attention. Without conscious thought, he retrieved the tire iron from the grass and went to investigate, waving to her reassuringly

80

before disappearing around the giant oak. Nothing. Except . . . Some of the long grass looked trampled. He poked with the iron. A fetid odor rose up. Noxious. He prodded some more, expecting to uncover an animal's rotting corpse.

She called to him, her thin voice holding the high edge of panic. He walked a few feet farther, examining the ground, but found no tangible sign of any animal, living or dead. Back at the car the pale blur of her face peered anxiously up at him. "Nothing but us chickens." The attempt to lighten the atmosphere failed. She began pulling at the seat belt again. "Let me. You might hurt yourself."

"I'm fine," she said, but she stopped her ineffectual movements nevertheless.

Sam leaned across her and poked and prodded, finally feeling the mechanism release. As the belt retracted she fell forward, into his arms. She felt soft. Holding her felt right.

"They had no heads," she said, and fainted.

Sam's reaction was primitive. Atavistic. He lifted her up and out of the car, then held her tight against his chest in a protective embrace. She was female and she was hurt. The urge to shield, to guard, to succor, overpowered him. Her safety and her survival depended on him. Warrior genes from a remote ancestor tightened his body into fighting readiness. Uneasily he swept the area with narrowed eyes, every sense alert for something, anything, out of the ordinary. But the enemy remained invisible, only the putrid odor to indicate another presence had been near. There was no one, nothing to fight.

Nevertheless, he hadn't felt so alive in a very long time.

Head injury, Sam kept thinking as he squinted through the windshield. The thought sent a shiver skittering down his spine. He drove slowly through town, knowing the nearest hospital was miles away, across the Kancamagus

Highway, not an easy drive even during the day. He hated mountain driving. Give him a nice straight flat city street.

The woman moaned and made a little snuffling sound.

"Easy. You're doing fine." Sam fervently hoped he wasn't lying.

The wipers were almost useless. He cursed as the right tires bumped off the road onto the rain-soaked shoulder. The curses became louder as he guided the car back onto the macadam. He risked a cautious glance at his passenger. Wrapped in an old plaid blanket he always kept in the trunk, she looked like a Scottish mummy. Then he saw the open eyes, big and dark, filling the still deathly pale face. The eyes were aware. Sam felt encouraged. "Hello," he said softly, "I'm glad you're back."

"Sam?"

"Yes," he answered, inordinately pleased she remembered his name, and risked another quick glance at her. She was struggling against the double restraint of the blanket and seat belt. "Relax. I'll get you to the hospital just as soon as I can."

"No. No hospital. I'm fine. Really. I've got to get to the inn."

Surprised, Sam shifted his attention from the road to the woman, and the car promptly swerved to the right again. "Damn it," he shouted, and saw her wince in the split second before he returned his attention to his driving. He didn't risk glancing at her again until all four tires were solidly placed on the pavement once more. "You had an accident," he said carefully. "Do you remember?"

"Yes." She shuddered.

"You must have hit your head. You were out cold when I reached you and you fainted again when I pulled you out of the car." *And before you lost consciousness you said something that can only come from a nightmare—or from a blow to the head.* He hazarded another quick glimpse at her. The paleness still prevailed, painted gorily by blood on the right side, but her features had hardened,

82

taken on a determined cast. "In between, well . . . you, er, you weren't quite rational. I figure you hit your head, probably on the side window. Could be a concussion. These things can be tricky, you can't take chances. You need a doctor, and that's where I'm taking you. Believe me, it's for your own good."

The last thing he expected her to do was laugh. The sound of it chilled his blood. It stopped, abruptly, and in the sudden silence he heard her sigh. *Hysteria*. Now he was truly out of his depth; he only had rudimentary first-aid skills.

"Sam—"

"Look, lady—"

"Alison. My name is Alison Fortune, and I don't blame you one little bit for thinking you've rescued a crazy woman. I have trouble myself believing what happened." She twisted sharply toward him, her body hampered by the restraints. "I only fainted after . . . after . . ." *They had no heads*. She closed her eyes and fought for composure. When she opened them seconds later he was regarding her gravely. "I know you don't believe me. Why should you? But I know what I saw and I wasn't hallucinating. It happened. It was real and I . . . Oh, God, please listen. Just listen."

"Okay. Easy. Easy, Alison."

"Pull over." He hesitated, and she didn't wait to press the slight advantage. "After you hear me out I promise you I'll go wherever you want. Willingly."

Sam wavered. She *had* to get to a hospital, PDQ if he was any judge, but . . .

Alison quickly took advantage of his indecision. "I give you my word."

"That's not necessary," he said rather gruffly, angry at himself for allowing her to sway him. Her agitation couldn't be doing her any good. He'd give her a couple of minutes and then nothing she said would stop him from taking her to the hospital.

He steered the car off the road into the first available place and switched off the engine. The rain immediately stippled the windshield, blinding them to the outside world, creating a snug haven.

The same feeling that he had experienced a little while ago, the urge to protect, to succor this woman, welled strongly within Sam. Against all the dictates of common sense he released her from the seat belt, feeling her body tense even through the blanket, although his touch was fleeting and impersonal. With a rueful smile, he gently tugged at the blanket, giving her the freedom to move her arms. "I'm probably the crazy one here. You could be in shock, and who knows what injuries you've sustained, but go ahead, tell me what you saw."

"Thank you," she murmured, "both for stopping to help and for this . . . for listening." She wriggled a hand free and immediately pushed her hair behind her ears. The fingers came away sticky with blood.

"Alison—"

"Sam, please."

He couldn't resist the appeal in both voice and eyes and he began to get an inkling that this woman could be very dangerous to him. He fumbled in his pocket and produced a handkerchief. He couldn't remember if it was clean. "Here, use this. You've got blood all over your face, too."

She wiped her fingers and began to swipe at her face. Without a word he reached over and flipped down the vanity mirror. The bright light ruthlessly made the mask of blood on her right side visible. The sight was frightening, should have produced at least a pull on her vanity, but all Alison did was try to wipe it off.

"Let me," he said, concerned that she was scrubbing too hard. "It's crusted. We need water."

"Leave it." She covered the mirror, returning the car to darkness. "Let me tell you what happened while it's still fresh in my mind."

84

Sam listened; he owed her that. He had promised, but it became increasingly difficult to keep incredulity from showing. He didn't want to touch off the hysteria again. The tale was fantastic; beyond that . . . unbelievable . . . inconceivable.

He realized she had stopped speaking, had been silent for some time. Time to get her to the hospital. "Uh, ah . . ." He cleared his throat and tried again. "I, uh—"

Her laughter again stopped him cold. He wondered if he could bring himself to slap her should she go into full-blown hysterics. She placed her free hand on his arm and leaned in close to his body. "It really does sound crazy. I don't blame you for what you're thinking. I'd do the same in your shoes."

Sam stared down at those bloodstained fingers and the compulsion to protect rose strongly in him again. "I'm not an expert," he said carefully, "but I've seen this before. Concussions can be, well, ticklish. Once you're—"

"Sam. Stop. All this happened before the crash, except for that . . . that hellhound. It was scratching on the door after the car hit the tree." His muscles tightened under her hand. Her eyes narrowed. "What? Did you see it?" He shifted on the seat and she clutched at him, digging her fingers into his arm. "Did you?"

Honesty, and the memory of the putrid odor and the desperate pleading look in her eyes, forced him to admit that he had seen something. "It was no more than a shadow, though, an impression of—"

"A big dog."

"Could be."

She sighed in relief and leaned her head back on the headrest. "Thank God."

She sounded so relieved, Sam hated to disillusion her. "Alison, I drove up in time to see you skid. If there had been something like this coach, I'm sure I would have seen it. It would have had to pass me."

"That's all right, Sam. You saw the dog. That's enough

85

for me." She smiled, a sad little smile, in the process cracking the dried blood on her face.

That vividly reminded Sam it was well past time they were on their way. "Hospital," he said firmly. "You promised."

"How about taking me to Dr. Cutter? He's a lot closer than the hospital and he's this side of the Kancamagus."

She was gracious enough to pretend she couldn't hear him cursing all the way back into town.

II

Dr. Henry Cutter lived in an old Victorian house. A discreet sign at the foot of the drive announced his profession. "He has his office in the house?" Sam asked, used to New York City where such an occurrence was as rare as a good steak east of Kansas.

Alison laughed. Sam noted with relief that there was no trace of hysteria in it. "Wait until you see it. It's like looking at a cover of the *Saturday Evening Post*."

Suddenly Sam wasn't so sure this was such a good idea. He had envisioned a modern emergency room equipped with ultra-sophisticated machinery, not a relic of a house with gingerbread trim.

He didn't realize he was frowning until Alison spoke. "He's really very good."

Sam thought about the Kancamagus and the time it would take to get across it. "Okay. Sit tight. I'll come around for you."

"No need. I can walk."

Sam's large hand briefly squeezing her shoulder told her argument was useless. He had her out of the car and on the porch before she could get very wet again. They both looked at the small sign giving the doctor's office hours that was pasted onto a pane of glass in the front door. "We're a little early," Alison said.

Sam shifted her more comfortably against his chest. "Stop stalling and ring the bell, please. I have my hands full."

Which was exactly what Dr. Henry Cutter said a short time later. Clad in a red-yellow-and-black striped robe over green pajamas, he wrenched the door open and gave the pair a thorough look before stepping back and opening the door wider. "Looks like you've got your hands full there," he said, and waved them inside, going immediately down a short corridor.

"Why, it's Alison!"

Sam looked up and saw a woman dressed in a faded terry-cloth robe leaning over the banister of a rather steep staircase. Old-fashioned hair rollers decorated her head. He didn't stop, closely following the doctor into the examining room. He placed Alison on the table, and with gentle hands unwrapped her from the blanket. He took several seconds to study the room. Norman Rockwell would have been right at home. He squeezed Alison's shoulder, this time reassuringly, and told her he would wait outside.

The woman in the terry-cloth robe was standing right outside the door of the examination room. A young woman, slippers flip-flopping noisily on the wooden floor, hurried down the corridor toward them. "Why, hi, Mr. Chandler," she said in a breezy voice teasingly familiar to him. He frowned. "I'm Jennifer."

Of course. *Sweet, blond Jennifer Cutter.* Sam made the connection in his mind as soon as she stepped into the light. Unfortunately he said it aloud. "Yogurt. You left a carton of apricot yogurt in the refrigerator."

"I couldn't find it."

Sam almost told her it was behind the beer, but another look at the older woman, obviously her mother, made him think better of it. "It's there," he told Jennifer blandly, then held out his hand. "Mrs. Cutter? I'm Sam Chandler, project manager of Dragon Meadow." Not that he was keeping score, but that was the third time this evening he had said something similar.

"Dorothy Cutter. Dottie." She had a firm handshake and the slightest of accents. "What happened to Alison?"

"Car accident."

"Poor dear. Henry'll see to her. You, Mr. Chandler, look like you could use a hot cup of tea."

Sam realized several things at once: Dorothy Cutter's accent was English and he was bone-tired and wet. "Please."

The kitchen was huge and outfitted with modern appliances. Gleaming copper pots and pans hung from hooks above a central island. Jennifer went directly to the work station and put a kettle on, while her mother rummaged in the refrigerator. It looked like a well-rehearsed act.

Sam was grateful for the tea and the lemon meringue pie, but was more grateful for the company. Twenty minutes later Henry Cutter came and wearily sat down at the table. Dottie placed a cup of tea in front of him before he could ask for it.

"How's Alison?"

A spare smile lit Henry's face. "Nothing too serious. Bruised knee. Possible concussion. The face looks worse than it is. The branch cut a furrow through the scalp. Those things bleed like sons a bitches."

"Did she tell you about the . . . er . . ." Uncomfortable, Sam raked a hand through his hair.

The doctor peered at him through his bifocals, sharp gray eyes missing no detail. "Jennifer," he said, "go and see if Alison needs any help getting dressed. Don't let her get off the table."

Apparently Jennifer took no umbrage at being dismissed, however gently. Her father waited until they heard the distant sound of a door opening and then closing again. The doctor calmly sipped his tea and then reached across the table and took his wife's hand. "Dottie's my nurse, but if you think she should leave, there'll be no offense taken."

Sam shrugged helplessly. "I don't have the faintest idea what's right or wrong. I thought she would have told you about what she thought she saw. Perhaps she's already forgotten about it."

"I think you'd better tell me what this is all about. If it will help me make a more precise diagnosis, I want to hear it."

He had no choice. Sam knew it, yet he felt that in some peculiar way he was betraying her. No, not her. Perhaps the trust she had placed in him. But . . . With as few words as possible he told the Cutters everything Alison had told him. When he finished speaking the big kitchen was silent except for the faint buzzing coming from the fluorescent light above the sink. Sam transferred his gaze from the bottom of his cup to the silent couple. It had been easier to talk of Alison's hallucinations without looking at anyone. The doctor appeared thoughtful, but his wife . . . "Mrs. Cutter?"

Her face was chalk white; her pupils were dilated so that only a thin rim of her iris showed, making it impossible to tell their color.

"Dottie! What is it?" The doctor automatically sought his wife's pulse. "Do you have pain?"

"The death coach! Henry, she saw the death coach!"

The fine hairs on Sam's body crackled as if an electric current had passed through him. "What . . . ?"

Both the doctor and his wife ignored him. Mrs. Cutter had a death grip on her husband's hand. "Someone has died. The death coach comes for the souls of the dead."

"Nonsense," Dr. Cutter said. "That's your old granny talking. More of her Cornish superstition."

Dottie shook her head vehemently. "No." The old-fashioned rollers bounced. "It's not superstition, it's real," she said stubbornly. "And the hound she saw—"

"Dottie!"

"What about the hound, Mrs. Cutter?"

Dorothy Cutter looked at Sam as if surprised at his presence. She blinked and then swallowed noisily. "The hound?" she repeated parrotlike.

"Did your grandmother say anything about it?"

The doctor's wife took a deep breath and then let it out. She seemed to shrink in size. "It's a dandy dog. One of the Devil's dandy dogs. The Devil is in Draconia tonight," she said, and for the second time that night Sam watched as a woman fainted.

Her head hurt, her throat was parched, and her eyelids felt as if they had coins on them. Heavy coins. *I'm dead,* Alison thought, and groaned. A hand touched her forehead, moved to her cheek, and then briefly pressed against the side of her neck. A deep voice told her to wake up, to open her eyes. It was a struggle, but she finally got her lids to lift. Worried eyes with little crinkled lines around them stared down at her. Green eyes. Very nice eyes. "Hello," she said. Her voice seemed to come from some distant place; it sounded hollow. She was vaguely aware that there was something she should be remembering.

"Hello yourself. How are you feeling?"

His voice was deep and gravelly and filled with concern. He sat down on the bed and leaned over her, bringing the nice green eyes close to her face. That was when Alison knew she was asleep, that he existed only in a dream. There hadn't been a man sitting on her bed in a very long time.

"Who are you?" she asked.

He gave a dry bark of laughter. "I should be wearing a sign."

She frowned. It hurt.

The nice green eyes narrowed. Alison decided that this

was probably not the best time to tell him how much she liked them. He leaned closer, blocking out the light, and the first hint of unease skittered through her mind. She could recognize his scent, a combination of essences: of soap and a woodsy cologne; of something his alone, his *maleness*—primitive, exciting; and also . . . rain. He smelled of rain, and with the thought came the next one, unwelcome, that she could *hear* it, hitting the windows . . .

He was real. She was in the inn; in his room; in his bed. Sam. Her fingers plucked at the soft smoothness of the percale sheet covering her.

The rain, furiously pounding . . .

Pounding.

No dream. This was no dream, and with the realization came memory and with memory came fear. Deep, bone-chilling fear.

Headless.

They had no heads.

"Oh, God. No. Sam . . . ?" The next instant found her sobbing her fear against a solid shoulder. Strong arms held her close; a gentle hand smoothed tear-damp hair away from her face. He rocked her and comforted her as if she were a baby. When the storm of weeping passed she lay limply against him, the pain in her head now a monstrous throbbing. She pictured it as a balloon filling with blood, swelling obscenely, threatening to burst through the wall of her skull. "My head. Hurts." She could barely get the words out past the pain.

"I know," he said, and gently lowered her to the pillow. "Tomorrow. Hang in until tomorrow. Dr. Cutter said no painkiller tonight because you might have a concussion. I'm sorry, sweetheart. I'm sorry." He wiped the wetness from beneath her eyes with the pad of his thumb, then he offered her water, the only thing he had to give. She drank thirstily, greedily. "Sleep now. Sleep's the best medicine."

"Sam?"

"Sleep, Alison. We'll talk tomorrow."

But something inside her, something stronger than the fear, something that penetrated even through the haze of pain, would not let her rest until she gave it voice. Alison Crandell Fortune did not have flights of fancy. She had had an accident, had seen what caused it. There had to be an explanation. Now all she had to do was find it.

"Sam—"

"Hush, Alison. Sleep. Sleep, sweetheart."

Her world was gray mist. She sank into it, dimly aware of a hand brushing the hair away from her face, of the tender press of firm lips against her forehead. *Sweetheart.*

12

Sam yawned, a great lip-stretching yawn, and then rubbed his eyes, which felt grainy from lack of sleep. He yawned again and shook his head to clear it. It didn't work.

The door of the trailer opened and then banged shut, admitting a rush of cool air. Rufus McClain entered and gave Sam an amused scrutiny. "Mornin', boss. You look like hell. Rough night?"

Sam regarded his foreman with a jaundiced eye. "Not like you mean."

"I kinda thought, maybe you and Angie . . . ?" He arched a brow. The gesture made him look like a middle-aged Mr. Clean.

"Well, you thought wrong."

McClain clomped to the table in the rear of the trailer where the coffee maker was kept. He pointedly didn't ask if Sam wanted a refill.

"Sorry," Sam said. "I didn't get much sleep."

Mollified, the foreman held up the carafe with the bitter brew everyone favored. "Coffee?"

Sam pushed his mug across the desk toward McClain and spoke around another huge yawn. "Yeah, thanks. Bring yours on over and sit for a while. I could use the company."

Sam accepted the refilled mug with a grunt that passed for thanks and immediately wrapped his long fingers around it, trying to pull the heat of the coffee into himself. He felt cold, and not just because of the chill dampness of the early morning. The entire fantastic, unbelievable night had drained him.

Rufus emptied his mug before he broke the silence. "Care to tell me what's bothering you?" A thought suddenly struck him. He banged the mug down onto Sam's desk, capturing his full attention. "I sure as hell hope you didn't lose any sleep over what I said last night."

"What?"

"What I told you at Sonny's, about the men being spooked and all."

Sam had forgotten about that conversation, or, rather, more urgent matters had pushed it out of his conscious thought. He wished it had stayed buried. If the men ever got wind of what Alison had seen ... But they wouldn't—at least not from him.

"No." Sam chopped the denial out, fast. It was the truth—as far as it went. He gave a short grunt that could have passed for laughter with someone less astute than McClain. "Actually, it *was* a woman and she did keep me up all night."

"Must have been a wild one." McClain looked pointedly at Sam's bandaged hand, which had been fascinating him. "What did she do? Take a bite out of you?"

"How did you guess?" Sam asked sourly. A grim smile tautened his lips. "But that was the least of it. Listen, the damnedest thing happened," and then he told his foreman an abbreviated version of his night. "And Dr. Cutter—by the way, he's Jennifer's father—made it clear that she needed to be checked periodically to see if she had a concussion. What else could I do?"

Rufus grinned at him. "What else?"

Sam grinned back. "Indeed." It had been an instantaneous reaction. The second he had seen Alison through the rain-speckled window, unconscious, blood pouring down one side of her face, she had brought out the protector in him. Besides, as he had told himself last night, he was a sucker for a damsel in distress.

Sam busied himself with paperwork after McClain left. He would have preferred to be outdoors, walking the site, even though the air was damp and the ground was muddy from the heavy rain.

Shortly after nine o'clock Jennifer poked her blond head inside the trailer. "Morning, Mr. Chandler."

Grateful for the interruption, Sam flipped his pencil so that he was holding it by the tip and drummed the eraser against a manila folder in a rhythmic beat. "Hi, Jennifer."

Jennifer smiled, and Sam could have sworn the room brightened. "Do you mind if I show my father around a bit? He hasn't seen what you're doing here yet."

"No problem," Sam said, then stared thoughtfully at the spot where Jennifer's shining golden head had been. It didn't take him long to decide he could use a little fresh air.

He found the pair easily by following the trail to the area near the river where they were clearing land for condominiums. Before making his presence known, he stopped in the shadow of an elm tree and observed father and daughter for several minutes. Jennifer bubbled with high spirits, talking almost nonstop, waving her arms about in her enthusiasm. Her father appeared to be distracted.

When Sam left his observation post and approached them, the doctor jerked his head up and offered a strained smile. Sam knew at once that his hunch had been correct. Henry Cutter had not come to the complex just to look around.

The doctor got down to business almost before the normal greetings were exchanged. He asked about Alison and briefly examined Sam's injured hand, lightly pressing the bandage to check for swelling and tenderness. "Good," he said, "very good. Keep it covered for another day and then let nature take its course. Best healer there is."

The three of them began to walk, Sam content to let Jennifer do most of the talking while he surreptitiously studied her father. The man unmistakably had something on his mind.

"Isn't that right, Mr. Chandler?" Jennifer pivoted to face him, her fresh young face shining with zeal. "You're going to try to save as many trees as you possibly can, aren't you?"

"That's the plan." Sam believed in preserving as much of the land as possible.

The day was warming up, although the sun would have to gain strength to firm the mud. They walked slowly, following the river, which was higher and ran faster because of the previous night's downpour. The path took them away from the activity, down to the old mill.

"They won't start on this for several weeks," Jennifer told her father. "It needs to be gutted and the brickwork reinforced before anything else can be done. Right, Mr. Chandler?"

"Right," Sam acknowledged, privately amused at the breadth of Jennifer's information. Such detail could only come from a member of the crew. Idly, he wondered who the lucky man was.

Dr. Cutter took several steps closer to the derelict building. "When I was a kid you came here only on a dare. It was the closest thing to a haunted house that we had in Draconia."

Jennifer giggled, the sound pure, innocent, in the clear

mountain air.

Her father looked at her sharply. "You never—"

Jennifer giggled again. "Not me. I wasn't brave enough, but I heard that some of the older boys once spent a night inside. Jerry Treadwell and his gang. Yuck, who would want to?"

Both men laughed at the very feminine response. At the mention of Jerry Treadwell's name Sam made a mental note to call him about Alison's car just as soon as he got back to the trailer. Lucy had recommended Treadwell, and he had promised her he would see to it.

Sam came out of his introspection to notice that Jennifer had moved too close to a crumbling wall for his comfort. "Careful."

He called the warning just as Jennifer wrinkled her nose. "What an awful smell."

It was, and it came from inside the old mill. Sam identified it at once, and knew that the doctor had also when he suddenly gripped his daughter's arm and dragged her back—away from the sweetish, unmistakable odor of death.

"Dad?" Jennifer's face had lost some of its brightness.

The doctor dropped her arm and gazed at Sam. They both knew what was in the old mill.

"I'd better have a look." Sam cast his eyes about the area until he spotted a long, thick branch partially hidden in the tall grasses. He picked it up and hefted it to determine its weight, much as he had the tire iron last night. He cautiously used it to poke at a sagging, water-swollen wooden door. With a bit of effort he got it to move several inches. Then he stepped back and gave the door a solid kick, which forced it open about a foot more.

The smell rushed out to meet them. Sam swallowed convulsively, stepped inside, the doctor moving to stand right behind him. The scent of corruption pervaded the old building, laced with another odor, putrid also, but not the odor of something dead. A rustling noise came from the darkness in a far corner. Startled, Sam took an involuntary step and slipped on something. He did a little dance to keep his balance and then looked down. Bile rose in his throat. He felt rather than saw the doctor peer around him, heard his sharply indrawn breath.

Another noise came out of the corner. Sam's eyes had adjusted to the dim light. He saw a shadow, sensed the presence of an animal. A big animal. It moved again, and two nightmare-colored red eyes gleamed briefly, then disappeared as it faded back into the shadows. They heard nails clicking across the floor, and then there was silence. It had left. Without exchanging a single word, both men stepped out into the sunshine.

Jennifer looked apprehensive and pale. "Dad?"

"An animal." He narrowed his eyes at his daughter. "For heaven's sake, Jenny, stop that scratching. My bag's in the car. Go and get it."

"But—"

"Right now, young lady. Wait for me in the trailer and I'll give you a salve for that hand before I leave."

Jennifer nodded and hurried away.

Sam waited until she was too far away to hear before he spoke. "You saw it?"

Henry Cutter looked even paler than Jennifer had. "Yes."

"I think that was the creature Alison saw last night. I recognized the smell. Your wife referred to it as a dandy dog. One of the Devil's dandy dogs, I believe she said. It . . . it must have been feeding on that . . . that—"

"Raccoon, I think. Hard to tell anymore."

Sam wished he had never looked, but he knew that the rotting corpse had been food for some larger animal. It had been savaged and torn apart; the remains were nothing more than a few pulpy masses of glistening red meat.

Even the bones had been gnawed.

"Chandler?"

Sam focused on the doctor, who was nervously combing his sparse hair with his fingers. "What?"

"It's Dottie. My wife. I . . . er, we had some night last night, ah, after you left. She, ah, wouldn't listen to a thing I said. I finally sedated her; she was still sleeping when I left." He paused, and Sam knew the doctor had finally come to the real reason for his presence at Dragon Meadow this morning. "I'd like to, ah, ask a favor. Not for me, mind, but—"

"I know." Sam's tone was weary. "I figured it out as soon as I saw you. Don't worry, I'll keep what your wife said to myself."

They both turned and looked at the old mill, knowing they shared a similar thought. Whatever secret they pledged this morning would not be long kept. Something savage was in Draconia and getting bolder by the hour.

Deirdre Treadwell

Using only the tips of his fingers he traced every inch of her body, learning the curves, the hollows, the hidden secrets of her femininity. Slowly, slowly he stroked, caressing, fondling, arousing, heightening desire until she became wild with need.

She trembled. It was pleasure; it was agony; it was unbearable, this slow, maddening arousal. She pressed herself closer to him, reveling in the contrast of their bodies: she was silky-smooth flame; he was hot, pulsing, hair-roughed velvet over steel.

"I want you. Now."

He ignored the command, used his clever tongue on her burning, sensitive flesh to drive her to a higher peak.

Panting, she knew she would have to beg. Her legs parted invitingly. "Please."

A laugh of pure masculine triumph rumbled through his chest. "Not yet," he said, and resumed the exquisite torture.

Wild with need, she slipped from his grasp and slid down the black satin sheets until she reached the foot of the bed. Hurriedly she swung her long, shapely legs over the edge and stood up. She would make him want her as desperately as she wanted him.

"Come back here," he growled.

She smiled—saucily, temptingly, wickedly.

A new excitement flared between them, sparked by her ploy, sharpened by an increased awareness as she turned gracefully, took flight, boldly leading him into further adventure. He stalked her silently, surely; careful to keep pace, not to outdistance her; to prolong the tension.

The stimulating hunt ended in the kitchen. Without a word he captured her, his large hands seizing her by the waist, lifting her up, placing her on the edge of the sink. The metal felt cold on her heated flesh. He forced her knees apart, then left her, opened wide, and went to the pantry. Soon he returned with a jar in one hand and held it up before her eyes. She watched as he opened it, plunged his tongue deep inside.

Her breathing became rapid; hoarse little panting cries filled the air. He lifted one of her legs and then the other, carefully placing them so that her heels were firmly pressed against the counter. One strong arm supported her back. Her breath caught in her throat. She was completely open to him. Vulnerable. He dipped two long fingers into the jar. They came out glistening, oozing strawberry jam. She closed her eyes.

He touched her. "Now," he whispered and . . .

The loud banging of the back door slamming shut ripped through the fabric of the fantasy. "Deirdre? Hey,

101

Deirdre, I'm home. Where are you, babe?"

Jerry Treadwell's voice boomed unexpectedly through the eerie quiet of the house. Deirdre trembled in rage. This was just one more filthy trick life was playing her. She began to laugh, the sound cold, hard, completely devoid of humor. It led her husband directly to her.

"What's so funny?" Jerry's eyes swept over her, then narrowed as they came to rest on the table next to her chair—on the rectangle of glass with a faint, telltale residue of white powder. "Isn't it a bit early for that?"

Deirdre shrugged and stood up, casually belting her ivory silk robe more snugly about her waist. "What else have I got to do?" The hours of her day were long and empty; she filled them as best she could, with daydreams and erotic fantasies, enhanced by the all-consuming white powder that made the images in her mind more vivid, more exciting.

Jerry clenched his hands and opened his mouth, but the words he wanted to say got no further than the back of his throat. What was the use? They had all been said before. Deirdre didn't want a family yet, and he refused to let her work. Old-fashioned of him, perhaps, but no Treadwell wife had ever worked. Not that Deirdre showed much inclination for it.

Belatedly, Deirdre took an interest in him. "What are you doing home? Did you forget your lunch?"

Jerry did his best to ignore the sneer in her voice. She hated that he ate his lunch out of a brown paper bag, but that was the way it had always been. Treadwells ate with their employees; one of the men.

"No."

A sudden light kindled in her eyes. She crossed her arms around her chest and hugged herself, the action pushing her breasts upward invitingly.

"Deirdre . . . babe—" He had only stopped by for his bowling ball.

The refusal made her waspish. "So what's so important? Did Milly Edgehill back into a parking meter again? We wouldn't want the mayor's wife to drive around in a dented car, would we?"

Jerry sighed, knowing they would soon have to resolve the problem of his work. He should tell her he sold the tract of land he inherited to the Mountain Venture people. But if he did, Deirdre would be after him to sell the business and go into something where he wouldn't get grease under his nails. Again, Jerry sighed; he *liked* working with his hands.

"Deirdre—"

"Forget it." She lit a cigarette and blew a plume of smoke past his right ear. "Nothing ever happens around here anyway."

She walked past him and went down the hall, into the kitchen. He could hear running water, then the kettle banging against the side of the sink as she filled it. He followed, stopping in the doorway to admire her. She was some sight, with her red-brown hair and her ripe, lushly curved body with its long legs, legs that seemed to go on forever. He walked up behind her and drew her into a tight embrace.

Deirdre turned in his arms and placed one perfectly manicured hand on his chest. "Jerry?"

The nails were painted a deep reddish-purple. Looking down he saw that her toes were tipped in the same color. "What, babe?"

"Stay."

The invitation tempted him, but he had things to do. He lifted her hand from his chest and kissed the fingertips. "I can't." She snatched her hand away. He dropped his arms and watched as she deftly stepped away, out of his reach. "You're wrong, babe, things do happen here. It seems Vera Alderbrook has gone and run away."

"Good for her."

Jerry ignored her sarcasm, opened the door to the utility closet and bent down, looking for his bowling ball. "I've got to drive to Laconia this afternoon. The Ford people down there say they've got some of the parts I need for Alison's car. While I'm there I'll probably order the glass for her, too. It's an old model and I'm sure neither Eddie nor Abe carries it in stock." He straightened up, his bowling ball in one hand, the duffel with his shoes and league shirt in the other. "I knew I left these in here."

Deirdre focused on the one thing of interest to her. "Alison?"

"Alison Fortune. You know, Richard's ex. Drove up here in the rain last night and had a little accident. Went into one of those big oaks on the notch road."

"Was she hurt?"

"Fella who called didn't say. Chandler, the architect out at Dragon Meadow." Jerry shrugged and shifted the duffel to the hand holding the bowling ball, and with his free hand grabbed his wife's chin, tilting her face up for his kiss. "Bye, babe, got to run. I won't be home for dinner."

Deirdre barely heard him. The morning had purpose now.

An hour later, dressed casually but wearing full makeup, her thick mane of straight copper-colored hair brushed into gleaming docility so that the blunt-cut edges grazed her shoulders, Deirdre was ready. She left the house by the back door. Early morning clouds had given way to a pale-blue sky. A wan-looking sun climbed slowly past the ridge of the Presidential Range. It didn't yet have the power to dry the waterlogged earth nor to evaporate the moisture from the grass and trees. Every leaf and blade of grass in the backyard dripped. A red-winged blackbird flashed across the space, landing in a clump of tall grass. Deirdre looked right through it,

104

missing the beauty of the bird and of nature. Her thoughts were directed inward; eyes gleaming with wicked anticipation.

Deirdre hummed happily. Life was good.

13

Alison awoke with a start, going from sleep to wakefulness with no apparent transition. She knew immediately she wasn't alone; knew it was Lucy, not Sam sitting in the chair near the bed. The scent of lavender that always clung to her aunt perfumed the room, mingled with the sweet smell of wet grass wafting in through the open window. She took several moments for herself, lying without moving, listening to her body, testing it for injury, finally knowing that whatever hurt she had sustained in the accident was minor. Her head ached dully, but nothing like the throbbing agony of the previous night. She blinked, watching the changing patterns a gently swaying tree outside the window made against a rectangular patch of pale sunshine on the ceiling.

She knew where she was without having to think about it. The Dragon View Inn held no secrets for her; she would recognize every room, every stair, every nook and corner of the old building even in the dark. It had been home since shortly after her seventh birthday, when her recently widowed father brought her for a visit and then left, ten months later, saying his sister Lucy would be a better parent. Ethan Crandell had been right in his judgment, but the decision had hurt. It still hurt, if she let herself think about it.

Her father, her husband: the two most important men in her life had left her with more bad memories than good ones. Often during times of introspection Alison acknowledged that she fought a constant battle against bitterness. Now, silently, she admitted she hadn't come to the inn to wallow in self-pity.

"I know you're up. No use trying to fool me."

The tart tone was vintage Lucy. Alison turned her head toward her aunt. The sight shocked her. In the months since she had last seen Lucy the flesh seemed to have melted from her frame, resulting in a new, frightening, fragility. Alison took in the changes in one sweeping glance, careful to hide her reaction, unsure of what to say, even unsure if saying anything was appropriate. Until she saw Lucy's eyes. Nothing of age or illness or infirmity dwelled there, they shone bright and aware and shrewd: experience and wisdom mixed with native intelligence. Lucy was right. She could never be fooled.

Alison didn't even try. "I expect you've heard."

Lucy checked her watch. "By now I expect just about everybody in Draconia has heard about the accident. I'm only grateful Samson assured me you were all right." She paused and then went on the attack. "What you and that meddling old fool Bertha thought you were up to, going behind my back, trying—"

"Trying to help the person we love. You can glare at me all you like, Lucy, it won't change a thing."

"You were almost killed! And all because of a fool's errand."

Alison laughed. She couldn't help it. Lucy was a master at manipulation. "Better not speak of fools."

"Watch your tongue, missy, I'm still due some respect."

Alison sat up and swung her long legs over the side of the bed. "I both love and respect you, Aunt Lucy, that's why I'm here. I've come to ask you to respect *me* and what I feel for you. And you can start today. It's very simple; all you have to do is take care of yourself." Anticipating at least one of the arguments Lucy could use, Alison angled her chin up. "I don't care if it's blackmail. I'll do what I have to do to get you to take proper care of yourself. And," she admonished, "don't think to only pay me lip service. I'm not leaving here until I know that you'll be all right."

"Alison." With shaking fingers Lucy gently traced the thin scab on Alison's right cheek. "Sam told me what happened before he left this morning. I called that old woman, Henry Cutter, and he said you would look a lot worse than you would feel. He also said there would be no scar." She pursed her lips primly. "I choose to believe him."

Alison laughed. Lucy was—Lucy.

Silence descended while they eyed each other warily, a silence that was suddenly, shockingly shattered. The savage call of a wild animal pierced the serenity of the morning. Lucy's body jerked violently, and before Alison could stop her, she jumped to her feet and rushed to the window.

Alison was right behind her. "What is that? I've never heard anything like it before," she whispered, suddenly afraid she knew, had seen it, up close.

Lucy shivered. Alison put her arm around Lucy's thin shoulders and squeezed lovingly. Lucy patted her niece's hand. "I don't know what it is, child, and I'm almost sure I never want to find out."

Alison thought of a waking nightmare, of a large black coach pulled by a horse with no head. "Lucy—" she said, wondering wildly how she could ask, what she could say, and not sound mad. Had Lucy seen them? Or had Sam told her about them? The fearful apparitions . . . and the beast with fiery eyes . . .

Gently Lucy disengaged herself from Alison's embrace. "I'm nothing but an old lady." She offered Alison the ghost of a smile. "And an old lady who is used to getting her own way, I might add."

Lucy had returned to her customary tart tone. Alison carefully kept her face blank. Too much had been thrown at her at once. She needed time to think.

Lucy suddenly was all brusqueness. "Get up and get dressed," she ordered. "We can't wait all day to clean this room. Of course, you will be moving in with me."

As an exit line, it couldn't be beat.

Richard Fortune stared at the telephone. He reached a hand out, almost touched the smooth beige plastic of the receiver, then quickly snatched his hand away.

Sweat beaded his forehead, although the little office in the rear of his store was cool. He looked at the wall clock and then back at the telephone, trying to picture what she was doing. God, he needed her. He would explode if he didn't have her soon. The bitch. Like all women, never satisfied, always wanting more. Well, she would see. Soon. He wasn't someone to be trifled with. In a short time she and all the other bitches like her would be fighting for a piece of him.

Before he could change his mind he picked up the receiver and dialed. He began to sweat in earnest the instant it started to ring. Once. A trickle of sweat rolled down his temple. Twice. His hand began to shake. The ringing stopped. A woman's voice answered, then paused. Richard pressed the receiver so tightly against his ear that it hurt. Then the recorded female voice continued.

Richard slammed down the receiver. Bitch! He shifted his position in the leather swivel chair, picked up a pencil and sorted through the papers scattered over his desk until he located the list of the winter items to be put on sale. He priced a dozen before the tip of the pencil snapped off. Swearing loudly, he hurled the pencil at the wall.

"Hey, keep it down. You're scaring the customers." Blond blue-eyed Art Bergstrom laughed and casually strolled into the office, seating himself without invitation. In the winter he was the darling of the bunnies on the ski slopes, in all seasons the favorite of women in every lounge and bar within a fifty-mile radius.

Richard glared, but failed to intimidate him. "Fuck the customers."

"Not even a desperate man would want to touch the two old broads who just came in."

Richard ignored him, hoping he would take the hint and go away. The walls seemed to be closing in on him. How he hated this store and everything in it. Including Art. Hated him and hated his money even more.

The whole thing was Daniel's fault. Daniel, his older brother, who wouldn't give him seed money just one more time. That he, a Fortune, had needed to take a partner, albeit a junior partner, to open even this crummy little business, was an acid that ate at his soul. He'd show him, Daniel the hotshot accountant. Soon he would get out of this nowhere place and go big time.

It was only a matter of months, now that they had broken ground for the complex. Dragon Meadow. *His* idea. Just as soon as the mall was completed he was going to open a big all-weather athletic-equipment store, using the money from the sale of his shares of the mill. Maybe he'd even sell some condos. He'd heard there was big money in real-estate commissions. But if it wasn't that, it would be something else. Adrian Blaise had promised.

Just then the telephone rang, and to Richard's chagrin, he flinched.

Art sniggered, an unpleasant sound.

Richard felt rage building within him, threatening to erupt. He was about to vent it, to tell the smug-faced bastard exactly what he thought of him, when the intercom gave a tinny beep. He punched down on the flashing red button and snarled a "Yeah?" into the speaker.

"Richard? Call for you on line one."

"Who is it?"

"You don't pay me enough to screen your calls," Joyce, part-time clerk, saleslady, and cashier, replied loudly before breaking the connection.

Richard's face turned a dull red.

Art smiled nastily, then slowly levered himself out of the chair, testing Richard's small store of patience to the utmost. "Keep your shirt on, I'm outta here," he said, then strolled from the office.

Richard viciously jabbed the button. The ensuing conversation was brief. Richard was in no mood to deal with a salesperson trying to solicit an appointment to show a new line. Then he sat and stared at the wall until Art poked his head inside the office, disturbing him again. "Get out," Richard growled.

A sly smile went no further than Art's lips. He leaned nonchalantly against the doorframe and held up a jogging suit in hot pink. "Lady in dressing room one wants to try this on."

A choked sound of rage rumbled low in Richard's throat.

Art stretched the sly smile a little wider. He held up his free hand palm out. "Peace. She asked specifically for you."

Richard abruptly stood up, sending the chair crashing back against the wall. He snatched the suit from Art's hand and rudely brushed past him, barely restraining himself from shoving his leering partner out of the way. Striding purposefully toward the front of the store, he pushed his way through the display area crowded with racks of merchandise. An overweight matron gave a startled gasp and scurried out of his way. A second woman glared at him, but she also stepped aside hastily. Cows.

He rapped once, loudly, on the slatted wooden door of the dressing room, then jerked it open without waiting for a response. Deirdre Treadwell stood there wearing a lascivious smile and very little else. In the mirror behind Deirdre, Richard saw the overweight woman's lips purse into disapproval as she eyed Deirdre's near-naked voluptuousness, barely covered by a scanty crimson teddy.

"Hello, Richard," Deirdre purred, and with a wink for the outraged matron, drew him into the small dressing room and shut the door.

Richard couldn't take his eyes from the sight of her breasts, creamy smooth, swelling in luscious mounds over the delicate red lace bordering the top edge of the silk teddy. His body tightened into an almost painful awareness.

Deirdre watched him through slitted eyes in which more than a hint of deviltry danced. She placed a hand on his chest and ran it meaningfully down his hardening body. "Umm, nice," she murmured, squeezing him gently, and laughed when he grabbed her wrist and wrenched her hand away. "Whatsa matta, honey, don'tcha wanna play?" she drawled.

"What the hell's the matter with you?" Richard ground out, trying to control the automatic responses of his body.

Deirdre leaned in close, pressing the fullness of her soft, scented breasts against his chest. He could feel their obvious arousal through the thin barriers of her silk garment and his cotton shirt. "Nothing's the matter with me." She drew one long leg up his body and hooked it around his waist.

Startled by the blatantly erotic action, he lost his balance and sent them both crashing against the thin wooden barrier separating the dressing rooms. "Have you gone crazy?" He pushed her leg down and disengaged himself, distancing himself from her as far as the limited space allowed.

"I'm just trying to have a little fun. Where's the harm

in that?" She tilted her head, a calculated movement that allowed her heavy mane of coppery hair to swing forward, framing her face. Her voice lowered seductively. "Jerry's going bowling tonight."

Suddenly acutely conscious that there was no noise coming from outside the dressing room, Richard lowered his voice to a whisper. "So?"

"Sooooo," Deirdre drawled, and raising onto her tiptoes, flung her arms around his neck and pressed her lips to his ear to tell him in specific, intimate detail precisely what she had in mind. Richard didn't have to say a word; she could feel his reaction. "Tonight?" she whispered huskily.

"Maybe." He shrugged out of her embrace. No one was going to take Richard Fortune for granted.

"Bastard." Despite the cramped quarters Deirdre had little difficulty slipping into her slacks and sweater. Richard made no move to leave, but stood watching her from under half-closed lids. Rummaging in her purse until she found her comb, she watched him obliquely as she deftly rearranged her hair into its usual sleekness. Finished, she dropped the comb into her purse and closed the zipper. Slowly.

"Leaving, my pet?" Richard detained her by grabbing her wrist in a tight hold. "Surely it would have been simpler to use the phone to make a date. But perhaps you had some other purpose?" His grip tightened. He could feel his fingers grating against the delicate bones in her wrist.

"As a matter of fact, I did. I thought a friend should be the one to tell you . . ." The provocative pause didn't work. Deirdre was getting tired of the game, and it was obvious Richard was fast losing what little patience he possessed, so she related the juicy news of Vera Alderbrook's disappearance.

Richard's reaction was typical of his disinterest in anything unrelated to himself. "So what?" Vera had made a play for him several months ago, but he had no interest in silly girls. He wanted, needed, a woman; a woman who understood and was willing to cater to his special desires. He thought of the soft leather straps he kept in the trunk of his car. Maybe tonight he'd let Deirdre tie him to the bed. She always became a wild tiger when they enacted that particular version of the master/slave game.

Deirdre recaptured his attention with a single word. "Alison," she said, and told him about the accident. Her satisfaction came by observing the color come and go in his face. Richard didn't even realize when he let her go. She pushed open the door and was amused to see the two middle-aged women customers and Art standing in the near vicinity. Settling the strap of her purse over her shoulder, she smiled at each in turn.

Art surveyed her with a bold smile. "You don't want the jogging suit?"

Deirdre laughed, a throaty sound that showed her appreciation of a kindred soul. She winked at him and started toward the front door.

Richard came up behind her and again grabbed her wrist. "Is this another one of your little games?"

Deirdre twisted out of his grasp. She stood rubbing her sore wrist. "Oh, Alison's back all right, for all the good it'll do you. Why don't you face the facts, lover? She put 'paid' to your account four years ago. Anyone else would have gotten the message by now." She marched to the door and opened it. Bells tinkled merrily. "About tonight . . ." she said over her shoulder, supremely confident of him, "call before you come over."

"Bitch!" Richard muttered, knowing she knew him all too well, knowing that he wouldn't pass up an opportunity to spend an evening in her bed. Then he thought— *Alison!*—and a slow smile decorated his face. Deirdre was wrong in thinking they were through. Everyone thought it—hell, even Alison did—but they were wrong.

114

They didn't know the one thing he did, the one thing he had, the thing he clung to, that made all their suppositions untrue. He had a promise from Adrian Blaise, and unless Richard was very much mistaken, Adrian Blaise was a man of his word.

Although a bit wobbly, Alison showered, unwrapping a cake of the hard-milled lavender-scented French soap Lucy provided all her guests. A nice touch, but she noted with amusement that Sam hadn't used it, preferring instead the large bar of soap that hung from a rope.

Sam. A clue to his personality. A smile curved her lips, even managed to stay in place when she realized her suitcase was still in the trunk of the Mustang. That meant she would have to put on the same clothes she had been wearing the night before. Thankfully there was no blood on either the jeans or sweater.

Alison worked through the tangles in her hair, careful of the neat bandage just above her right ear. The face in the mirror was too pale, the eyes too wary. She worked on it with cosmetics, mentally thanking Sam for having the presence of mind to bring her purse along last night. Nothing would help her eyes; they had seen too much.

Alison sighed, pushed the thoughts away. Lucy was sharp; she didn't want to worry her. Ready to leave, she had her hand on the doorknob when the telephone shrilled loudly. Intrusively. It was an odd, almost misplaced sound in the quaintly furnished room. All the fears and uncertainties she had come to associate with such an ordinary occurrence flooded into her consciousness, choking her reasoning power. To her, the usually innocuous ringing was as frightening in its way, as earlier, the wild call of the animal had been.

Ring followed ring. Such an innocent happening, nothing to cause trembling or an overall weakness that had little to do with the body and everything to do with the mind.

"Coward!" The epithet unfroze her. She strode to the instrument and snatched up the receiver, barked a terse "Hello."

"Alison."

Her name. Only her name. Alison felt her stomach clench with the sick feeling the obscene calls always produced. Now it would start, the silkily seductive voice, hypnotizing, sapping her will, pouring erotic suggestions, descriptions, into her unwilling ear. She didn't know which she hated most: the lurid pictures the insistent voice produced, or the loss of control over her *self*, the thinking, reasoning part of her. Her body, poised for invasion, visibly flinched when the voice came again.

"Alison? I'm sorry, I told them not to wake you."

"Sam!"

"I thought for a moment there you had already forgotten me." A chuckle spilled into her ear, a warm, endearing, very male sound. "And after the night we spent together."

She gasped, she couldn't help it, and a slow red flush crept up her neck to her cheeks. She would never forget. Another chuckle, this one decidedly wicked, warmed her ear.

"How's the headache?" he asked, as if he hadn't been so outrageous a moment before.

"Pretty much gone. The problem now is hunger."

"I won't keep you," he promised. "I wanted to know how you are and also to tell you that I called Jerry Treadwell this morning and asked him to pick up your car. Lucy suggested him. I hope it's all right?"

"That's fine, Sam. Thank you for taking care of it."

"No problem. I, ah, had a look at it this morning."

"You didn't have to do that."

"I wanted to," he said, which was only half the truth. The other half was that he wanted to have another look

116

behind the tree. He hadn't expected to find anything, but still . . . As anticipated, there had been nothing to see, nothing but the trampled grass, sodden from the downpour. Even the fetid odor had dissipated; the air clearwashed and pure.

"Most of the visible damage is glass. Oh, while I was there I picked up your suitcase. I thought I'd be able to get it to you before you woke up, but I got tied up. I'm sorry."

"No problem. Really. You've, ah, done more than enough. I, ah . . ." She paused, nonplussed. How do you thank a stranger for taking care of you?

He must have sensed her discomfort, for his voice smoothly interrupted her thoughts. "Treadwell said he'd call you with an estimate."

"That's fine."

An awkward little silence descended.

"Sam . . ."

"Alison . . ."

They laughed. The momentary insecurity passed. "You'd better go and get something to eat. I don't want to find myself feeling the sharp edge of Lucy's tongue."

"You know her then?"

"Yes." The fondness in Sam's tone was genuine.

"Sam, about last night. I . . . what I saw—"

"No!" There was a pause, then his voice came, laced with something she couldn't readily identify. "Later. Let's discuss it later when I see you."

Alison stared at the phone for long moments after she hung up. Something had happened, something new, to put that cautious tone in Sam's voice. Uneasily she wondered what it was, then pushed the worry to the back of her mind. It wouldn't do to face Lucy with a troubled face. The one thing her aunt didn't need was something else to worry about.

The hall outside Sam's second-floor bedroom had the familiar waiting stillness Alison always associated with the inn. She had always believed that if she listened—with her being instead of with her ears—she would hear the sounds of those who had come before. The stiff portraits of long-ago Crandells that lined the hall and marched down the staircase reinforced the fancy. They gazed out from oil-glazed eyes, solemnly watching, eternally present, yet long gone. She had never been more conscious of her position as the last of their line than she was at the moment.

She checked her appearance in the huge gilt-framed mirror that graced the short wall on the turn of the first landing, then proceeded down. The third step from the bottom protested her weight. She smiled. It was comforting to know that the more things change the more they stay the same.

Jessie Gilford, the housekeeper who had been at the inn for over twenty years, looked up at the sound and motioned for Alison to wait. Alison was happy to oblige while Jessie gave directions to a couple. Then the tourists left and Jessie came rushing out from behind the front desk. She hugged Alison, hard. "Sorry you had to wait. That couple wanted directions to the old cemetery." She made a sound of distaste. "I'll never know why people poke around a place like that."

"They take rubbings of tombstones. It's a hobby."

"I know, but I can't say I approve. The dead are entitled to their rest." She hugged Alison again, then stepped back to examine her. "Enough about that nastiness. Let me get a good look at you. We've all been frantic since we heard. How are you, dear? Should you be up? I peeked in early, but you were sleeping like a lamb, although too pale, I thought. But after what you've been through, the shock of it—" Alison blanched and Jessie clicked her tongue. "How stupid of me to remind you. Why, it's a wonder you weren't killed in that accident. Such a terrible night to be out. So sweet of you, dear, rushing here to be with your aunt. You're a good girl and I told Lucy that very thing, just ask her if I didn't."

The words gushed from her in one breath. Alison marveled at it, grinning down affectionately at her. Jessie was a short dumpling of a woman, with wide hips, a pillowy bosom, and kind brown eyes. Her comfortable appearance belied a sharp mind and a tongue that could be biting if the occasion warranted. Jessie and her husband Luke had made the inn their home. Alison was well aware that they could be the answer to Lucy's problem, if Lucy didn't let her stiff-necked Crandell pride get in the way.

Lucy, though, was as stubborn as any Crandell, in a family known for its obstinacy. Alison knew she had a fight on her hands. She also knew a seventy-nine-year-old woman who had suffered two strokes in four months shouldn't be running an inn by herself. Alison knew it, and Lucy probably knew it, too. The trick was to get her to admit it, then they could go on from there.

Her face must have reflected her thoughts, for Jessie gave her arm a pat. "You're worried, I can see it. Perhaps the old Tartar will surprise you. Just go easy."

"Thanks, Jessie, I will." Alison sniffed the air, then grinned. "Something smells wonderful. I'm starving."

Jessie beamed. "I'll just go on in the kitchen and tell Luke. Dr. Cutter told Lucy you're to eat lightly. Will poached eggs do?"

"Nope. I want whatever is producing that heavenly smell." Jessie assumed her militant look. "Okay. Poached eggs. On English muffin. Oh, and plenty of coffee."

"Weak tea," Jessie corrected firmly. "Now go on into the bar, you'll find your aunt there."

Alison stopped in the shadow of the arch dividing the lounge from the bar area. She wanted the advantage of seeing Lucy before being seen herself. Lucy wasn't hard to spot. She sat at a small round table, a calculator and a spreadsheet before her. She wasn't alone, but she was studiously avoiding her companion. Alison almost laughed out loud. Sometimes Lucy was so predictable.

Lucy looked up and grunted when Alison bent to give Bertha a kiss on her wrinkled cheek. The old lady's skin felt dry and papery. She smelled of lilacs and powder and hair spray.

"Thanks for calling yesterday," Alison murmured, ignoring Lucy's critical stare. "I like your hair. It's a new style, isn't it?"

Bertha patted the underside of her tightly crimped, nut-brown hair with a hand so age-spotted it was almost the same color. "Thank you, Alison dear, it's good of you to notice it. Fact is, I think the color may be a bit too dark."

Lucy snorted and mumbled something under her breath. Both Alison and Bertha ignored her, the latter reaching for a half-empty glass of wine.

"I think it looks nice." Alison noticed a distinct tremor in Bertha's hand as she took a delicate sip and then placed the glass carefully back down onto the table.

"It 'taint the wrapping, but what's in the package," Lucy muttered darkly, leaving no doubt about her negative intent.

"She's not speaking to me." Bertha calmly took another sip of wine.

Alison hovered between amusement and exasperation. In her experience, egos got testy past the age of sixty-five. She endured more than she wanted of the sniping, for the two women shamelessly used her as a backboard. They seemed to enjoy it all enormously.

Jessie arrived with Alison's breakfast in time to hear a particularly antagonistic remark of Lucy's. The housekeeper forcefully slammed down the plate with the two picture-perfect poached eggs. The pot of tea came down hard right after it. She used less force with the cup and saucer. "Shameful," she said to her employer with the familiarity of many years. "You're one of the lucky ones.

120

There are those who haven't got a soul to worry over them."

Lucy mumbled something. The only audibly clear words were "suffer" and "fools."

Jessie stomped off. Bertha took another sip of wine. Alison ate her breakfast. To her relief, they observed an unspoken cease-fire while she was eating.

It ended the second she finished.

"More tea?" Lucy asked, and when Alison politely refused another cup, launched an immediate offensive. She was grateful for their love and concern. She would listen to their advice. She would then, as always, do exactly as she wished. Of course, the last was not said aloud.

Alison wondered what Lucy had cooked up.

Bertha ordered another glass of wine.

"Oh, Derek, meet my niece," Lucy said when the bartender returned to the table with Bertha's Chablis. Alison and the young man exchanged polite nods. "Derek's been with me two months now," Lucy explained loudly. "Breaks a lot of glasses, but he knows his sports. Got a head stuffed full of statistics. The customers like that, especially the sports fans. Good for business."

The telephone rang and Derek went to answer it.

"Nice young man," Bertha said.

"You only like him because he fills your glass to the top," Lucy snapped.

Bertha smiled serenely. "It seems we're speaking again."

Alison sighed. This was no place to talk. Lucy was at her most recalcitrant. She silently counseled herself to be patient. She had known it wasn't going to be easy. Lucy Crandell had been called a "managing female" all her life, now, near the end of it, she wasn't about to change her ways—at least not without coercion.

"Aunt Lucy, I didn't come here to fight with you. I would like you to think about something. Just think

121

about it. We can talk about it later." Alison took a deep breath and then, because she knew no other way to say it, blurted the words out. "Sell the inn."

They fell like rocks into a still pond. Lucy recoiled as if the ripples they made physically hit her.

Alison picked up Lucy's gnarled, blue-veined hand with her own smooth-fleshed one and gently squeezed it. "Just think about it. That's all I ask."

"It's too late."

"What?" Alison had to lean forward to hear. The noise level in the bar had increased dramatically as the lunch time rush began.

"The inn will be yours soon, to do with as you see fit. Times are changing, child, especially here. Strangers are coming, strangers and . . ." For a few moments her eyes focused on something beyond, and then returned to look at her niece with love shining from their depths. "Don't ask me to explain. I can't. I only know what I feel inside." She sighed. "I don't have long, child, I feel it in my bones. Don't look like that. I've done what I wanted. I have no regrets." Her eyes softened, a hint of moisture making them look glassy. "I had you, didn't I? That no-good brother of mine did me the greatest favor of my life the day he walked out of here without you."

A tight, squeezing sensation in her chest made it difficult for Alison to breathe. Lucy had never spoken this way. She had never been a fatalist, but a fighter, a ranter against time and tides. Alison knew that for as long as she lived she would remember this moment, this second out of her life when her only living relative admitted she was only human, prey to mortality. Little, ordinary things impressed themselves on her consciousness. Out of the corner of her eye she saw Derek pick up the telephone. Outside the nearest window a brightly plumaged blue jay flew from one tree to another, disappearing into the foliage near the top of the second tree. From the dining rooms came the murmur of voices, the sounds of silverware clinking against china.

Lucy squeezed Alison's now-clammy hand. "Perhaps I'm wrong, but . . ." She turned to the window; to the notch; to the mountain. There was a funny little smile on her lips when she again faced Alison. "You mean well, child, but I don't think there's any need for long-range planning. Ever since I heard about this thing with the mill I knew deep inside I'd never live to see it. The inn will be yours then, Alison, yours to do with what you want. The Crandell name dies with me. Maybe that means it's time for new blood at the inn."

"Lucy!"

"Everything comes to an end. Don't be so shocked. Perhaps I don't *want* to live to see the changes that are coming." Bertha squirmed on her chair and Lucy pounced. "Hit a nerve, huh? Why—" She broke off as Derek came to the table. "Yes? What is it?"

He looked at Alison. "Mrs. Fortune? Telephone call."

"Thank you." Alison pushed back her chair. "That must be Jerry with the estimate on my car."

She walked to the bar and was reaching for the telephone when Bertha's voice came plainly to her. "You've got no right, Lucy Crandell, scaring Alison with that talk of death."

"Mind your own business," Lucy grated. "It's for her own good."

"Hello?" Alison said, wondering what her aunt meant by that last remark.

Static crackled over the line.

". . . *Allliii—son.*"

14

Deirdre was surprised to find Leavitt's relatively empty for the middle of the day. Just inside the door Draconia's mayor stood at the check-out counter gossiping with the clerk as she rang up his order. J. Norbert looked up and caught sight of Deirdre. He beamed her his patented vote-for-me smile. "How are you today?" he asked in his genuine political I-care-about-you voice.

"Just fine, Bert." She was amused to note the mayor's purchases were all snack foods. Like a child who can't wait, he had already opened a box of chocolate-covered doughnuts and was eating one, heedless of the crumbs dropping onto his jacket and the chocolate smear on his fingers.

"Have one," he offered, proffering the box to Deirdre, who refused with a shake of her head. The mayor shrugged and took another doughnut before closing the box and handing it to the clerk. He took a big bite, chewed happily, then asked a seemingly casual question. "Jerry back from Laconia yet?" It was Deirdre's turn to shrug. "Too bad about the accident. Alison was lucky. Richard must be relieved."

"I expect so," Deirdre said in a neutral tone, squarely meeting the mayor's sharp-eyed gaze. There were precious few secrets in a town as small as Draconia. Deirdre

124

knew that even if the mayor guessed her relationship with Richard, he didn't—couldn't—*know*. And that made all the difference. Inwardly she smiled. Life without the tang of excitement would be unendurable. With a casual wave she headed down the closest aisle.

As always, Deirdre immediately felt a slight tug of claustrophobia. The old-fashioned aisles were very narrow, crammed with staples and delicacies and household items, assembled with no discernible system. She wandered aimlessly, stopped when the deep rumble of a man's voice, an answering tinkle of feminine laughter, came from the aisle behind her. Intrigued, she quickly rounded the head of the aisle, in her hurry bumping into a pyramid of cans in the congested space. "Damn," she exploded as several cans fell and rolled away. She lunged, barely managing to prevent the entire edifice from tumbling down.

"Here, let me help."

"Thanks." When the cans no longer teetered alarmingly, Deirdre looked at her helper. "Oh, hi, Michele."

Michele Tanner's green eyes were bright. Her skin was flushed and her lips looked slightly swollen, as if she had just been thoroughly kissed. To someone with experience, there was only one conclusion to reach. Fascinated, Deirdre peered beyond Michele, but the aisle was empty. Deirdre couldn't help the knowing smile that played around her lips. Who would ever have suspected that prim and proper Michele, wife and mother of three, would take a lover? And in her own backyard.

Michele bent and retrieved another can. As Deirdre took it from her, a bright red mark on Michele's palm drew her attention. "That looks like a bad burn."

Michele curled her fingers over it. "It's not a burn." She looked at her watch. "I've got to run. I would like to stop at the inn and see Alison before I pick up the kids. Have you heard about the accident she had last night?"

"Jerry told me."

"Oh, yes. Of course."

Deirdre didn't like the sound of that, the slight undertone she thought she perceived in Michele's voice. Damned snob. They were all that way, all the descendants of the original twenty-three families. The Fortunes. The Crandells. The Starks. The Tanners. They always stuck together, like Alison and Michele. Then she remembered that there had been a Treadwell among the founders, and Deirdre lifted her chin to a defiant angle. "You'd better get going then, hadn't you?" It gave her satisfaction to be the one to end the meeting. "I expect you and Alison have a great deal to talk about," she said meaningfully, allowing Michele to see the knowing smile which was so much better than words. Let her run to her good friend Alison. Let her wonder how much she had seen and heard.

The elated feeling fled too soon. If she lived in Draconia a hundred years she would never belong. Not the way Michele did.

"Mrs. Treadwell. Deirdre, isn't it?"

Startled, Deirdre whirled around, caught her breath. A tall, well-built, handsome man stood close beside her. She hadn't heard him approach. Strange, for so large a man to move so quietly.

"Did I frighten you?"

His voice whispered intimately in the confined space. She had to tilt her head up, straining her neck, to see his face. He seemed immense.

"Don't be alarmed," he said in a smoky, seductive tone as he gently took her right hand.

Deirdre's self-possession returned with a rush as she recognized him. This was a man—no more, no less—and men were creatures Deirdre understood. Coquettishly, she smiled up into his handsome face. "I'm not in the least bit afraid—Mr. Blaise."

"Good," he said, and bent his dark head over her hand.

Deirdre melted as his hot, slightly rough tongue branded her palm. Her body primed itself for love; her insides softened to the consistency of molten honey. She wanted . . . needed . . .

"Oh!" she said, slightly breathless, more than a bit confused, unsure of what had happened. Adrian Blaise stood several feet away. Her mind must be playing tricks. Her thoughts touched her escape, the white powder of delight, then shied away. "I . . . ah . . ."

Adrian placed a jar in her hands, smiled. Then he was gone, after a slight bow and words murmured low. "*À bientôt.*"

Deirdre slowly looked down. Strawberry jam. A shiver traveled the length of her spine. Without understanding a word of French she knew he had told her he would see her soon.

"That's it for me." Sam shoved his chair back and got up so fast the papers on his desk fluttered in the sudden eddy of air.

Jennifer stopped typing. "Going to lunch, Mr. Chandler?"

"Yup." Sam wasn't particularly hungry, but he had promised Alison her suitcase. He could grab a sandwich and a beer in the bar while he was at the inn.

Jennifer looked at the clock on the wall and then returned her clear gaze to Sam. "I'm on the last page of the supply/cost estimate report. It shouldn't take long if you would like to wait."

"No problem. I'll look it over when I get back." Sam knew that on any other day Jennifer would have had that report finished an hour ago. But this hadn't been an ordinary day; it had taken time for them to settle in after the grisly discovery in the old mill. Thank heavens it was Friday. That thought begat another. "If you've got a heavy date this evening you could leave a little earlier today. No need to wait for me to get back. I know how long it takes you girls to get ready." The few times his daughter had been allowed to visit him he had been amazed at the time she spent preparing to go out.

A lovely rose color bloomed on Jennifer's cheeks. "Yes . . . no . . . it's all right, Mr. Chandler."

Sam winked at her, wondering as he had earlier, who the lucky man was. Jennifer deserved the best.

The air felt good after the stuffiness of the trailer, but it was still heavy with moisture. Sam frowned up at the sky. It looked like it might rain again. He couldn't start pouring cement until the weather cleared and the ground dried. A worried frown creasing his forehead, he bent and scooped up a handful of earth, squeezing to test its moisture content.

McClain walked up and did likewise. "Too wet. I think we should wait."

Feeling frustrated, Sam threw down the dirt and brushed his hands. "It looks like more rain. I think I'll call the weather boys up on Mount Washington this afternoon. See what they've got long-range."

McClain nodded. "Sounds good."

"Hey, watch out!" yelled one of the crew.

Startled, both Sam and Rufus looked up to see a mud-spattered car traveling too fast on the rutted dirt road, barreling straight toward them. They ran for the relative safety of the trailer's steps. The car screeched to a halt, and narrowly missed plowing into them.

"Where's the fire?" Rufus mumbled as he followed Sam back down the steps.

The transmission made a grinding sound as the gear lever was heedlessly thrown into park. The driver's door sprang open and a middle-aged man half leaned, half fell out.

"Got a phone? It's an emergency," he yelled, his voice thin, trembly, verging on panic-stricken.

Sam noted that although the day was still cool the man was sweating profusely, his hair plastered to his skull in lank strands. His face was a pasty white, giving him the appearance of an egg wearing a toupee of wet wool. Obviously he was holding a tight rein on himself.

The men nearby had all stopped working and were staring in their direction. Sam motioned to the trailer. "Go on in. Help yourself."

Abruptly, the man ducked down and stuck his head inside the car. "Be right back, Ethel honey."

A wail came from the female passenger. They could all hear it, a high, thin ululation. *"Herrrb—"*

"It's all right. You stay put, now."

The passenger door opened before he finished speaking. The woman tumbled out in her haste, staggered, and grabbed onto the door for support. "You're not leaving me here," she screamed.

Out of the corner of his eye Sam could see the men moving closer. He caught McClain's eye, knew they were both thinking of last night's conversation. "Let's go inside." He urged the couple to move, an inner sense warning him not to let the crew hear anymore.

It was too late.

The woman was paler than her companion and totally without his control. "There's a dead girl in the cemetery," she shrieked.

For one wild second Sam thought it was a joke, that the two of them were part of some juvenile prank cooked up by the men. But all the powder in the world could not achieve countenances so dead-white, so bloodless, nor could the best acting create the panic that poured from them in waves.

The trailer door creaked open and then banged shut.

129

Jennifer stood on the top step, a sickly expression on her face. Her lips barely moved in a whisper, but they all heard; all knew.

Vera.

Vera was dead, and all Sam could think about was his daughter. Mandy. It could have been her, sprawled under the merciless sun, innocent in death. Never to laugh; never to cry; never to bloom; never to share the sweet perfume of her soul with someone she loved. He couldn't bear thinking about it; he couldn't think of anything else.

"If only I'd insisted she come with me last night," he told the first state trooper to respond to the call.

The trooper shook his head sadly. " 'If only,' Mr. Chandler, are words I've come to hate. Don't punish yourself, there's no sense in it."

Sam heard the words but also saw the awful truth. Even he, veteran of many such encounters, could not keep the pity from his eyes, the hard-come-by knowledge that suffering cannot be turned on and off like a tap.

After more than three hours, Sam finally got away. Exhausted, he drove straight to the inn and parked in the small tree-shaded lot behind the building. He got out of the car and stretched tense muscles. A squirrel ran part way up a tree, then paused to study him with bright, curious eyes before scampering out of sight in the thick foliage. A hawk cruised the sky.

Sam sighed. Life continued. He walked around to the front entrance and let himself into the inn. As always, the hushed calmness, the sense of endurance and time-lessness the inn conveyed, soothed him. He closed the door and paused to let his eyes adjust to the dimness.

A soft voice said "Hello," and there was Alison, standing in front of the desk. She was pale, and when he got close he could see sadness and anxiety in her eyes; still, she remained a beautiful woman.

"Hello." He returned. "Should you be up?"

"I slept the morning away." She put out a hand as if to touch him, then let it drop back to her side. "Sam . . . I want to thank you for what you did last night. Without you, I—"

Embarrassed, Sam waved her gratitude away. "I only batted five hundred last night." His voice held both bitterness and remorse. Alison tilted her head, puzzled, and he sighed heavily, knowing he had to explain. "Have you heard about Vera?"

"Yes. If anything, bad news travels fastest of all."

"I saw her last night. Vera. Out on the road. She must have been on her way to—" His voice cracked and he thought for a split second he was going to lose control.

"Sam—"

"I thought of my daughter, my little girl, and . . . ah—" He stabbed his fingers into his thick reddish-blond curls. "I stopped, wanted to give her a lift. I should have insisted."

The green eyes Alison had found so alluring in the early-morning hours showed pain. "Sam . . ." she said softly. "I'll bet that you could use a drink and some food. Did you have lunch?" When he shook his head she lightly touched his arm. "Come."

Sam willingly followed her into the bar. Even at this off hour there were customers. Alison led him to a small table by the window. The view was pastoral, soothing. Green grass rippled across a wildflower-dotted meadow. In the distance hulked Dragon Mountain, darkening into a somber blue-green as the sun rode low and red in the sky. Sam ordered Scotch, and Alison told Derek to bring the bottle to the table. After he left, she asked Sam what he would like to eat.

Sam looked at his watch. "The kitchen's closed."

131

A hint of mischief crept into Alison's eyes. "I think I might manage something for you. I'm related to the owner, you know," she whispered dramatically.

Sam shook his head, the simple motion requiring almost all his strength. "Not right now." He reached for the bottle, poured himself another drink. "Where is Lucy?"

"Napping, I hope."

Sam grinned. "How did you manage that?"

"Blackmail."

Sam looked skeptical. "And that worked?"

"Okay, so I begged and groveled."

"Smart girl. You do what you have to, to get the job done."

"Right." Anxiety tightened her features. "That's what Dr. Cutter said."

"Henry was here?"

"This afternoon. The police tracked him down, they wanted him to, you know . . ." Her voice trailed off. She looked stricken for having reminded him.

Sam did know. He had been there, since the police wanted to be sure Vera was the same girl he had spoken to last night. All he had been able to see was Mandy. Once again he damned himself. Mandy. He didn't realize he had said it aloud until Alison spoke.

"Tell me about your daughter, Sam."

The softly voiced request helped him regain his equilibrium. "Mandy is sixteen going on thirty-four, hostile to authority, any authority, and dissatisfied with everything." He sighed, the sound tearing from deep within him. "She's run away from home four times."

"Ah . . ." Alison said, helpless.

Sam shrugged, a small gesture that said more than words. There was no way he could adequately convey the feeling of powerlessness he felt where Mandy was concerned. "She's home now, and last time I spoke to her she sounded more content. Her mother says it's a stage. According to her, Mandy is no different from other teenagers." He snorted derisively. "If you ask me, that's just more of her California talk, and nothing more than the old ostrich head-in-the-sand syndrome."

Alison frowned and Sam laughed, the sound harsh and hurtful. "Mandy lives with her mother and stepfather in California. Denise remarried almost ten years ago. God, that's a different world out there. Everyone's got an analyst, even the dog." Again he laughed. "You heard me right, the damn dog's in therapy. Bootles or Bootsie, or whatever the little beast's name, had an identity crisis, it didn't know it was a dog." He finished the Scotch in one long drink. "Believe me, it's true. That's why I stopped to talk to Vera. All I could see was Mandy. Alone. It was so dark. I thought . . ."

"You tried, Sam. That's more than most would have done. You could hardly force her into the car."

"But she's dead, and I —"

"And you couldn't have done more. No one abducted her. No one molested her. She had an accident. It was an awful night, she probably slipped and fell. The ground was slick from the rain. You remember."

Sam remembered. He also remembered the slick verge of the notch road; a fetid odor; a shadow. He remembered Alison describing a black coach, a headless horse, a headless man. He remembered Dottie Cutter talking about a death coach coming for the souls of the dead. Vera was dead. "Ahhhh, no," he whispered, unwilling to believe, more unwilling to share his thoughts with the girl looking at him so compassionately. She also had seen a beast, and this morning, in the old mill . . .

"What is it?" Alison spoke sharply, sensing something wrong.

He had promised Henry Cutter he would keep Dottie's outburst a secret. For how long? Didn't Alison have a right to know? "Nothing. I'm tired, is all. It's hard to think straight."

Alison's face clouded. There was something he wasn't saying. She gazed out the window, remembering Lucy's fascination with the view, the odd look on her aunt's face and her fatalistic words. *It's too late.*

But Alison wasn't buying that. Lucy simply had the natural depression that sometimes followed illness. Especially in the elderly.

At that moment Alison had never felt more like a Crandell. A problem was a challenge. She had come to solve the problem of Lucy's illness; she would do it. The other problem . . . She straightened her shoulders and cleared her throat.

Sam raised his eyes from his glass. There was a firm set to Alison's jaw.

"About last night," she said, her voice gaining strength as her thoughts solidified. "I've been thinking about it all day, about what happened, what I saw." She raised bright eyes to him. "I wasn't hallucinating. I know I wasn't. It was real. It happened. And," she brought her hand down flat on the table for emphasis, "I'm going to find out what it's all about. Someone, somewhere is playing a joke, and it's not funny. It smacks of Ichabod Crane and Brom Bones and I'm not buying it. This is the twentieth century and people aren't as gullible as the ones in Washington Irving's Sleepy Hollow." She looked at him somewhat defiantly. "What do you think?"

He hesitated, wanting to share what he knew, bound by his word. He needed sleep; perhaps then he could think a bit clearer, but he also needed to give her an answer.

"I don't know what to think, Alison—yet. Will you give me some time? Trust me a bit? Believe me, I'm as anxious as you are for some explanation."

He could see that she liked his answer as little as he

did, yet she was polite enough not to push. Almost absentmindedly she rubbed her temple.

"Headache?"

The compassionate tone was familiar to her from the night. "It's not so bad. Henry said to expect it for several days."

"She should be resting, just like she made her aunt do. I heard the doctor tell her."

Jessie, a disapproving frown puckering her forehead, had come up to the table so quietly that neither Sam nor Alison had noticed her until she spoke.

"Jessie—"

"Don't you 'Jessie' me, young lady. You're not as strong as you think you are. Even Crandells get tired, like normal folks, although they won't admit it. You're the same as your aunt, just a mite less mulish, to my way of thinking—but you're young yet," she added.

Alison looked indignant, and more like Lucy than she knew. Sam unsuccessfully tried to hide the amusement crinkling his eyes.

"Lucy's quite a gal," he said.

Jessie frowned at him, then returned her attention to Alison. "Why don't you go on out of here, honey? Everything's covered. Adele came on time for once, so we're full strength. The Dragon View Inn will manage for one evening without you or your aunt." When her words seemingly had no effect, she appealed to Sam. "Maybe you'll be able to persuade her. After the time she's had. First the accident, which I'm sure I don't have to tell you about, then having to deal with that stubborn aunt of hers. Not to mention that nasty call this afternoon—"

"Jessie!" Alison spoke sharply, warningly.

"What call?" Sam asked.

But he didn't get an answer, for both women were staring at the archway separating the bar area from the

135

sitting room. Sam twisted about and immediately recognized Richard Fortune just as he felt Alison flinch. His tired mind finally made the connection. He knew Richard through the complex at Dragon Meadow, knew he should have recognized the relationship sooner.

Richard came directly across the room toward them. Dark eyes surveyed Jessie, dismissed her, spent a few moments studying Sam before settling on Alison. Hungrily.

Sam recognized the look, recognized it and reacted to it so strongly that the power of it momentarily shook him.

"You're back," Richard said to Alison.

"For a few days." Alison's voice was a flat, carefully controlled monotone.

For several moments desolation was visible in Richard's eyes. Then he transferred his attention from Alison to Sam and his manner, even the body language of his stance, became truculent. "You're the guy who spent the night with my wife."

Jessie gasped, took a step closer to Alison, like a mother hen rushing to protect her chick.

Sam slowly pushed the bottle of Scotch to one side. "Is that so? I was under the distinct impression you don't have a wife." His voice was deceptively calm.

"He doesn't. Not anymore." Jessie folded her arms under her bosom and positively glared.

A dull red flush stained Richard's cheeks. Ignoring both Jessie and Sam, he turned toward Alison. "It's all over town, you know. Everyone knows you spent the night in his bed."

The only sound in the sudden stillness was a clinking from the bar where Derek was putting glasses into the overhead racks as people turned, drawn to the drama.

The blood rushed from Alison's head, leaving her feeling so dizzy she thought she would faint. She knew only

136

too well Richard was right. Michele had taken pains to point it out to her that afternoon. She closed her eyes and then she felt the familiarity of Sam's hand on her shoulder, an almost imperceptible squeeze, comforting.

Taking his time, he rose to face Richard. "So . . . ?" he invited in a voice laden with menace.

"So she should have had more sense. This isn't New York where—"

"That's enough." Although Sam had pitched his voice low, the effect was as if he had roared. He took a step closer to Richard, intending to intimidate, and had the satisfaction of seeing the other man step back. "Listen, Fortune, and listen hard. I'm only going to say this once. It's true Alison spent the night in my bed. She was in pain, suffering from shock and concussion. I did what I could for her, which was damned little." Again he took the step that brought him toe-to-toe with the other man and lowered his voice still more. "Do you want to make something of it?"

Richard hunched his shoulders, a puny shield against Sam's wrath. He did want to make something of it, but a spark of self-preservation helped him to understand that this was not the time. He held on to one thought: Adrian Blaise would make everything right.

With a sound akin to a growl Richard pivoted and walked away. Jessie, acutely aware that they had created a scene, walked to the nearest table and asked the couple there if they were ready for another round. Derek struck up a conversation with a customer. Within seconds the room returned to normal.

Blood rushed in a red haze behind Alison's closed lids. It was no surprise to discover her headache had come back with a vengeance. The air stirred near her, she felt a light touch on her hair, smelled the woodsy cologne that had both soothed and excited her the night before. And then she heard Sam's voice, pitched low and intimate, close to her ear.

"Something else happened last night, Alison." She opened her eyes. Sam was hunkered down next to her chair, his face on a level with her own. "I made myself a promise, while I sat there helpless, watching you suffer. I promised myself that should I ever be so lucky again to have you in my bed, you would feel nothing but pleasure. Now I give you the same promise, sweetheart."

He brushed his fingers gently down her cheek and then was gone, leaving her alone with a jumble of thoughts and impressions. She sat and stared sightlessly out the window where night was rapidly claiming the view. Her life, her world, was spinning out of her control. She took a deep breath, remembering. *Sweetheart.*

Deirdre awoke with a heavy weight across her waist and legs. With her eyes still closed she inhaled, pulling the scent of him deep within her lungs. It excited her. She opened her eyes to find his own on her, fathomless twin pools of black, as dark as a moonless night. "You're beautiful," she murmured, and still imprisoned by his arm and leg, ran her hand down his hair-roughened chest to his belly. He caught her questing hand and guided it lower; she felt his power, his readiness. "Again?" she asked in awe, and was treated to his laughter, deep and dark and tinged with a hint of the forbidden.

Deirdre couldn't resist. Although she ached, especially between her legs, her body tightened, her senses coming alive, ready, greedy for more. He stroked her, expertly, seeking and finding all her pleasure points. Deirdre's cat-lithe body writhed sinuously, expecting, accepting, demanding more. But suddenly he sat up and rolled away from her. Through ecstasy-blurred eyes she saw him standing by the bed, fully aroused, heavy with need; pri-

138

meval; the sight of him stole her breath away.

Deirdre held up her arms and opened her legs. Wide. Invitingly. Her lips pouting suggestively, she slowly rotated her hips. Tantalizingly.

He smiled. In a movement so swift she had no time to protest it, he leaned over and captured her ankles, turning her so she faced him, and began pulling her toward him until her curved bottom reached the edge of the bed. Then he bent down and placed her feet in her high-heeled mules. Strumpet slippers, Jerry called them, because they were nothing more than a wide band of pink satin covered with fluffy pink feathers. "Come," he said, and held out his hand.

"Where are we going?" Breathless with desire, Deirdre hardly recognized her own voice. But as he led her from the bedroom and headed down the hall, a new sensation lodged in her chest, a prickling of unease.

As if he sensed it, he halted and took her in his arms. Reaching down, he cupped her alluringly firm buttocks in his large strong hands. Then he lifted her, brought her up and in, pressed close to the heat of his body.

Deirdre felt him stirring against her, and in that moment forgot all caution, abandoned herself completely to him. With a wild cry of mingled desire and surrender, she wrapped her legs around his waist. Thus entwined, he carried her down the stairs, along the hall into the kitchen, and put her on the edge of the sink.

Deirdre knew what came next. For a moment she tried to puzzle how he knew, felt again the touch of unease, but he was parting her legs, opening her, and she forgot to care. Fantasy melded with reality.

The kitchen was quiet, hushed in the murky light of late afternoon. It was peaceful—save for the hoarse little panting cries coming at regular intervals from Deirdre's throat . . . and for the thin, whining, snuffling sounds coming from behind the back door.

Through a haze of passion Deirdre watched him dip his fingers into a jar, knew they would come up covered, oozing, dripping with crimson jam. Strawberry. He painted her breasts, circling her, following his fingers with his tongue. Again, and then again. He used her like a canvas—creating, erasing, designing—grew bolder, more lavish, moved down.

Deirdre trembled, moaned, and thought she would die . . . if he didn't touch her . . . in her most sensitive place. "Now, now," she begged, knowing this was where it had ended, the aborted fantasy. "Please."

His fingers returned to the jar, scooped, came up covered in sticky jam. He touched her throat, drew a line, straight as an arrow, down between her breasts, past her perfect little navel, through the nest of copper-colored curls between her thighs until his fingers touched her where she wanted to be touched, mingling the luscious strawberry jam with her own sweet honey.

A sound tore from Deirdre's throat. Wildly abandoned, having lost all inhibitions, she touched herself and then reached for him. He let her capture him, pressed close, teasing her, but withheld the final thrust. Deirdre rubbed her hands over her breasts, priming them with the slippery preserves. She held out her hands, tried to grab him again, to guide him into her.

He came close, then withdrew. She begged. Again he pressed to her, hot, hard, everything she wanted. She was panting again, loudly. She closed her eyes; she could not bear to have him tease. He was gone again; she waited, knowing he would soon return.

She whimpered, needful. A voice answered; high, whining, inhuman. She felt a draft of air.

Deirdre's eyes snapped open. Shocked, she stared, for a moment forgetting her position, her vulnerability, poised on the edge of the sink with her knees spread wide.

140

Nightmare! Fantasy gone awry. Shadow slinked to shadow beyond the now-open door. A snarl, the sound of scrabbling, and then they rushed in, a sea of moving shapes, huge, black, flowing horrors with bright-red saucer eyes. They yelped, the sound thin, unholy, as they rushed to him, their master—naked, unafraid, the center pole to their mad dance. One detached itself from the pack, padded across to Deirdre, snorted a spurt of crimson flame.

Deirdre felt the heat, felt it and knew for sure that fantasy was gone and in its place was nightmare. The beast sat before her, blood-red eyes unwavering. Horrified yet strangely fascinated, she finally tore her eyes from it, lifted them to where he stood. He appeared taller than before, immense, still rampantly aroused, surrounded by the pack, excited by the scent of fear. Her fear. A silent command, the raising of his hand, set them toward her. Whining, they crouched low, began to stalk.

Deirdre looked across the room, saw him by the door, the beasts by the hall, and knew she was trapped. Slowly she slid down, off the sink; heard the click as her heels touched the tiled floor. Her palm itched, she scraped it against the edge of the sink, leaving behind a streak of sticky red jam.

Now. Inch by inch she moved, sideways, a tiny thread of hope giving her the courage to go on. Two other doors in the room, one the closet, the other the stairs to the cellar. To safety.

Jerry had remodeled the house, made an inside entrance to it. She would get there. Slowly. The huge dark shapes paced her. Slowly. Panting. Them or her? Another belch of fire, the tongue of flame brushing along her naked thigh. Hysteria welled suddenly.

Almost there. Inching along the wall, she felt the edge of the doorframe beneath her questing fingers. A few

141

more steps, she could grasp the handle.

A creak, a groan, a rush of cold, dank air.

The door was opening; by itself swung wide.

No!

Had she screamed it aloud? What matter? Relentlessly they advanced, the huge black nightmare beasts with blood in their eyes and the promise of blood on their tongues. Hers.

They rushed her then, jumped across the space, hurtling bodies, snapping, snarling, stopping her heart and snatching her breath. She whirled about, leaped for the stairs. Miracle. She landed safely, shoved at the door.

Too late.

Hide.

Down the stairs, rushing headlong into the dark. Almost there.

The thin heel of her slipper missed a tread; her foot twisted, her knee gave way. It seemed like a long way down. To darkness. To eternity. Deirdre knew it wasn't long enough.

15

Richard sat nursing his anger in the corner of a booth in the smoky dimness of Sonny's Tavern. Damn that big bastard Chandler. Damn him. Damn him. Damn him. Interfering where he had no right.

The room was noisy, fast filling to capacity with a boisterous Friday night crowd. The jukebox blared rock and country, the volume so loud the floor vibrated. The air was thick with the smell of cooking meat, the acrid odors of hot oil and sweating bodies secreting cheap aftershave lotions and dime-store perfumes. The older, staler smells, of beer and disinfectant and other, less savory ones, mingled uneasily to form a pungent blend. Richard stared straight down into his bourbon, oblivious to everyone and everything. He couldn't drag his mind from the single thought: Alison was his. His woman. Damn that Chandler.

A voice broke into his dark reverie, snide, taunting, mockingly enjoying. "What a surprise. This is the last place I thought you'd be."

Richard felt rage, a different, sharper fury than he harbored for Sam. "Fuck off!" he snarled at his unwelcome visitor without raising his eyes from the dark-amber liquid in his glass.

Art Bergstrom smiled nastily and slid his body onto the bench seat across the booth from Richard. "Strike out, lover boy?"

Richard raised hate-filled eyes. His life was a mess, and the smug-faced son of a bitch grinning at him so nastily was a big part of it. He wanted to smash his glass into the smirking face, wanted to have the satisfaction of feeling skin stretch and split, bone splinter and break. He wanted to see blood spurt, spread in a flowing tide, obscure the hated features. Instead, he took a long swallow of bourbon and repeated his invitation. "Fuck off."

Art was seemingly oblivious, or unconcerned, with the blatant hatred being directed at him. "That Deirdre looked like a hot little number. If you don't want her . . . ?" He left the rest unsaid.

Deirdre! The name shot like a burning arrow through Richard. He had completely forgotten about her.

Art squinted through the curtain of smoke to the clock above the bar. "The leagues will be starting to bowl just about now. Seems a shame that a little lady like that should have to spend the night on her lonesome. Say the word, Fortune, and I'm outta here. The chick looked like she has a short fuse."

Richard realized that Art had eavesdropped earlier. He narrowed his eyes while his brain began to function again. First he would rearrange pretty boy's features, then he would keep his date with Deirdre. His mind flicked to the leather straps in the trunk of his car. Maybe he would tie her up this time, frighten her a little. She liked it rough.

"Ready to order?"

Caught unaware, Richard whipped his head around so fast, his neck snapped. Angie stood in front of the booth, bony hips pressed against the edge of the table, her order pad raised and a pencil poised above it. About as subtle in her wants as Art in his. Friday night was second in tips only to Saturday. Take up a booth and you had to pay.

Richard got up, drained his drink, fumbled in his pocket, and threw some bills on the table. "Stay out of my face," he warned Art, "or you'll be wearing that smirk over your ear."

"Nice guy," Angie observed as she automatically slipped the pad into her pocket with one hand and the pencil behind her ear with the other.

"The best," Art agreed as he watched his partner shoving his way through the crowd toward the exit.

The banging of a door and the sound of loud laughter pulled Sam from a deep sleep. After all the weeks and months he spent in the field, he should be used to waking up in strange places, in strange beds.

Still groggy, he rolled over, reaching out for the travel alarm clock he kept on the bedside table. His groping fingers knocked it to the floor. "Damn," he said, and fumbled for the bedside lamp. A cone of soft yellow light illuminated a small area, leaving the rest of the room in shadow. He checked his watch and then retrieved the clock from under the bed. They both said the same thing. It was almost eight. He had needed the sleep, but had only intended to nap for an hour. Again he was too late for the inn's dining room.

Resigned to Sonny's menu for another night, he showered and shaved and dressed and then went through the familiar ritual of putting wallet, keys, handkerchief, comb, and small change in his pockets. Ready, a nagging sense of something forgotten, or undone, plagued him. At the door he hesitated, patted his pockets in a typical male routine. Everything seemed to be in place.

No one was behind the front desk in the foyer. A neatly lettered cardboard sign inviting customers to ring for service was propped against a bell. Sam peeked into the sitting room, half hoping to spot Jessie and beg for a table, but she was nowhere in sight. Several parties waited to be seated; the room rang with talk and laughter. He didn't have to count heads to know he didn't have a hope.

"Evening, Chandler."

Sam swiveled about and met the full force of J. Norbert Edgehill's beaming smile. "Hello, Mayor. I didn't see you."

J. Norbert shook hands firmly. "Me and the missus are waiting for a table. We come out most Fridays," the mayor confided man to man. "It's a treat for Milly." Then, like a chameleon, his entire aspect changed. "Terrible business about Vera today. Terrible."

"Yes, it was." Sam's voice was cold. He didn't intend to discuss the accident with Draconia's mayor.

J. Norbert, for once sensitive to the nuance of another's tone, changed the subject with admirable dexterity. "I hear tell you boys had some excitement down at the old mill this morning. Wild dogs, wasn't it?"

Sam shrugged noncommittally, thinking J. Norbert didn't miss much. "Are strays much of a problem hereabouts?"

This time the mayor shrugged, his neck all but disappearing with the motion. "We get a few, nothing we can't handle. Problem comes when campers deliberately let 'em go or lose 'em in the woods. The bigger ones can turn feral after they've had the first taste of fresh blood. I've heard tell they even form packs, hunt together." He paused, stared off into space for a moment, then transferred his gaze back to Sam. His voice took on a hard edge. "Anything's possible."

146

"I suppose," Sam returned mildly. The mayor's none-too-subtle suggestion intrigued him. He wondered if it could possibly be a warning. It wasn't very surprising the politician had learned about the grisly discovery. The crew had cleaned out the old mill and nailed new, sturdy boards over every opening in the structure. Any one of them could have talked about it.

Just then Jessie hurried up to them. "Your table's ready, Bert. Sorry you had to wait." She eyed Sam distractedly, then consulted a piece of paper. "I don't see your name here. Did you make a reservation?"

"I'm afraid I forgot," Sam admitted. "Again."

"Join us, Chandler," J. Norbert invited. "Milly and me would be glad of the company."

"Thank you. Perhaps some other time," Sam said.

The mayor lingered a moment. "Dragon Meadow is very important to Draconia. Nothing must interfere with it. I myself personally assured Mr. Blaise that nothing would." He stuck out his hand, and Sam automatically extended his own. "Don't stand on ceremony, Chandler. You hear? I trust you'll remember," he said, and they both knew it had nothing to do with a dinner invitation.

"What was that all about?" Jessie asked as the mayor ushered Milly into the dining room.

"Damned if I know," Sam said. *But I sure would like to find out.* Another puzzle. Something else to worry about, although heaven knew he had enough to keep his mind occupied. Again the sense of something undone, overlooked, assailed him. He strained his mind toward it, but it remained elusive.

"Oh, no," Jessie muttered, inadvertently distracting Sam, "there are the Millers, half an hour early."

She hurried off to greet them, leaving Sam free to go. Once outside he inhaled deeply, his thoughts still full of J. Norbert, wondering if he was reading hidden meanings into a totally innocuous situation. The air felt good—crisp, clean—untainted. He stared up at the sky, marveling at the myriad of stars, then lowered his gaze, straining to see through the blackness, back into the notch.

The dark bulk of Dragon Mountain brooded over everything, a huge, densely wooded, lightless place. Mysterious. He shook his head at the fancy, so unlike him, and took another deep breath, inhaling the clear, chill air with its tinge of pine and balsam. Not a hint of a rain cloud, he noticed, pleased, pushing the puzzle of Draconia's mayor to the back of his mind. If the weather held through the weekend they might be able to pour concrete on Monday. If they couldn't, they would fall behind schedule.

A well-worn path wound around the inn to the parking lot in the rear. Sam followed it more by instinct than anything else, for trees screened the moon and only dim light spilled out of the windows, dappling the ground. The bar-lounge area looked very cozy and inviting from outside. Tall slender white candles in hurricane lamps graced every table, lending the room an aura of warm intimacy.

Sam had almost passed the appealing scene when something made him halt and step off the path, out of the light and into the shadow. With eyes narrowed, he studied a couple sitting at a small table near the window. Jennifer's bright blond head was like a beacon in the subtly lighted room. Her companion was a dark contrast.

Sam studied the man's profile. Something was making him uneasy. What was it? Why should he be concerned? Despite feeling like a voyeur, he hesitated, hidden in the dark. Jennifer said something; the man tenderly placed his hand over hers, like a lover.

The man—Richard Fortune!—brought Jennifer's hand

148

to his lips and kissed her palm.

The breath whistled from between Sam's teeth as he fought the urge to rush inside and drag Jennifer away. From all that he knew about Richard, the man was no fit companion to her.

She's not your daughter, Chandler. The silent warning delivered, he forced himself to walk away, although he couldn't resist one last look over his shoulder. From this angle Richard looked very big, very broad, as he leaned over the table toward Jennifer's slim figure. Like a big black spider engulfing its prey. The thought flashed through Sam's mind at the very instant he realized that the man was not Richard.

"Ah, Jennifer," he said, sadly shaking his head, "perhaps you would be better off with Richard after all." From what he could see, she was completely out of her league.

When he was four houses away from the Treadwell place Richard recalled Deirdre telling him to call before coming over. Screw it, he thought, the nearest pay phone was in Draconia proper, not counting the one on the highway near Treadwell's garage. The idea amused him, calling from a man's phone to see if the man's wife was available for screwing, but he wasn't in the mood to waste time. Besides, he didn't take orders from her. He didn't take orders from anyone.

To be on the safe side, though, he drove by her house, slowing down and looking for signs that Jerry had forgotten his passion for bowling and boozing with the boys and had chosen to stay at home with his wife on this particular Friday night. The Treadwell place was dark. Odd, that, but Richard figured Deirdre was taking no chances, either pretending she was out or in bed early.

He grinned in the dark, the green luminescence from the dashboard giving his skin a sickly glow. One of her reasons would soon be true—he'd see that Deirdre was in bed early.

After parking on the street behind the Treadwell house, Richard opened the trunk and took out the small package with the leather straps, then cut through the Rowlands' property and approached Deirdre's house by way of the backyard.

The ground was still soft from last night's rain; with each step his feet squelched down into wet grass and mud. The thought of ruining his expensive shoes in this fashion, sneaking around like a cheap back-door Romeo, did nothing to improve his disposition. He reached the small patio where Jerry had laid down flagstones two summers ago. An offensive, foul odor hovered over the area. After the first whiff Richard tried not to breathe through his nose.

The back door stood ajar. Richard rapped loudly on it at the same time he peered into the kitchen. It was too dark to see anything; the moon was not yet risen.

He pushed, and the door creaked open another couple of inches. "Deirdre!" he called in a loud whisper. "Hey, Deirdre!" Silence greeted him. Almost out of what little patience he still possessed, his feet starting to itch in the damp loafers, Richard boldly shoved the door all the way open and walked into the kitchen. The air inside was rank. He gulped involuntarily, his brain automatically trying to place the odor. Charnel house, a house of the dead, popped into his head, but although it conjured a grisly picture, he had no idea what it would smell like.

Where the hell was Deirdre? He wasn't in the mood to play games, at least not this kind of game. Tonight he needed an outlet, a good workout to release his tensions, sexual and otherwise. From experience he knew that Deirdre's bed technique was better exercise than an aerobics class—and a hundred times more fun.

The house was quiet; waiting. A prickling unease finally penetrated Richard's egocentricity. Something was wrong. At last he experienced a stab of concern for Deirdre.

"Deirdre?" He listened, but all he heard was a faint buzzing.

Scenes from movies flashed through his head. The quiet, the smell, the dark, the sense of *waiting* . . . for him to walk down the hall, push open a door, to find—what? Butchery? The handiwork of a crazed killer? A bloody, mutilated corpse, mortal remains signifying death's calling card?

Jesus, he had to get out of there. Panicked, he swung around, for a moment so disoriented he forgot the direction of the door.

The droning, buzzing sound increased. Richard backed up until he banged against the wall, his shoulder hitting the light switch. Instantly the kitchen flooded with cold fluorescent light. His eyes scanned the room. Nothing out of place, except . . .

Flies. A whole goddamn bunch of flies. The stupid bitch must be stoned again to leave the door open, he thought disgustedly. He shook his head, faintly ashamed that he had let himself get so out of control. Flies, for crying out loud, but . . . There were so many of them. Big black cluster flies, busily, greedily feeding on . . .

Blood. They were drinking blood. He could see it, bright-red blood, smeared on the counter. *Goddamn fucking bloodsucking vampire flies.* Richard felt his intestines squeeze, his stomach do an uncomfortable flip-flop.

Then he saw the jar, the top off, the enterprising insects crawling all over it, feasting on the sugary contents. He walked close, looked at the label. Jam.

Stupid bitch, leaving something like that out.

Angry now, sure Deirdre dreamed, lost in her own personal Xanadu, he stormed out of the kitchen, down the hall. He'd find her and make her sorry she freaked out on his time. He knew the house well. One glance in the dining room, then the living room, and he was on his way upstairs, certain he would find her there.

He flicked on the light in the bedroom. The bed was rumpled; the scent of sex permeated the air.

This betrayal, on top of everything, was just too much for Richard. "Stupid, cheating bitch," he shouted, deeply aggrieved. His voice bounced off the walls, echoing eerily through the empty rooms. Not for one moment did he think Deirdre had spent the afternoon in that bed with her husband. No, the two-timing slut was shafting both of them. He clamped his teeth together, exerting so much pressure that his jaw ached with the force of his anger. No one, especially not a little thrill-seeking tramp, was going to play this game with him. Not with Richard Fortune.

Fury flooded him, blood pumping into his head, creating a red haze before his eyes. Not stopping to think what he would do when he found her, he went into the bathroom, expecting to find her there, passed out.

The bathroom was empty. So were all the other rooms on the floor. Puzzled, shaking, having no outlet for his tension, Richard rushed back downstairs, not caring how much noise he made, leaving a trail of lights behind him.

Back on the ground floor he did a more thorough search, even opening closets and looking under furniture. Made mindless by the drug, she could have crawled anywhere. She could have overdosed; anything was possible.

That thought sobered him, took the edge off his anger. But if she had, then where was she? Had her lover called the police?

"That's it, I'm gone," Richard muttered to himself, his anger disappearing as suddenly as it had come, leaving him drained of emotion, totally depleted both mentally and physically. His body felt heavy, unutterably weary. An all-too-familiar depression insinuated itself into his mind, nibbling at his self-confidence.

The flies were still devouring the jam when he went back into the kitchen. He cast them a disgusted look, then noticed something he had overlooked. The door to the cellar stood slightly open, showing a wedge of blackness. Richard wanted desperately to be away, but his feet had yet to get the message. They carried him across the floor until he stood directly before the partially open door. For some reason the flies sounded louder over here.

Unnerved, wanting to run, he nevertheless pulled the door all the way open and found the light switch on the inside wall. A frugal sixty-watt bulb bathed the stairs in dull yellow light.

Richard took one look and froze in place. Then he heaved, his stomach reacting in the seconds before his mind could assimilate what his eyes saw. The sight was bad enough, but the sounds . . .

Flies. More flies than he had ever seen. Buzzing. Droning. Crawling all over . . . *Naked. Sprawled obscenely. Jeeesus, she was naked and covered in blood and the little fuckers were sucking and drinking and . . .*

No! Jam. It was jam, and what the fuck did it matter? She was dead, any fool could see that and they were . . . *Oh God they were crawling between her legs. Delving into her. They were . . .*

Bile rose in his gorge; sweat popped out all over his

153

body, ran down his forehead into his eyes, stinging, blinding . . . But not soon enough. Not nearly soon enough. He had seen and he would remember. Deirdre. He knew it was Deirdre. He recognized her frivolous pink-feathered slippers.

16

"I'm sorry about the suitcase," Sam told Alison for the fourth or fifth time. "I knew there was something I was forgetting." They were sitting at one of Sonny's small round tables, as far from the jukebox as possible so that they could hear each other. He had just finished a meal of fried chicken and french fries. Alison had refused to be tempted into having anything since she had eaten earlier. Sam ordered onion rings anyway, to go with her beer, and was amused at the way she daintily picked at them. He had Lucy to thank for not being alone again tonight. She had all but pushed Alison out of the house when he had stopped by with the overlooked suitcase.

"Forget it. You had more important things to worry about." Alison chewed on an onion ring and looked around with interest. "I haven't been here in so long. I don't recognize more than a handful of people."

Sam surveyed the crowded room and chuckled. "I do. Three-quarters of them are in my crew."

"Ah, you're the boss then. I wondered why you get all those little polite nods of greeting."

"Goes with the territory." Sam shrugged, then broke out in a huge grin. "Here comes the antithesis of 'polite,'" he said out of the corner of his mouth.

Amos Hubbard materialized out of the bluish-gray smoke haze like Frankenstein out of the pit and cackled in a high-pitched voice. "Why, if it ain't the city fella. Fast worker, ain'tcha boy?" He leered at Alison. "Heard you was back, girlie. Almost got yerself killed doin' it."

Alison grinned. "How are you, Amos?"

"How should I be? I got one foot in the grave and th'other wantin' to follow it." The old man smirked at Alison and then looked hopefully at Sam. "Right good ball game on the TV."

Sam never took his eyes off Alison. "Not tonight. Catch you another time."

"Ayuh." Amos winked lasciviously and wandered away in the direction of the bar.

By her second beer, Alison was feeling more relaxed than she had in a very long time. Sam was very easy to be with, despite the astounding thing he had said to her that afternoon. Every time she thought of it she blushed, but instead of pushing it away, she kept coming back to it. That alone would have made her uneasy as recently as two days ago. Two days ago. Before nightmare and insanity became real.

Alison surreptitiously studied Sam's profile as he followed the old man's weaving path through the boisterous Friday-night crowd. Instinctively she knew he was a man people liked, trusted. She gave voice to the thought. "Amos likes you."

Sam swung his gaze back to her. "Lucky me."

Alison laughed. It was the first time Sam had heard her laugh, an amused laugh, not one tinged with hysteria. It was a good, pure sound. He decided he would like to hear it again, but another man was approaching the table.

"Hiya, Alison." He pulled out a chair and made himself comfortable.

"Hello, Jerry." She turned to Sam. "Do you know Jerry? Jerry Treadwell?"

Sam extended his hand. "Chandler. Sam Chandler. I called you this morning about Alison's car."

The two men shook hands across the table.

Jerry helped himself to one of Alison's onion rings. He knew everyone and everything connected with Dragon Meadow. It was his future, just like everyone else's in Draconia. But around strangers he had the inborn reticence of most small-town people, so his reply was laconic. "Seen you at the station. Lincoln, isn't it?" He didn't need Sam's confirmation. He ate two more onion rings, carefully wiped his fingers of grease, and got down to business. "About the Mustang, Alison, I'm sorry I didn't get back to you earlier." Then he started to tick items off on his fingertips.

Alison looked dazed when he finally stopped. "How long?" He shrugged. "How much?" He shrugged again. "Jerry," she wailed, more dismayed by the prospect of being without transportation than by the cost of the repair.

"I'll work up an estimate. How about I drop it off sometime tomorrow? You staying with Lucy?"

"Yes."

Sam waited until Jerry was on his feet before telling him that the bill for the Mustang's rear window was his. Alison opened her mouth to protest, but Sam didn't let her get the words out. "I broke it. I'll pay for it." He could see the interest in Treadwell's eyes, but he didn't intend to satisfy it—at least not tonight. Right now he thought the most important thing was to get Alison on the dance floor, just as soon as a song with a slow beat came on. He wanted to know how she felt in his arms.

The record changed, and to Sam's delight it was a slow, sensuous tune. "Shall we?" He indicated the miniature dance floor and felt like a teenager when Alison hesitated just a shade too long for his ego, finally accepting with a shy little nod. Sam didn't pause; he took

157

her elbow and had her up and out on the dance floor and into his arms in one smooth motion. It was no great surprise to find that she felt good pressed up against his body. Better than good. She was shy and a bit skittish in his arms, but that would change. He'd make damn sure it did.

In the middle of the dance a hand tapped Sam's shoulder. None too pleased at the interruption, Sam whirled around to find his foreman grinning at him.

Rufus nudged Sam with an elbow in the ribs, his eyes examining Alison curiously. "Hello, pretty person. Might you be the little lady who took a bite out of the boss here last night?"

Sam stiffened and wished Rufus anywhere else on earth. He was about to suggest McClain take a hike, but then Alison offered Rufus her hand. Sam watched it disappear inside the foreman's huge mitt.

"Guilty as charged, but I only bite St. Bernards or men who come to my rescue in downpours. You're quite safe with me, Rufus."

Sam still had his arm around Alison. Despite her light tone he could feel the tension creeping through her. The mellow mood had fled. McClain had brought the nightmare back.

They left Sonny's by mutual consent soon after. Sam damned himself for bringing her there. He should have taken her where they could have had privacy. He should have braved the mountain roads, taken a chance on getting served without a reservation in one of the fancy new restaurants in the resort and condominium complexes clustered around the western end of the Kancamagus, even though he disliked those developments and shunned them as much as possible. Wild, wooded expanses had been bulldozed bare to make way for concrete, steel, and boxlike buildings. The land had been raped. Dragon Meadow would never be like that. He would see to it.

In the blessed quiet of the parking lot he tried to explain. "I only told him about the accident. Nothing else."

Alison's practical New England upbringing and her Crandell genes would not let her be anything but pragmatic. "He wouldn't believe you if you told him the whole thing." She made a sound faintly reminiscent of Lucy's ladylike snort. "You had to be there."

Sam smiled at the attempt at humor, then swiftly sobered. "There's something you should know." Quickly he told her the Cutters knew what she had seen. "It was a judgment call. I thought at the time that you, er . . ."

"Had a pretty good knock on the head that made me nuts."

"Something like that." Gently he squeezed her hands. "I'm sorry."

Alison's eyes were dark and unreadable in the dim light. With every atom of his being, Sam wished this was a normal night so he could say and do all the normal things a red-blooded man who has been too long without a woman wants to do. More than anything he wanted to make good on his promises: the one he had made to himself; the one he had made to her.

But this was not a normal night. They needed to talk. Because he didn't quite trust himself to be alone with her and at the same time to keep his hands off her, he invited himself back to Lucy's house for coffee. He damned himself for being civilized, but it was the only place where he would have to exercise self-control and still have privacy. After all, he couldn't make a move on Alison with the old tartar sleeping upstairs. At least he hoped he wouldn't.

Jennifer Cutter

Jennifer quietly closed the front door of her parents' Victorian house and tiptoed across the polished wood floor toward the staircase. The house was quiet and dark, which meant that her parents were already in bed. That suited her just fine. She didn't want to see them; she didn't want them to see her.

Since childhood, when she raided the kitchen late at night, Jennifer knew exactly where to walk so as not to step on any squeaky floorboards. When she reached her room she didn't turn on the light, making her way surely to the cushioned window seat. She knelt on it and pressed her forehead against the glass, crossing her arms under her breasts and tightly hugging herself. Keeping the memories inside.

Trembling, she closed her eyes. Her body ached. With her eyes closed the pain intensified, the pain that had brought so much pleasure. It was wrong; she knew it, but God help her, she knew no way to stop it. It was like nothing she had ever known, like nothing she had ever dreamed about. The things he did to her. The things she did to him. Memory alone caused her body to tingle.

"Adrian," she murmured, the movement of her love-swollen lips another kind of pleasure-pain.

"Jen? Are you awake?"

Jennifer's eyes flew open and her lissome body twisted to face the door. "Mom? I'm tired. Can we talk in the morning?"

"Shh, I don't want to disturb your father." Dottie entered the bedroom and carefully closed the door.

Jennifer inched away from the window, not wanting even the light from the moon to fall on her face. She could never fool her mother, had never before even tried to go behind her parents' backs, but she couldn't—*wouldn't*—stop seeing Adrian, and if they knew . . .

Jennifer shivered, unsure of just how this had happened, how she had been drawn like a foolish moth to the flame. He was a fever in her blood, an irresistible

160

wildness, the forbidden, dark side of passion. She was addicted.

Desperation made her plead. "Please, Mom, can't it wait? I'm really very tired."

Dottie was so upset she failed to recognize the alien tone in her daughter's voice; the slyness that was not Jennifer; the closemouthed hesitation; the underlying note of panic. Instead, with shaking fingers, she pressed something smooth and cool into her daughter's hands. "Wear this. Don't take it off. Promise me, Jen, it's very important. Wear it and watch. Should it shatter you'll know."

Fear of a different kind shook Jennifer. "Know what?" she whispered.

"Danger. You'll be in danger."

Wide-eyed, Jennifer watched as her mother reverted to another time. There was no mistaking the gesture. In the quiet darkness Dottie punched the air in the age-old sign used to ward off the evil eye. "Now you. Do it. You've got to protect yourself. Do it!"

Jennifer's slim body swayed like a reed. Her head started to ache; her arms felt like lead weights hanging from her shoulders. She couldn't move them, not even to scratch her hand. The center of her right palm itched unbearably.

Ice-cold fingers touched Jennifer's hand. "Do it!"

Jennifer could barely breathe. Her voice croaked eerily through the dark. "I can't."

17

Alison and Sam were approaching the turnoff to the inn when a wild cry shattered the night. Alison jumped and unconsciously grabbed Sam's arm. "Did you hear that?"

Sam did and knew this was his chance to see what animal was making the infernal noise.

They passed the Dragon View Inn and sped farther back into the notch. The feral cry repeated as they approached Dragon Meadow, the sound lifting the fine hairs on the nape of Sam's neck. The damn animal sounded very near. His thoughts were grim as he twisted the wheel sharply and, with a squeal of protesting rubber, the car made the turn onto the access road to the construction site. The Lincoln shimmied out of the turn; Sam floored the pedal, jouncing them down the rutted road at a dangerously accelerated speed.

"Sam?"

Sam stole a quick look at Alison. Her eyes were wide and staring, two black holes in a pale face.

"Hang on." He returned his attention to the muddy, rutted road. As soon as the car shuddered to a stop Sam had the door open and was halfway out when he realized Alison was also getting out. "Stay here a minute. I've got to check the old mill. Lock the doors. You'll be safe."

"No! I'm going with you."

Sam hesitated and then nodded. "Okay. Wait a second, I need to get something." He went to the trunk for the big heavy-duty flashlight he always kept there, also picking up the tire iron. "Let's go. Keep close to me." Alison glanced from the weapon up to his taut features, but didn't say a word.

Keeping the flashlight beam low to the ground, he quickly plunged down the path toward the river, Alison right behind him. When they neared the old mill he stopped so abruptly she almost crashed into him.

"What is it? Do you see anything?" Her breath was coming in short gasps.

"Listen."

Alison concentrated, but all she could hear was the rushing river and the loud thrumming of her heart. "I don't hear anything."

Neither did Sam. Although the memory of a large black shape, two fire-bright eyes gleaming through the dimness of the derelict mill, the savaged, mutilated corpse of the raccoon, made him reluctant to encounter the animal face-to-face, he wanted to see it. Perhaps it was nothing more than pets turned wild, as the mayor suggested. But wild dogs or not, he didn't want them using the old mill as a lair. Playing the flashlight across the ground, he grunted with satisfaction when he found several large rocks. "Insurance," he told Alison, and threw them one by one against the wall of the old mill, listening intently between each throw. Nothing. Finally satisfied there were no surprises ready to spring out at him, he did a fast survey of all four walls.

"Those boards look new," Alison commented when he was through with the cursory inspection.

Sam switched off the flashlight and the night immediately closed in. He couldn't make out her features. "They are. We put them up this morning."

"Why?"

He took her arm. "Let's go back to the car." As they walked he told her what he and Henry had found in the mill that morning.

"You think it was the same animal I saw last night?"

Sam shrugged and opened the car door for her. At that moment another eerie howl sliced through the night. Alison jumped back, her shoulders making hard contact with Sam's chest. He put an arm around her waist, felt her body go rigid as another voice joined the first, and then another and another until the night rang with high-pitched, piercing howls.

The only thing keeping Alison from surrendering to superstitious dread was the feel of Sam's solid strength against her back. "Oh, God, it sounds like a pack of wolves baying at the moon."

"They're not close."

Alison tilted her head. "No. They sound as if they're moving away."

"Come on. I want to see if we can get a look at them." He urged Alison inside the car and threw the flashlight and tire iron into the back. At the notch road he turned right. The howling paced them as they sped through the dark.

"Lucy and I heard cries like this earlier today."

"Did she say anything?"

Alison stared straight ahead. Lucy had said many things, strange things, but nothing specific about the savage cries. "Not about this."

"Lucy heard it before. We both heard it last night, just after I returned to the inn to shower and change. After I met Vera."

Alison began to feel very afraid.

Sam slowed the car. "Listen, it's growing fainter." He steered onto the grassy shoulder and stopped, opening the window before turning off the headlights and engine.

Innocent sounds greeted them. The wind soughed through the notch, rustling grass and leaves, a plaintive voice whispering a familiar tune. Insects whirred and chirped. A bird sleepily called to its mate. Nothing but the normal springtime night noises. Draconia Notch lay peaceful under the ink-black shadow of Dragon Mountain.

"Damn it, we've lost them." In frustration Sam whacked the steering wheel with the heel of his palm. So close. The whole pack could not just disappear. There had to be some evidence of them.

Alison peered through her side window and then drew hurriedly back. "Sam, look where we are."

The old cemetery lay just to their right, the smooth-humped tombstones gleaming like dinosaur teeth under the rising moon.

Sam mumbled a curse and again whacked the steering wheel with his palm. "I don't like this. It's just too damn coincidental."

"You think Vera . . . ? You think the two are connected?"

Sam's voice was grim. "I don't know."

"Vera's death was an accident."

"Yeah," Sam said, but he was thinking that an old cemetery was a very peculiar place for a young girl to be alone in late at night. He reached for the door latch. "I'm going to take a look."

The world was suddenly too dark, too quiet for Alison. "Out there?"

Sam recognized Alison's growing panic by the squeakiness of her voice, the rigid posture of her slim body. "I'm just going to look, nothing else. God knows I'm no hero, Alison, but I've got to see what we're dealing with. Whatever these creatures are, they're roaming the Dragon Meadow site, and I can't have that. They're spooking my crew." He reached over and gently squeezed her shoulder.

"It's probably a pack of wild dogs. If I can find the direction they took, maybe the park rangers can do something about them. Wait here a minute, I'll be right back." He reached into the back and picked up the flashlight and tire iron.

But Alison was right behind him when he walked through the gate and into the cemetery. He didn't turn on the flashlight; the moon was high enough to give light. They moved silently, Alison never more than two steps from his side.

It didn't take them long to explore the old cemetery. The ground was spongy from the rain, making the going slick and dangerous. Alison didn't need Sam's low-voiced admonition to watch her step.

They came upon a spot where the ground was churned and rough, and she knew that this was the place where Vera had died. Sam turned on the flashlight and played it over the area, across the ground, and over the ancient markers.

Alison grabbed his arm and directed the light onto the nearest granite tombstone. The letters sprang out of the dark: ALD RB OK.

"Here? Vera was found here? Right in front of her family burial plot?" Alison whispered the questions, her hushed voice disbelieving.

"Yes."

They both thought *coincidence*; rejected it. Sam stepped forward and traced his fingers over the worn stone. "It says Alderbrook, all right." He focused the light lower. "The other names are less distinct."

Alison knew the monument. "This is Noah Alderbrook's grave. He was one of the founders of Draconia. Well, it really was New Hope then."

"Oh. I've noticed the cemetery's name is New Hope, but I thought it had some religious significance."

Alison shook her head. "No. New Hope was the name

166

of the town. They came here to get a new start. Just about everyone had an interest in timber, either logging it or milling it or transporting it or using it for end products like lumber and paper and pencils. New Hope wasn't a big place, but the entire town, everybody, was in business together, sort of like a modern co-op. Except for some farms, everyone depended on timber."

She ran her fingers down the weathered stone. "Strange that Vera should have died here."

Sam stepped carefully over the grave and tugged at Alison. He wanted to be away, needing to put distance between himself and this spot of recent, untimely death. "Whatever those animals were, we've lost them." Silently he determined to come back in the morning when he could do a more thorough search. A wisp of white, ghostly in the silvered dark, caught his attention. "What's that over there? It looks like ground fog."

Alison shivered. "It's the gate."

Puzzled, Sam moved the flashlight in a wide arc. The beam of light cut across tombstones and trees, disturbing the dark. "Didn't we come in from back there?" he asked, then swung the light forward, aiming it toward the misty area. An opaque whiteness swallowed the bright beam. "Ground fog clings to low places. There's got to be a dip in the earth, probably a sunken grave over there."

"No. It's always like that."

"C'mon, let's take a look."

Sam strode away before Alison could tell him not to go near the gate. But she was too late and Sam was getting farther away with each second. She hurriedly moved toward the beam of light and to the reassurance of his presence.

Alison found him standing before the low stone wall bordering the cemetery. As she approached he clicked off the light because the mist was throwing it back.

"Strange," he said, "I thought this gate was a back exit, but it's not in the wall, it's completely outside the cemetery. Why is that?"

"No one knows."

Sam put the flat of his hand on the waist-high wall and vaulted over. Carefully placing the flashlight and tire iron down, he leaned over and put both his hands on Alison's waist. She was swung high, up and over the wall before she realized his intent.

Sam didn't put her down right away, but held her, close to his chest. Then he slid her down the length of his body until her feet touched the ground. His hands still had not left her waist. A new awareness crackled between them; a tenseness that had nothing to do with the circumstances of time and place. After several breathless moments Sam sighed and let her go, his only consolation knowing there would be another time. He would make sure of it.

To cover the sudden surge of emotion, he turned away and surveyed the gate. The sinuous fog rolled around its base, weaving in and out of the long green grass, obscuring the ground. The moon shone down on it, its rays catching the gleam of glossy black paint on the bars; higher up the glow of gold on the spikes. Silver light illuminated the twisted iron, the Gothic letters spelled across the arch.

D R A C O N I A

"Impressive," Sam said, "and very mysterious. A gate without a wall. A gate that serves no purpose."

"Let's go," Alison said, edging backward toward the wall. Being this near to the gate made her nervous.

Sam came back to her and she thought he had listened, that they would leave. But he reached around her and picked up the flashlight and the tire iron, handing her the light and telling her to keep close by his side.

168

Alison obeyed, not because she shared his curiosity, but because she feared being left behind. The closer they got to the gate the less she wanted to take another step, even more so when she became aware of a noxious odor. She sniffed and made a face.

"Rank, isn't it?" There was a new tenseness to Sam, a sense of controlled excitement. "That's the same smell that was near your car last night and also in the old mill this morning. Whatever we've been chasing has been this way."

Suddenly Sam crouched down and told Alison to put on the light. She swept it along the ground, revealing an area of trampled grass and mud.

"Hold it!" Alison dutifully steadied the beam as Sam gingerly pushed a clump of grass to one side with the tire iron. He studied the ground for a long time before lifting his gaze and staring fixedly at the gate. "Strange," he muttered, and taking the light from Alison, walked a slow circle around it. Then he reached out and grabbed one of the bars and shook it as hard as he could. The gate didn't budge.

"It's never been open. Never." Alison cautiously moved to his side. Every instinct told her to run, to run fast and far, and to never look back.

"Hmm," Sam said.

Alison didn't like the sound of that. "Believe me, it's locked. It's always been locked. Everyone knows that. Besides, what difference does it make? You can see right through it. There's no mystery. You know what's on the other side."

Alison was frightened, so frightened she only wanted to leave, to run away, maybe all the way back to New York. But New York wasn't the safest place for her, either. There were the obscene calls, night and day, until she could hardly keep from screaming each time the phone rang. And now the calls were here . . . But that problem paled next to this new one . . . This enigma of impossibilities.

Blindly she reached out for Sam. "Let's go. Please." Her voice was a thin wail.

Sam clicked the light off. The moon was hidden behind a cloud and he used the covering blanket of darkness to reach out and take Alison into his arms. She stiffened at the contact, but made no move to escape. "In a moment, sweetheart, I promise. First let's try to understand what we have here." He stared at the gate long and hard over Alison's head. A frown creased his forehead and he began slowly, musingly, to speak his thoughts aloud.

"There are signs of many animals here—also deep depressions, tracks, like narrow wheels would make. You saw them. The wheels of a coach, perhaps?" Alison shuddered; Sam tightened his arms. "Only in front of the gate. There's no sign of any disturbance behind it. So? You tell me. Where did they go?"

Alison struggled in his embrace, but he held her firmly. "No. I . . . no . . . I don't know." She bit her lower lip to keep it from trembling. "This whole thing tonight . . . last night . . . Oh, God, it's impossible."

Gently he brushed a wayward strand of hair off her cheek. "Look around, Alison. They were here. Where did they go? You heard them, you can't deny it." He loosened his hold and turned her about so that she faced the gate. "The tracks end here. Where did they go? Think. Help me find out what happened."

She stepped out of his grip and spun around to face him. "It's impossible." *As impossible as a headless horse. As impossible as a headless coachman. As impossible as a dog with eyes of fire.*

Sam refused to end it. "Where did they go? Into thin air? Into the ground? Or, did the gate open? What happens when the gate is open? *Did they somehow go*

170

through it?"

Alison trembled. "But . . . but . . . That's impossible. Crazy. Look. You can see. There's nothing here."

Silver light etched Sam's features as the moon reappeared. He didn't look like a crazy man, he looked just like what he was: a rational man faced with a seemingly irrational puzzle. "Crazy? Maybe." He stabbed his fingers through his hair in a gesture Alison was coming to know. "Mysteries have solutions," he muttered, then suddenly relaxed his tense muscles, threw her a grin. "Impossible? We'll see."

Amos Hubbard

Amos Hubbard slid off his favorite barstool, the one with the best view of the television, and stood swaying next to it for several moments. All the beer he had guzzled had failed to deaden the pain in his joints, although it had done a better job of numbing his mind. He peered through the haze blearily, looking for Sonny. Friday and Saturday nights were his least favorites. Too many young people, yelling and screaming at each other over loud music. In his day the mating rituals had been a lot quieter. Although he liked to look at all the pretty young things, some of them—wearing their clothes so tight and so short—it made it easy for him to remember what the good Lord had made females for, there was only so much noise and hubbub an old person could take.

"Right noisy in here tonight," Amos complained when Sonny finally moved down the bar to settle his bill. His voice was a thick wheeze, a result of the combination of smoke and beer and the ravages of old age.

Sonny whisked Amos's empty glass out of sight and swiped at the wet ring it left with his bar rag. "Gotta make a living. Lord knows a body can't survive on the business an old fart like you brings in."

Amos grinned and thrust his arthritis-swollen hand into his pocket. "Smart-mouthed wop. Whadda I owe ya?" The two of them always ended an evening with a few good-natured insults.

Sonny made a big production out of adding the tab. Amos extracted the money from his pocket, carefully counting it out, laying the notes on a wet spot on the bar. Sonny rolled his eyes, scooped the money up and wished Amos good night over his shoulder as he walked away.

Amos raised his hand in a farewell salute, an ill-considered movement, for it unbalanced him and sent his frail body stumbling into the next barstool. He connected with solid flesh.

His volatile temper not improved by having struck out three times that evening, Art Bergstrom welcomed the opportunity to vent his frustration. He shoved Amos upright and gave him a powerful shake. "Keep the fuck away from me, old man," he snarled, "or I'll put you out of your misery."

Amos was old and thin, but his muscles still retained the wiry strength attained over many years of hard physical labor. He knocked the younger man's hand away. "Stupid young pup. 'Pears t'me ya ain't much of a threat to no one. All these here young things with their tits hangin' out jest pantin' fer it, an' ya cain't even git yerself laid. I been watchin' ya. Sittin' here all night, breathin' heavy." Amos cackled with glee as Art's fair complexion rapidly darkened with hot blood.

"C'mon, that's enough." Angie slipped between the two combatants and glared at each of them in turn. Art made a growling noise but retreated back to his barstool when Angie stood her ground. Then she turned to Amos, who was grinning spitefully at Art. Without taking her eye off him, she shouted down the bar to Sonny. "Amos all square with you?"

"Yeah. Show him out," Sonny yelled back.

"Tough guy," Art sneered, "bounced by a dame."

"Why you—" Amos spluttered.

Angie latched onto his arm. "Fun's over." She deftly steered Amos toward the entrance and waited to see him through the door.

Amos found himself standing outside in the dark. He felt an uncomfortable fullness in his bladder, briefly contemplated going back inside to use the john, then gave up the idea when he thought of the effort to weave his way through the crowd of hot, sweaty bodies gyrating on the dance floor. He could make it home in the same time.

Fortunately his Chevy pickup was not too far away. Amos lovingly patted its dented side, opened the door, and climbed painfully inside. God, he ached tonight, but nowhere as bad as in his back. It felt like someone had stuck a heated metal rod up his spine. "It ain't right, an old man should have ta suffer so," he muttered, then in deference to his bladder, started the engine and roared out of the parking lot, taking the turn onto the road so fast that a shower of gravel flew up in his wake.

It was close to midnight and Draconia was quiet, the roads empty, the Chevy's heavy engine laboring up the ridge road the only artificial sound in the night. At the top of the hill Amos pressed his foot to the pedal and raced down the quiet street, past dark houses, shuttered and locked for the night. His house was near the end of the paved road, back where the houses were not shoulder to shoulder, where a man didn't have to draw his shades if he didn't care to.

Halfway there he realized he was in a race with his bladder. "Damned plumbin'," he mumbled, and gave the truck a goose. It shot forward and Amos had to struggle

173

not to cross the center line. He swore but didn't let up on the gas. "Mitchell place," he said as a big, yellow-trimmed Colonial flashed past. That meant he was almost home. Just the Slavins, the Mercers, the O'Rourkes, and the Drakes on this side; the Gebharts, the Treadwells on the other side of the road; then the long empty stretch before the Jacksons, the Saywards, and then his place.

To distract himself from his discomfort he started to sing, a raunchy song he had learned five decades before on a naval ship steaming toward the coast of France. That also had been June and on that long-ago night he had had the same fear of wetting his pants.

"Aw, shit," he said, and jammed his foot down on the brake. The remembered fear of the night before the Allied invasion did him in, and he knew he wasn't going to make it home. In haste, he tumbled from the cab, already unzipping. He identified his location by the bed of petunias he was about to water. Fat Martha Gebhart put a lot of stock in her petunias. If Gebhart caught him he would shoot his ass full of bird shot.

Amos aimed and let fly. He hoped he could finish fast, but this, among other things, did not work as well as it had when he was younger. As relief crept through him a new worry surfaced. He should have remembered to turn off the engine. The steady sound of it throbbing in the otherwise quiet night was a finger pointing directly to him should Gebhart haul his rear end out of bed and look out the window.

Amos tried to hurry, but nature could not be rushed. The throbbing sound was getting louder. The truck . . . but it wasn't the truck . . . Twisting his torso, he peered down the road.

Something else was abroad in the night. Something coming down the road. Amos squinted. Coming from the Treadwell place. Something big and black, moving

174

down the road . . . hooves pounding . . .

A nightmare apparition thundered toward him. Amos opened his mouth to scream, but the breath was caught in his throat. All his bodily functions stopped, frozen by horror.

On it came, a black nightmare, swooping out of the dark; loathsome unholy.

Between the moment when his heart stopped and started again, Amos saw the whole. Unwanted details froze in his mind. Mentally he pushed at them, tried to drive them out, but it was too late. Much too late. The big black coach drew near, coming straight down the road, never swerving, never veering, although . . . Blood, black under the high, cold light of the moon pumped from the thick stump of the horse's neck. A whip was raised, cracked down, lashed against the bloody wound.

The coach flew by. Amos raised his eyes, gagged, and moaned as he followed the line of the whip past the hand, the arm, up to the shoulder, the neck . . . The head . . . NO HEAD. NO HEAD. SWEET JESUS I HAVE SINNED. I'M DEAD. I'M DEAD I'M DEAD I'M DEAD, DEAR LORD. I DIED.

The coach flashed past. Amos squeezed his eyes shut. Too late. Too late because he had seen. Had seen and wished he had not. The head. The coachman's head. On the bench next to him. Leaning close, snug against his thigh.

And worst of all, it winked. IT WINKED, SWEET JESUS, THE MOTHERFUCKER WINKED.

Everything started to work again at once. Amos retched as beer followed by hot bile poured up his throat, out of his mouth, spouting from him in an ocean of foul-smelling vomit. His interrupted stream restarted, running down his leg.

As soon as he was able, he was back in the truck, roaring down the road. Toward his home . . . his haven

175

. . . his Remington.

There would be no sleep for him. Not tonight.

Amos had seen and he knew. A nightmare prowled the notch.

Part II

18

Alison stared down at the note, written in black ink in a bold hand on one of the inn's paper napkins. " 'When you have eliminated the impossible, whatever remains, *however improbable,* must be the truth.' Sir Arthur Conan Doyle believed that, sweetheart, and so do I. Sam. P.S. I have to go to Dragon Meadow. Wait for me."

"What did he say?" Lucy asked the moment Derek, who had delivered the note, was out of earshot.

"Who?" Alison asked teasingly.

Lucy refilled Alison's coffee cup and placed the carafe back on the table with an audible thud. "What did Samson say?"

Alison sighed. Lucy was like a dog with a bone. "Oh, nothing much." She never lied to Lucy, but this time she felt justif'ied in the evasion. Telling a convalescent that real nightmares stalked the dark hours could not be the best medicine.

"Why, that's not . . ." At Alison's suddenly suspicious look, Lucy snorted and reached for the note, tugging it out of Alison's hand. All innocence, she put on her reading glasses and scanned the hastily penned lines, nodding approvingly when she reached the end of the short note. "You'll do as he asks, won't you? You'll

177

wait for him?"

"Lucy, I didn't come up here to ... ah ..." She shrugged, decided to state her true feelings unequivocally. "I wish you'd stop matchmaking."

Lucy tilted her head, giving her a birdlike appearance, and smiled slyly. To Alison's dismay, she completely ignored the request. "Something's going on between you and Sam. Now don't you go denying it, child, there's no fooling me." Meaningfully, she tapped the note with a finger.

Alison blushed, no more able to stop the hot blood from flooding her face and neck than she was to erase the knowing look from her aunt's eyes. Lucy was right. There *was* something going on between them, and Alison simply did not know if she could handle it.

With nervous fingers, she picked up the note and spread it open. Her mental faculties were not their sharpest after spending a disturbed night with little sleep. Glumly she contemplated the bold black letters. The apparition she had seen on the notch road Thursday night could be explained. *Everything* had an explanation. *There are more things in heaven and earth, Horatio/Than are dreamt of in your philosophy.* "Easy for you to say," she mumbled, unaware she had said the words aloud until Lucy spoke.

"What?"

Hastily Alison gathered her scattered thoughts. "Uh, nothing." Shakespeare was good, but he never had to deal with a New Englander.

"You going to do like the boy asks? You going to wait for him?"

Straight forward, uncompromising, tenacious. Alison loved Lucy, but sometimes she made her want to scream. She *did* want to see Sam, to explore the growing feelings between them, but hard on that thought came the knowledge that Sam would want to pursue the search they had started last night and she didn't know if she could face that. Besides, she had come to Draconia to see to Lucy's welfare, and that purpose was far from being accomplished. Mentally she winced, knowing that part of her was using Lucy as an excuse.

"Well?" Lucy asked, running out of patience.

Alison shook her head, not having to feign the regret she felt. "I'm afraid not. You and I have some serious talking to do."

"I'd rather see you sort out your own affairs. It's time you got on with your life, Alison, way past time. Don't waste any more of it."

That got Alison's attention. She looked hard at her aunt and saw the determination in every line of the familiar features. That and something else—something foreign to Lucy's nature, almost a deviousness, a smoke screen. "Not this time, Lucy," she said. "You're not getting rid of me that easily. I came up here to talk with you, to see if we can't get this thing settled."

"This *thing*, Alison, is my life. As I told you yesterday, there's no need for a discussion about it."

"Have you at least thought about it? About selling the inn? Jessie and Luke would be perfect owners. They love the old place, they wouldn't turn it into a roadside bar or a disco."

A devilish light crept into Lucy's eyes. "The Dragon View Inn can be turned into a whorehouse, for all I care. I told you, dead is dead. What's done after I'm gone won't bother me the least little bit." Alison stiffened, and Lucy leaned over to pat her on the hand. "Have I shocked you? I didn't think I'd brought you up to be a prude."

Alison knew Lucy too well to let her slide away from the real issue. "Nice try, but it won't work. We've got to talk, and right now is as good a time as any."

But Lucy was shaking her head, her neat silver curls catching the sunlight pouring in from the big window behind the bar. "Can't. Now, don't go and pout, child,

179

I really can't. The Historical Society is meeting here today and I've got to see to the parlor and then to the table arrangements for the luncheon. Last month Sarah Mercer was put next to Carol Drake by mistake. The meal was about as much fun as dinner on the *Titanic.*"

"The Historical Society meets on a Thursday, doesn't it?" Alison asked suspiciously. She would not put it past her aunt to invent a make-believe meeting just to escape the discussion.

Lucy dropped her eyes and fiddled with her coffee cup. "They . . . ah, waited until I . . . ah, was home." Then, as if fearing Alison would seize the admission to force the issue, she got up and firmly pushed her chair under the table. "I've got lots to do." She passed behind Alison's chair and put a gentle hand on her niece's shoulder. "I meant what I said before. Don't you go burying your future in the same grave as your marriage to Richard." She felt the slight tightening of Alison's muscles under her hand, squeezed her shoulder reassuringly. "You stay here and finish your coffee. I'll tell them at the desk to let Sam know where he can find you."

Alison found herself alone with her thoughts and a rapidly cooling cup of coffee. Neither gave much comfort. Her time was not really her own. As sympathetic as the firm seemed to be, she knew that their patience and understanding was finite. As soon as the car was fixed she would have to leave. She was so preoccupied that when Derek tapped her on the shoulder, she jumped.

"Sorry, Mrs. Fortune, I didn't mean to startle you." He indicated the bar phone with a nod of his head. "There's a call for you." Alison's body stiffened and the color drained from her face. Derek's voice seemed to come from a distance. "Mrs. Fortune! Mrs. Fortune, are you all right?"

"What's the matter?"

Alison heard the scrape of a chair and then felt a large hand grip her arm. She turned her head to see familiar green eyes worriedly studying her face. Strange how much better she felt, just having Sam near. Giddily she thought how happy that would make Lucy. The crafty old fox.

"Hi. I waited."

"So I see," Sam said dryly. "Aren't you feeling well? Does your head hurt?"

"No. I'm fine. Honestly. I guess I'm just tired."

"Should I take a message?" Derek asked. "There's a call waiting for Mrs. Fortune," he explained to Sam.

"I'll get it." Before Alison could think of a way to stop him, he had picked up the telephone. Helpless, she waited for him to slam down the receiver in disgust. It never happened. A wicked light gleamed in his eyes when he finished the short conversation and came back to the table. "Isn't that nice?"

Alison knew she shouldn't fall for so obvious a ploy, but they both knew she couldn't resist. "What's nice?"

"Michele's heard so much about me that she invited me to her party tonight." Alison gave a good imitation of Lucy's snort. Sam grinned, crinkling the skin around his eyes. "She invited you also, so I accepted for both of us."

Alison had to work hard not to grin back at him. It took no stretch of the imagination to know why Lucy liked him so much. Idly she wondered just when she had fallen down the rabbit hole.

"It's six minutes past ten," Amos Hubbard complained.

"Hold your water." Ben Mercer bent down and tried to fit the key into the lock, but Amos's shadow made it difficult for him to see. "Move back. I cain't see with you in the way."

"Where ya been? I've been waitin' on ya." Impatiently Amos hopped from foot to foot, his anxiety rising with each passing moment. He wouldn't feel safe until he got what he came for.

Ben finally succeeded in fitting key to lock, gave a twist, and pushed the door of his shop open. Amos almost knocked him over in his rush to get inside. Ben stood in the doorway and scratched his head in perplexity.

"Come *on*. Move yer ass." Amos went straight to the gun counter. "Yer supposed ta open at ten."

"What's the all-fired rush?" Amos's anxiety was finally getting through to Ben. "Seen the Cropsey monster?"

Amos's thin body jerked. The Cropsey monster was a favorite campfire story used to frighten kids. Ben had inadvertently come close to the mark. "I've come to get me some o' them hollow-nosed bullets. The kind that'll mushroom out an' blow a hole the size o' Toledo in whatever it hits."

Ben slammed a box down on the counter. "This'll do ya. Blow the fuckin' shit out of a moose."

Amos grabbed for the box. "Ain't no moose."

Ben's hand came down flat over the box before Amos could pick it up. He leaned across the counter. Even the sour odor wafting from Amos could not deter him, so rampant was his curiosity. "If it ain't no moose, jist what d'ya plan to get with these?"

Amos told him.

Ben hardly waited until Amos was out the door before picking up the phone and dialing his wife.

19

Alison wasn't the least bit surprised when Sam said he wanted to go back to the cemetery. She had been expecting it, but still a slight shudder rippled through her when he put it into words. They probably had missed details last night—but details of what? During the small hours she had convinced herself she did not want to know.

Yet, here she was again, Sam by her side. The cemetery looked quaint. Peaceful. Most of the graves were very old, the tombstones thinned by wind and weather, the inscriptions almost obliterated. Some stones canted at odd angles; some had sunk partway into the ground. Except for the fresh Alderbrook tragedy, all the sorrows of death had faded and the ancient dead slept quietly under a blanket of green.

"Looks different in daylight," Sam remarked.

Alison nodded agreement. "Almost charming."

The entire aspect of the place was improved by the bright sunshine. A light breeze blew down from the mountains, sweeping through the U-shaped notch, rustling the long grass and setting branches and leaves to tremble. Alison tucked her hair behind her ears to keep it from blowing into her face. There was a hint of moisture in the air and the quality of the light was that clear translucence that sometimes precedes a storm. When she mentioned this to Sam, he groaned.

"I hope you're wrong. The ground is still wet from the other night. I was counting on some good strong sunlight to dry it out over the weekend. Any delay at this stage of construction could set us back weeks."

Alison knew that the area had some of the most severe and unpredictable weather in the world. She squinted up at the sky. "The clouds are moving fast. At this time of the year that usually means rain."

"Terrific."

Suddenly Alison couldn't resist a little tongue-in-cheek teasing. "It could be worse. Scientists believe that if the summers around here get even a few degrees colder the snow won't melt in some of the deeper ravines and glaciers would form. The most famous glacial valley around here is Tuckerman's Ravine over on Mount Washington. Maybe you should go over there and take a look."

"Better and better. Any more good news?"

Alison laughed, surprised that she was so relaxed, suspecting that Sam's easygoing manner had much to do with it. They wandered for some time in companionable silence, broken only when one of them pointed out an interesting inscription or Sam asked one of his frequent questions. More often than not Alison didn't have an answer for him.

"If you truly want to satisfy your curiosity you should come out here with Bertha Rice. She knows quite a bit about the cemetery and Draconia's history."

Sam looked thoughtful and then nodded his head. "Perhaps I will."

By now they were near the southeast corner of the cemetery. Sam stopped beneath the shade of a cluster of huge white pines whose gnarled roots had swallowed up several stones. He pointed to the rounded tops, the only indication left of the graves. "Poor bastards. Gone for good with not even a name to tell us who they were."

Poignancy welled inside Alison. "Surely their families, their descendants remember them." She frowned. "There is a poem that puts it quite elegantly. Something about never dying as long as someone remembers your name. I can't put my finger on it. Damn!"

"It doesn't matter. I understand." Sam took Alison's hand and wove their fingers together as if it were the most natural thing to do. "Where are your people?"

Alison pointed with their coupled hands. It was a strangely intimate gesture. "Over there. The Crandells sleep beneath the hackmatack tree."

"Okay, smartie," Sam said, looking down into her twinkling eyes, "I give up."

"Tamarack, or eastern larch, to you, but I've always preferred the Indian name. Much more romantic."

"Nice word."

Alison met his clear green gaze, knowing he didn't refer to the tree. She was the first to break eye contact. They walked to the cluster of Crandell graves in silence. Alison brushed her fingertips lightly over the largest stone. "Abel and Sarah. They built the Dragon View Inn." She wandered over to four small stones nestled in the shadow of Abel's large monument. "Seeing these little graves makes me feel so sad. I can't begin to think how Sarah felt."

"So many children died in early infancy in those days. I think the people were better able to accept it then. It was a fact of life."

Alison's eyes blazed with emotion. "Look. Sarah buried Rachel, age fourteen months, eleven days, only six days after baby Judith. Enos died eight months later, and Abel two years after that. Not one of those four children reached the age of five. Do you think a mother who isn't sick at heart would have them carve the dates like this? Each one has the years, the months, and the days."

Sam moved to stand directly in front of Alison. He was so close she had to tilt her face up to see his expression. His eyes were dark with emotion. Gently he cupped her face in his big hands. "Alison," he said huskily, and bent his head to hers.

He held her loosely; Alison knew she could pull away. Instead she waited, suddenly breathless, fiercely wanting the feel of his lips on hers. When it came the kiss was soft and tender . . . and brief. Too brief.

Sam raised his head and gazed down into her eyes. "I didn't mean to do that. Not here. This was no place for our first kiss." He smiled. "But you'll get no apology. I wanted some of that fiery passion for myself." An unremitting honesty forced the admission.

"Sam—"

He kissed the tip of her nose and then dropped his hands, only to put his arm around her shoulders and draw her close. Then he returned to the previous subject, as if the moment of intimacy had not happened. "You're right. Just because something was a common occurrence did not make it any easier to bear." He gave her a friendly squeeze, then let her go. "It wasn't only the children who died young, but quite a few of the women, too, and many men seem to have been buried with more than one wife."

It took Alison a moment longer to switch mental gears. Not only had she welcomed Sam's kiss, she had ardently desired it. Silently she marveled that in so short a time she had let him get closer to her than any other man since . . . Like magic the name she was mentally trying to avoid caught her eye.

ELEAZAR FORTUNE was cut deep into an impressive marble headstone. Sam read the name aloud. "He's got the biggest tombstone; he must have been important. Richard's great-great-something?"

"Yes."

186

"Rufus—you met him last night, remember?—brought his name to my attention recently. He said there's some local legend that old Eleazar here trafficked with the Devil to save the mill."

That brought the ghost of a smile to Alison's lips. "Not only Eleazar, but twenty-two others as well. Most of them are buried in this cemetery."

"Do you know the story? Were they devil worshipers? Did they have a coven?" Sam knew the story, remembered every word McClain had spoken, but he wanted to hear Alison's version.

"Hardly. It all happened in one night, the way I heard it. Exigency forced them to do what they did. The river was flooding, threatening the mill, and as if that weren't enough, a landslide started in the mountains. It was heading straight for the mill and would have destroyed not only the mill but the entire town if the Devil hadn't dammed the gorge. Remember, the mill was the lifeblood of the town. Without it, everybody would have been wiped out."

"So they conjured up the Devil and made a deal?"

This time Alison laughed out loud. "As I heard it he just happened by."

"And . . . ?"

Something in his tone alarmed Alison. "And what? That's all there is. The tourists love the story."

Sam was staring thoughtfully at Eleazar Fortune's grave as if the answers he sought could be found there. The ease Alison had experienced with him disappeared, leaving her feeling drained and slightly depressed, prey to the doubts and fears that had plagued her all night.

"Sam?" She hated the plaintive note in her voice but was powerless to change it. "What's the matter? What are you thinking?"

"I was wondering why you married Richard."

Surprised at the unexpected direction of his thoughts, Alison could only stare at him.

"I suppose that you could tell me it's none of my business, but we would both know you'd be wrong." He jerked his thumb at Eleazar's grave. "From all accounts that guy was a leader of men, whatever the path he chose. I've known Richard for several months now, and to all appearances he, ah . . . Oh, hell. There's no good way to ask why you married him."

Somewhere in the back of Alison's mind she had known that one day she would have to answer the question—for herself, if not for another. Sam said he had the right to an answer; in her heart Alison agreed. Yet knowing this, she still had to force her lips to move. "He . . . he was different . . . very different. He was young, full of hope. Life held promise. Then things . . . disappointments in business . . . he wanted—" She shuddered, seemed to contract within herself. "I couldn't," she whispered, "I just couldn't . . ." She began to shiver, as if the memories leeched the heat from her body.

Sam's hand was on her arm. She could feel the warmth of it through the layers of sweater and blouse. "It's all right, sweetheart, it's all right," he murmured, and took her into his arms.

Alison relaxed into his embrace, letting the comfort he offered flow from his body into hers. One of his hands drew lazy circles between her shoulder blades while the other one rested against her lower spine, slowly urged her nearer. She pressed her forehead to his shoulder.

Gradually the nature of the embrace changed. Desire tightened Sam's muscles as Alison's body flattened against his larger, harder frame. He brought her in closer, watched as she raised her head, saw the gleam of awareness in her eyes. His own eyes gleamed with satisfaction as her arms slowly crept up around his neck.

This time the kiss was hard and hot and wildly exciting. Alison trembled with the force of her surging emotions; gloried in the reemergence of long-buried needs and wants. It felt natural to be held in Sam's strong arms, to feel his tongue sweep exploringly through her eager mouth. Each searching stroke awakened dormant senses, built desire. Greedily she burrowed against him, seeking more, now answering his questing tongue with her own.

Sam groaned at the sweetness of her response. She was flaming in his arms; another few minutes and he knew he would lose control. Reluctantly he drew back, placed hungry little kisses on each closed eyelid, her forehead, over the throbbing pulses in her temples. Then he whispered in her ear, whispered promises; silken, tempting, erotic. Alison moaned breathily. "Later," he said, and gave her one more hug.

Alison's senses reeled. Sam had to steady her when she opened her eyes. The reality of Eleazar Fortune's big weathered tombstone struck her like an ice-filled snowball, unkindly plummeting her back into the world.

Strong callused fingers lifted her chin. Understanding green eyes bored into her. "Again I offer you no apology. This, between us, is natural and good. Exciting. I'll fight for it, even if the one I have to fight is you." He gave her no chance to reply. "Let's take a look at the Draconia gate, and then get some lunch. I'm starved."

Somewhat numb, Alison went with him, her hand in his. When they reached the stone wall at the rear of the cemetery Sam followed the same procedure he had the night before. Alison didn't protest when he lifted her over the wall and set her down in one fluid motion, nor did she say a word when he took her hand again and walked right up to the gate. It was when the unpleasant odor hit her that she tugged at his hand, trying to back away. "Ugh," she said. "It's stronger than last night."

"You'll get used to it in a second." Alison started to tell him that she didn't want to get used to it when Sam grunted. "I was right. This gate must have opened. Look. Along this edge. Do you see it? The paint's flaked off." He dropped her hand and walked around the gate, his eyes glued to the ground. "Look at these tracks. I'm sure this second set wasn't here last night. They're deeper, as if this thing was heavier on the way back. See?"

He sounded excited by the discovery.

Suddenly it didn't matter to Alison that the sun was shining, that she could hear birds singing, insects clicking and chirping and the droning of a bee in a nearby clump of wildflowers. Dread, the same dread that had paralyzed her two nights ago filled her so that she thought she might suffocate. Evil. She had seen evil— but some part of her still hoped and prayed that she was wrong.

Suddenly the itch in her palm flamed to life. Alison slowly lifted her hand, stared at it. The mark in the center pulsed blood-red.

Richard couldn't stop shaking. He was cold, deep down bone-chilling cold. Hot showers, steaming cups of coffee, and more than enough liquor to make an elephant dizzy had no effect. He couldn't get warm. But that wasn't all he couldn't do. He couldn't eat; he couldn't sleep; he couldn't do anything . . . but remember.

Pink feathers.

And flies. With his eyes closed he saw them . . . crawling . . .

He shuddered, swallowing convulsively, had to use all the force of his will to keep his gorge from rising. Inside his head he still heard them . . . buzzing . . . droning . . . Disgusting little bastards. He should have . . .

A sharp rap on the door of his office snapped his head up. He should have stayed home, he thought as Art walked into the room and sat down without a word. But he couldn't give in to himself, he couldn't stay holed up, staring at four walls, wishing he had never started with the two-timing little tramp in the first place. Everything had to look normal . . . especially now.

"Well?" Richard demanded, although his tone lacked its customary snarl. He didn't seem to be able to muster the strength for it.

Art opened his mouth, but no words came out. For once he wasn't wearing his sneering expression.

Richard knew what was coming; knew it and feared it. He had no other recourse but to play the innocent, so he picked up a thick pile of invoices. "I'm busy. State your problem and then hustle your ass back out there with the customers where you belong. Show them some of that no-fail Bergstrom charm. Maybe we'll break even this month if you do."

"Richard . . ." Art nervously shifted, raised his hand, then let it drop. "Uh . . . one of the customers just told me that . . ." Sweat glistened on his forehead. He swiped at it with the back of his hand. "Listen," he said, "that chick . . . uh, Deirdre . . ." Richard tensed, a reaction Art took as part of his usual hostility, so he spoke faster, the words tumbling out. "Listen, it's not what you're thinking. It's not about . . . Look. She's dead. I'm sorry, man. I really am. I didn't know how else to tell you."

Hearing it like this made it seem as if she had died all over again. How long had she lain there, the flies crawling all over her . . . feeding on her . . . worming into her? Richard gagged, made a moaning noise deep in his throat, and leaned forward, dropping his head into his hands.

191

Art got up and clumsily patted him on the shoulder. "I'm real sorry, man, you know I am."

Richard raised his head. "How . . . ?"

"She musta been stoned. Fell down the cellar stairs. That ditsy broad Ellie Berger," he jerked his thumb toward the outer room of the shop, "said Jerry found her wearing her birthday suit." His eyes narrowed, malicious interest sharpening his gaze. "She was smeared all over with jam and . . ." he paused deliberately, "there were flies crawling all over her. All over her," he said once more for effect.

Richard shuddered, abruptly pulled open the bottom drawer of the desk, and took out a bottle of Dewar's White Label. He poured his coffee into the wastebasket and filled the cup with Scotch, then gulped a mouthful, shuddering again as it traveled down to his empty stomach.

"Ellie said Jerry didn't find her until way past midnight."

There it was, the question Richard knew Art couldn't wait to ask. He took another gulp of the liquor, stared down into it, shook his head. "I rang the bell last night, but she didn't answer. She must have been . . ." *God knew that was the truth. All the time he was running through the house, looking for her, she was . . .* His hands began to tremble; he needed both of them to raise the cup. Draining it, he reached for the bottle, looked up, and saw that Art still stood next to him. Richard had had enough. "So, all right, you told me."

Art grabbed the bottle and took a swig from it. "Not everything. Listen, this'll curl your toes." Richard was staring blindly into his cup when Art finally got to the end. ". . . and the *really* interesting part," he concluded, "is that the old fuck Hubbard said these things with no heads came from the Treadwell house. Can you beat that?"

Richard didn't even want to try.

"They never should have messed with the mill."

Bertha daintily lifted her glass and took a ladylike sip of Chablis. "You're talking nonsense again, Lucy."

"It's the Devil's work. I told you it was, way back in February." Suddenly chilled, Lucy clutched her cardigan close around her neck. "Seems to be too much of a co-incidence in a town this small to have two girls die in fatal accidents one day after the other."

"They're saying down at Leavitt's that Deirdre used drugs."

Lucy shrugged. " 'Twouldn't surprise me none, but I don't believe that's what killed her." With a professional eye, she surveyed the cozy private room set up for the Historical Society meeting. It had been dusted and swept and the table set by Adele under her direct super-vision. Everything was as it should be, yet Lucy couldn't help going to the table and moving a placemat and fiddling with a precisely folded napkin.

The ploy didn't fool Bertha. "Stop that twitching and say what you mean." It took great effort to keep her tone tart. The fear that had invaded her mind on the night of Lucy's first stroke, the night of the town meet-ing to approve the zoning changes that made Dragon Meadow possible, entered her body and chilled her bones. Lucy said some strange things that night; she was talking the same way now.

Lucy let her hands fall still. "I've already said what I mean, you just don't believe me."

"Now, Lucy, you're not going to go on about that old story, are you? Are you feeling all right? You're not dizzy or anything?"

"There's nothing wrong with me save I'm surrounded by doddering old fools who can't see what's right be-fore their noses. Something's wrong in Draconia and it has been ever since that smooth-talking man started up with the old mill. It should have been torn down long ago." A shudder rippled through her.

"Sit down, you're getting yourself all upset." Bertha gently nudged her toward a chair. "You've been ill, it's only natural to feel a little depressed, to imagine—"

Lucy impatiently shook off Bertha's hand. "Don't treat me as if my mind's gone wandering. There's nothing wrong with it. The Devil's here, I tell you, and if you won't believe me then you're the fool. Two girls are dead and there'll be more. You mark my words. More girls will die and I don't intend for my Alison to be one of them."

"Calm down. Nothing's going to happen to Alison."

Lucy's eyes took on a strange unfocused look which scared Bertha more than the strained, hoarse whisper. "He's got everyone fooled, but not me. I know who he is. I know *what* he is."

Lucy sounded so sincere, so sure of herself, that a prickling unease lodged itself in Bertha's mind. She very much feared that the strokes had permanently damaged her old friend in some way. "Perhaps we should postpone the meeting," she murmured, concerned. "What with the accidents and all."

"It's too late," Lucy snapped, "the food is already prepared. Besides, I called Phyllis Sayward this morning and she said to go ahead. As president, it's her decision."

Ten minutes later all the ladies were present except for Sarah Mercer and Dottie Cutter. Mary Alderbrook, of course, would not attend. Vera had been buried that morning.

The usual gossip was ignored as speculation about the two deaths took precedence over everything. Carol Drake said that it was no secret that Vera had been seeing Jerry Treadwell. "Who do you think she was waiting for in the cemetery?" she demanded truculently when Phyllis Sayward told her that she wouldn't get her facts straight if they were printed on a billboard in letters ten feet high.

For once Martha Gebhart agreed with Phyllis. "Jerry had no time for anyone save Deirdre, God rest her soul. From what I hear she was more than enough for him." She took another glass of wine and let her eyes slide to where Lucy was helping Adele place a tray of canapés on a side table. "Deirdre had her interest fixed elsewhere."

Lucy didn't need eyes in the middle of her back to know they were all staring at her. She straightened her spine. "Richard is a single man, has been for almost four years now. What he does is strictly his own business."

Martha twitched her shoulders righteously. "I didn't mean—"

"Oh, yes, you did." Bertha, finishing her second glass of wine, used her cane to lever herself out of her chair. "I wonder where Sarah is? I'm getting right hungry and we still have to get through the presentation. Whose turn is it?"

"Mine." Milly Edgehill's voice was whispery and thin. Nervously she clutched a glass of wine in one hand and a crumpled lace-edged handkerchief in the other.

Bertha leaned heavily on her cane and stared piercingly at the younger woman. Milly, in her estimation, was a limp noodle who let herself be pushed around by just about anyone.

Milly dabbed at her temple with the handkerchief, as usual feeling a little bit gauche in this gathering. Some of the women thought the society should be limited to members of the founding families and made no secret of it. The Edgehills had arrived in Draconia shortly after the turn of the century, too late for inclusion in the inner circle. Time had not healed the resentment this created nor ameliorated the inevitable feelings of inferiority that increased with succeeding generations.

195

Bert saw Dragon Meadow as a way to change all that.

"What's your presentation on?" Bertha asked, having to check her tongue. What she actually wanted to know was how long it would take. When the mayor's wife was slow to answer, she impatiently tapped the floor with her cane.

Milly unconsciously patted her purse. "The Effect Of The Great Fire In The Profile House In Franconia Notch In 1923 On Tourism In Surrounding Areas, Specifically in Draconia Notch" had been written in her blood. The subject was innocuous; no one, not even the most rigid stickler among the founding families, could object if Milly stuck to the twentieth century. She was about to recite as much of the title as she could remember after two and a half glasses of wine, but the words died in her throat when the door banged open and Sarah Mercer burst inside.

The buzz of conversation stopped abruptly. All eyes turned toward her.

"Listen," Sarah said, slightly breathless, excitement causing her gaunt body to vibrate. "Ben called, and he said that Amos Hubbard told him . . ."

They listened. They listened and they heard, but they didn't believe.

Phyllis Sayward sniffed disdainfully and picked up a celery stalk stuffed with cheddar. "I always said that old man would go stark raving mad one day." She shuddered delicately. "I do hope now they'll do something about him."

Her autocratic voice released the others from their thrall. A babble of noise swelled to thunderous proportions in the small room.

"He's obviously dangerous," Martha Gebhart proclaimed in her loud voice, "and he lives right near to me."

"There's nothing wrong with Amos," Lucy shouted, catching their attention. "Why, I—"

"Lucy . . ." Bertha said warningly, afraid her friend would say something rash.

"She's right," Dottie Cutter shouted from the doorway. There was a wild look in her eyes that instantly drew their attention. "She's right, there's nothing wrong with Amos. He only had the misfortune to be in the wrong place at the wrong time. Just like Alison."

Lucy paled and swayed from side to side, gripping the edge of the table to keep upright. "What has Alison got to do with this?"

Too late Dottie remembered Lucy's fragile health. "Sit down," she said brusquely, "you might as well hear it from me. By nighttime the story will be all over the notch."

Bertha gave Dottie a sour look as she guided Lucy to the nearest chair. "Proper nonsense," she said gruffly, but remained close to Lucy, offering her support. "Say what you have to," she ordered.

Once again the ladies of the Historical Society listened. When Dottie stopped speaking, Bertha rolled her eyes heavenward. "And it was your grandmother who told you all about these, er . . . myths? The death coach? The Devil's dandy dogs?"

Dottie bristled but stood her ground. "My grandmother, Molly Pengelly, was an honest, God-fearing woman. She lived a hard life and wasn't much given to fancies. Where she grew up, Cornwall, in England, they believe these things. They've seen them." She paused for emphasis. "Just like Alison and Amos."

Milly pressed the wadded ball of her handkerchief against her throbbing brow and closed her eyes, thinking of Bert . . . his plans for Draconia . . . for Dragon Meadow . . . for himself. The throbbing in her head made her nauseous. "No," she whispered, "it's . . . impossible."

Dottie rounded on her. "Deny it all you want. I don't care. I told you. I gave you fair warning." No one

197

spoke. Their silence released the pent-up emotion inside Dottie. "This isn't the first time the Devil's walked this land. He's been here before and been made to feel welcome. You know I've got the truth of it. It's your ancestors who did it. Why don't you check those papers you're all so proud of? Look in those diaries hidden in your attics. You'll see. You'll find it."

"What?" Milly breathed.

Dottie seemed to collapse inside herself. Her lips barely moved. As one the group leaned forward to hear. The answer came on a sigh. "Proof."

20

"You look very pretty. I like that on you."

Alison frowned at the only dress she had brought to Draconia, a softly pleated red-and-purple floral print silk skirt with a matching silk-and-cotton sweater. "I don't know if I should wear it. Suppose they barbecue?"

Lucy gave one of her patented snorts. "Then you'll stay away from the grill."

Alison laughed and hugged the old lady. "Whatever am I going to do with you?"

Lucy dove into the opening like a killer whale jumping through a hoop at an aquarium. "You're going to go back to New York and leave me to live my life." Alison withdrew as if she had been bitten by something with very sharp teeth. Lucy gently smoothed Alison's hair away from her face. "This is no place for you, child. Surely you know that now."

Alison could be as stubborn as her aunt. "Lucy, I came here to help—"

"Then do as I ask. Help me to have a quiet mind and go back to New York. There's danger here."

There was a long silence during which Alison thoughtfully studied her aunt. Tonight Lucy looked every one of her seventy-nine years. The ravages of illness were all too apparent. Her skin appeared fragile, translucent, a thin papery covering barely concealing the bones beneath; her body was rail thin, as if it could no longer take nourishment, but it was her eyes that showed the greatest change. They brimmed with the familiar intelligence, but sadness crowded them also, sadness and a strange, frightening knowledge—a *knowing*. Life, for Lucy, was no longer a mystery.

In the end there was no need for Lucy to say another word. Alison knew she was giving in to more, much more than a simple request. She sighed and tried one last time. "It really means that much to you?"

Ever the opportunist, Lucy didn't even hesitate. "It's the greatest gift you could give me, to know that you're away . . . safe."

Alison sighed again, bent down, and placed a kiss on Lucy's pale cheek. "Then I'll go home. My car should be ready sometime Monday. I'll leave then, all right?"

Tears glistened in Lucy's eyes, her voice was a whisper. "Yes."

Sam hadn't felt this nervous before a date since his high school days. Lucy's knowing grin when she opened the door didn't help to alleviate the peculiar feeling.

"Come on in." She eyed his tie critically, her grin widening when he automatically checked to see if the knot was straight. "Leave it be," she said, and the grin took on a hint of mischief as she surveyed his tall frame from the top of his head to the tips of his brightly shined shoes. "You're a right good-looking young man. You and my niece make a handsome couple. Just see that you do right by her."

Sam bit back his own grin and solemnly assured her that he would treat Alison with the greatest respect.

From halfway down the stairs Alison took in the scene with one comprehensive glance. "Secrets?" she asked softly. Lucy set her lips firmly together. Alison laughed at the familiar expression, kissed her on the cheek, and admonished her to go to sleep early.

Once in the car, Alison gave Sam directions and then let several minutes slide by in silence. She wondered how to warn Sam about Lucy's proclivity toward matchmaking without seeming indelicate. Finally, she sighed and twisted sideways toward him. "I can make a good guess what Lucy was whispering about tonight. I would like to remind you that . . . well . . ."

Her perfume floated toward Sam, recalling Thursday night. He tightened his hands on the wheel. "It's all right, sweetheart. Lucy didn't put anything into my mind that wasn't already there."

Alison shifted away from him. "Lucy made me promise to leave Draconia."

"When?"

"As soon as my car is ready. Monday, I'd imagine."

Sam didn't comment, concentrating on driving the unlit road. Soon they turned into a winding country lane and three-quarters of a mile later pulled into the driveway of the Tanners' two-story Colonial. Set back on an acre and a half of semiwooded land, it was impressive. Sam surveyed the house professionally, then whistled through his teeth. "Not bad. What does he do, rob banks?"

The question, delivered only half facetiously, made Alison laugh. "Nope. He's a dentist."

"Same thing," Sam mumbled as he took Alison's arm and escorted her up the flagstone walk. Now that he knew Alison was leaving, he wished they had gone someplace where it was just the two of them, someplace romantic. Damn that Lucy. She had fanned a flame that needed very little to ignite into a roaring blaze.

Ed Tanner, fortyish, with receding hairline and burgeoning paunch, opened the door and drew Alison into an enthusiastic hug. Keeping one arm around her shoulders, he shook hands with Sam as if they had been friends for years and then cheerfully ushered them inside. "Everyone's on the patio. You know them," he said to Alison. "Go right on through and help yourself to the bar. I'll be right with you after I give Michele a hand in the kitchen."

Alison led the way, pausing for several seconds before sliding open the glass doors leading to the patio. Sam gently touched her arm. "We don't have to stay, you know."

Alison laced her fingers through his. "Oh, yes, we do. This is your party, remember? I'm only your date." The discussion was rendered moot when a thin stylish redhead let out a controlled shriek and advanced on Alison with open arms. The embrace was socially brief. "You're looking well, Rita," Alison said, and immediately introduced Sam to the woman who had once been her sister-in-law.

Rita Fortune made no secret of the fact that she was impressed. "Wherever did you find him?" she drawled.

"*I* found *her,*" Sam said easily, sliding a hand around Alison's waist.

"Oh, yes, the accident. We were just talking . . ."

"Rita . . ." a tall, handsome man said warningly. He smiled at Alison, kissed her cheek, then shook hands with Sam. "Daniel Fortune. I've been meaning to drop by Dragon Meadow one of these days, I just haven't had the time."

"I'd be glad to give you the fifty-cent tour any time."

"You'll stay far away, if you know what's good for you."

As one, they turned toward the speaker. Dottie Cutter was standing on the edge of the patio, the shadowed lawn and dark silent woods behind her.

Sam's eyes narrowed. "What do you mean by that?"

Dottie jerked her head up to meet his gaze. "Don't

tell me you haven't heard the stories?" Her voice was loud and harsh.

Unbidden, a picture of big, solid, dependable Rufus McClain jumped into Sam's mind. Oh, yes, he had heard the stories. Uneasiness tightened the muscles in his neck and back. "I've heard them." He shrugged, unwilling to say more.

Daniel put a drink in his hand. "Vodka and tonic okay?"

"Fine," Sam said, noticing that, without asking, Daniel had handed Alison a glass of white wine.

Dottie was apparently unwilling to let the subject drop. A bleak expression settled over her face, an older, fading version of Jennifer's. "They're true. You don't need me to tell you. I know what you and Henry found in the mill yesterday morning."

Sam took a long swallow of his drink, winced as he felt the alcohol burn its way down. "The mayor seems to think it might be wild dogs, abandoned pets—"

"Bert's a fool. He knows we're not dealing with anything like that."

"What are you talking about?" Rita lit a cigarette and waved it at Dottie.

"I'm talking about the Devil!" Dottie screeched.

Several seconds passed when no one moved, no one spoke. The only sound was the rustle of the wind through the bushes and trees.

Then Rita laughed nervously. "Surely you're not giving credence to that old tale? Why, we all know it's nothing more than a fairy story. It brings in tourist dollars, that's all."

"If you believe that, then you're as big a fool as the mayor."

"I think that's enough," Henry said, and put a calming hand on Dottie's shoulder.

Eyes bright, glittering with emotion, she immediately shrugged it off and rounded on him. "No, it's not.

Why can't you listen? Are you all so in love with the almighty dollar that you can't see what's right in front of you?" She gave a short bark of laughter. "That's really a stupid question. You don't want to see. You're all greedy, just like Bert. You've all been seduced by the promises that smooth-talking oily man made. You think you're going to be rich. But nothing's for free, nothing in this world. You'll see. It's started. Already two lives have been sacrificed."

Callously Rita waved her hand in dismissal. "Surely you're not linking the deaths of Vera and Deirdre with Dragon Meadow? Why, everyone knows Deirdre had a coke habit that would choke a horse. The wonder of it is that she didn't fall down the stairs and break her neck sooner. She was an accident just waiting to happen."

"And what about Vera? How do you explain her death?"

Rita shrugged. "She was a silly little besotted fool, simply in the wrong place at the wrong time. Playing with fire, if the rumors were true."

"I tell you those girls didn't die by accident." Dottie pointed at Alison. "Tell them what you saw Thursday night. You've seen the death coach, Alison. It comes for the souls of the dead. Tell them! Tell them about the dandy dogs, perhaps they'll believe you."

"Hey, this is supposed to be a party," Daniel protested.

Alison smiled gratefully, remembering all the times during her marriage when she had wished that Richard could be more like him. "It's all right. I saw something . . . 'grotesque' is the only word to describe it. But everything has an explanation, and I'm sure we'll find one for it."

"You know . . ." Rita said musingly, then shook her head dismissively. "No, that's crazy."

"I doubt it could be any crazier than some of the

things that have been going on around here lately," Sam said encouragingly.

Alison wryly noted how Rita seemed to arch under his regard like a pampered feline; a self-deprecating laugh purred from her lips. "It's nothing, really, except . . . Had you thought of the coach over at Franconia?"

Daniel handed Rita a refill. "What a good idea, darling." He shifted his attention to Sam. "There is an old Concord mail coach on display in the Flume Visitor Center. I guess it's possible someone's borrowed it for . . . nefarious purposes." Oddly, he looked relieved.

"But wouldn't we have heard if someone's purloined it?" Henry asked. "It would be rather difficult to keep a thing like that quiet."

Sam shrugged, but he looked thoughtful. "They could always say they took it off display for maintenance. That's what I'd do rather than admit I'd been careless enough to lose something that large. I expect it is valuable?"

It was Daniel who answered. "As a surviving piece of early Americana, it's probably priceless—"

"Oh, why won't you listen?" Dottie broke in. "The coach itself isn't the issue here. It's him, the Evil One. He's here in Draconia with his hellhounds, hunting human souls, and whatever you think, by my count he's already got two."

Ed came out of the house in time to hear Dottie's impassioned speech. "The Evil One? Sounds like you people are a couple of drinks up on me." He laughed, but nobody joined him.

"I presume you're talking about *the* Devil, Satan himself?" Rita asked Dottie, unable to keep the cynicism out of her voice. "Doesn't he have better things to do than hang around a dull town like this?"

"Sneer all you want. I tell you the Devil is in Draconia. You're in danger, whether or not you choose to believe it."

Alison thought about Lucy's odd attitude. Suppose illness wasn't its source? Had the renovation of the old mill, the start of construction on Dragon Meadow, stirred up hidden fears in the people of Draconia? Was this mass hysteria? Like the Salem witch hunt?

Ed chuckled. "The Devil, hmm? Have I met him?"

Dottie bristled, hissed in impotent fury. "Adrian Blaise. Adrian Blaise is the Devil himself, and he alone knows the price we've got to pay for Dragon Meadow."

A loud crash made them all jump. White-faced and glassy-eyed, Michele stared at Dottie. A tray dangled from her hand and broken plates and spilled food littered the area around her feet.

Far off thunder grumbled over the mountains. Michele quickly recovered her aplomb and knelt to clean up the mess. Ed and Daniel went over to help. Alison stared at Daniel, marveling how two men who looked so alike could be so different. Richard never would have volunteered.

When they finished, Michele came over to Sam, her hand outstretched. "Sam Chandler, I presume, or is it Sir Lancelot?"

Sam took her hand. "I believe Alison referred to me as a St. Bernard."

Michele laughed, then grimaced, quickly withdrew her hand, and rubbed the palm against her thigh.

Sam was quick to apologize. "I'm sorry. Sometimes I forget my strength."

"No, it's not your fault. It's nothing." Thunder rolled, this time louder, closer. A moisture-laden wind picked up her hair and blew it across her face. Impatiently, she brushed it out of her eyes.

"Your hand . . ." Alison gasped, her eyes fixed on the bright red mark on Michele's palm. She didn't have to look at her own hand to know the two marks were identical.

Just then, Adam, Brian, and Tiffany, aged eight, six,

and five, erupted out of the house. Michele turned to them eagerly, leaving Alison to wonder at the look of relief that quickly passed over her face. It was another small puzzle.

By the time they sat down to dinner, Alison had pushed it to the back of her mind. Talk at the table was lively, with much of the attention focusing on Sam, the only new face. He fielded so many questions that Ed finally intervened good-naturedly. "Hey, give the guy a break," he said.

Daniel laughed. "Will you listen to him? What does he know about breaks? You should see the bill he sent me last month."

"Someone's got to cover my mortgage," Ed retorted straight-faced.

"You've got a nice place here," Sam said.

Alison smiled, remembering Sam's earlier comment.

Ed looked very pleased. "Thanks. Do you design homes?"

"Not anymore. I specialize in malls."

Henry tilted his head to the side. "Why do I get the feeling you don't like them?"

"I don't."

"If you feel that way about it, why do you work on them? Surely an architect can choose his projects?" Michele asked.

"We specialize, just like doctors."

"But why pursue an area you dislike?" Henry persisted.

Sam chuckled deprecatingly. "I guess you could call it vanity. In architecture, as in everything, there is more than one way to do something. As far as working on malls and shopping centers, I like to fool myself into thinking that I can make a difference, however insignificant." Then he spoke passionately, denigrating strip malls, glitz malls, shopping centers, and anything that leeched the character from the land. "For the most part

207

these places are clones. Once you're inside you can't tell if you're in Washington or Wisconsin or Connecticut." He broke off, embarrassed. "I didn't mean to bore you. I'm no crusader."

"I've seen the plans for Dragon Meadow. It won't be like those other places." Daniel took a sip of wine, glanced at Dottie. "There's been an effort to preserve—character was your word, I believe? From what I can see the new buildings will conform to the land, keeping the landscape as natural as possible. Your work?"

Sam nodded modestly, wanting to say that it was Adrian Blaise who had made everything possible, but not wanting to be the tinder that ignited Dottie's short fuse.

He didn't need to say it. Dottie half rose from her chair, her face purpling with frustration. "You people just won't listen. Dragon Meadow is the Devil's work! You don't have to believe *me*. Just wait. You'll see."

A rumble of thunder followed a bright streak of lightning. Rain started to pound hard against the windows. The fancy little bulbs in the chandelier flickered and went out, just like in a Grade B melodrama.

"Sit tight," Ed said. "I'll see if it's a fuse."

They could hear him walk down the hall, hear his curse when he walked into a piece of furniture. It took only a few minutes until he returned, playing a flashlight before him. "Lightning must have hit a power line . . ." he began when a high, piping voice interrupted. He swung the light toward the doorway. Tiffany stood there, rubbing her eyes, tear streaks on her cheeks, a much-loved teddy bear clutched to her thin chest.

"Mommy," she wailed, "Adam and Brian are gone."

21

Lucy did not want to go to sleep early. What difference could it make if she coddled her old, sick body? A month? . . . a week? . . . an hour added to her life span? Three days ago it would have mattered, but no longer. Now she had only one purpose left: to safeguard Alison.

She stood for long moments in the hall after the door closed behind Alison and Sam. The house seemed empty without them, a silly fancy, as she had been living alone since Alison's marriage. Living alone and liking the freedom.

If she didn't go to bed she could watch some television, or listen to music, or read the scandalously erotic romance Deirdre lent her. Deirdre! Lucy's thin frame shuddered. Whatever she had been, whatever she had done, the poor foolish girl had not deserved to die. Certainly not as a victim, for victim she had been, Lucy was sure.

Standing in the hall, unsure of what to do, Lucy remembered the meeting that afternoon, the tension in the room. Dottie had been scared, wild-eyed with it. What had she said, right at the end? Something they all could do? Something they *had* to do? Lucy sighed, forced herself to relax, to let the thought come. God, how she hated being old. Why, just ten years ago—five even—she would have been able to . . . Proof! That was it. Dottie had said there must be proof, tucked away, hidden in a diary, a letter—written by someone long ago, someone who had been alive when the Devil had first come to Draconia. No, to New Hope.

Lucy looked at the stairs, thought of the three flights up to the attic where all the detritus and memorabilia of the Crandells was stored. In the distance she heard a rumble of thunder; a gust of wind snaked in through the cracks around the door. It was going to storm, and all at once her cozy bed held great appeal. Shaking her head, Lucy began to climb the stairs, not even pausing as she passed the second floor and continued up to the attic.

"Needs a right good cleaning," she muttered when the lights strung across the center beam revealed neglect. It was not too bad near the door, where she had placed the most recently discarded items, but dust and cobwebs held sway farther back, where the older dressers and trunks and suitcases were stored.

Armed with an old feather duster she found lying atop a pile of books, she cleaned off several trunks and boxes and went to work. An hour later she knew the job was too big for her; at least for this evening. Her back ached from bending and shoving and sorting piles of what could only be called junk. A grim smile stretched her lips. Very soon the treasured items of her life would be relegated to the attic. Briefly she wondered if Alison would think her memorabilia worthless. "Sentimental old fool," she chastised and forced herself to search yet another box.

The ventilation in the attic was poor, the air stuffy. Thunder rumbled overhead. Lucy's head began to ache. Defying illness and old age could be done only for so long.

Wearily she left the attic, hating the frailty of her body. The sudden, sharp shrilling of the telephone sliced through the quiet, making her jump. Quickly she glanced at her watch, saw that it was still relatively early; nevertheless her heart thudded heavily against her breast as she hurried to answer it.

"Hello?" she said, her voice betraying anxiety, listened to Bertha's greeting, then huffed angrily. "Nothing's wrong, I just didn't expect to be disturbed at this hour. I expect you've got a right good reason."

Bertha replied, her voice sounding tinny, a pesky insect worrying Lucy's ear. "I thought you'd want to know right away. I found the strangest reference in a diary. Here, let me read it to you."

Lucy waited impatiently as Bertha coughed, rustled pages, then finally came back on the line. "Let me see . . . Here we are. Now, I want you to know that the writing's poor, full of fancy curlicues, besides being so faded it's hard to read, but far as I can make out the writer, Amanda Rice—"

"Do the best you can, Bertha," Lucy cut in, strangling a protest at her friend's slow, detailed description.

"Yes. Well, Amanda Rice says here, on October 23, 1923, that, and this is a direct quote now, 'Mary Beth Winslow's paper was included in the centennial publication celebrating the founding of Draconia, *despite the very justified protests of the good men and women of the town who held to the belief that such dredging up of unhappy memories can serve no useful purpose.*' "

Lucy had no trouble hearing Bertha's emphasis; her voice became higher and she spoke very fast.

"Lucy? What do you think? It could be a reference to . . . you know—what Dottie was talking about this afternoon."

Bertha's excitement was palpable. Lucy's gut tightened. She had seen a book about the centennial celebration . . . somewhere. A slim volume. Paperbound.

Thunder rumbled, static crackled on the line. Bertha remembered an open window. After she hung up, Lucy stared thoughtfully into space, willing herself to remember. She *knew* she had seen something about Draconia's centennial, and not too long ago. Frowning, she went downstairs and searched the shelves in the living room, but all the books were novels.

A jagged streak of lightning lit the night. Through the window Lucy could see the inn, clearly defined. The solid bulk of the first story, with stones worked in a bricklike pattern, gave way to the more graceful lines of the second and third stories, where gables peaked sharply into the sky. Then the night returned to dark, and with the darkness came the rain, slanting hard against the panes, driven by a wind that swooped down the mountain and swept through the notch.

Lucy stood as still as stone, in her mind a clear picture of where the book was: in the inn, tucked on a shelf in the sitting room. She had dusted it the other day.

The rain had increased, in density and force. Lucy didn't hesitate, obeying a sense of urgency, of not a single second to waste, that drove her out into the storm. The umbrella she snatched from the stand in the front hall was torn from her grip before she took ten steps outside. She was immediately soaked to the skin.

A sensible woman would have retreated, would have marched right back into the house, up the stairs, into a hot tub, but Lucy, sensible her entire life, disregarded ingrained habits and mulishly proceeded. A voice in her head whispered she had no choice.

The door to the kitchen stuck, but she managed to force it open. Luke looked up in shock to see her standing there, water puddling at her feet.

"Miss Lucy, ma'am! Are you sick?" He rushed to her side. "Here, let me help you sit down. I'll go get Jessie. Is the phone out? I'll go for the doctor right away." His large, capable hands, so graceful when they stuffed a fowl or decorated a cake, pulled at the strings of his apron so clumsily they broke.

Lucy held up a hand, the gesture commanding. "There's no need. I'm fine. I just want to get something."

Luke simply stood and stared as she regally walked out of the kitchen.

Lucy marched straight to her objective, heedless of the squelching sounds her shoes made. The material of her dress, completely saturated, clung clammily to her skin. "Aha!"she exclaimed, and pounced upon a slim, paperbound volume leaning against a cookbook of New England dishes. Plucking it from the shelf, she made a clucking sound with her tongue against her teeth, and took it to the nearest chair. Her hands shook, but she ignored it, as she had everything else; as she would anything that hindered her *knowing*. The old book flopped open, the spine flaked and cracked so that the pages lay flat.

Lucy stared down. Providence! Mary Beth Winslow's name leaped off the page, burned into her retina. In that moment Lucy knew it had been meant to be, the mad, heedless rush through the rain. She skimmed the pages excitedly.

"Well, you've gone and done it now."

The voice came from another dimension. Reluctantly Lucy looked up, blinded to everything but her inner thoughts.

"Lucy! Are you sick? Should I call Dr. Cutter?"

Dimly Lucy perceived Jessie's voice as she would the whine of a mosquito. A sense of unreality covered her mind like a pall, blessedly numbing her. She had just read confirmation of her fears. Miserable, she understood that this time there was no joy in being right. As her vision cleared she saw that Jessie stood before her, a militantly bristling hen spoiling for a fight. Only the fearful expression on her face indicated her apprehension.

In the next second Jessie's expression grew even blacker, her dread that something was wrong intensifying

213

into certainty as Lucy sprang out of the chair and clutched her chest. The book fell unnoticed to the floor. Horrified, Jessie lunged toward her, snatching her into her arms to prevent the fall she suspected was imminent.

With surprising strength, Lucy's hand came forward, pushed the younger woman away, and pointed past her shoulder. Her lips worked, but no words, only a thin, mewling sound, issued from her throat.

"Oh, dear God," Jessie moaned, certain Lucy was having another stroke.

An inarticulate screech tore from Lucy; fury darkened her eyes; she began to shake. Then, before Jessie could restrain her, she darted straight toward a couple leaving the bar.

How dare he! And in her inn! Lucy skidded to a halt in front of him, the tall, darkly handsome man with amusement glowing from eyes as black as pitch. A sardonic expression played over his features. So great was her rage, Lucy could not speak. Glaring up at him, her thin body swayed, gripped by a passion so strong it kept her erect when her knees felt so weak they could barely support her weight.

"Miss Crandell! What's the matter?" Alarmed, Jennifer reached toward Lucy.

Lucy tore her hate-filled gaze from Adrian Blaise's amused one. The look she turned on Jennifer was so intense, the young girl involuntarily retreated. "Go home, Jennifer. Now. This man's evil. Don't stand there. Leave!"

Adrian laughed, the sound low, silkily beguiling. Lucy thought of rich dark chocolate. "Your tricks won't work on me," she snapped. "I know who you are; I know *what* you are. Beast! Fiend! Loathsome goat!"

For a split second Adrian's urbane mask slipped. Cold dark rage leaped from his eyes. Impaled by the stark fury, Lucy's indomitable will allowed her to glare right back.

Jennifer made a small sound of distress. Lucy grabbed her arm and shook her. "Do as I bid, Jennifer. Leave now, else he'll destroy you." For emphasis she gave her another fierce shake.

Stunned, Jessie rushed up and pried Lucy's hand away. "Come sit down," she ordered, then spoke apologetically to the other two. "Go on, I've got her. Everything will be all right. I'm sorry. I'm sorry. I don't know what's come over her."

"I think she's having some sort of seizure. At her age it could be fatal."

Lucy endured the dark, mocking gaze of her nemesis as Adrian delivered a — *warning?* — in a falsely sympathetic tone. She cast him a murderous look. If he could die, she would kill him; the regret that it couldn't be was plain for him to see.

If death for him was not possible, then she could act as spoiler. Using a large portion of her remaining strength, Lucy broke free of Jessie's grasp for the second time and again pleaded with Jennifer. "He killed Vera and Deirdre, and you're next. Listen to me. Listen. I know how he holds you with the sins of the flesh. It's his way. He's the great seducer, the despoiler, the . . . ah, no . . . not now," she whispered, stricken, as a sharp pain lanced through her left shoulder, traveled quickly down her arm. Crushing pain moved inside her chest, squeezing the breath from her. Slowly she started to crumple.

It was Adrian who broke her fall, who lowered her gently to the floor, who solicitously bent over her. Lucy's failing sight saw crimson flames flash deep in the black depths of his eyes and knew he no longer had any reason to hide his triumph from her.

But Lucy had her own triumph. She raised her head, by the gesture indicating the need to talk. He bent his ear to her lips. "You took me. *Me!* You've lost. Crandell . . ." she murmured and lost consciousness.

"Call your father," Jessie screamed to Jennifer as she

215

dropped to her knees. Tenderly she lifted Lucy's head onto her lap, stroked the silvery curls.

Adrian followed Jennifer to the telephone where he brushed the petal-smooth skin of her cheek with the backs of his fingers while she frantically stabbed at the buttons. She bit her lip, wondered why the slightest contact with him made a molten desire flow hotly through her veins. As the phone begin to ring, she leaned forward anxiously, the motion causing the triangular dark-green malachite pendant she wore around her neck to swing forward. It struck the telephone, shattered into pieces. Jennifer stared down at them, mesmerized. *Danger!*

Adrian repeated the caress.

Lost in the brilliance of his smile, Jennifer forgot her mother's warning.

Brian Tanner

The world was big and dark and unfamiliar and . . . *scary.* Nothing looked the same as it did in the daytime—the *normal* time. Why, *anything* could be hiding, *anywhere,* ready to jump out, to scream *BOO,* to *pounce* and . . . But here Brian Tanner's six-year-old imagination balked. He didn't want to think what that awful something *was,* much less what it would do once it had him.

Because he didn't want to think about it, that was all he *could* think about, like a jury told not to picture a pink elephant. Brian's pink elephant had big bulging eyes and green skin with scales and long pointed fangs and . . . *it was hiding behind the bush the big one on the corner of the Sheffield house the one he never liked to walk past even during the day because you knew there just might be something hiding behind it and now . . .*

Thunder rolled over the mountains and a sudden gust

of wind made the branches of the trees sway, bent the long grass over and rattled the bushes. Enough for him to see *it* was not hiding behind the bush. No. That would be too easy. Brian knew to be wary of that bush.

If only he had remembered earlier, but remembering was something he wasn't too good at. His mother always said he would forget his head if it wasn't attached to his neck; his father usually just looked disappointed.

But Adam . . . Adam probably would beat him up— no, Adam *definitely* would beat him up, maybe even *murder* him should he ever learn that he had left Adam's soccer ball, the one he got for his birthday, in the schoolyard. Oh, yes, Adam would beat him up, especially because Brian had forgotten to ask permission to take the ball. Well, not exactly forgotten—just sort of overlooked it, since Adam probably would have said no. Adam *definitely* would have said no.

In the distance lightning forked brightly to the earth. It lit up the mountains for long seconds, then the world again got dark, the mountains *hulking,* big and black, going on forever, even up to the deep dark blue sky. Another rumble of thunder reminded Brian he had better hurry. He was more than halfway to the school, even closer if he took the shortcut, but that meant taking the path past the Sheffield house and cutting through their backyard. Past the bush.

Brian thought of courage and that reminded him of his favorite hero. Indiana Jones would take the path. Of course, something positively *gruesome* would leap out at him, but Indiana would only laugh, look bored for a second, then go on, straight down the path. *Nothing* stopped Indy.

Brian smiled, started forward, screamed high and loud and long in pure fright when a hand grabbed his arm. Brian Indiana Jones Tanner balled his right hand into a fist and wheeled about, smashing it into the creature's gut. It said "Oof" and collapsed, Brian on top. Brian/

217

Indy didn't hesitate: with a fury born of desperation he punched and kicked and tried to gouge out the creature's eyes.

Until the creature screamed directly into his ear.

"It's me, Adam! Let me up, you jerk."

Brian landed one more good punch . . . maybe for Adam frightening him so . . . maybe just because he wanted to. In either case, it felt good.

"You're a cretin, did you know that?" Adam asked. He swiped at his nose.

In the dim light Brian saw that his brother's nose was bleeding; blood that looked black smeared his upper lip and his fingers.

Adam pulled up a clump of grass and wiped his nose and fingers. "Well, cretin, what're you doing out here?"

Indiana Jones whispered cunningly in Brian's ear. "What're *you* doing out here?"

"I'm following you, jerk. You made so much noise climbing out the window you woke me up." Adam sniffed experimentally, tested the area beneath his nose with his fingers. They came away clean. "Boy, are you gonna get it when Mom and Dad catch you."

"So will you."

The logic of this had Adam stymied for only a second. "Nope. I'm only here because you're a jerk."

Brian thought that Adam didn't know the half of it, which brought him right back to his problem. Only now it was worse, *much* worse. Right then the scaly creature with the bulging eyes and the big fangs would have been a great deal more welcome than his older brother.

Adam got up and hauled Brian up after him. "Where you goin'?" Then, noticing where they were, he squinched up his eyes and regarded Brian with dawning suspicion. The younger boy's guilty expression was easy to read. "You left something at school again, didn't you? What?"

Brian squirmed, refused to meet his eye.

Adam mentally reviewed their day. It didn't take long. "My soccer ball," he screeched. "Why you—"

He reached for Brian, but Brian was gone, running down the path, real fear supplanting make-believe. Adam *was* going to murder him.

Brian ran past the Sheffield house, safely negotiated the turn past the bush, then trickily left the path and fled into the darkness of the backyard, headed for the safety of the woods. Just as he reached them, a bright jagged bolt of lightning lit the sky, followed immediately by a hard, driving rain. It took just a few seconds for Brian to be soaked to the skin.

"Wait, moron!" Adam yelled.

Brian could make out his figure, still on the path, standing with hands on hips. All Adam had to do was cut across the yard and he could intercept him. The two-year difference in their ages showed to Adam's advantage in longer legs.

"Wait up! I'll go with you," Adam shouted, started to run.

Brian hesitated, wavering, afraid of Adam but more afraid of the unknown dark, the vastness of the night. The familiar won. "C'mon," he screamed above the rain, and confident of his brother's compliance, waited until Adam approached and then ran into the woods.

When he burst out the other side, Adam was hard on his heels. Now that the scariest part was past, Brian was none too sure he wanted Adam this close. Putting on a spurt of speed, he sprinted across the track and raced out into the middle of the soccer field. A streak of lightning lit the sky; the field was almost as bright as day, each dandelion and blade of grass plain to see. Brian looked to his left; the north goal appeared to be empty, although he thought he saw something move. Just a flicker of movement, enough to make him feel uneasy.

He squinted to see better, but just then Adam shrieked and ran to the right. With the next flash of lightning

219

Brian saw his brother scoop an object out of the net of the south goal and knew that the precious soccer ball had been found. Adam turned, his prize clutched tightly to his chest, and in that instant Brian thought he saw movement behind him; a shadow, a *something*, creeping up behind Adam.

Quickly Brian spun around and stared at the other goal. The *something* was there, too, and it HAD RED EYES THAT GLOWED.

Brian snapped his eyes closed.

"I'm gonna get you, you creep," Adam yelled, his voice full of menace now that he had his ball back. "You're gonna be hamburger, HAM-BUR-GER, you little jerk. Just you wait."

Brian stood rooted to the spot, unable to move, incapable even of opening his eyes.

Adam was closer now. "You're gonna be sorry, Bri-an, sor-ry you were born. Yessir, Brian baby, baby Brian, are you ever—"

Silence.

IT ATE ADAM! Brian *knew* it and *knew* that he was *next*.

"Brian?"

It was a panicky whisper, but it was the sweetest music Brian had ever heard. His eyes popped open and there was Adam, Adam his brother alive and uneaten . . . and looking so scared Brian wished he had never opened his eyes. Adam was so close Brian could see his eyes, two huge black circles in a dead-white face staring at . . .

Brian sobbed and reached for his brother's hand as the *somethings* came padding forward, big red saucer eyes unblinking.

Adam took a step to the side and pulled Brian with him. One of the big black beasts howled, fire flaming in a long deadly stream from its mouth. Brian got a glimpse of huge sharp teeth. A disgusting smell, like something was *dead and didn't know enough to lie down and rot* made him gag. He began to tremble, so badly he was afraid he would fall down. Adam was shaking so much his teeth were chattering.

"RUN!" Adam suddenly screamed.

But it was too late.

The creatures came forward, silently, relentlessly, massive jaws agape.

"They're gonna eat us!" Brian yelped, and that was the goad that enabled them to run. Adam took off and yanked Brian's arm so hard the younger boy almost fell. They got no more than five feet when the big black beasts circled in front of them again and moved in.

Brian inched closer to Adam, tears and rain streaking down his face. He began to hiccup, great wrenching internal stutters that jerked his body spastically. Eyes squeezed closed, he gripped Adam's hand as tight as he could. One of the creatures howled. Brian could feel the fire of its breath on his face and his whole body stiffened with fear. Any second those huge fangs would *crunch* into his body, through his bones, and . . .

"Look!" Adam whispered.

Brian responded to the shaky note of hope. He peeked through slitted eyes. A man was coming toward them *and the creatures were letting him walk right through their circle!* Brian forgot to breathe, opened his eyes wide, and looked up. Looked up and up and . . . HE'S EIGHT FEET OH NO HE'S TEN FEET TALL . . . AND . . . AND . . . *AND HIS EYES ARE GLOWING RED.*

"Well, well, well . . . what have we here?" the stranger said, and smiled.

22

"Gone?" Michele whispered, her face rapidly draining of color. She jumped to her feet so fast her chair crashed back against the wall. "What do you mean *gone?*" she demanded, the question spoken on a rising note of panic as she rushed to her daughter, knelt before her, and gripped her shoulders, hard.

Everybody started to talk at once. Alison looked at Michele, saw the dawning horror in her bright green eyes, and felt her pain slice through her. Shaken, she looked to the rain-streaked window, to the darkness beyond. Two little boys were out there . . . Was *he?* Was Dottie right? Was Adrian Blaise the Devil?

Within seconds the men were running through the house, while the group in the dining room was silent. They could hear their footsteps hurrying from room to room, the sounds of doors and closets being opened and banged closed. And then they were back and no one needed to ask what they had found. Tiffany, quiet until then in her mother's embrace, opened her mouth and bawled.

Thunder shook the window. Michele swiveled, Tiffany clutched tightly in her arms, caught her breath in a half-sob at the hard-driving rain. Lightning dazzled, made her cringe. "My babies are out there and . . ." In a hoarse voice she beseeched Dottie. "Tell me it's not true. He's not . . . He couldn't be . . . He . . . he wouldn't hurt babies, would he? *Tell me he won't hurt my boys."*

Rita, herself the mother of two boys, told her in a gruff but kindly voice to pull herself together. Then she suggested Michele get on the telephone and start calling the neighbors on the chance that someone had looked out a window and seen the boys.

The rest of them organized a search, roughly dividing the area into quadrants. Sam offered his crew as a search party, knowing he would find most of them at Sonny's. Ed agreed to join if they did not find the boys in half an hour.

Sam grabbed Alison's hand, tugged her after him, out into the rainy night. "You'll have to help me. I don't know the area." She got into the car, and seconds later he joined her, handing her the flashlight. "I never should have put it away," he said with grim humor. The tires screeched as he backed out of the driveway and paused on the road. "East is . . . ?"

"To the right," Alison said, and lowered her window to shine the flashlight along the edge of the road.

"What's down this way?"

Alison frowned, concentrating. "Let's see, there are a few more houses and beyond them a farm . . ."

"What kind of farm? Every time we dig into the soil at the site we reap a shovelful of stones."

"It's a tree farm. You know, for landscaping."

"Sewall's? That's the outfit we're using for Dragon Meadow."

"Sounds familiar." Alison hunched her shoulders, intent on scrutinizing the verge.

It did not sound too promising. Sam checked the clock, then concentrated on driving. He doubted the boys had taken the road, but somebody had to make sure they were not on it. He had been chosen because he didn't know the woods. "We don't want to have to look for you, too," Daniel had said, and that was that.

Suddenly Alison yelled to stop, startling him. Sam hit

223

the brakes too hard; the car went into a controlled skid. "Sorry. What did you see?"

Alison didn't answer, was already out of the car and running toward the side of the road, playing the flashlight along the base of the trees that edged it. When Sam reached her she was holding a sodden tennis sneaker. By its size he saw it could not have belonged to a child.

She looked so disconsolate that Sam pulled her into his arms, gave her a fierce hug and a quick kiss. "They'll be found. They're not the first boys to pull a stunt like this."

Back in the car Sam put on the defroster. "Damn rain," he mumbled, thinking about Dragon Meadow and its developer. Adrian Blaise. The Devil? Granted, some mighty peculiar things were happening in Draconia, but . . .

"Sam?"

"What?" He had to strain to hear her. Alison's body was twisted so she could look out the window. Wind and rain were streaming onto her; every so often she pushed her sodden hair out of her eyes with an impatient gesture.

"How long?"

"Couple of minutes. Then we'll turn back."

"What do you think? About . . . you know . . ."

Sam knew she wasn't referring to the boys. He sighed, decided to be brutally frank. "I think that Dottie Cutter sounds like she's got a screw loose."

Alison flinched as if he had struck her with a metal-tipped bullwhip. "Then you think Lucy—"

"I think Lucy is one of the most levelheaded individuals I've ever had the pleasure to meet." He stopped, knowing he tread on treacherous ground and had to choose his words with care. "I also think that she's very emotional right now, after her illness and—"

"I thought that, too," Alison interrupted, "but now I'm not so sure."

"Oh?"

"Everything's too . . . *neat,* is the only word I can think of. Did you know that Adrian Blaise is a client of the law

224

firm I work for?"

"So what? That hardly makes him the Devil, does it?" Alison threw him a look over her shoulder that plainly told him she was in no mood for levity. "Sorry, that was uncalled for. Look, it seems to me that we have two problems here." He stabbed his fingers through his hair. "The first problem, as I see it, is whether we believe in the Devil."

His use of the plural pronoun warmed Alison. She stole another quick look at him over her shoulder. "The second?" she asked, then snapped her attention back to the side of the road.

"The second problem is tricky. It really depends on the answer to the first. Well, I guess it really doesn't . . ." He paused, peered at the road ahead. "That must be the tree farm." He steered the car to the side of the road and shifted into park. "Last stop."

Alison closed the window and turned to face him. Gently she touched his arm. "The second problem . . . ?"

"Hell!" he exploded, then laughed. "Appropriate word. Listen, this whole situation is crazy, but it seems to me that whether or not we, personally, believe in the Devil, it is possible that he exists, and . . . if that is true, then he could be Adrian Blaise — as well as any other man." He shook his head and then grinned at her. "My whole world has been topsy-turvy since I met you."

Alison took it seriously. "I wonder," she said slowly, "if you haven't just hit upon the key. After all, everything started Thursday night. I don't think *everything* can be coincidence."

"Perhaps. Now we'd better get back. I'll put in that call to McClain and he'll have men combing every inch of this area within the hour." As he started to make a U-turn the headlights picked up a side road. "Where does that go?"

Alison frowned, concentrating, then shook her head. "I really don't know. The entrance to the nursery is about a half a mile farther up."

"What's behind the farm?"

"Woods. The boundaries of the state forest snake in and out around here. Over there," she waved her hand, "is the district combined school."

"School?" Sam looked thoughtful for a second and then backed the car up and turned onto the unpaved road. "Let's see if we can get there from here. This may be a back road to the school. Anyway, it's worth a chance."

The rain had made a quagmire of the rutted road. Sam had to grip the wheel tightly to keep control. Half a mile later it went from dirt to pavement with potholes in every size dotting its surface, but it was an improvement. Sam increased speed, even though it was raining so hard the road was difficult to see. He swore every time they hit a hole.

"You're ruining your car."

"It's only a car," Sam grunted. A bolt of lightning lit the sky. He narrowed his eyes and squinted at a vague shape. "What's that? Over there to your right."

"It's the school, the back of it. The athletic fields are—"

Sam swerved the car off the road so sharply that Alison's teeth snapped together with such force she bit her tongue. Tasting blood, she turned to Sam, got one good look at his face, and then peered out the window. In the next second her heart stopped and her breath froze in her lungs. Shadows moved and shifted as the strobe-light effect of the lightning lit the area. Great big shadows. Beast-like.

"Hold on," Sam yelled, and steered across the field.

Alison had the door open before the car came to a stop. Sam shouted a warning to wait for him. She ignored it. "Adam!" she screamed. "Brian! It's Alison."

Two small figures turned toward her. Sam had left the headlights on, in the light she could see their white faces, eyes huge and staring. She skidded to a halt next to them, looked quickly to the left and then to the right, puzzled. She could have sworn . . . But then the boys were in her arms and she was hugging them and Sam came up to stand

226

beside her and nothing mattered except that Adam and Brian were safe and . . .

The smell. A repulsive odor made it difficult to breathe. Alison straightened, a boy tucked firmly under each arm. For one mad moment she expected to see the pack of wild animals they had chased last night, but instead of wild-eyed, slavering beasts, there was only a man. Sinfully handsome, elegantly attired, he looked as out of place on the rain-soaked athletic field as an exotic butterfly on a Manhattan street. He stood silent, watching.

"Sam!" she whispered, tightening her hold as both little boys pressed closer.

Sam stepped in front of them, his attitude plainly protective. "I see him." He stayed there, waiting for the other man to come to him.

Adrian Blaise crossed the muddy expanse separating them as if the soggy field were the finest Persian carpet. He seemed uncaring of the rain plastering his dark curls against his temples and soaking into his suit. A faintly amused, slightly mocking smile lifted his lips. "Ah, Chandler, I didn't know the boys were yours."

"They're not." Sam's voice was low and gruff, his tone just short of rude.

"No, of course not. You've got a girl, in California, if I remember correctly."

Sam stiffened. "Yes." He gestured to Alison. "Let's get these two home." He took each boy by the hand and started for the car.

"Mrs. Fortune," Adrian Blaise said in the deep, smoky voice Alison remembered from the one time they met, long months ago in December, "I heard you were in Draconia. I can't tell you how happy and relieved I am to see you came to no harm from your unfortunate accident. I trust you are suffering no ill effects?"

His voice! She knew his voice! It had whispered in her ear, obscenely taunting, strangely compelling.

The dark night, the rain, receded, faded into insignificance as he smoothly captured her hand, lifted it to his lips, performed the same continental ritual he had on that day in December.

Alison stood rooted to the ground, mesmerized, mentally braced for the remembered erotic assault to her senses. Only this time, when his tongue touched her palm, there was only the briefest flicker of something dark and dangerous, forbidden, yet deliciously enticing. Surprise shone in her eyes, surprise and a fleeting hint of disappointment. Nervously she moistened her lips with the tip of her tongue, acutely aware he was watching her, amusement narrowing his gaze. Her palm tingled and she knew without looking that a small spot in the center glowed a bright ruby red. Sudden anger made her tremble. She snatched her hand from his. "I'm fine."

He smiled. "I'm glad."

Only seconds had passed, but for Alison it seemed as if an hour, perhaps a lifetime, had elapsed. She tore her eyes from his and ran for the car without a backward glance.

Sam met her halfway there. "I thought you were with me." His voice was hoarse with concern. "What did he want?" he demanded.

Alison did not have an answer.

Michele was standing in the open doorway when they raced up the drive. Her expression went from anxiety to joy as Adam and Brian tumbled from the car, launched themselves at her, burrowed into her embrace. Thin bodies shivered with sobs as reserve broke and the terror of their experience overwhelmed them.

"Thank you," Michele whispered, her own eyes glassy with tears, "thank you, thank you." Still holding her sons, she started inside. After only a few steps she stopped, turned to Alison. "Oh, God, how selfish of me," she wailed. "I almost forgot. Jessie called—" Her stricken look said it all.

* * *

"She's alive." Jessie's voice sounded tinny, strain evident.

White-faced, Alison pressed the receiver closer to her ear. "Where . . . ?"

"They took her to North Conway."

"Henry—"

"Dr. Cutter is already on his way. Didn't Michele tell you?"

Alison closed her eyes and shook her head, then remembered that Jessie couldn't see her. "No. We had some excitement here, I guess she forgot." She paused, gripped the receiver so tightly her fingers went numb. "I'm going right over. I'll . . . I'll call you."

The sound of Jessie clearing her throat came over the line. "Alison? Tell Lucy—" Jessie stopped, emotion clogging her throat. "Tell her I love her," she whispered.

After she hung up, Alison stood for long moments with her head bowed, fighting the sting of tears. Then she straightened and slowly turned around.

Ed had returned, and he and Sam were holding a low-voiced conversation. As soon as they noticed she had finished the call, they broke it off.

"Sam told me everything. I can't tell you how grateful I am you found the boys . . ." Ed paused and placed his hand on her arm, "or how sorry I am to hear about Lucy. Anything I can do?"

Alison pushed her damp hair away from her face. "I hate to ask, but I need to borrow a car. They took Lucy to North Conway."

"Forget it. I'll drive you."

Alison blinked in surprise, bewildered at Sam's brusque tone. Even in a sodden state, his jacket wrinkled and his white shirt so soaked she could see the warm tone of the flesh beneath, he radiated an aura of command. She stiffened, immediately resenting his assumption of authority.

Sam completely ignored the spark of anger that sent spots of color to her cheeks and began to discuss the fastest route with Ed.

Michele chose that moment to come downstairs. Almost as if she could read Alison's mind, she patted her on her arm. "He's a good man. It's all right to accept help."

"I don't like to depend on anyone. Not anymore." Alison knew it was churlish of her to resent his take-charge attitude, but her hard-won independence was not easily set aside.

"You're a different woman than the one who was married to Richard. You're strong now. Accepting help is a long way from dependence. Now go," she said. "He's waiting."

Soon warmth and light were left behind. The hard rain had given way to drizzle; patchy fog hampered visibility. Sam was forced to a slow pace as he carefully watched for the route through Crawford Notch. Tired and tense, he would have liked some music but was afraid of disturbing Alison. Each time a finger of fog floated in front of the car he cursed fluently but softly.

They had the road to themselves, and after the last lights of Draconia winked out behind them, it was as if they left had the world they knew and entered a world of long ago. Here there was nothing but the elements: earth and air and water and mountains and fog and dripping trees and blackness and . . . Something dashed toward them, something big . . . hooves pounding . . .

Alison screamed. Sam swore. Alison screamed that it was the death coach, drawn by the big black horse with blood spurting from its neck; that Lucy was dead; that the Devil had sent his headless coachman to fetch her soul.

This time when Sam cursed there was nothing quiet about it. "Alison! It was only a deer. Now calm down."

Alison made a strange little sound. Sam risked a quick glance at her. "It was a deer," he repeated firmly. "The damn deer almost got us killed. Hang on, sweetheart."

They raced through the night. Within Crawford Notch the mountains crowded the road, rising steeply on both sides. Clouds wreathed their tops, hiding them, constantly shifting shape, first lacy smoke rings, next trailing winding cloths, twining sinuously through the trees.

"This is where the Willey house was, you know, the one that was swept away by a landslide. It rained so hard that the mountain gave way. All the people were lost." The words gushed out, uncontrollable, spawned by Alison's nervousness. "It must have been a night like this."

Sam sensed, rather than saw, her shiver. "Nice thought," he said dryly.

"Oh, God, Sam, I'm sorry."

"Nothing to be sorry for."

"But there is. There is. If it weren't for me you wouldn't . . ." She paused, then came to a sudden decision. "Look, I think you're in danger by being with me."

Sam laughed, the sound rich and full in the confines of the car. "You've got that right, sweetheart." When she sat tense and quiet he reached out and captured her hand, squeezed it reassuringly. "But I'm a big boy. I know what I'm doing."

Alison smiled despite the anxiety gnawing her insides. Sam was a special man. If only they had met under different circumstances. If only . . . But 'if onlys' were for fools. She had been raised to confront problems head on. She had also been raised to be honest. "I'm not talking about that. I wish I were."

This time Sam chuckled, gave her fingers another squeeze. "There's nothing wrong in talking about *that*. There's no denying the attraction between us. I know I felt it in you. I hope you felt it in me. I certainly made no attempt to hide it."

Four days ago Alison would have had difficulty even imagining such a conversation, much less having it. But with Sam it felt all right; more than all right, it felt natural. Despite all her worries, her fears, the dread of what she would find when they reached the hospital, there was a part of her that glowed warm and happy. She had thought that part of her dead—murdered, laid to molder in the

231

grave of her marriage. Now Sam had come into her life and shown her that she was still a woman, still capable of feeling, of wanting. It made her both giddy and sad. Timing was everything—timing and luck. Alison sighed, very much afraid she and Sam had neither.

As if he could read her mind and didn't like what he found, Sam sobered. "I give you fair warning. I won't tolerate anything coming between us, spoiling our chance to build something together. I know this is premature, but I know what I want, and I want you."

They made the rest of the drive in silence. Sam pulled into the hospital parking lot and drove Alison to the entrance. "Go on ahead. I'll follow."

Alison took a deep breath and walked through the door with her head held high. A bored-looking woman directed her to the intensive care unit after taking what seemed to be an inordinately long time looking up Lucy's name in the computer. Though Alison wanted to reach across the desk and punch the keys, she kept a tight rein on herself. Then she was running down the indicated corridor, conscious of the sleeping hospital, the nighttime sounds of pain and suffering, the smells of illness and disinfectant and anesthetic. The fear that she was late—perhaps only seconds late—was an acid burning through her soul.

Henry Cutter called to her from the doorway of a waiting room adjacent to the intensive care unit. "In here," he said, all trace of the convivial dinner companion gone, "I want to talk to you."

His voice said it all. "Is it . . . is it another stroke?" Alison managed to ask past the lump in her throat.

"No. Not this time." Henry took Alison's arm and led her to a sofa, urged her to sit. She resisted, but he gently forced her down. "She's had a heart attack, a massive one, I'm afraid."

Alison moistened her lips. "Then . . . ?" Henry shrugged, a doctor's most useful evasion. Alison read the belief in his eyes. "May I see her?"

"Five minutes, no more. Then you should go home. Get some sleep." Alison snorted. "Rest then," Henry advised.

Lucy looked old and frail and . . . empty, lying still under the white hospital sheets, burdened with IV's and leads from monitors. With tentative fingers Alison touched Lucy's hand, gently stroked the pale skin. It was wet; it took Alison several moments to realize that the moisture was her own tears.

Sensing Alison's presence, Lucy stirred and opened her eyes. They shone—no, they positively gleamed with . . . *triumph* was the word that sprang to Alison's mind.

Lucy lifted her hand, the fingers searching. Alison carefully enfolded it, trying to infuse all her love and need into the fragile contact. "You're safe," Lucy whispered. "Safe. Tricked him. Me. Took me. Crandell. Safe," she murmured, and fell asleep.

Henry and Sam were talking in low tones when Alison came out into the corridor. "I'm going home now, Alison. There's nothing more I can do. She's holding her own," Henry added, throwing a crumb.

When they were alone Alison suggested Sam also leave. "I thought we'd gone beyond that," he reproved and led her into the waiting room, where he waited until she wearily sank down onto the sofa and then told her not to move, he would be right back. He quickly reappeared and handed her a cup of coffee. "It tastes like boiled tar, but it's the best I could do."

Some time later Alison felt the cup being taken from her hand, but she was too drowsy to open her heavy eyelids. She dozed, fitfully, her sleep plagued by dreams in which she was running from something, but in slow motion. She forced herself to wake. The lounge was shadowed; only one lamp was burning and someone had turned off the bright overhead lights. She took in the cracked vinyl furniture, the magazines with the covers missing, the smell of stale smoke . . . of despair.

Sound asleep, Sam was sprawled at an awkward angle in

one of the chairs. Even in the dim light the signs of exhaustion on his face were plain.

Alison felt remorse; they were almost strangers, she had no business entangling him in her affairs. Squinting at her watch in the dim light, she saw that only about thirty minutes had passed. She ventured out into the silent corridor, searching for water, finding a fountain around the second bend. The water was warm, but she forced two aspirin down. Then she splashed water on her face and behind her neck, closed her eyes and leaned against the wall, trying to think.

It didn't take her long to realize she wasn't helping Lucy by staying. Her mind made up, she moved resolutely back down the corridor. After checking that Lucy still slept, she made sure that the nursing staff had her telephone number and would call her immediately if there was the slightest change in her aunt's condition.

Sam was waiting for her outside the doors of the intensive care unit. Alison looked up into tired green eyes filled with worry and compassion. She held out her hand to him. "Let's go home."

The rain had turned the parking lot into a shiny black lake. "Wait here, I'll get the car." Sam walked away before Alison could offer to go with him. She shivered in the chill air and reflected that there were aspects of a man-woman relationship that she had missed. It felt good to be pampered.

The car was warm. Alison settled back with a sigh, closed her eyes and let the low strains of a Bach cantata soothe her.

"Does the music disturb you?" Sam asked.

"No, I like it," she replied, and those were the last words she said until she found herself being lifted up and out of the car and hugged close to Sam's broad chest.

Groggily Alison noted her surroundings, made no protest as Sam carried her into Lucy's house and up the stairs. "There, that one," she said, pointing to the door of her room.

Sam, however, had other plans. He kept walking until he found the bathroom, used his foot to kick the door open and his elbow to flick on the light switch. Alison blinked in the sudden glare, made a small sound of protest deep in her throat when he released the arm under her knees and let her feet slide down and find the floor. He steadied her until she regained her balance, then stepped back. "Strip and get in the shower. Do you need help?"

She stared at him stupidly, wondering why she hadn't realized he could be cruel. "Sleep."

"You need to get warm first. Your clothes are still damp." He went to the shower and turned on the water, only returning to her side when billows of steam started to fill the white-tiled room. His lips lifted in a small smile; his fingers went to the hem of her sweater, started to tug it upward.

Alison swayed into his body, her mind too numbed to immediately comprehend his actions. The fact that he was systematically relieving her of her clothing came home to her when he curtly ordered her to raise her arms so that he could slip the sweater over her head. She blinked owlishly up at him and belatedly tried to bat his hands away.

He sighed and released his hold. "If I leave will you give me your promise that you'll be in the shower in two minutes?" Solemnly she nodded. "Two minutes, or I'll be back to put you in myself." He kissed her on the tip of her nose and left.

Alison wasted precious seconds staring at the door. Sam, she knew, would keep his word. She hurried into the shower, leaving her clothes in a heap on the floor.

The water felt heavenly; she stood, unmoving, letting the hot stream flow over her. Her eyes closed, her body swayed slowly, operating on its last reserve of energy. Lethargy produced by tiredness and the soporific hiss of the warm shower lulled her, until a sudden draft alerted her that she was no longer alone.

Dimly she heard rustling sounds, then the shower curtain was pushed to the side and Sam stepped into the tub. Naked. Broad shoulders, slim hips, long, heavily muscled thighs and calves, all bare, save for a thatch of golden hair furring his chest, arrowing down past his waist to his abdomen and below, where it broadened to define his masculinity.

Alison stared, unable to drag her gaze away from his sex. He began to stir under her heated regard. All at once the large, old-fashioned tub seemed too small. "Uh," she said, sluggishness fast fleeing.

Sam took in her appearance with one long, thorough look. Her flesh, pinkened by the heat, was firm and smooth and gently curved. He grinned when he realized she couldn't tear her gaze away from his arousal. Cupping her chin with his hand, he lifted her face up. "Relax. Despite appearances, everything is under control." He laughed when she blushed a fiery shade of crimson, drew her close, kissed her hard and released her.

Alison didn't have time to think, much less to move away. Sam picked up a bar of soap and worked it into his hands. Soon they were foamy and then they were on her, all over her body, soaping her with gentle care. He was thorough, intimately so, and after her first startled stiffness, she quickly came to enjoy the feel of his touch on her skin. It was something of a shock when he carefully pushed her under the water, rinsed her, then offered her the bar of soap. When she blushed and hesitated, he shrugged and quickly soaped himself and then nudged her aside so that he could rinse.

Alison caught her breath at the play of taut muscles beneath smooth skin when he twisted about to turn off the taps. The silence assaulted them, harsh and humming with unspoken wishes, unfulfilled desires.

The bathroom was steamy, redolent with the smell of

soap, the mirrors fogged. Alison picked up a big fluffy bath towel, only to have Sam take it from her. She stood docilely while he blotted the moisture from her face and neck, then moved the towel over her shoulders, down her back. A tightness began to build in her belly, a tightness that had nothing to do with fatigue or fear, but had everything to do with sensual awareness, with the beginnings of hunger and need.

His hands stilled on her body as he sensed her mounting tension. "Alison?" Sexual appetite and a dawning hope tightened his voice into gruffness. A groan tore from his throat when she leaned forward, daintily licked droplets of moisture from his skin. "Alison," he said again, grasped her upper arms and held her away. He was trembling.

"I want you. Is it wrong?"

She was shaking. Sam folded her into his arms, brought her into the heat of his embrace. "No. It's not wrong."

A hot tear fell into the curve of his neck. "Lucy . . ."

"Shh, sweetheart." He was hot and heavy and throbbing with his need of her. "Nothing between us could be wrong." She didn't say anything, burrowed closer against him. He groaned and pushed himself into her damp cleft, letting her feel the full force of his arousal, holding his breath lest she either pull back or reject him out of shock.

Alison did neither. Instead, she widened her stance, accommodating him, welcomed him into her warmth. "Now? Here?" she whispered.

For answer he swung her into his arms, went striding down the corridor to her bedroom. The room was night-chilly and damp, the rain still driving against the multipaned window. Alison looked at the bed, saw he had turned down the comforter and sheet, and shivered.

Sam squeezed her tightly, bent his head to nuzzle the tender skin of her neck. "I'll warm you, sweetheart."

The huskily whispered promise raised goose bumps on her flesh. He found the pulse point beneath her ear and pressed his lips to it. As he lowered her to the bed an unwelcome flutter of panic made her tense involuntarily. She had had time to think; passion was fleeing with remembered pain.

Sam stilled, his powerfully muscled body suddenly alert. "Alison?" Embarrassed, she pushed her hot face into the curve of his neck, her arms convulsively clutching his broad shoulders. He straightened and hugged her close. "Look at me."

Compelled by the calm authority of his tone, she raised her eyes to meet his gaze. Emerald-bright eyes, fired by passion, searched her face, their heat and hunger burning into her.

"It's . . . been so long."

"I won't hurt you."

The words that had been meant to reassure had the opposite effect. She flinched, seemed to shrink into herself.

"Are you afraid?"

"No . . . no . . . yes. Yes! You won't . . ." Thoroughly paralyzed by shame, she turned her head away.

He sat on the edge of the bed and cradled her on his lap. "I won't what?"

She should have known Sam would not give up easily. She also should have had more sense than to let her emotions run away with her common sense. After avoiding all intimate situations for four years, she felt gauche now.

"I won't what?" he prompted, his voice low and intimate, one hand lightly stroking up and down her arm. She closed her eyes, shuddering with the sensations he produced. "Answer me, Alison. What won't I do, sweetheart?" Her breath caught in her throat when his hand found her breast. "Tell me."

She involuntarily arched into his hand as he shaped her breast to fit his palm. "Funny. You won't . . . make me do anything funny." Her voice was so low he had to bend his ear to her lips to hear it.

Bemused, caught between two worlds, the old one of memory, of emotions and control gone awry, and this new world, of sensation, of passion, of natural beauty, she missed the small hitch in his breathing, the indrawn breath when he realized her hesitation was rooted in pain.

His hand stilled, then resumed its gentle kneading. "I won't *make* you do anything." He wanted to know precisely how she had come to fear, although his imagination supplied him with several scenarios.

Alison had her eyes closed. "Look at me." When she did, staring at him wide-eyed, he hesitated, choosing his words with care. "I won't do anything you don't want me to do. I promise. We're partners in this. Will you trust me?"

Trust. Alison took a deep breath, inhaled the aromas of clean soap-scented skin and the musky smell of an aroused male—the scents of Sam, who was opening new vistas for her, who should not have to shoulder the weight of her problems. With a blinding clarity she realized she would never be free unless she freed herself. Reaching deep within her being, she discovered she had the courage to take what she wanted. "Yes." Her voice was tremulous. She firmed it. "Yes. I trust you. I *want* you." She wound her hands around his neck and wove her fingers into the springy curls at his nape, slowly pulled his head down to hers.

Sam let her take the initiative, intuitively realizing how important it was for her. When their lips met, hers were shy, tentative. He let her play, welcomed her tongue when it slipped past the barrier of his teeth, until the tension in him forced a faster pace. His lips firmed, his tongue took deep possession of her mouth, and to his delight, she answered him, the fire that was hidden beneath the surface flaming into a bright, white-hot inferno.

He placed her in the center of the bed, immediately coming down beside her. His hands roamed her curves, followed by his lips and teeth and tongue. All the while he learned her body's secrets, its hills and valleys and crevices, he praised her, her beauty, her courage, and told her what

239

he wanted to do, what he wanted her to do, what they would do together.

The heat of her own response surprised Alison at first, but as passion built and desire engulfed her, she had no time to think. She could only feel, as she drowned in sensation, and a spiraling need threatened to rip asunder the fabric of her being.

Through a haze of delight she heard his voice, whispering love words, rough words, some words that would have made her blush had not her skin already flushed with need as he drew the knot in her belly tighter and tighter with each stroke over her love-damp skin. All of a sudden it wasn't enough, to lie passive, accepting. She rolled over, pushed him down, treated him to a fevered exploration with fingers and lips and tongue.

Stunned, Sam let her have her way, glorying in her obvious delight, until, panting with need, he urged her onto her back and covered her with his eager body.

Outside the storm renewed, found new intensity. Thunder boomed over the mountains, slashes of lightning intermittently lit the room, rain drummed against the window. Throbbing with need Sam pressed against Alison, withholding himself for one last agonizing moment while he studied her face in a blinding flash of light. Her eyes were open, staring into his. He held her gaze, pressed forward, entered her. She surged upward, taking him deep, canting her hips to help him push high.

A groan tore from deep within his chest. He took her lips, possessed her with his tongue as his hips started to move, leading her in the dance as old as time. Fast and furious, shed of modesty, bereft of finesse, they came together in a frenzy as powerful as the storm that raged outside. Alison cried her final passion into his mouth; he soon followed with a hoarse shout that signaled an almost painful fulfillment.

For long moments he lay above her, trembling, dazed by the force of their joining. Then he remembered his weight, her fragility, and rolled to the side, taking her with him. His large hands, work-roughened, delicately stroked damp strands of her hair back from her face. His lips placed butterfly-light kisses on her temple, her closed eyes, her lips. He smiled in the dark when he heard her sigh, murmur his name, then fall asleep with the ease of a child.

In the unfamiliar dark Sam tightened his arms around Alison, knowing it was a woman he held, a woman he would fight for, a woman he would protect. His commitment made, he followed her into sleep, his hand protectively on her hip.

23

Sunday, June 16

Alison opened her eyes to murky gray light and the soft sound of rain drizzling against the window. For several heartbeats she lay in the netherworld of half-waking, then consciousness kicked in and memory flooded her, overwhelming in its intensity. She made the smallest of sounds, no more than a hurried intake of air, but it was enough to signal her wakeful state.

A large warm hand slid up her leg, crested her hip, and came to rest on the soft mound of her belly. Then he drew her slowly backward, until her naked rear connected with his larger, harder body. She wiggled that part of her experimentally, eliciting a sharply indrawn breath and another, more intimate reaction. The hand on her belly started to move in slow circles, ever widening, until it roved the territory of quivering breasts to the delta of soft, silky curls between her thighs.

Alison twisted and tried to turn, desperate to press her tingling breasts into his hair-roughened chest, to ease their ache by the abrasion. He denied her wish, keeping her facing away, his hand teasing, tormenting flesh already flushed with desire as he opened her legs by sliding one of his between them. Strong teeth gently nipped her earlobe, the point of his tongue entered her ear, delicately probed, sending sharp arrows of sensation skittering down her spine. Then he nudged aside the strands of sweet-smelling hair from her nape, tasted her skin along the ultrasensitive column of her long, slender neck. She shivered; even the feel of his breath on her was an erotic caress that caused hot, molten honey to prime her passion.

She wanted—needed—to feel his hard possession. Again she tried to turn, met resistance. A low moan escaped her throat, eliciting a faster tempo from his questing hand. At its downward sweep his fingers sought and penetrated her hidden recess, testing, finding her more than ready.

Driven to a dizzy plateau, she began to pant, her breath loud and harsh in the early-morning hush. As if it were a signal he had waited for, he began to murmur in her ear, telling her how sweet she was, how very much he wanted her, how soon his hard flesh would be buried deep within her.

Alison squeezed her eyes closed and let the spell he wove enmesh her. There was nothing in the world but the magic of his hand, the music of his voice, the excitement of anticipation and, finally, the breath-catching mindlessness that came when he lifted her leg and positioned himself against her. She jerked convulsively. He steadied her with honeyed words, with the promise of fulfillment, then pressed himself forward, slid smoothly into her, up high, filling the aching, empty void with throbbing-hot steel.

She groaned, the sound torn from her depths as only a few powerful deep strokes brought her to the brink. Teetering on the edge, almost maddened by the need to find relief, she felt him slide his hand down her belly, part her black curls, stroke the sensitive bud that was the key to her release. Then there was nothing for her but wild abandonment, a freedom such as she had never known, a few seconds out of time when she took what he offered, found what she sought, and tumbled into a world of exquisite sensations, dizzied by exploding colors, almost suffocating on a poignancy that welled from deep within her soul.

Sam waited, sheathed deep, tense and pulsing with the need for release, while she drifted back to reality. Then he spread her wider, gave her more of his weight, rode her with long, powerful thrusts which again ignited her passions so that she joined him in frenzy, finding a second, blinding fulfillment as he exploded deep within her.

He was trembling, his heart an erratic tattoo, his breathing harsh and labored. When he was able to move he turned her, gently kissed her sweat-damp temples, worked his way down to her mouth where he captured her lips in a sweet kiss of pure contentment. Drawing back to look at her, he stroked her hair, watched her eyelids flicker. "Sleep. Sleep, sweetheart," he murmured, gathering her close so that he could feel the beat of her heart.

Sated, Alison fell into a sound, dreamless sleep, safe and secure within the circle of his arms. The time for dawn came and went, the world outside the window only lightening a degree as rain and fog wreathed the mountains and poured down into the notch. The old house, swollen with damp, creaked and groaned, but it was the jangling shrill of the telephone tearing through the quiet, shredding the peace, that pulled her from tranquility into instant, mind-numbing fear. She bolted upright, her body tense, filled with a familiar dread.

Slower to awaken, Sam slitted his eyes open and ran his index finger down her spine. "Aren't you going to answer it?" She stiffened, but didn't reply. More alert now, he opened his eyes fully, took in her tense posture. "What's wrong?"

Alison sat mute, her eyes appealing for help. With a muttered curse, Sam got out of bed and strode naked from the room. The telephone sat on a little mahogany table in the hall. He snatched the receiver off the hook and growled into it.

The voice that poured into his ear was at first slightly taken aback, then apologetic. "No, no, that's all right, Jessie. She should have called. She was so exhausted she must have forgotten." He listened, then said good-bye. When he replaced the receiver he stood and stared at it for long moments, wondering what part of the puzzle the ringing of a telephone played in the picture that was beginning to form in his mind. The answer was only yards away.

Alison took one look at Sam and immediately assumed the worst. "Lucy?" she whispered. "Was it the hospital?"

Sam put his own impatience on hold. "No. Lucy's the same. That was Jessie. She called the hospital first thing. It was you she was worried about."

Acute embarrassment attacked Alison. She drew her knees up, taking the sheet with her, cocooning herself into its minimal protection.

Sublimely unconcerned with his nakedness, Sam folded his arms across his chest and regarded her with a mixture of expectancy and exasperation and tenderness. The time for evasion was past. Long past. "Why are you afraid of the telephone? Does it have something to do with what's been going on around here?"

Alison licked her lips to give them much needed moisture, looked everywhere but at him. Events were rushing at her, overwhelming her. Too fast. Things were happening too fast. She needed time to assimilate them, to come to terms with them.

"You might as well tell me. I don't give up easily."

Despite the intimacy of their situation, his nakedness intimidated her. Alison squeezed her eyes shut and tried to think. He grasped her chin and tilted it up. When she opened her eyes it was to find Sam's face only inches away. Inanely, she blurted out the thought that was at the front of her mind. "You're not dressed." To her mortification, she sounded like an outraged virgin.

Amusement crinkled the corners of his eyes. "You noticed." He let her chin go and stepped back, absentmindedly raking his fingers through his hair as he did so often. Casually he looked around for his pants and then remembered that he had left them in the bathroom. "Okay," he said after several moments of thought, "I'll go back to my room and shower and change. Then I'll pick you up, say in a half hour. That's your reprieve, sweetheart. The only one you're going to get."

Less than an hour later they sat facing each other across a table in the town's only coffee shop. Sam had just polished off waffles and bacon; Alison had eaten half a blueberry muffin. While in the shower earlier she had come to terms with herself. The time for withholding facts, thoughts, suspicions—whatever—was over. She waited for the waitress to refill their coffee cups and leave them alone, then she started without any preliminaries.

"Do you remember what I told you last night? About your being in danger by being with me?"

Sam hunched his shoulders, started to speak, but she cut him off.

"No. Don't say anything until you've heard me out. It's only fair."

Sam narrowed his eyes, wondering where she was going. Carefully he put his coffee cup down in the saucer. He had a feeling he would need all his concentration.

Alison wiped her lips with a paper napkin and then crumpled it into a ball. "You made a joke of it, what I said, but I was serious. Deadly serious." She leaned forward, lowered her voice. "Dottie is right. She knows what she's talking about. I found that out last night. Adrian Blaise is the Devil. He's the Devil and he wants me." Her palm started to itch. She balled her hand into a fist. "He wants me but I'll be—" she smiled sardonically, "*damned* if I'll go without a fight."

"Okay. Tell me," Sam said, his tone calm, steady, as if the subject under discussion were ordinary.

Alison told him, sparing a moment first to reflect appreciatively on his open mind. She addressed herself to only those things she knew firsthand, starting with the office party in December, the first time she had seen Adrian Blaise. "And last night," she said, conviction strengthening her, "I recognized his voice. Definitely." She clutched the balled napkin convulsively. "I know Adrian Blaise has been making obscene calls to me since January."

Sam picked up his cup; just held it. He stared past her, deep in thought.

Now that she had told him, Alison wanted him to believe her. "Months ago I thought . . . well, I thought it *might* be him, but there was no reason for it. The idea was really off the wall. Crazy. But now I have no doubt. None at all. In fact, I think he *wanted* me to know."

Sam's eyes narrowed.

"Don't you see? He's playing with me. He's playing some monstrous game, some cat-and-mouse game. He's toying with me . . . before . . ."

Sam replaced his cup in the saucer. "Calm down. He's not going to hurt you."

Alison hunched her shoulders, a defensive, submissive gesture. "The Devil always wins."

"No, he does not." It was a controlled roar. Several heads turned their way, curious eyes took in the picture of a distraught woman, an angered man. "Sorry," Sam said, sounding anything but contrite. He took Alison's hand, pried the napkin from it, and wound their fingers together. "Where's the girl who just said she'd be damned if she'd give up without a fight?"

Alison looked down at their joined hands, wondered at her bad timing—meeting a man like Sam now! He squeezed her hand reassuringly. Alison remembered her Crandell genes. "She's here," she said, meeting his gaze.

247

"She's just afraid."

"Good. I think that's a good way to be, given the circumstances."

"Do you believe me? About the Devil? About Adrian Blaise?"

Sam released her hand to drum his fingers on the table. "Anything's possible. At this point I can't say more than that. It's pretty hard to, er, . . . believe in the Devil, much less to put a name to him."

"Look, he's already killed Vera and Deirdre. And Lucy—"

"What about Lucy?"

"Didn't I tell you? Last night she said some rather strange things. Taken by themselves they mean nothing, but in light of the other happenings—"

"What did she say?"

"She said I was safe. Something about tricking him." Alison picked up her cup and took a sip, grimaced, and hastily set it down when she realized the coffee was cold. "It could be nothing, merely the ramblings of a sick woman, but . . . if you put it together with the other two. Look, Vera was an Alderbrook, a descendant of one of the original families of New Hope. Deirdre married one. The Treadwells were here from the beginning. Lucy's a Crandell. All women."

"Are you suggesting some ancient vendetta?"

"I'm not suggesting anything. It just seems . . . *peculiar* that all the victims are female, are somehow either descendants of New Hope families or connected to them."

Sam grunted. "You're painting a pretty broad canvas."

"Maybe not so broad." Alison held up her itchy right hand, palm toward him. Without looking she knew the mark in the center glowed a bright ruby red. "I think you've seen something very similar to this. Remember?"

Sam's entire body tensed. He certainly did remember. Michele bore an almost identical mark and . . . With the delicacy of a surgeon probing a wound, he touched a finger to it. "Does it hurt?"

"It itches."

Memory teased him, then firmed. Jennifer had an itchy palm.

"He's branded me. Us. I don't know when Michele got hers, but this mark has been on my palm since the day in December when Adrian Blaise touched his tongue to it." Alison spoke in a low, controlled tone, but her voice had no emotion. "I bear the names of two original families. Michele does also. She was a Stark. Ed's family and hers were among the first twenty-three. Perhaps there is some sort of . . . pattern after all."

Sam's eyes grew cold and hard. He stood up and reached in his pocket. "Let's go see if Lucy can talk to us. I want to hear exactly what she told you. If you don't mind, though, I'd like to make a few stops first."

Alison didn't mind. She was feeling much better, now that Sam knew everything. As if to mock her, a prickling in her palm reminded her that she hadn't told him everything. She shoved the offending hand into the pocket of her jeans, but that couldn't make the fear go away. Deep in her soul Alison knew that should Adrian Blaise wish it, she was his. Should he whisper dark erotic words, seduce her with forbidden desires, she would go to him. That had been her fear every time the telephone rang. There was no way she could tell that to the man with whom she had just made such beautiful love.

Ever since his divorce, Sunday was the worst day of the week for Richard. Usually he spent the better part of the day recovering from the night before, but this week he didn't have the luxury of mindlessness until midday. To add to his depression, it was a gray rainy day, with no chance of seeing the sun. Richard hated the rain, hated it even more now that he was alone. It made him think, and that was something he tried to avoid.

Since Friday night, when he had found Deirdre's body, he hadn't been able to find any escape. Not in sleep, which evaded him, nor in liquor, although certainly not for lack of trying.

The thoughts that crowded his mind couldn't be. It was impossible. Such things didn't happen in the twentieth century, in America. Such things didn't happen—but if they did, could they be set in motion by a business deal?

He had heard the rumors. How could he not? If he didn't hear them from some busybody wandering into the shop, he was sure to hear them from his good ol' buddy Art, The Fastest Mouth in the East. Richard grinned evilly. That wasn't exactly how big-mouth Art described himself.

Sternly he reminded himself to stay on the subject. It was easy, all too easy, to lose himself in hating Art.

"State the question, Richard," Miss Amelia Dutton, terror of the third grade would say, impatiently tapping her metal-tipped pointer against the chalkboard. If he closed his eyes he could hear her voice, the snickers from the other children, just waiting, hoping he couldn't do it.

"The question is whether the Devil is in Draconia, and if he is, did he come here because I made a deal with him?"

"Correct, Richard," echoed Miss Dutton's voice down a dusty corridor of his mind.

Richard sat and thought about the question, then thought about the answer to the question. Sat and thought and drank vodka, neat. The more he thought about it, the more he thought he knew the answer. It was so simple. All the evidence was before him. Everything he wanted, everything he dreamed about, was coming true.

Finally he couldn't avoid the truth. "Holy shit," he cried, "the Devil is in Draconia. He's here because of me."

The idea electrified him.

"There's no such thing as a free lunch," Miss Dutton whispered in his mind.

Immediately Richard pictured Deirdre covered in flies. Ridiculous. What had she to do with him, with what he wanted?

"Things are not always what they seem," Miss Dutton gently chided.

"Fuck off, you friggin' old bitch," Richard screamed. Miss Dutton wavered, disappeared, leaving behind an image of pursed prune lips. That, and a well-placed seed of doubt.

Richard's vodka-soaked brain needed reassurance. There was only one place he could find it.

In a hurry now, he took a quick shower, shaved and dressed in slacks and a sport shirt. Searching impatiently through his closet, he finally located his favorite jacket underneath his terry-cloth robe. Three fingers of vodka further primed him, and then he was on his way.

The day continued gray and filthy. Fog wisped across the road; a fine mist stippled the window. Shivering, Richard turned on the heat. He passed the inn, thought of Alison, wanted to stop and tell her it was all for her, everything he did, had done, but knew he lacked the courage. A tremor made his hands jerk on the wheel.

The road to the old Justice farmhouse was just up ahead, less than a mile from the access road to Dragon Meadow. Overgrown with weeds, the cracked pavement was so studded with potholes he thought his axle would crack even though he slowed the car to a crawl. His nerves were wound tight when he came to a stop in front of the house. Weathered gray boards in need of paint, cracked windows, sagging steps leading up to the porch. Unimpressive.

The front door opened, although he didn't remember knocking. The hall was dark, then suddenly flooded with brilliant light. Richard stared, taken aback.

On the outside the house looked derelict, but on the inside everything was rich, even opulent. The door closed behind him. Richard moved farther into the hall and stopped, catching a glimpse of the front room. Luxurious Persian carpets, expensive antique furniture.

"Beautiful, isn't it?"

Richard whirled toward the deep voice coming from above him, hearing a faint edge of amusement and . . . contempt. He didn't wait for Adrian Blaise to descend the staircase, couldn't wait lest he lose his nerve. "Tell me the truth," he said. "I want to know."

Adrian reached the bottom of the stairs. Richard looked up, way up, into dark, unfathomable eyes. "Truth? You had no need to come to me. The answers are with you. Look within yourself." He laughed, a low, menacing sound. "Look deep within your soul."

Richard looked, helpless to do otherwise, and recoiled in horror. *"Nooooo."*

"Yes." Adrian Blaise inspected the cuff of his sleeve, straightened a heavy-looking gold cuff link. "If that is all . . . ?" he suggested politely. "I've got an appointment. You really should have called, you know."

"Alison," Richard croaked. "You promised."

Adrian paused in the act of shrugging into his suit jacket. "Ah, yes, the beautiful Alison. So desirable." He turned to Richard, speared him with his black gaze. "You wanted her here. She is."

"But—" Sweat popped out all over Richard, ran like a river during spring thaw until his entire body was damp. "That wasn't all I wanted."

Adrian Blaise closed the distance between them with one giant stride. His dark eyes mesmerized, bright crimson flames within their depths fascinated, lulled. "Yes?"

Richard managed to stand his ground. "She's mine. Alison's mine. I want her."

"So do I." He smiled.

Jennifer brushed her hair until it shone, then dressed with more than her usual care. She could hear her parents moving around the house and wondered how she could leave without running into them. They would ask questions, questions she wasn't prepared to answer.

As if drawn to it, Jennifer went to the bureau, opened the drawer in which she kept her underwear, and pushing several nightgowns aside, stared down at the pieces of green crystal. She shivered, remembering her mother, how she had looked when she gave her the triangular malachite pendant. *"Wear it and watch. Should it shatter you'll know. Danger. You'll be in danger."*

Jennifer slammed the drawer closed. *Danger.* Danger was dark and exciting, a feast of the flesh, an addiction. Merely thinking about it made her go soft with longing. The lure of Adrian was like a fever, heating her blood, robbing her will.

A cunning, foreign to her nature, allowed her to tiptoe down the stairs and out of the house. Her mother rushed out onto the porch, just as she started her car. Jennifer ignored her. Nothing could keep her from Adrian. Nothing.

24

Rufus McClain

Rufus McClain was surprised to see Sam open the
door of the trailer, more surprised to see Alison follow
him in. He was quick to hide it, figuring it was none
of his business. To cover the first few awkward moments, he busied himself providing them with mugs of
coffee. He was amused by Alison's polite fiction that
the coffee was fine. "It's liquid mud, ma'am, but it's
what the crew favors. I kind of got in the habit of it."
He hesitated, cleared his throat, then asked her how her
aunt was doing.

"She's holding her own," Alison replied, failing to
control the quaver in her voice. "We're on our way to
see her. Thank you for asking, Mr. McClain."

Sam frowned at his foreman. "How did you hear of
it? Lucy took sick late last night."

"No mystery. One of the paramedic fellas was in Sonny's when the call came through." The trailer hummed
with sudden silence, save for the motor on the beer-
filled refrigerator. "Something I can do for you, boss?"

"Nothing. I didn't expect to find you here, is all."

Rufus laughed, a hollow sound. "That goes for me,
too." When Sam remained silent, he shrugged. "No big
deal, just thought I'd check around." His eyes darted to
Alison, quickly shifted away.

"Why?" Sam rapped out.

Alison's body jerked slightly at the harsh tone. "Go ahead, Mr. McClain. I'd like to hear whatever it is."

Rufus stole a glance at Sam before answering. "Okay," he said, then wiped the back of one big hand across his forehead, and grinned a little sheepishly. "I let that old character Hubbard spook me. He was talking wild. About this place, among other, er, things. I just thought I'd better come on out and look about a bit."

"Find anything?"

McClain scratched his bald head. "Nothing." He shifted his bulk; the springs of the chair creaked protestingly. "You?"

"Same thing. Wild talk, from some of Draconia's leading citizens." Sam pushed his mug aside, held out his hand to Alison. "If there's nothing to worry about here, we'd best be getting on our way." At the door he turned back to Rufus. "You'll lock up?"

"Sure thing."

It didn't take long for Rufus to put everything in order, the coffee carafe and mugs washed and dried, ready to be used again first thing in the morning. After carefully testing the padlock on the trailer door, he stood and looked around. The day was gloomy. Although it wasn't actually raining, everything dripped. He turned up the collar of his heavy flannel shirt and started for his car, stopping only five feet away from it. Something didn't feel right.

He had checked the site. Thoroughly. Still . . . He'd better check it again. Just to be sure.

Thirty-seven minutes later he was back at his car, more puzzled than before. There was not a thing out of place. Nothing was missing. Yet the feeling that something was wrong refused to go away.

Rufus silently told himself not to be a fool. The bottoms of his jeans were sopping wet from pushing his way through bushes. He could use a hot meal and a change of clothes. Instead, he drove his car into the cover afforded by a thick stand of pine, shut the engine off, and settled down to wait.

Bertha Rice

Miserable, her age-spotted hands nervously twisting a lace-edged handkerchief, Bertha repeated the same sentence she had spoken on the average of every two minutes since she arrived at the inn. "If only I hadn't called her last night."

Jessie refilled their teacups, poured a good dollop of brandy into Bertha's, and shook her head. " 'Twouldn't have mattered none. Same thing would have happened. Just later, is all."

"Fate," Bertha muttered darkly, took a healthy swallow of tea, and reached for the bottle of brandy. "I don't believe in it. There's things that can be changed."

"She seemed almost happy." Jessie produced a tissue and dabbed at her eyes. "After she had her attack, that is. Before it, she was excited, almost wild with it. And then that business with Jennifer and that nice Mr. Blaise. Why, I—"

Bertha grabbed Jessie's arm. Startled, the housekeeper sloshed tea all over the table. "Blaise? Adrian Blaise was here? Tell me about it."

Something in Bertha's expression told Jessie she had better satisfy the old lady first and ask questions later. Bertha drank in every word as thirstily as she sipped her brandy-laced tea. Jessie's voice broke when she described Lucy's attack and she had to use her tissue more than once to blot up the tears which welled from her eyes, but she managed to get the story told.

Bertha sat in silence, deep in thought, barely acknowledged when her cup was refilled. "Lucy isn't one to do something without a reason. Tell me what happened again, only this time, start from the beginning. I want to know everything Lucy did last night."

"Again?"

Bertha ignored Jessie's dismay. "Again. It's important. Very important."

Jessie obliged. Unhappily. But Bertha was Lucy's dearest friend, and she was so obviously suffering, and . . .

Bertha pushed her chair back so violently she almost overturned it. She plucked at Jessie's sleeve. Her lips moved but no sound came out.

For one awful moment Jessie thought Bertha was having some sort of attack. Then she saw the excitement sparkling in her eyes. "What is it? Was it something I said?"

"Yes. Oh, yes. You mentioned a book. Come show me. Show me the book she was reading." Impatiently Bertha thumped her cane as she waited for the younger woman to get up. "Don't you see," she said, "Lucy must have found the proof."

Alison frowned at the dripping vista. "The Kancamagus is probably shrouded in fog. We'd best go via Crawford Notch again."

"No problem, that's the way I want to go anyway. I'd like to check out some things in Franconia Notch State Park. It shouldn't take long."

When they pulled into the parking lot below the Flume, Alison knew Sam was taking everything very seriously. He headed straight for the Visitor Center, ignoring the pretty waterfall that ended in a pool beneath the wooden plank bridge from the parking lot. Alison found a coin in the pocket of her jeans, tossed it into the pool as they passed. Sam stopped and stared at her, then gave her a warm smile. "Playing tourist?"

Given a choice, Alison would have liked nothing better. She shrugged and returned his smile, only to lose it the second she stepped inside the building. She had hoped . . .

Sam could tell by her face, but he asked anyway. "That isn't the coach you saw?"

"No."

He had to make sure. "It was very late, remember? And the rain was exceptionally heavy . . ."

"No. None of that matters. There's no way that was the coach I saw, the one Dottie calls the death coach." She took the hand he offered and let him lead her closer to the exhibit.

"What's different?" Gently he nudged her. "Alison? Tell me, sweetheart."

"This coach is bigger, wider." She pointed to a plaque in front of the exhibit. "The picture shows it being drawn by four horses. The dea—, the other coach was narrower, and both Amos and I only saw one horse, and it was black. Everything was black. I couldn't have made a mistake about that." They both stared at the pale lemon-lime of No. 431, built in 1874, decorated with pictures of New Hampshire's Old Man and Franconia Notch on the passenger doors and the American seal on the front, the eagle with a ribbon in its mouth. "And it didn't say U.S. Mail or Valley Line or anything else."

Abruptly she turned her back on the exhibit as disappointment ate at her. She had so hoped that what was happening in Draconia was someone's idea of a joke—albeit a sick one. That was something that could be handled.

Sam had her hand again, and then she was outside, breathing deeply of the moisture-laden air. This time she didn't even spare a glance at the coin-dotted pool. A fine misting rain dappled her hair with droplets of moisture by the time they reached the car.

When they were inside he reached over and tucked several wet strands behind her ear. "It was a long shot."

She sighed, tried to shake off a sudden despondency. "I know. Where to now?" she asked dispiritedly as they followed a minivan filled with teenagers onto the parkway.

"The hospital." He didn't tell her, but he thought it more important than before that he hear exactly what Lucy had to say.

25

Rufus was beginning to wonder just what kind of fool he was, sitting in a cold car in wet clothing, when he heard the sound of an engine. His car was well hidden, but still he scrunched down, and with infinite care, rubbed a clear spot on his side window. He watched as a familiar car braked to a stop in front of the trailer and Jennifer Cutter got out.

Breath escaped his lips in a near-silent hiss. She was one of the last people he had expected to see. Observing her as she warily looked around, his earlier uneasiness intensified. When she left the clearing and walked into the trees he wasn't far behind.

It was raining again, the air colder than normal for June. "You're getting too old to sneak around," he mumbled, but not being a man given to fancies, he trusted his gut instincts. Something was wrong. He would bet his next paycheck on it. He shivered, blaming it on the chill wind that penetrated the layers of his clothing.

The rain curtained his movements. The ground was soggy, creating a cushioning sound, and as they neared the river, the rushing water effectively masked any other noise. Jennifer walked purposefully, looking straight ahead, intent on reaching her destination.

Closing the gap between them, Rufus skirted the path,

uttering a low-voiced curse when he brushed against a branch and ice-cold water doused his head, trickled down his neck under his collar. He was still muttering imprecations against the trees, the rain, the mud, and anything else he could think to blame for his uncomfortable condition, when he realized that Jennifer had stopped walking and was looking about uncertainly.

Quickly Rufus hid his bulk behind a tree. Jennifer resumed walking, but a bit less surely. Some of the bounce had gone out of her step.

He waited before following. Her destination was plainly the old mill. If she was heading for a romantic assignation it was a strange place for it. Idly he speculated about the kind of man who would insist on meeting in such an out-of-the-way place. He could only think of one answer: a married one.

When the old mill came into sight Rufus looked around for the best vantage point. A thick-trunked beech afforded ample cover while offering an unimpeded view of the derelict building and a good portion of the area surrounding it. He was no Peeping Tom, would wait only long enough to see that Jennifer met her date, if indeed that was her purpose in coming here.

Rufus studied the terrain, surveying the entire area of earth and sky with a knowledgeable eye. The river ran fast at this point, usually green-bellied underneath, white-laced on the surface where rocks from pebbles to boulders interfered with its flow. Today everything had a gray cast, reflecting the sky. Even the bright spring green of new leaves and bushes and grass was subdued.

Jennifer had halted approximately ten feet from the near side of the mill. Behind her was the river, but she barely gave it a glance, peering instead back up the path and then looking at her watch.

Sheltered behind the beech, Rufus grew indignant. Not only was this fellow forcing Jennifer to sneak around, but he even had the audacity to keep her waiting. He had a good mind to go and tell her that whoever this fellow was, whatever her feelings, she could do better, when a flicker of movement several yards behind her caught his eye. He blinked, looked again, and in that instant his mind grew numb with shock. He stared, aghast, as hugh black shapes slinked around the far corner of the building, advancing upon the unsuspecting girl.

For long moments he stood, rooted to the ground as firmly as the ancient beech before him; then the temporary paralysis gave way and he picked up several rocks and stepped out into the open. Jennifer spotted him immediately. Words of warning crowded his throat, but he bit them back, afraid of precipitating an attack before he was close enough to help.

Something must have alerted her to the danger, for she whirled about, her body going rigid when she saw the great preternatural beasts. They were nightmares from a madman's brain, with their eyes the color of blood, their mouths filled with long, sharp-pointed teeth and . . . Rufus gagged as he caught their scent, like spoiled meat.

Jennifer's slim body was shaking like the leaves of a silver aspen in the wind. She produced a low, moaning sound. It raised the fine hairs on McClain's body. The sound stopped abruptly, and she gave a terrified scream when one of the beasts snorted a thin stream of fire that sizzled through the damp air.

Her cry sliced through Rufus like a fingernail down a chalkboard, but he didn't stop his steady advance. More of the loathsome beasts rounded the side of the mill, silently padded close to the trembling girl.

"Jennifer," Rufus whispered as he approached, "listen to me." She gave no sign of hearing. He sharpened his tone, raised his voice. "Jennifer! Listen! Take a step backward. Slowly, girl, I'm here to help." His immediate goal was to reach her, to put her behind him. He refused to think past that.

The beasts had formed a rough semicircle before her, and although they milled about and showed signs of restlessness, they came no closer.

As he slowly advanced, the beasts watched him with fire-bright eyes. Jennifer still stood motionless, apparently petrified. He focused his attention on the one thing he had to do, not even sparing a thought for the consequences. He reached out and grabbed her by the arm, roughly swinging her about and shoving her behind him. "Run, girl," he screamed, "run!" After several seconds during which he feared she wouldn't—or couldn't—obey, she took off and sped back up the path.

Too many years and too many beers prevented his own escape. He whirled about, took a stance. The beasts were crouched, ready to spring. The rocks were heavy in his sweaty hands. Just before he threw, he glanced up and saw a man. The sight chilled his soul.

Jennifer had the trailer in view when she heard it, the sound that tore through the trees, echoed around the hills, flew up to the cold gray sky. Ancient, savage, a primal cry of battle engaged. The lone human voice was immediately joined by others—frighteningly inhuman.

And then—abruptly, terrifyingly—there was silence. Jennifer jumped in her car and fled.

Lucy was sleeping when they got to the hospital. A nurse refused to let Alison even so much as peek in at her. There were rules, she maintained—and one of them was that there was no visiting until the afternoon. That said, she let the door to the intensive care unit swing closed in Alison's face.

"Damned martinet," Alison mumbled, glaring at the door.

Sam took her arm. "Let's get some coffee. We'll come back later."

Alison wasn't prepared to give in just yet. Not when her peace of mind depended upon just seeing that Lucy was resting comfortably. "I'll be right back," she announced, and pushing the door forward with the flat of her hand, marched into the restricted area.

She was back in no time, escorted by the same nurse. "She seems to be sleeping peacefully," Alison said, and then thanked the nurse as if she had done her a favor.

"Coffee now?" Sam asked, happy to see that the minor skirmish had restored some of her Crandell spunk.

The rain was falling steadily again. They left the hospital and headed south, toward the center of North Conway. Sam wanted doughnuts with his coffee.

They proceeded at a snail's pace, caught in a traffic jam that rivaled the Long Island Expressway at rush hour. Except here, there was only one lane for traffic in each direction, both directions sharing a center lane for turns. As they inched closer to the main business district, Sam's mood grew blacker and blacker, until finally he could no longer contain his disgust. "Just look at this mess."

Alison roused herself to look. "What?"

Sam made a sweeping gesture with his hand, then slammed it down on the horn when a car tried to pull in front of them from the turn lane. "Damn chiseler," he growled, "but who can blame him. This whole situation is an abomination. The entire area is just too damn small to handle an influx of cars and people and businesses on this scale." He swore at a truck that forced its way into the line of cars from a minimall of outlet stores. The truck was only in front of them long enough to reach the next line of discount stores, where it swerved into the parking lot. "If you think this is bad, you should see what goes on up in southern Maine. Some of the stores in Freeport are open twenty-four hours."

Alison narrowed her eyes at a cluster of outlet stores. "Why, there used to be a house there. It was charming, with gables and . . ." Her voice trailed off. "That was what you were talking about last night, isn't it? Developers with no eye to anything but big bucks."

Sam grunted. "You've got it, sweetheart. What you're looking at is part of America's newest shame. I only hope people will wake up before it's too late to save some of the beauty of this land." He grunted again as the long line of cars came to a stop. "Perhaps I'm wrong; maybe this is what everyone wants. Stores certainly bring jobs to an area."

"I guess that's true enough. Down near Manchester there's a retail center that's built around the idea of an Austrian village. I read the developer is planning another one, a French village. He couldn't do that if the local people objected. They must know what they're giving up, how it will change the area and, ultimately, their lives." Alison stared out the window, at the cars, the people, the stores. "It was the same with Dragon Meadow, wasn't it? It never would have been started without the people of Draconia wanting it. Whatever the price, they're just going to have to pay it. Oh," she gasped, as the double meaning of her words hung in the air.

Hours later she was still thinking about what she had said, thinking and wondering. Could it be that simple? Quid pro quo? Had the people of Draconia *known* what they were contracting for? Who they were contracting with? Had they *all* known? Did this particular real-estate deal demand payment in blood?

Her troubled thoughts must have shown, for the instant Lucy was awake she demanded to know what was the matter.

"I'm worried about you," Alison gently chided.

"And pigs have wings" was the tart retort. Sharp eyes peered past Alison. "Is that Samson behind you? Come closer, boy, I want to see you."

Sam stepped to Alison's side and took the thin hand Lucy offered. "You're looking fine."

"I'm dying," Lucy replied. She squeezed his hand, pulling him down until she could whisper in his ear. "I did it for Alison. For my Alison."

Sam would have liked to question her, but he could see how weak she was, how exhausted those few words had left her. A big buxom blond nurse hurried over and clucked reprovingly. Neither Alison nor Sam needed to be told they would have to leave.

They had dinner at a roadside restaurant and then drove home through another drenching rain. "Damned weather," Sam complained, adding the worry of falling behind schedule to all his others. He parked the car in front of Lucy's house and went inside with Alison. She flicked on the light switch and gasped.

Sam reached for her, his body automatically preparing to fight. At first he thought he was hallucinating, for he thought it was Lucy sitting there in the gloom. It wasn't Lucy, it was Bertha, sitting in a cane-back chair, clutching a slim volume in her age-spotted hands. Those hands trembled as they lifted toward Alison. "Here. Mary Beth Winslow's article. It's the proof."

26

Monday, June 17

It felt natural to Alison to turn to Sam in the hush of early morning. While she was in his arms the world and all her troubles receded. Pressed to his side, her cheek resting on the broad expanse of his chest where she could hear the thunder of his heart slowly return to its normal rhythm, she wanted nothing more than to stay there—safe, protected. She sighed with the thought and he hugged her close.

"Penny for them."

She rubbed her cheek against his hair-roughened skin, damp from their recent lovemaking. "They're not worth that much."

He lifted her chin so that their gazes met. "I'll be the judge of that." Slowly his hand stroked down her side, over the curve of her hip. Alison produced a catlike sound of contentment deep in her throat. His hand reached her knee and began an upward journey, traveling along the sensitive skin of her inner thigh. Alison's breathing quickened and the little purring sound intensified into a moan of delight. Sam's head descended, his lips hovered over hers. "Two pennies," he murmured.

With his fingers tantalizing her it was easy to share her thoughts, for now they were of nothing but him and the pleasure they soon would share again. She whispered them into the space between their lips, the final words felt rather than heard, for suddenly his mouth covered hers, hard with renewed need.

Desire leaped between them, raw, demanding, so hot that neither could wait. With a groan that came from his core, Sam pulled her eager body onto his, helped her to find him, then let her set the pace for their loving.

A passion so wild it overwhelmed every inhibition allowed Alison to ride him with abandon. When she reached her peak he was with her, rolling her over at the last, hoarsely crying out his own release from above her into the gloom of another rainy morning. Trembling in the aftermath of exertion, he moved to roll away. Alison clasped her arms around him, refused to let him go.

"I'm too heavy for you, sweetheart, let me up." She only hugged him tighter. Still joined to her, he slowly eased over until they were lying on their sides. "What is it?" She refused to answer, and he knew then that there was nothing for him to do but to hold her.

Feeling safer, she drifted off to sleep, finally waking to the sound of the bedroom door closing. She shot out of bed and ran out of the room, calling Sam's name. Then she heard the sound of the shower, and without a moment's hesitation, went into the bathroom.

A huge grin of pure male appreciation lit his face when he saw her. Green eyes raked her figure, from the crown of her head to the tips of her toes; the grin widened. "Did anyone ever tell you what beautiful toes you have?"

Needing to satisfy his curiosity, Sam drove into town to the library before going to work. After getting directions from the librarian, he selected the most promising books and set to work at a table in a secluded alcove. It didn't take long. Only three books yielded information. One was a catchall work listing everything considered even remotely occult. It mentioned the death coach and the dandy dogs. The other two dealt with myths and superstitions and offered several different versions of a pack of dogs associated with the Devil.

He was deep in thought as he headed out of town, only remembering as he was passing Treadwell's that he wanted to stop there. A young boy wearing a rain-slick parka ran out of the office. His blond hair was plastered wetly to his forehead, yet he greeted Sam as cheerfully as if the sun shone brightly. While he was busy at the gas pump, Sam got out of the car and went over to the service area. Two mechanics were working on a late-model Cadillac in the first bay. A van was up on the lift in the second bay, parts of a tailpipe lying on the concrete beneath it. The third bay was empty.

The older of the two mechanics straightened and wiped his hands on a rag as Sam approached. "Mornin'. Help you?"

"I hope so. I promised Mrs. Fortune I'd check on her car. But I don't see it here."

The mechanic turned his head and spat, then carefully wiped his lips with the back of his hand. His eyes flickered to the younger mechanic, who had stopped working and was openly listening, then shifted back to Sam. "That the Mustang?"

Sam recognized a stall when he heard one. He answered the question with a hard stare and a demanding silence. The mechanic hawked another wad. Sam stood his ground.

Finally the younger man broke the uncomfortable silence. "It's around back. We wuz told not—"

"What Ralph is tryin' to say is we're waitin' on parts."

Sam's eyes narrowed as Hobart, the older mechanic, jerked his head at Ralph, motioning him back to work. "I'd like to speak to Treadwell. What time is best?"

Hobart lifted his shoulders and let them fall. "Ain't been comin' in regular since his missus got herself killed. Try later, why don'tcha?"

The incident put Sam in a foul mood, and uncomfortable thoughts accompanied him to the construction site. No matter how he tackled it, from whatever angle, he was left with an uneasy feeling.

His temper wasn't improved when he drove into Dragon Meadow and found the trailer dark and locked and most of the crew milling around aimlessly in front of it. "Where the hell's McClain?" he barked at Tommy Russo, an assistant foreman. When he received a shrug in reply, he unlocked the trailer and stormed inside. He easily located the work sheet with the daily assignments, and within five minutes dispersed the men. Alone, Sam grumpily brewed coffee and tried to settle down.

His thoughts wouldn't let him. The minutes ticked by, going no faster despite the frequency with which he looked at his watch and checked it against the big electric clock on the wall. He called McClain, listened to the unanswered ringing, then slammed the phone back down. The refrigerator hummed, annoying him; the rain tapped against the window, reminding him of the threatened work schedule.

Not only was McClain late, but Jennifer had also failed to show. With a sigh, he called her, but there was no answer there, either. Idly he wondered if they could be together, then dismissed the thought. He called McClain a second time, with the same result.

A little after ten o'clock he picked up the telephone and called Alison. "How's Lucy?" he asked almost immediately, his voice reflecting the tension and uneasiness he couldn't shake.

"She's holding her own. That's a direct quote." Her voice quavered. Sam waited silently while she struggled to control it. "The nurse I spoke to wouldn't tell me anything more."

"Damn!" He raked his hand through his hair. He had promised Alison he'd drive her to the hospital in the afternoon, but with McClain's unexplained absence, he was going to be delayed.

It was easy for Alison to tell he had problems of his own. "Don't worry about me, Sam. I'll see if I can borrow a car if mine isn't ready."

"No. I'll take you," he said, about to tell her that she couldn't expect the Mustang to be fixed anytime soon, when the door creaked open. "Hold on," he told her, expecting Rufus or Jennifer.

Instead, one of the young local men McClain had hired lurched against the doorjamb, his face chalk white. "I found McClain," he said, and vomited all over his shoes.

27

Jennifer ignored the telephone when it rang. She sat, huddled into herself, staring out the window, her haunted eyes seeing not the neat sweep of green lawn but the old mill and . . .

She shuddered, wondered if the chill would ever leave her soul. She could almost feel sharp teeth sinking into tender flesh, feel the spurt of warm blood . . .

Was that how it had been for Rufus? Was he dead?

Of course he's dead, a voice inside her shrieked. *He's torn to shreds, and it COULD HAVE BEEN YOU. FOOL! IT WAS YOU HE WANTED ALL ALONG!*

All yesterday afternoon . . . all night . . . all this morning . . . she had sat and stared, seeing nothing, picturing him lying out there, the rain falling on him, soaking into his clothes, sliding down his flesh, washing away the blood . . .

The telephone rang again. Jennifer tried to block the sound. She knew who was calling. She knew what he wanted. She also knew she couldn't resist, even now, after she had put it together.

How long could she hide in her room?

The ringing stopped, then started again. Something inside Jennifer snapped. She watched her hand reach out, saw it pick up the receiver.

"Yes?"

Question or acknowledgment? She would never know. As still as stone she let the dark voice flow over her, into her, become one with her. It was irresistible; where it summoned, she went.

He was waiting for her, standing in the rain, a being of such compelling power that, even afraid, she went unhesitatingly to him. He took her hand and led her into the woods, following a well-trod trail, stopping when they reached a deep, swirling mountain pool of pure stream-fed waters.

"The Devil's Dam," she whispered, the words unheard in the mighty roar of its waterfall cascading down the slick-sided gorge. Beautiful. Mesmerizing . . . Until she shivered in the sudden knowledge that she stood alone. "Adrian!" she cried, wildly looking about.

He stood not far away. When he raised his hand she thought he beckoned her, and started toward him. His fingers snapped, a command, and then she felt it, the prickling of her body hair, warning . . .

They were there, the loathsome beasts . . . crouching silently, slavering, waiting . . .

A menacing growl came from behind her. The creatures were circling, closing in. Still he stood and watched.

Too late, fury sparked. She hurled herself toward him, fingers stiffened into clawlike shapes. That handsome face would bear her mark, as she bore his.

He never moved. Never so much as flinched.

Jennifer saw that much before the dandy dogs howled rhapsodically, an unholy choir. Set loose, they turned on her. Spewed bright ribbons of flame.

Searing heat engulfed her. Fire crinkled her flesh. Charred it. Maddened by pain, she dove into the pool.

28

While looking for a pen, Alison found the slip of paper Clare Bauer had handed her on Thursday, a hundred years ago. One call and her obligation would be fulfilled. Quickly she punched out the numbers and asked to be connected with Mr. Peter Carmody, senior partner of the local law firm representing the Mountain Venture group.

"Mr. Carmody's in conference. May I help you?"

Alison recognized the ploy, was absurdly grateful for it. Not for one second did she let herself forget that this man represented Adrian Blaise. With a little finesse she wouldn't have to speak to him at all. She launched into a succinct explanation, ending with the hopeful admonition that it was unnecessary for Mr. Carmody to return her call unless there was something specific he wished her to do.

Then, feeling virtuous, she called her own office and asked for Winda, wanting to speak to her friend before reporting to Clare. The familiar voice vibrated across the miles. "Hey, girl, what's shakin'? How's your aunt doing?"

Alison resisted answering the first question. Winda wouldn't believe her, would probably think she was on drugs if she told her even one little bit of what was going on. So she only told her of Lucy's heart attack, listened to Winda's words of genuine regret.

Winda summed up the situation. "Bummer. You need me for anything other than a sympathetic ear?"

"Actually, I need to speak to Clare."

"Why'd you want to do a thing like that, girl? Give me the message. I'll tell her she wasn't at her desk when you called."

Alison laughed and readily complied. "Thanks, Winda. I'll be in touch."

Feeling better for having spoken to her ebullient friend, Alison made herself a cup of tea and then took it into the living room. Armed with a yellow legal pad and a pen, she set to work, frequently referring to Mary Beth Winslow's article. An hour later she had several lists, many questions and absolutely no idea how to set about getting answers.

A growling in her stomach let her know it was time for lunch. Rather than eat alone, she threw a cardigan over her shoulders and hurried through the rain to the inn. As she had hoped, she found Bertha sitting in the cocktail area, a glass of Chablis on the table.

"You look mighty peaked," was the old lady's greeting as Alison kissed her cheek. "Come sit down and have a glass of wine." She waved to Derek. "There. Now we can talk. Did you read it?"

"Yes." Alison thought of all the lists she had made. "I read it and reread it."

"And . . . ?"

"I just don't know." Alison shrugged, then thanked Derek as he brought the Chablis to the table. She took a sip of the cold wine. "Obviously Mary Beth Winslow was convinced that the twenty-three men who founded New Hope made some kind of pact with the Devil. Made a pact and paid a price. Over and above the usual one of their souls, that is."

Bertha leaned forward. "The mill is the key. It's the heart of the town. It was then . . . and it will be again, once this fancy new complex is finished." She drank her wine slowly and then carefully placed the glass down. "Alison dear, you must realize . . . well, stated quite boldly, it is quite clear you are at risk. Doubly, if that Winslow woman knew what she was talking about. You are female and a Crandell."

"So is Lucy," Alison whispered.

Startled, Bertha almost knocked over her wineglass. "You think . . . ?"

Alison never had a chance to answer, for at that moment she glanced up and saw Jessie standing in the archway. One look at her face told her that Lucy was dead.

Part III

29

September 1823
New Hope

Susannah Justice

The house was quiet, eerily so, even with the children sleeping upstairs. Usually Susannah would have blessed the peace, used it to catch up on some of the endless mending, or dipped candles, or done any one of the untold chores, but tonight was different. Tonight there was no peace in the quiet. If what Jedediah had told her was true, then there was no peace in all of New Hope.

Susannah shivered and drew her shawl more closely around her shoulders. Surely Jedediah was wrong. He had to be wrong.

The sound of a wagon approaching the house sent her rushing to the window. Her hand trembled when she pushed the curtain aside. With relief she recognized the bulky figure of Silas Parrott. She had the door open before he could knock. "What brings you out tonight?" she cried.

Silas took one look at her white face and knew that Jedediah had not kept silent. He sighed, removed his hat as he stepped inside. "I've come to fetch Jed. He's needed."

"Now? Tonight?"

"Aye."

"He's in the barn. He didn't like the look of the cow."

Silas nodded. "Thank'ee. I'll be about finding my own way."

But Susannah followed, suspecting something else had

happened, something terrible, and she couldn't abide not knowing what it was. She ran directly to her husband's side. "Here's Silas come to see you," she cried, fear lacing her voice.

Jedediah slipped his arm around her waist. "Go back to the house, Sukey, it's cold out here." She stubbornly refused, daring him with her eyes. Finally he turned to Silas. "She knows. You can talk."

"Aye. I figured." He avoided looking at her when he spoke. "I've come about James. He's hung himself. Left a note saying he didn't want to live without Mary. You're needed to help with the burying."

Susannah gasped, grew even paler. She clutched Jedediah's arm. "No! Don't go!"

He shook her off, reached behind him to the peg in the wall for his jacket and hat. When he was dressed he took her by the arm and walked her toward the house. "That's five, Sukey. Five. Don't you see? He said it would be five. It's over. It's all over."

An unnamed dread almost closed her throat. She had to force the words out. "But why must you go now? Tonight?"

Silas hastily backed off. "I'll be by the wagon. Don't tarry," he warned.

Jedediah hurried Susannah into the house. " 'Twill be no ordinary burial. It's best to do it fast."

"But at night? With no minister?"

"He's not like the others. The women. Surely you realize that?" Quickly he strode into the kitchen, checked to see the door was barred, then moved quickly back through the house. At the front door he drew her close, kissed her cold lips. "Come. Take heart. This is the last."

"But . . ."

"Bar the door behind me. I'll try not to be too long."

At first she jumped at every sound, started at every creak, ran up to check the children so often she grew tired from climbing the stairs. John, Jacob, and the baby, Deborah, slept the sleep of the innocent. When she wasn't watching the children, she wrote in her diary. Finally, worn

278

out, Susannah dozed in the rocking chair before the fire.

The fire was reduced to embers when she heard the sound of hoofbeats nearing the front door. "Jed!" she breathed, struggling to shed the weariness that weighed her down. At the door she hesitated, some innate cautiousness staying her hand from the bar. "Silly woman," she chided herself. "Who could it be save your husband?"

Still, she went to the window. The scream that rose in her throat died stillborn. The children. She mustn't frighten the children. The thing outside stamped its foot, tossed its neck . . . "Nooooo," she moaned, refusing to believe it had no head.

"Oh, God, no! Jed!" She put her hand in her mouth to hold back the scream. Transfixed, she stared as another— thing—came down off the coachman's bench and opened the coach door. As if he could see, a man with no eyes, no head, he bowed. The moon sailed out from behind a cloud. Susannah moaned as she saw the blood as black as tar dripping from the raw stump.

Somehow she found the will to move. Slowly, she backed away from the window, concentrating on each step. The kitchen door opened and then closed. Her heart leaped wildly against her chest. Jed was home! She was safe!

Then she remembered . . . The bar across the door. "Jed?" she whispered, still hopeful, as she heard the sound of footsteps crossing the kitchen floor.

He came into the room and she could see by the dying fire that he was beautiful. Although she had never seen him before, she instantly knew who he was. The stranger. The stranger who had started it all.

Her thoughts flew to her children, asleep above. She stepped close to him, head held high, daring anything for them.

Dark eyes held her, eyes that saw right through her, deep into her soul. "Your children are safe."

Her breath leaked out in relief. But now noises were coming from the kitchen, the sound of nails clicking across the floor. Shadows flowed along the ceiling, bathed in crimson

279

from the embers' glow. Monstrous shadows, of creatures not of this earth.

Susannah cringed. He took her hand, turned it palm up for his lips. Wild ecstasy stabbed through her at the touch of his tongue. He raised his dark head and she stared into his eyes. "I'm going to die," she said, seeing it there.

"Yes. But first I'll be your lover."

Slowly his hand came up and cupped her breast. Susannah trembled, then moaned as he gently squeezed. Eyes glazing with awakening desire, she moved more fully into his embrace.

He smiled.

30

It was raining again. Alison thought it fitting, to say good-bye to Lucy under a sky as gray and weeping as her heart. Above the yawning grave stood the hackmatack tree; tombstones of Crandells crowded close. Lucy would be the last Crandell to slumber here. Next to Alison, Bertha sniffled and leaned heavily on her cane. Grief furrowed her face, but there was an acceptance there that Alison could not find.

The service was mercifully short. Lucy had wanted it that way. Everyone was being kind, was saying the right things, but Alison could find no consolation. Lucy had died for her. It was a burden beyond bearing.

Behind her, Sam's solid presence lent her strength. She felt him take her elbow, try to draw her back from the grave. "It's over," he murmured in her ear. She wondered.

Lucy's friends and neighbors came back to the house, filled the rooms with reminiscences about her while they ate the food and drank the wine that Jessie and Luke had set out. Alison found a quiet moment to pull Jessie aside. "Thank you," she said, indicating the spread. "Lucy was lucky to have you, both you and Luke." She poured a glass of wine and forced Jessie to take it.

"That's the way Luke and I always felt about her. She was family."

Alison nodded, a lump in her throat. "We'll have to talk. Soon."

Time passed. The rumble of voices, the ache of unbearable loss that memories stirred, combined to give Alison a headache. The other talk, the whispers and speculations, made her blood run cold. Names drifted to her: Vera, Deirdre . . . Rufus. Just as people were beginning to leave, the mayor walked in the door, looking even more self-important than usual.

Bertha sniffed disdainfully. "Something has sure set a fire under Bert's nose."

Alison wasn't paying much attention, for she had caught sight of another late arrival. Richard stood in the doorway, hesitating as if unsure of his welcome. He looked terrible; his eyes were bleary and his complexion had an unhealthy grayish tinge. She watched as he restlessly scanned the crowd, knowing he searched for her. When at last their gazes locked, it was like a physical blow. His eyes were haunted . . . pleading.

A buzzing broke her concentration. Voices were talking loudly, the interest centered on J. Norbert. She wrenched her attention away from Richard. Impressions flew at her, swamping her so suddenly she couldn't sort them out. All she knew was that something dreadful had happened again.

Jennifer. The name raced through the room. *The pool . . . dead . . . drowned in the Devil's Dam.*

Alison found the tale too terrible to comprehend. Bertha shoved a glass of wine into her hand. The cool liquid slid down her throat.

Richard's face swam out of a haze. He gripped her arm, leaned down to whisper directly into her ear. "Don't worry. Don't worry."

The wine had made her dizzy. She clung to him, for a moment forgot her aversion to him. "About what?"

But he wouldn't say. Daniel came over, and after one look at his brother's face, led him away.

At Bertha's urging, Alison sipped more wine, not protesting when one glass was exchanged for another.

Amos Hubbard, wearing an old black suit, shiny and threadbare in spots, came to kiss her cheek. He smelled of whiskey and age. "Stubborn old fool," he said, his epitaph for an old friend.

Again the voices buzzed, then abruptly stilled. Amos froze, his expression one of outraged disbelief. Dimly Alison heard a familiar voice, then the thump of Bertha's cane. The voice came again, closer, greeting J. Norbert. Recognition struck; it was no surprise to look up into Adrian Blaise's dark, compelling eyes.

He took her hand, shook it in a normal way. There was no jolt of desire, no urge to a dark, forbidden passion. The words he spoke were faultless, appropriate to the situation. "My sympathy on your loss. Ms. Crandell was . . . special."

"Yes." Alison thought there might be a hidden message—a confirmation of sacrifice?—but her brain, fuzzed by alcohol, couldn't be sure.

Adrian looked perfectly at ease, as if the people near them weren't watching with avid curiosity. He was the stranger in their midst; not one of them was unaware of the rumors, the wild talk. Dragon Meadow. The old mill. Four deaths—no, *five,* with Jennifer.

Alison remembered her role of hostess, indicated the food and wine with a wave of her hand. Relief spread through her when Adrian declined, said he couldn't stay. The sooner he left, the better, for from the corner of her eye she saw Sam approaching, fury sparking from his eyes.

The two men faced each other: Sam, thin-lipped, hostile; Adrian, politely aloof, sardonic. Silence eddied; effectively isolated them.

Adrian broke it. "McClain's death was shocking."

"He was murdered."

J. Norbert insinuated himself into their presence. "I warned you about feral animals, Chandler. Surely you must remember?"

Sam ignored him, his attention wholly on the other man.

283

"I know what killed him."

"Indeed?"

Adrian smiled. The air hummed with unspoken thoughts, unnamed hostilities. Finally Adrian reached into a pocket and drew forth a small book. He gave it to Alison. "I found this at the Justice place. I thought you might like to have it."

Alison stared at the small leather volume, trying to think what to say. Her head was pounding. She felt sick.

Sam's large hand gripped her elbow. "It's enough. Come with me."

Upstairs was blessed quiet, a surcease from examining eyes. Alison let Sam undress her, down to lacy panties and bra, and didn't protest when he threw back the covers and ordered her to lie down. The sheets felt cool beneath her skin. He left her and then returned with two aspirin and a glass of water.

Alison gratefully swallowed the tablets, drank thirstily of the water. "I don't want to be alone," she said, ashamed of the need in her voice, the hot tears that slid down her cheeks.

Without a word Sam removed his jacket and tie, then took off his shoes. The bed dipped under his weight when he lifted the covers and lay down next to her. He pulled her close, her back to his chest, and murmured soft words into her ear.

After a time she shifted to face him, raised her heavy-lidded eyes to his. "It's over, isn't it? Mary Beth Winslow wrote that there were five . . . five deaths—the same as now."

For a moment Sam's features tightened with pain, then they eased into a more normal set. "It's over." He stroked her hair, dipped his head, and kissed her. "It's over, sweetheart, now go to sleep."

Jerry Treadwell

The world had become a cold, empty place for Jerry

Treadwell. His home was a constant reminder of what he had lost; his work no longer interested him. Not that there was much of it today. Not even fill-ups. Most of the people had gone to Lucy's funeral.

His eyes filled with tears. Lucy had been old. Not young like Deirdre. God, he missed her. Now she'd never know what a great deal he had made, how rich he was going to be. He should have told her about the land he'd sold to the Mountain Venture people, the share of Dragon Meadow he'd bought with the profit. Too late. God, what a stinking world it was.

He wiped his eyes, smearing grease across his face. The clang of a wrench on concrete, the harsh curse of Hobart, the senior mechanic, floated to him through the door that separated the dingy little station office from the garage. He found himself walking to the door, a sudden, unreasoning anger flooding him, making him violent. He stormed into the garage, looking for trouble. He found it immediately.

Ralph was suddenly in the wrong place at the wrong time. He looked up from draining the oil from a Chevy to see grief gone amok shining from Jerry's eyes. A large fist slammed into his chest, sending him sprawling.

"Hey!" Hobart yelled, picking up the wrench and running toward them.

Jerry turned his rage on him. "What the fuck am I paying you lazy bastards for? Why the hell isn't anything in here?" He pointed to the empty lift in the third bay. Ralph took the opportunity to slide out of his reach.

"Hey, take it easy." Hobart hefted the wrench.

"Answer me," Jerry roared. "Why aren't you lazy bastards earning your keep?"

"There's nothing waiting, boss. 'Cepting that Mustang out back. You told us to hold off on it. Remember?"

The black rage ebbed, leaving Jerry feeling depleted. Emptier than before. He remembered all right. It was a favor, not working on the Mustang.

Without a word he went to his car and drove out of the

station so fast he left tire marks across the pavement. In the rearview mirror he could see the men staring after him. He didn't give a damn.

By the time he pulled into Sonny's parking lot he had forgotten all about them. Sonny's was dark and cool and nearly empty this early in the day. "A boilermaker," he told the barman, a skinny kid who usually washed the dishes and did odd chores. He needed oblivion, fast. The kid served him, hung around. "Hey, what'cha staring at, kid?" he snarled belligerently.

The youth mumbled something, swiped at the bar with a rag. A shadow at the other end of the bar stirred. Jerry ignored it, signaled for another drink. "Keep 'em comin', kid, until I tell you to stop."

"Drowning your sorrows?"

Jerry stiffened when he recognized the voice. He swiveled around, stared up into Richard Fortune's tortured eyes. "What's it to you? Whyn't you crawl back into your corner."

Richard sat down on the stool next to him. He watched as Jerry tilted his head back, drank the whiskey neat. "It won't help, you know. Nothing will. Believe me, I've tried."

Jerry seared him with a look of hatred that would have shriveled another man. "Don't think I didn't know about you and Deirdre. I knew, but . . ." He groaned with remembered pain. "I knew she needed other men. If it made her happy . . ." His hand balled into a fist.

"Go ahead," Richard said. "It'll probably make us both feel better."

Jerry went for him with a roar that made the skinny kid run from the room. Jerry's fist made sickening contact with Richard's face. Skin burst; blood spurted. Jerry punched him through a red haze of hate. Again and again; until his arms grew tired. Then the realization finally came that he had met no resistance. None at all.

His vision cleared. Richard lay sprawled on the floor. Jerry grabbed his shirt and shook him. "What the fuck's the matter with you? I could've killed you, you crazy bastard.

286

Do you want to die?"

Richard tried to answer, but his voice was weak. Jerry bent down and listened, listened to what Richard had to say. When the voice stopped, Jerry let him drop. Richard's head bounced against the hard wood of the floor. Jerry went stumbling from the bar, hating Richard more than he had before.

Hating himself even more.

Sam waited twenty minutes to make sure Alison was soundly asleep before getting out of bed. She sighed, but didn't awaken. Tenderly, he tucked the covers about her shoulders, the protectiveness she always evoked welling up in him. He picked up his jacket and tie, bent down for his shoes, his gaze coming to rest on the little leather book on the table by the bed. The book Adrian Blaise had given her. He took it and left the room.

The house was hushed. Everyone had gone, save for Jessie and Adele, who were busy clearing away the remnants of food and drink.

"Is she all right?" Jessie asked when she saw him.

"Yes. She's sleeping. I've got to go back to work. I'll leave her a note."

Jessie nodded. "I'll be at the inn if she needs me."

The trailer was empty. Someone had made coffee. Sam tried to avoid looking at McClain's desk, at Jennifer's covered typewriter. He settled heavily into his chair, knowing he should work, but knowing he wouldn't. Not until he had read the book.

As he had surmised, it was a diary. An old diary, the ink faded and hard to read. *Susannah Justice, 1823* was boldly written across the first page, underlined. The next page was headed January 1. Sam settled down to read.

It didn't take long. Susannah's life was filled with ordinary things: a husband, three children, a house to manage while Jedediah worked the land. She was happy, although

287

her life was hard. Work done and work to do filled the pages. Social visits were rare and greatly treasured. An epidemic of fever in early March had her fearing for the children. Three children of New Hope died. In April, Mary Jones had a sixth miscarriage. Susannah grieved.

Sam put the diary down and got up to stretch. He went to the door and opened it, saw that the rain was heavier than before, and shook his head with disgust. It was no longer a question of whether they would fall behind schedule; now it was a matter of how much. In the distance he could see Tommy Russo talking to Charlie Pugh, the civil engineer. Something would have to be done there. Russo was too inexperienced to step into McClain's shoes.

Shoving that problem to the back of his mind, he refilled his mug and went back to the diary, determined to find out why Adrian Blaise had given it to Alison.

Susannah was too busy in the spring months to write often. In the summer she grumbled about the weather. Sam riffled the pages, saw the last entry was in September. He forced himself to go back and read each page in order.

The door to the trailer banged open, startling him. Charlie Pugh came in, bringing the rain and an earthy smell from the mud clinging to his boots. A taciturn man, he nodded and went to the table along the back wall where the blueprints were kept. He selected one, then cleared his throat. "River's rising, Sam. Thought you should know."

"Shit." Another problem, this one potentially serious. He had warned them from the beginning that the old mill was too close to the riverbank. At least they had listened to reason about the condominiums and mall. They would be situated far back, safe from any threat of flood. "Have the men pull all machinery back. If it continues to rise I'll have to contact the boys upstairs. Let them decide how much effort they want to put into saving the mill."

"Sounds good to me." Charlie went out, leaving mud clumps on the floor.

Sam returned to New Hope, 1823. September was a rainy

288

month. Harvest was upon them. Susannah worried, at first because Jedediah did, but later because the entire town did. The rain caused the river to rise. Sam hunched his shoulders; it made uncomfortable reading. Save for the time of year, the circumstances were eerily parallel.

He found out just how close they were in the next entry. It was all there; everything Mary Beth Winslow had chronicled, only firsthand. Susannah wrote of the night of the big storm, the fear that gripped the town, the heroic effort to save the mill from flood and landslide. Her joy when they succeeded was only exceeded by the wonder of not losing their crops. " *'Tis a miracle. Truly,*" she wrote.

The deaths began two days later. Patience Breed was found dead beneath *"a Wondrous Gate, newly erected by an Unknown Hand."* Mary Jones, pregnant again, died soon after, as did Rebecca Alderbrook, wife of Noah, and Dinah Leavitt, sister of Ezra, proprietor of the general store.

Susannah was nervous, more so because Jedediah had turned sullen and withdrawn, sure signs to a loving wife that something was wrong. She confronted him, cajoled, threatened, finally pleaded, until he talked. *"It is too Terrible, Diary, to write. They have done an Abomination, an Unholy Thing. I fear for Jedediah. I fear for myself."*

There was one more entry. September 19th. Sam stabbed his hand through his hair and resumed reading. Susannah's faded writing took him back to a dark night when she sat anxiously waiting for Jedediah to return. *"This Night it is Over, Diary. At Last! James Jones has taken his Own Life. Hung himself. over the Grief of losing Mary. Silas Parrott fetched Jed to help with the Burial. Although I cannot Rejoice that James is Dead, he is the Fifth, and Jed assures me that is the Number Adrian Blaise requires to satisfy his Unholy Lust. That and the new Name for the Town. DRACONIA. After Tonight the World shall know we Belong to the Devil."*

Sam carefully closed the diary and stared into space. Susannah wrote of five victims: Patience, Mary, Rebecca,

Dinah, and James. *Vera, Deirdre, Rufus, Lucy, and Jennifer.* Sacrificed to Adrian Blaise. Was it his vanity that prompted him to give the diary to Alison? Or was it for some other reason?

Questions. Questions without answers. What of Susannah? Why did the diary stop with that last, telling entry?

Another question, but perhaps this one had a ready answer. Making a swift decision, he found the telephone book and easily located the number he wanted. Then he placed the call.

31

The telephone pulled Alison from a deep, dreamless sleep. Conditioned to dread, her stomach clenched. But then she remembered Lucy, and anger burned away fear. She stormed out of bed, fed up with being manipulated.

The air was chilly in the bedroom, colder in the hall. Clad only in scanty lingerie, her skin prickled into goose bumps. Instinctively she knew the house was empty; Sam had gone. She snatched up the receiver, expecting the worst, but it was Clare Bauer's voice that poured into her ear, murmuring condolences. Alison was so surprised, she sat down abruptly in the ladder-back chair next to the table, listening with only part of her mind, the other part busy wondering how Clare knew. Had Jessie called the office without telling her? Had Sam?

The answer came so suddenly, it made her gasp. Adrian Blaise! Following that came the next question: Why?

"Who told you about Lucy?" she snapped, rudely interrupting Clare. There was the slightest hesitation on Clare's part. Alison read her own interpretation into it. "It was Adrian Blaise. He let you know, didn't he?" It was imprudently said, yet Alison couldn't stop herself.

Again, Clare hesitated. "Mr. Metzger authorized this call, Alison. In view of your aunt's death, he thought you might wish to take some extra time, to, er, see to her estate

291

while you're up there."

Alison translated that as meaning Adrian Blaise wished to have her remain in Draconia. As if in confirmation, her palm started to itch.

"Alison? Did you hear what I said? Mr. Metzger is being very understanding. What with people starting to take vacation time, we're shorthanded as it is. Better to wrap everything up now."

To Alison's suddenly sensitive ears, Clare sounded almost desperate. Snippets of a conversation came back . . . Adrian Blaise helping Clare place her autistic grandson in a special school.

"Alison?"

"I can't think right now, Clare. You'll have to excuse me." Her voice quavered when she said good-bye. Clare belonged to the Devil.

She waited five seconds and then dialed the number of Neumann, Fox, Greenbaum, Deutsch, Metzger, and Simonson. When the receptionist answered, Alison disguised her voice by pinching her nose and asked for Winda Green, making her voice as nasal as possible. The ruse worked, for Winda answered in her business voice. "Winda, it's Alison," she said. "Please don't say my name. It's important."

"May I help you?"

If Winda had been in front of her, Alison would have thrown her arms around her and hugged, "Listen. Clare Bauer just called and as much as told me to stay here."

"I don't think I quite understand."

Alison squeezed her eyes shut. This was the hard part, saying it out loud. "Winda, Lucy died. The funeral was this morning." Winda drew her breath in sharply, but mercifully didn't say anything. "Did you know?"

"I'm sorry."

"Then you didn't know?"

"No, I didn't, and I don't see . . ." Winda caught herself, then went on, her voice even once more, carefully impersonal. "I think you'd better explain."

"You're not going to believe it."

"Try."

Alison talked. There was silence when she finished—total, unnerving, *dead* silence. Then Winda sighed. Alison braced against being told she was crazy and needed psychiatric help. She supposed that was what she herself would advise a friend telling such a tale. All at once she couldn't bear another second's wait. "Well? What do you think? Crazy, huh?"

"Probably."

Alison felt as if she had just been punched in the stomach. If you left out the fantastic—the death coach, the Devil's dandy dogs, the Devil himself—you still had the incontrovertible fact that five people had died. Five. Perhaps Winda hadn't understood that, given the incredible nature of the other information. "But—"

"But there is no sense in taking chances. Leave. Leave that place. PDQ."

Alison hung up, shivering with more than the cold. Winda had confirmed her own conclusion: she must leave Draconia with all haste. But first, she had one more call to make. She dialed the number, and while she waited, stared at the glowing mark in the center of her palm.

When Sam got to the cemetery Bertha was already there. He had a momentary qualm when he saw her through the rain stippling the windshield of her ancient Buick. She looked every one of her eighty-three years. What the hell was he doing involving an old lady in this madness?

Bertha didn't give him long to agonize over the question. She motioned for him to get in the car, and when he did, held out her hand. He placed the diary in it, opened to the significant entry. Bertha read Susannah's faded writing carefully, moving her finger down the page, occasionally saying a word aloud. When she finished she closed the slim volume and handed it back to Sam.

"Four women and one man. The same as now." Bertha shifted in the seat so that she could look out the side window. "Poor Lucy was right after all. And I doubted her." She inhaled deeply, then let the breath rattle out in a loud sigh. "Thank goodness it's over."

"Is it?"

"Why, you read the diary. Susannah specifically said five victims were all he took."

"That we know about." Sam struggled to keep his voice calm, to keep the nagging worry that ate at him from overwhelming his ability to reason. Bertha shifted uncomfortably, reacting to his palpable tension. "What happened to Susannah? Why did she stop writing in her diary? Why did Adrian Blaise give it to Alison?"

Bertha's face took on a pinched look. She reached for her cane and umbrella. "Susannah's in there." She nodded toward the cemetery. "You'll have an answer soon enough."

Alison had been right when she told him that Bertha knew the cemetery. Going slowly, hampered by the slickness of the wet grass, she nevertheless led Sam straight to the spot where Susannah lay. The small, thin slate stone, greened by lichen, canted to one side. Two rosettes, representing immortality, were joined by a leafy vine across the rounded top. Beneath, the inscription was hard to read.

SUSANNAH
Wife of
JEDEDIAH JUSTICE
Died Sept. 19th, 1823
AE. 29

Bleakness threaded Sam's voice, bleakness and sorrow, even though Susannah had long ago gone back to dust. "She died that night, the night she made the last entry in the diary." Then fear gripped him, black, numbing, wholly consuming, making it difficult for him to breathe. "There were six victims. She was number six." He bent down and traced the date with his fingers. "She thought she was safe. Poor Susannah."

Bertha sniffed. "Five women. One man. The man hung himself." She took one look at Sam's face and sniffed again. "Now, don't you let your imagination go running away with you. We know nothing for certain." Her attention was caught by something in the right lower part of the tombstone. Using her cane, she pushed aside the long grass that covered the base. "What's that? You're going to have to do the bending, boy."

Sam got down on one knee, heedless of the moisture seeping through his pants. "There's something else chiseled into the stone. Part of it has sunk beneath the ground." As he spoke, his hands were busy, pulling out clumps of grass, digging the earth away from the stone. Finally he removed enough of the hard earth to see the inscription. He drew his breath in sharply, rocked back upon his heels.

Bertha, grown impatient, prodded him on the arm with the tip of the cane. "Move aside, boy. I can't rightly see." Sam got up and stepped out of the way. Bertha squinted, then frowned. "What is it? I can't seem . . ." Suddenly she tapped the tombstone with her cane. "Why, it's a V. Now why would they put that there? Unless they didn't mean it, seeing as how it's so far down, away from everything else."

"Oh, they meant it all right." Sam clenched his jaw so hard his teeth ached. "It's a Roman numeral. It stands for five. Susannah was the fifth."

Vera. Deirdre. Lucy. Jennifer.

Neither one of them had to say the names aloud. They wove through the air, silent, sad ghosts.

Bertha, ever practical, turned to the left. "The Alderbrook plot is over that way. Susannah mentioned Rebecca. Let's go see if there is a mark on her tombstone."

Sam knew where the Alderbrooks were buried, remembered all too well. The image of Vera wouldn't go away.

"She was only twenty, poor girl," Bertha said when they stood before Rebecca's grave. "She died on September 17th."

"Two days before Susannah." Sam ran his hand over the sunken stone. Rosettes and a leafy vine.

"There's no extra mark. No numeral." Bertha sounded relieved, but she was talking to Sam's back. Hunched down, he was busily scraping earth away from the base of the stone. Nothing appeared. "We're wrong," she said when he stood up. "Thank goodness. I've never been so happy to be proved wrong."

Sam looked around. "I need something to dig with. This stone has sunk much deeper than Susannah's."

"Here, take my car keys. You'll find a trowel in the trunk. No, don't look at me that way, boy. I didn't know we'd be needing it today. Bought it two days ago when I got the idea to put in asters this year. I misplaced the one I've been using for years."

Sam found the garden tool and was back by the grave in no time. Bertha hadn't moved. Without a word, Sam set to work. His efforts soon revealed "I's"—three of them.

"Number three," Bertha said when Sam stepped back. Her voice sounded thin. She was trembling. "Who else are we looking for?"

"Why don't you go back to the car and turn on the heat. I'll tell you what I find."

Bertha glared. "No."

Her tone brooked no argument. Sam didn't even try.

Dinah Leavitt's tombstone was not as sunken as Rebecca's. It only took Sam a couple of minutes to reveal the mark. They stared at the Roman numeral four.

"It's the same, all right. Look at the rosettes and that vine." Sam took Bertha's arm. "We don't need to see anymore. They're all the same."

"No." Bertha stubbornly scowled at him. "We need to

296

see them all. I have my reasons."

Once again Sam didn't argue. They located Patience Breed's grave. Sam uncovered a single "I."

"One more. Mary Jones. Over that way, I believe." Bertha pointed with her cane.

It was no surprise when he found a Roman numeral two.

"That's it then. There's the mark. Mary was the second victim." He moved to the stone next to hers. "It's not her husband. I wonder where he's buried?"

"Oh, they wouldn't have put him here. Not if he died by his own hand. They couldn't put a suicide into sacred ground."

Something inside Sam snapped. "Sacred ground!" He pointed. "That's Eleazar Fortune's grave over there. That bastard and who knows how many others started this whole thing. Who knows when it will be through—if ever." He waved his arm toward the gate. "Sacred! Look over there. That thing was put up by the Devil. It's probably a portal to hell."

"I'm worried for her, too." Bertha clicked her tongue reprovingly when Sam stiffened and looked wary. "Now don't go denying it. We're both thinking the same thing. Let's start back, it's getting right chilly for an old body to be wandering about."

As they walked, Bertha talked. Sam had to stoop down under the umbrella to hear. "The first and third victims were twenty years old—Patience and Rebecca, right?" Sam nodded. "The second was Dinah, and she was thirty-eight."

"She was the fourth victim. Mary was the second."

Bertha turned, the motion bumping the umbrella into Sam. He had to put up his hand to save being poked in the eye. "Okay, but the order isn't important." They reached Bertha's car, but when he moved to open the door, she stopped him. "In a moment. I think you know what I'm getting at, but it needs to be said. *All those*

297

women were under the age of forty."

"Then you're saying that Lucy—"

"Lucy doesn't count. She thought she tricked him, but *he* tricked *her.* He's a loathsome, lying beast. Poor Lucy should have remembered that." Moisture pooled in her eyes, but she blinked it away and confronted Sam with her usual tartness. "Your friend Rufus doesn't count, and neither does Lucy. There have only been three victims. Don't you see? Three."

Although fear burned like a fiery finger in his gut, he tried to calm her. "We don't know that for a fact. You yourself just said it. The Devil is a trickster. We can't know anything for sure." In his mind's eye he saw the blood-red mark on Alison's hand, a similar one on Michele's. He remembered Jennifer, scratching her palm.

"You and I know he wants Alison. I'm afraid I'm too old to do anything about it. You're young, boy. Take her and run. If you have to, run to the ends of the earth. Don't let the fiend get Alison." *Don't let him get Alison."*

"Leave? Have you lost your mind?" Michele sucked in her breath, looked apologetically at Alison. "I'm sorry, I know you're under stress."

"It's okay. Let's talk on the way." Alison firmly steered Michele out of Lucy's house and into her car. She felt better the instant the motor roared to life and they drove away.

"Where are we going?" Michele eased her foot off the accelerator.

"Drive," Alison ordered. "We're going to get your children." She checked her watch. "School doesn't let out for forty minutes. Is Tiffany with a sitter? We'd better pick her up first."

"I dropped her off with Ed's mother. I didn't know what else to do. You sounded desperate when you called."

"I was. I am."

Michele swerved to the side of the road and turned off the engine. "I'm not going anywhere until you tell me what this is all about. You're scaring me."

Alison grabbed her friend's right hand, turned it palm up. Then she lifted her own. "Take a good look, Michele. We've both been branded."

Michele snatched her hand away, curled her fingers into her palm. "I don't know what you're talking about."

"Cut the crap. This is me. Your friend. Oh, God, there's no time. Listen, Michele, I know you've got something going with Adrian Blaise—"

"Alison, I'm warning you. There's nothing—"

"And there's nothing you can say that will make me believe otherwise. Stop lying, at least to yourself. Your life's on the line."

"No!" Michele's green eyes darkened with emotion. She shook her head vehemently. "No! He wouldn't—"

"Oh yes he would. It's exactly what he *would* do. Adrian Blaise is a monster. A demon. He's the Devil himself."

"No!"

"Yes! I know what he does to you. I know all about it. He seduces you. He can do anything he wants with you. With him you know passion, like never before, like with no one else. Right? *Right?*"

Michele averted her face. Alison whispered the words that hurt, yet might save a life. "Vera. Deirdre. Jennifer. You've heard the rumors. They're true—every last one of them. It's his way. He seduces, then kills. *And you and I are on the list.*"

Michele whirled around, green eyes blazing through a haze of tears. "What about you? Has he gotten into your pants? You're jealous! That's it, isn't it?"

Alison took a deep breath. "No." *But if he gets close enough to touch me, if he places only one finger on my skin, I know I'll be lost.* All at once it was an effort to continue. Something treacherous within her whispered how easy it would be to give in. *He offers pleasure beyond your wildest imagining. He'll get you, you know he will. Why bother to fight?* "No!" she said forcefully, whether to herself or Michele, she had no way of knowing.

Huge, glistening tears were running down Michele's cheeks. "What about Lucy? Wasn't she a bit long in the tooth for an affair?"

"Stop it!" Alison reached out and touched Michele. "This isn't you. This is the poison he spreads. Think. You'll know I'm right."

Michele wiped her eyes, started the engine, and violently jerked the lever into gear. She started to turn the car around.

Alison gripped her arm. "I'm not going back. I can't make you leave, but I'll be damned if I'll stay." She laughed.

"It's not funny. You sound—"

"Crazy? Perhaps. Look, there's no time. If you won't come with me, please take me to Treadwell's. If my car isn't ready I'll hitch a ride out of town."

Michele brought the car to a screeching halt in front of the gas pumps. A bell sounded, alerting the attendant to a customer. "What about Sam? Ed and I thought that maybe you two . . You know."

Alison *did* know. She hadn't been able to reach him, so she left a note. "He wasn't at work when I called and there's no time to track him down. He's in no danger, Michele. Just you and me." She thrust her palm in front of Michele's face. "Take a good look. There's no denying it." Swiftly she opened the door and got out. Michele stared at her through the window, then drove away.

"Hey, where'd the car go?"

Alison turned at the sound of the voice. A blond youth was staring at her. "I've come for my car. The Mustang that was in the accident. Where is it?"

"It ain't ready yet." The youth pushed the hood of his rain-wet parka back, scratched the hair above his ear.

It was then that Alison realized how hard it was raining,

300

that she was standing in the downpour without an umbrella, without even a raincoat. "Where's Jerry?"

He shifted his feet. "He came back a coupla hours ago. Looked like sh— uh, said not to bother him none." He wilted under Alison's stare. "He's around back, ma'am."

"Thank you." Alison walked around the pumps and headed toward the back of the garage. If Jerry hadn't finished her car, maybe he could let her have a loaner. If not, she would just have to hitch to one of the larger towns, then rent a car. She had to surround herself with people. The Devil couldn't send a pack of dandy dogs after her in a crowd. Could he?

She rounded the corner of the building. There was her Mustang, gaping holes where the windshield and the left rear window should have been. There was no sign of Jerry.

"Damn!" she said, and turned to go. That was when she saw the movement, saw it and registered it, long before she opened her mouth and screamed. The screaming went on and on, sounding like it was coming from someone else, unceasing as she went around the car, up to the tree. The tree where Jerry Treadwell hung. The screaming continued—high, harsh, desperate . . . all the time her eyes went from the shoes, up the legs, past the hands, the arms, the shoulders, the neck . . . To the face . . . black with congested blood . . . the tongue . . .

Black and red and yellow swam in a haze before her eyes. Mercifully the screaming stopped the second she hit the ground.

Sam waited until Bertha's car disappeared around a curve in the road, then instead of going to his own car, he turned around and went back inside the cemetery. There were some things he wanted to see.

His feet squelched down into mud. The ground could no longer absorb moisture. Pools of water had formed where the graves were sunken. He squinted up at the mountains, hoping to see some sign of clearing, but fog had drifted down to form a low ceiling. When he looked toward the back of the cemetery he saw that it also wreathed the gate.

A coldness coursed through him. He told himself it was drenched clothing on clammy skin. It was only part of the truth.

He knew the way now. Still, the going was rough, the ground slick, moisture-laden bushes clawing at his clothing. He passed the graves of the Civil War dead. The flags near their footstones drooped limply, too wet to unfurl.

Eleazar Fortune's large marble tombstone drew him. Eleazar had outlived Susannah and Rebecca and the other three, outlived them by twenty-nine years, the total of Susannah's life, to die at the age of sixty-seven. "I hope you suffered, you bastard. I hope you remembered every day of your life, every second of every day, what you started here. I hope the memory tortured you."

The anger within him was growing, feeding like a cancer on his fear. What Eleazar Fortune had started over a hundred years ago was still going on.

He hunched his shoulders and walked away, toward the far humbler Justice plot. Skirting Susannah's grave he searched for Jedediah's, nearly missing it, finding it by tripping over an edge. It was a plain slab, no decoration, sinking at an angle down into the earth, almost as if Jedediah were pulling it into his grave.

Sam hunkered down, pulled up a clump of grass, used it to clean the face of the stone of pebbles and mud. When the date of death came clear, he stared. September 19, 1823. "Did you die trying to save her?" he whispered, knowing in that instant he would protect Alison with his life. Then he hung his head, thought of three children orphaned in one terrible night.

"No!" he screamed, at an appalling thought. Quickly he scanned the area, searching for other markers, smaller markers, such as had been used for children. To his relief he didn't find any with the name Justice. Susannah and Jedediah had had some luck in that then.

The fury within him now began to burn with a fiercer flame. Swiftly he made his way to the rear of the cemetery, easily vaulted over the stone wall.

The wind picked up, moaned an eerie song. It played through the trees, rustled the bushes, made the fog writhe and swirl. The gate loomed out of the murky half-light, shrouded in tattered mist.

He walked up to it and grabbed the smooth black bars. Around him, the air was still. Nothing moved; there was no sound. Beyond the gate he could see the swaying trees, the scudding fog. His hands tightened on the bars. "I'll get you!" he screamed into the dead air. His voice didn't sound; he heard it only in his head.

Sam gripped the black bars tighter and shook so hard his muscles ached, until at last he let go and stepped back. Ghostly laughter teased him.

He walked away, knowing he would be back.

Bertha would have liked nothing more than to have a glass of wine. It would chase the chill from her bones; perhaps would help her bear the burden she carried in her heart. Resolutely she drove past the inn. It was too soon. She hadn't yet completely come to terms with the knowledge that Lucy would never come back.

On the edge of town she passed Draconia's volunteer ambulance, sirens blaring and lights flashing. There was a crowd of people milling around the gas station. Pulling up at one of the pumps, Bertha struggled out of the car, juggling her cane and umbrella.

The mayor and Everett Hale were standing in front of the office. J. Norbert was subdued, his flesh pallid, hanging from him as if it had been stretched and then had failed to return to its original shape. Everett, however,

303

looked feverish, excitement making him hop from foot to foot.

Bertha wasted no words. "What's going on here?"

Everett could hardly wait to tell her. "Jerry's gone and hung himself. Right out back."

Bertha recoiled from his ghoulish enthusiasm. "He was in the ambulance?"

J. Norbert shivered. "Yes. I told them not to use the siren and lights."

"Yeah, Jerry's in no hurry," Everett said, showing his teeth in a humorless smile. Bertha clicked her tongue disapprovingly. Undaunted, Everett turned to the mayor. "As I was saying, Bert, I don't know why they put him in the ambulance. The girl would get more use out of it, to my way of thinking."

"Henry knows what he's doing" the mayor replied.

"What girl?" Bertha asked at the same time, although from the cautious way Bert was looking at her, she knew she wasn't going to like the answer.

"Now, don't go getting yourself upset. She wasn't hurt. Just had the bad luck of finding him."

"Alison," Bertha said in a flat tone, and leaned heavily on her cane. "What was she doing here? Do you know?"

"Came to get her car, according to the attendant, young Fred," Everett supplied helpfully. "Said she screamed so loud he thought she was being gang raped, er, beg your pardon." He was apologizing to thin air, for Bertha was already on her way.

"She's not here, Bertha," J. Norbert called out. "Henry took her to his house." Bertha stopped and turned to look at him. "She only fainted. She'll be all right."

"Thank you, Bert." Their eyes met, then the mayor's shifted away. Bertha returned to her old Buick as fast as she could. No longer could she remain passive. She was old, but she would do what she could to put an end to the slaughter. She owed it to Lucy to try. It was the mill, of course. Everything came back to that. To do something, though, she was going to need help and she knew just where to find it.

Fred, blond hair plastered to his forehead, blue eyes alight with macabre interest, came running up. "Fill 'er up? Did you hear what happened? I found her—"

Bertha brushed him out of her way with her cane, wielding it like a saber. She drove straight to Sonny's Tavern, exceeding the town's speed limit for the first time.

Amos Hubbard was at the bar. He regarded Bertha with little enthusiasm as she thumped the floor with her cane, attracting the barman. "Chablis," she ordered. "Bring it to a booth."

Amos snickered, then was sorry he had, for Bertha transferred her attention to him. He didn't care for the look in her eye, not one little bit.

"We must talk. Now. We have to think of some way to stop him."

Amos knew who she meant, knew it by his body's instant reaction. Liquid gurgled through his intestines. "G'way," he mumbled. In his mind he saw the dismembered head, the gruesome wink.

Undeterred, Bertha pushed her face close to his. "We're both too old to be afraid."

Amos thought of the big black horse, his raw, bleeding stump of a neck, the whip cracking down into the gore. He shuddered.

Bertha seemed to understand. She put her hand on his arm. "There's nothing to the dying, Amos, nothing to be afraid of. It's what comes after I fear. Lucy tried. I can't do less. Can you?"

She turned away and headed for the booth where the boy had placed her glass of wine. Reluctantly, with much misgiving, Amos followed.

32

Alison awoke to darkness in a small, unfamiliar room. More asleep than awake, she heard the sound of rain beating against the window. With it came the faint tinkle of bells. Disoriented, she sat up and swung her legs over the side of the bed, discovering she was fully clothed. She strained to remember where she was, but her brain was sluggish and . . .

A frantic mewling sound caught in her throat as memory flooded her—awful, paralyzing in its terrible clarity. Jerry's corpse dangled in her mind's eye before she could shut it out. No man should die that way, should inflict such a death upon himself. What demons had driven him? A low, bitter sound escaped her. The demon had a name and she knew him well. She had been running from the fiend when she found Jerry . . . The rest of her memory returned and she knew that Henry had taken her to his house, given her a sedative and . . .

Run! There was no time to waste.

Alison jumped up, swayed dizzily for a moment, and staggered against a table. She grabbed the edge until the world straightened, then swept her hand over its surface, located a lamp, and clicked it on just as someone knocked on the door.

Sam walked in, closed the door, and stood with his

back against it, taking in her appearance with a fast but thorough appraisal. The shock of finding Jerry was apparent in her pale complexion. He had expected that, but not the signs of incipient panic that made her slender body tremble, threatening to snap her control.

He was trying to find the right words when she seized the initiative. "I called you. There was no answer." The tone was accusatory.

"I know. I saw the note." He reached into his pocket and pulled out the diary. "I took this while you were asleep. I think you'd better read the entries for September."

Alison sank down on the edge of the bed. While she read she unconsciously pushed the hair behind her ears, touched the healing wound on her scalp. When she finished she closed the diary and looked at Sam expectantly.

"I was in the cemetery with Bertha when you called. Susannah was the fifth victim. She died the night she wrote that last entry."

The ethereal sound of wind chimes, wildly dancing, echoed through the house. The window curtains billowed out.

Alison looked about, saw her handbag on the table, and picked it up. "I've got to leave. I was on my way when I found . . ." She closed her eyes and willed Jerry's swaying corpse to fade. "Oh, God, Sam, I've got to get out of Draconia!" Quickly she told him about Clare, about Winda . . . about Michele.

Sam held out his hand. "Come on."

Henry was waiting, standing watchful in the dimness of the hall.

"We're leaving," Sam said. His voice sounded overly loud in the hushed atmosphere.

They all swung about at the sound of a floorboard squeaking. Dottie descended to the foot of the stairs and stood there, her arms wound tightly about her chest. Alison stared at her ravaged face, a face with grief etched so deeply, it had grown old overnight. Henry put his arm around her waist, winced when bells danced in a sudden draft.

"Demons are afraid of bells. They flee . . ." Dottie let her voice fade.

The tinkling followed them out into the night. It was raining even harder than before. The comfort of the big car was familiar to Alison now. At the end of the driveway Sam stopped and let it idle. He pulled her to him, kissed her roughly, then put the car back in gear. "Let's see what we can do."

After a while Sam turned on the radio, selected a station playing light classical music. Neither one of them spoke. Alison hardly dared to breathe. Could it be as easy as this?

The road wound before them, a wet black snake.

When it happened, Alison didn't realize what it was. She felt a bump, heard Sam curse, but felt no fear. That came later.

"We've got a flat," Sam said, interrupting his stream of blue words to explain. He maneuvered to the shoulder, shut off the engine, but left the headlights on.

"Do you have a spare?" Surely they could change the tire, be on their way again.

"Yes, I've got a spare." He sounded tired. Exhausted. *Defeated.*

Alison followed him out into the rain and stared at the highway. That was when she felt the fear, felt it slam into her, snatching her breath, robbing her of will.

Sam gently turned her around so she could see the road behind, then waited for her to face forward again. "It's a one-way road, sweetheart."

It was a beautiful sight. A deadly sight. Sharp, protruding, jagged pieces of glass studded the roadway as far as the eye could see. Probably all the way to hell.

The night loomed empty and endless to Michele. She hated the rain, hated to be alone, although technically she wasn't, for the children slept upstairs.

Pouring a glass of wine, her second after dinner, she took it into the den. She drank too much, but it was something to do during the long, lonely evenings when Ed wasn't home. The first thing she did was draw the drapes across the glass doors leading to the patio, closing out the night, the rain.

Had her feelings of dissatisfaction, of a lack of fulfillment, started with Ed's late hours? Or had they been born the first time she saw Adrian Blaise?

She shivered with the memory. She had been ripe for him, ripe for the plucking. Adrian, with his beguiling eyes, his fiery touch, his knowledge of how to pleasure, had only to crook his finger and she came running. He was the perfect lover. Giving. Taking. Sharing. Teaching . . . Oh, the things he had taught her, the joys of the flesh, sensual, sexual things that she never would have experienced without him.

Damn Alison! Michele gulped the wine, needing to feel a buzz, needing her reality softened. Of course her affair with Adrian was wrong. It was wrong, but it was necessary. Without him she was dead inside—a shell, with no hope. With Adrian she was alive.

Dreamily, she let her head fall back upon the couch, closed her eyes. The rain drummed against the window, lulling, soothing, hypnotic. Tapping a gentle rhythm . . .

The world fuzzed, tilted. Wind whispered . . . *Vera. Deirdre. Jennifer. Lucy. Vera Deirdre Jennifer Lucy. VeraDeirdreJenniferLucyVeraDeirdreJenniferLucy.*

"No! Go away!" Michele shouted. To the voice of the wind. To the image of Alison, eyes wide, fearful, sure—

so very sure—of deadly peril. Michele rubbed her itchy palm against her thigh, tossed off the rest of the wine.

From upstairs came the bang of a shutter, followed by a sharp cry, which quickly escalated into a wail.

Michele ran upstairs. Tiffany sat in the middle of her bed, the pretty big-girl's bed with the canopy of dotted swiss. Her eyes were round with terror, her mouth open in an endless howl. Outside her window a pin oak groaned under the weight of the wind, rapped with knobby knuckles against the panes.

As Michele secured the shutter, the rain drenched her head and arms. She lowered the shade and went to the bed, gathered the little girl close. "Hush, baby, it's all right. It's only a storm."

Tiffany clung, whimpering. "Big dogs," she cried, "with red eyes."

"A dream. You had a bad dream," Michele crooned, trying to recall where she had heard about them, but her brain was clouded by wine and she couldn't remember.

Tiffany's terror gradually gave way to sleepiness. Michele tucked her in, kissed her cheek, inhaled the baby-powder scent of innocence. She left Tiffany hugging her teddy bear.

The boys slept undisturbed. Adam lay on his side, the covers thrown back, completely exposed to the damp night air. Michele rolled him to one side, pulled the sheet and blanket out from under him and around his thin body. She brushed the hair off his forehead, planted a kiss. Then she tiptoed across the room. Brian was a small, boy-size mound under the covers. Michele unearthed him, kissed his cheek, and smiled when he sighed and rolled over.

The hallway and stairs were steeped in shadows. The house shook under the assault of the storm. Michele hurried through the murk, detoured through the kitchen, came into the den, a full glass of wine in hand . . . and stopped.

He was waiting for her, a smile lighting his dark, beautiful face. Wine sloshed over the rim of the glass, spilled over her fingers. It occurred to her to ask how he came to be there, but the magnetic pull he exerted brushed it from her mind. He was her lover; he brought the nepenthe she craved; she wouldn't—couldn't—stop to question, not when he offered surcease from all sorrow and worry, rounded the hard edges of life.

Her breath caught in her throat. Something was different tonight. Reproachful green eyes met blazing black ones. What she saw there made the fire that he had kindled inside her turn to ice. Instantly sober, without the mantle of alcohol to soften the blow, she read her fate. "Bastard," she hissed, but he paid no heed.

Moving to the glass doors, he drew back the drapes. The scene revealed was culled from a nightmare. Rain and wind scoured the earth. Lightning sizzled through stygian dark, lit the world, allowed a glimpse of densely forested, impenetrable mountains hovering in the distance. Closer in, trees bent, branches bowed, snapped under the mighty strength of the gale-force wind.

It wasn't the storm that caused Michele to gasp, strangling the scream for her children's sake. It was the other, the *things* that crouched outside . . . waiting. "Adrian," she implored, hating to beg, knowing it was useless. Alison had known, had given fair warning. But she, besotted and blind, had paid no heed. Now she was going to pay.

"Mom . . . my." The thin, frightened wail drifted through the house. "Mom . . . my. Mommy!" Demanding, imperative, the little girl's voice was joined by a baying, a chorus of howls that shriveled Michele's soul.

In that instant Michele knew she would do anything, but a part of her still wished to believe. Silently she entreated him, her erstwhile lover, the fiend in human

311

guise. He smiled.

Fear fled, swept out by an icy calm. She would slay the dragon and save her child, even though it meant giving up her own life. "Run, Tiffany! Run away!" she cried. Swiftly she bent, snatched up the wineglass from the floor, cracked it against the edge of a table. Then she sprang straight for him, brandishing the jagged glass.

A primal yell escaped her as she went for the kill. Suddenly an unholy din rent the fabric of the night as the glass doors imploded, shattered into fragments under the force of hurtling bodies. They crashed inside, the creatures of the night, impervious to the flying glass, bringing with them the wind and the rain and the stench of the fiery pit.

Michele opened her mouth to scream again, but the shower of glass was deadly. A sharp-pointed sliver embedded itself in her neck. The scream became a moan, a gurgle, a final, silent quiver. Her bright emerald eyes dulled.

The beasts milled about, whining, denied their prey. Their master snapped his fingers, herded them away. The hunt had just begun.

"We're trapped!" Alison cried as full realization hit her.

"Not yet we're not. Wait here a second." Sam got the flashlight and ran back to her. "Come on. We walk." He grabbed her hand and started down the road.

Glass crunched under their feet. They used the light from the headlights to find their way until they rounded a bend. Then Sam switched on the flashlight, played its beam from side to side. He figured Draconia to be about a quarter of a mile ahead. Alison had a tight grip on his hand. He squeezed it and picked up the pace, mumbling under his breath.

"What did you say?" She had to raise her voice to be

heard above the storm.

"Why didn't the state run this road through the notch?" It had always puzzled Sam that it dead-ended at the Devil's Dam. To get out of the notch they had to pass through town. "Every one of the other notches has a thruway. Do you know why an exception was made with Draconia?"

"No, I never gave it much thought. I—Oh!" She tugged Sam's hand excitedly as the lights of Draconia beckoned. "Let's go!" she shouted. Before he could make a move to stop her, she dropped his hand and ran ahead.

"Wait! Alison! Wait for me!"

She turned and motioned him to hurry. That was when he felt a tremor beneath his feet and heard a mighty roaring noise. It boomed through the dark, evoking a primal terror so great that he froze with superstitious dread.

"Alison!" he screamed as the ground bucked and the force threw him off his feet. The booming sound escalated and the earth shook until suddenly, in the space of a heartbeat, everything stopped.

Sam lifted his head. Quiet. Stillness. Except for the rain and the wind. *Too* quiet. He pushed himself to his knees, looked about wildly, his breath catching in his throat when he saw Alison sprawled on the road. He staggered upright, went stumbling toward her, only marginally aware that something was different; something to do with the road.

She was already stirring when Sam reached her. He pulled her into a tight hug before helping her to her feet; one part of him was still trying to figure out what had changed.

"What happened?" Alison asked.

"Landslide, just the other side of town, if I don't miss my guess," he said, and swore as he stared at the road, finally identifying what was wrong.

313

"Sam, look!" Alison was quicker than he was. She pointed at the road. The glass had disappeared. "This means that we can get through. We'll fix the tire—"

"Sweetheart, no. The landslide has sealed us in. Draconia is a dead end."

Of course.

33

September 1823
Draconia

Eleazar Fortune

The day was crisp and bright and sunny, not a cloud in the sky. Soon the forests would turn to red, then to burnished gold and orange, blazing in glory as the leaves died and left the trees barren for winter. In the spring there would be a rejuvenation.

But people were not trees.

Eleazar Fortune wandered through the cemetery, stopping at each new mound of raw earth. A brisk wind blew through the burying ground, stirring the leaves already fallen, urging others to drop from their branches and fly away. It would soon dry the mud, leaving the earth hard and caked. There were no markers yet, they were still being carved, but he knew each grave. It was over, the dying, but the bitter gall of its memory would not go away, would never go away.

His rambling walk ended in the same place it had yesterday; in the same place it would tomorrow. He always saved them for the last. The two graves snuggled side by side, a grim parody of how their occupants had lain in their marriage bed.

Jedediah and Susannah Justice.

Eleazar's broad shoulders slumped in sorrow under the pain of remembering how they had found Jedediah, lying in a pool of congealed blood, his body mutilated,

315

scoured by claw marks, his throat . . .

"I'm sorry, Jedediah, old friend," he murmured, "we didn't know, didn't guess. He's a lying snake. We know that now." He drew a deep breath and slowly let it out. Every day he tried to find an explanation for Jedediah—for himself. "You did what you had to, tried to defend her, but nothing could have saved Susannah."

He raised his face to the blue dome of sky and roared his pain and sorrow and remorse. Nothing was worth the terrible price they had paid. He beseeched the heavens for a sign that all could be made right. Dark laughter drifted to him, filled his head, twined around his shrinking soul, told him how futile was his effort.

Eleazar lowered his eyes, left the beauty of the blue sky, the purity of the light. These were not for him, ever again. He was not surprised to see Adrian Blaise leaning nonchalantly against the new gate, the obscene symbol of their fall from grace. Slowly he made his way to him.

For a moment, as he neared him, Adrian seemed to loom to a great size, then appeared once again as he had.

Eleazar felt a strange little quiver, deep in his gut. Surely he was nothing but a man? How could it be otherwise?

Then Adrian smiled.

The smile told Eleazar everything. All he feared was very real. "I want to make an end, an end to this unholiness," he cried, so loudly he startled a flock of small sparrows into flight.

"You made a pledge."

"Aye."

"Is your word not good, then?"

Eleazar looked him straight in the eye. He had lost everything; there was nothing more. "Better than yours, I'm thinking. The terms were not clear. Twenty-three men pledged to you, but you—you took our women. Our women! Vileness." Again the dark laughter squeezed his soul. Eleazar stood his ground, wondered, not for the

316

first time, how evil could be so fair of face.

As before, Adrian read his mind. "I am what you want, what you have made me. No more. Look well upon me. You see yourself."

The gate silently opened, then closed. Adrian was gone.

Rage filled Eleazar, mottling his face a purplish crimson. The veins of his neck bulged into twisted blue snakes, pulsing and writhing to the beat of his hate. He raised his fist to the gate. "Hear my pledge! I'll make this right. If it takes eternity, I'll see to it."

The wind swirled into an eddy about Eleazar. Dark laughter filled his head, mocking him. He knew it would be with him all the days of his life.

34

The Present — Wednesday, June 19
Draconia

"What now?" Alison asked.

Sam's tone was grim. "We find another way out."

"Susannah wrote of a landslide. It . . . it cut off the road. It took them more than two days to dig free."

"They didn't have earth movers." Sam pointed. "See that, those downed poles. They carry live wires. Whatever you do, don't touch them. They're the most immediate danger, but you also have to watch out for ruptured gas lines, sewer pipes, telephone lines . . ." Unspoken was the caveat: *If we should be separated.*

Alison shut her mind to the possibility. She started to walk toward town, but he caught her arm.

"I don't think that's a good idea. We've got to get out now. It'll take too long to break through."

His urgency communicated itself to Alison. "How, then?"

"I think our best bet is to head for Black Bear Junction. It's the shortest route to the outside." All they had to do was hike over Dragon Mountain . . . after they changed the tire and drove to the trailhead at the Devil's Dam. Dragon Mountain offered the shortest, most accessible route to the outside, to a town that didn't bear the Devil's name.

It only took a second for Alison to make up her mind.

"Let's go."

Sam put the spare on the car in record time, tossed the tools in the trunk and had the engine running before he closed his door. Water rippled across the macadam, sprayed up from the wheels as he made a U-turn and headed back into the notch.

They drove past the turnoff to the inn, then past Dragon Meadow. Briefly he wondered if Russo had called the men in earlier, was trying to salvage the old mill from the flooding river. Russo wasn't McClain . . . Soon the complex was behind them. Sam resolutely put it out of his mind. Survival was all he could afford to think about now.

Alison stiffened when the cemetery came into view, but couldn't drag her gaze away. The only light was from their own headlights, illuminating the low stone wall and the headstones closest to it . . .

NOT AGAIN! OH, GOD, NOT AGAIN!

For long seconds Alison sat frozen in disbelief, then her body started functioning again and, as if from a great distance, she heard herself scream.

Startled out of intense concentration, Sam quickly glanced over at her, then swung his eyes back to the road just as something big thundered out of the gray torrent. He had no time to think, only to react as it came at them, head on. He jerked the wheel to the right. They slued around as a big black coach dashed by and disappeared into the swirling mist.

Sam regained control, brought the car to a stop at the side of the road. He noticed his hands were shaking when he reached for Alison. No longer screaming, she was staring at him with unfocused eyes. He gripped her shoulders and shook her roughly. "Come on, come back. I need you." She blinked and awareness returned. "That's my girl."

"The death coach. You saw it?"

"I saw it." He offered her a grim smile, then put the car back into gear and inched them forward.

"Someone's dead." *Michele.* Alison knew it as surely as she knew her own name. She twisted toward Sam, her face a mask of agony. "It's Michele, isn't it?"

Sam didn't answer.

"Isn't it?" She sobbed, the tears burning her eyes, until the violent weeping gave way to a trickle. She fished in her handbag for a tissue and blew her nose. "Sam?"

"What, sweetheart?"

"You do believe now? In the Devil?"

Sam gave a short, harsh bark of laughter, thought of the big black coach with its gruesome horse and driver. "Oh, I'm a believer all right." He glanced at her. Her face was a pale oval disk in the gloom. He couldn't see her expression. "I believe in survival. I believe in you and me."

He took the turn into the parking lot for the Devil's Dam a little too fast. They skidded, the front wheels climbing the decorative stones lining the entrance. Sam started to curse, yanked the wheel hard, and gave a grunt of satisfaction when they bounced down onto the road again. He drove to the back of the lot, as close to the trail as he could, and shut off the engine.

Alison laughed nervously. "I think you're beginning to repeat yourself."

"Very funny," Sam growled, and picked up the flashlight. Then he pulled her close and kissed her deeply. "Let's go, sweetheart."

The storm was a fearsome thing. The wind slammed into them; the rain hammered against their exposed flesh. Sam fought against it, reached Alison and grabbed her arm. They staggered toward the head of the trail, grateful for whatever shelter the canopy of trees offered.

In the distance the emergency siren howled, cutting through the din of the raging storm. People were already

320

mobilizing, would come with all the technology of civilization. They would come too late for them.

The path was slippery with mud and rotting leaves and needles, made more treacherous by slick, wet stones and loose pebbles. The wind screeched unnervingly through the dense foliage. Before long Alison was breathing harshly as Sam pushed for the fastest pace she could sustain. Another landslide was possible.

Ahead they could hear a mighty roaring as tons of water poured down through the narrow gorge, over the immense tear-shaped rock, into the basin beneath . . . The pool where Jennifer had drowned.

They burst into the clearing where so many tourists had stood. Tonight no one would take pictures, would thrill to the story of a dark stranger saving a town. From here the trail went up; they would have to start climbing.

Sam stopped, told Alison to rest for a moment. She nodded gratefully and sank down onto the man-made ledge rimming the pool. He leaned over her. "You're doing fine," he said encouragingly.

Alison didn't waste her breath in a reply. The smell of wet earth filled her nostrils. All around them leaves rustled, bushes swayed. She didn't want to think what they could conceal.

"Ready?" Sam asked, and cupped her elbow, helping her rise. He faced the mountain, the cataract that foamed whitely into the churning, overflowing pool so that he couldn't see the large, dark creatures that came running out of the woods.

Alison saw them first as shifting shadows, then more clearly as the beasts of nightmare they were. She opened her mouth to scream, but no sound came out.

Sam took one look at her face and whirled around. It took less than a second to size up the situation, make a decision, act on it. He shoved Alison away and shouted at her to run.

Then he spun to face them, the pack of preternatural beasts that were already advancing, salivating as they surveyed their prey. He hefted the flashlight, a puny weapon, but it might buy some time for Alison to get away.

He now counted his life in seconds.

Tommy Russo

Tommy Russo swore and wondered for the thousandth time why Sam hadn't come. The river was rising rapidly and would soon boil over its banks and flood the whole godforsaken complex, destroying everything. And he would be to blame; merely because he was here.

The one good thing was that most of the men had come in on their own and were working to secure the site. The problem was the old mill, situated so precariously close to the river. He didn't much see the sense in saving it, but as Charlie Pugh had explained, the big-money boys considered it the focal point of the complex. Without it they wouldn't be interested in the project.

He played his flashlight over the river, trying to estimate how long they had. It could be any second, or an hour, or a day—as far as he could tell. The beam of light skipped over the inky water, picking out the angry white foam as it swirled by, sweeping logs and branches and sometimes a tree past at a dizzyingly fast pace.

Startled when a mud-covered figure loomed out of the sheeting rain, Tommy slipped and felt the sodden earth of the riverbank give way beneath his feet. A strong hand gripped his arm and hauled him back onto safer ground.

Charlie Pugh grinned at him, his teeth very white in his dirt-streaked face. "No time for a swim, boy."

Tommy was going to tell him exactly what he thought of his humor, just as soon as he could control his voice, when the night erupted into violence. The earth heaved and a nerve-shattering noise screamed through the air, drowning out all other sound.

Tommy was thrown to the ground, landed hard on his back, the air whooshing from his lungs. The mud beneath him began to slide, taking him with it, down into the river, a toboggan ride straight into a watery grave. There was no time to think, just to react. Twisting, he managed to grab some tough weeds. His arm felt like it was ripping out of its socket. He clung, his face pressed into the muck, pain scouring through him, alternately cursing and praying it would end. Whatever *it* was.

The end came so abruptly he didn't recognize it at first. The ground stopped shaking and the screaming freight-train sound ceased. Now he could hear the storm again, and the roaring of the river, but their voices were tame in comparison.

With the earth still, he was able to inch himself up, using the toes of his boots for purchase in the crumbling bank. Panting, his arm on fire, he finally hauled himself far enough up the incline to hook his other elbow over the rim. Exhausted, he rested a moment before painstakingly scrabbling the rest of the way.

The first thing he saw was Charlie, draped bonelessly over a rock. He stirred and then staggered to his feet as Tommy stumbled over to him. Completely unnerved, Tommy screamed in Charlie's ear. "What the fuck was that?"

"Slip, most likely. Big one, too, by the sound of it."

"What the fuck's a slip?" Tommy yelled, fearing that at any minute the whole thing would start again.

"It's what landslides are called in the notches. This whole area is volatile. Why, in Franconia Notch alone there have been at least eight major slides in the last five decades. You should know the area you're working, Russo."

"Yeah." On top of everything, he didn't need a history lesson.

"Could get another one, anytime now. Maybe more than one. No surprise, with all the rain we've been having."

"Yeah," Tommy said again, not feeling any better having his fear confirmed. He considered sending everyone home, each man for himself.

Charlie pointed past Russo's shoulder. "Sound came from that direction. It's a good bet the road's blocked."

"Shit," Tommy said. He'd better go have a look. But first he'd see to the men.

Scrapes and cuts and bruises comprised the injuries. No one was missing. Bobby Williams had broken a front tooth and his nose when he slammed facedown onto a rock. His nose was swollen and the skin under his eyes was already turning red. He gave Tommy a thumbs-up sign and a gap-toothed grin.

Russo sent him back to the trailer for first aid, and when he saw that the rest of the men were wet and miserable, gave them a coffee break. He stayed behind to check again that nothing was in imminent danger of collapsing.

Alone, Tommy suddenly remembered that this was where McClain had been found. With his throat torn out and his flesh chewed and . . . He swallowed convulsively, thought he saw movement from the corner of his eye. The hair rose on the nape of his neck. He swung around in a circle, wildly bobbing the flashlight up and down. The curtains of driving rain effectively concealed everything save the huge stacks of rain-soaked lumber and the hulks of glistening-wet machinery. And shadows. Shifting.

That was enough for Tommy. Shit on the responsibility. He hurried after the men, not looking back. He might see something he didn't want to.

324

The trailer's warm yellow light beckoned. About to leave the cover of the trees, Tommy stopped dead. He forgot about McClain. He forgot about the phantoms that might be at his back. He just stood and stared.

People were standing in the clearing in front of the office. Men and some women; old and young; a disparate group, united by one thing—the guns they had trained on the crew. An old lady seemed to be the leader of the gang. In one hand she held a big black umbrella, in the other a cane, pointed at the center of Charlie Pugh's chest.

This was just what he needed. Ma Barker and her gang. What the fuck did they want? He sure as hell didn't know; couldn't even guess. The only thing he *did* know was that this was the last straw. The goddamn last motherfucking straw.

35

"Sam."

That one softly spoken word froze him. *She didn't go.* It had never occurred to Sam that Alison would not go.

"There are more dandy dogs right behind me."

Rage flooded Sam, fed by the sudden loss of hope. His body twitched, he wanted to turn, but was afraid to take his eye off the dogs in front of him, lest that should trigger their attack. He kept his voice low. "Come over to me. Slowly. Easy does it."

Trapped. Nowhere to go. Nothing to do. They would never leave Draconia.

Alison crept to his side, almost hypnotized by the dogs' hideousness. The beasts avidly followed her movements, swinging their misshapen heads around.

Rain and an icy-cold sweat dripped into Sam's eyes. He didn't dare blink. He gripped the flashlight, was afraid it would slip from his moist grasp.

Any moment now.

Death seemed inevitable. The only question left was whether he could take any of the bastards with him.

Alison grabbed his arm. "I . . . I don't think they're going to kill us. Not . . . not now." Before he could say a word, she walked straight for the evil-looking pack.

Stunned, Sam followed, reaching her side within three

steps. Alison had her chin tilted upward at what he had come to regard as a Crandell angle. She took his hand and tugged him forward. The dogs snuffled and whined—but they backed away, shifting enough to allow a narrow path. A plaintive howl sliced through the night as they inched away. It was so close they could feel it cut the air. Once past the last creature, they ran.

Wet branches slapped at them as they crashed down the trail, the hellhounds in pursuit. It seemed to Alison as if they had been running forever. Her lungs screamed for air. The howling wind seemed to snatch it right out of her mouth. All of a sudden she slipped, her heart skidding into her mouth as she felt herself falling. Sam yanked her upright and dragged her until she regained her footing.

The creatures kept right on their heels, but made no move to outflank them. Sam wondered if it was a game, and if so, where it would end. Finally they burst out of the woods. He had half expected to see Adrian Blaise there, but the area was clear. The dandy dogs crashed through the trees seconds later, only to stop at the trailhead.

Sam and Alison ran free. At the car he opened the driver's door and shoved her inside, quickly following, pulling the door closed so fast he almost caught his leg. The pack came gliding out of the forest.

Sam twisted the key violently; the engine whined. He forced himself to be calm, started the car and drove away as fast as he could, sending sheets of water spraying up on both sides. The creatures paced them for a while before veering off and fading into the dark woods.

Alison started to cry. Sam put his arm around her and dragged her close. "Hush, sweetheart. Hush. You were very brave." He had to carefully control his voice to keep it from cracking. He checked the rearview mirror. There was nothing but rain, so he pulled over and stopped the car, leaving the engine running.

Now he had two arms to hold Alison. She was shivering, burrowed against him like a little furry creature seeking warmth. Warmth he could give her; it was little enough. He stroked her hair, and after a time she raised her head. "Feel better?" he asked.

"Um," she said, tucking the wet strands of her hair behind her ears. "I must look a mess."

Sam laughed. "You look beautiful. You'll always be beautiful to me." Inwardly he raged—to have found something precious . . . He groaned and tightened his arms about her, then lowered his head, seeking her lips.

But Alison pushed herself out of his embrace. "You think I'm beautiful?" Excitement glinted in her eyes.

"Very," he replied gravely. "Both inside and out."

"Sam," she said thoughtfully, "I wonder how Adrian Blaise views me. I mean, does he think I'm beautiful? Is that why he wants me? Or am I just part of the pact? That damn pact that was made in 1823."

Sam's gaze narrowed. "Not according to Susannah's diary. She specifically wrote of five victims. She was the fifth."

"Right. So there must be a new pact. Let's assume the terms are the same, since four women have died. Four young women. I'm . . . I'm not counting Lucy."

"Keep talking, sweetheart."

"I don't think *who* made the pact is important."

"Twenty-three pledged themselves to it in 1823," he said firmly.

Alison looked startled, then thoughtful. "I see. You're right. It could be more than one. I wonder . . . ?"

"Go on, you're doing just fine." Sam couldn't keep the growing excitement from his voice. Isolate the problem, analyze it . . . then act.

"It's the old mill, isn't it? This whole renovation scheme, the entire Dragon Meadow complex . . . The

328

heart of it is the old mill. My God, Sam, it's history repeating itself. Only this pact wasn't made for survival, but for profit." She began to shake, not with fear, but with rage. "It's disgusting! A real estate deal signed in blood."

A gust of wind shook the car. A keening howl pierced the storm, instantly reminding them of the present danger.

Alison clutched Sam's hand. Her fingers were ice-cold; her eyes burned hotly with excitement. "We've got to destroy the old mill! Don't you see? Without it, there can be no pact."

Sam hesitated. It wasn't that simple.

"Can you do it?"

"Alison, sweetheart . . ." He gripped her hands, held her fast when she tried to move away. "Think. If everything we know about the pact made in 1823 is true, then the Devil saved the mill by putting a rock in the gorge, creating the Devil's Dam. That stopped the mountain from sliding into the notch."

"So?"

"So, destroying the old mill wouldn't work. The Devil's part of the pact has to be abrogated. The rock has to be dislodged." He glanced out the window, at the ferocity of the storm. "Given the instability of this entire area and the rain we've had . . . it's possible that could destroy the notch and everything in it." Alison inched her chin upward. Sam stabbed his fingers through his hair. "Damn it! I'm worried about the people. We've got to warn them, ring the church bell or something."

Alison looked amused. *"Draconia* doesn't have a church. One was never built. Those who want to attend services go to the next town. For emergencies Draconia relies on a siren. I heard it go off. By now I expect most everyone's been warned. Besides, nobody could ignore that landslide."

Acid gnawed Sam's gut, but he refused to acknowledge the pain. "So let's get going. We'll need dynamite. We ordered some last month to remove some large rocks. We didn't use it all."

Alison threw her arms around his neck, hugged him hard.

Sam put the car back in gear and headed for Dragon Meadow.

Bertha felt uneasy. The situation could very easily get out of hand. Restless and afraid, it would take very little to turn the crowd of townspeople into a mob. There were too many people with guns, some of them hotheaded, like that Art Bergstrom. He looked mean, like he would enjoy hurting someone.

"Ma'am," Charlie Pugh said, striving for patience, "why don't you come inside. We can, er, discuss—"

"We ain't movin'. None of us." Amos Hubbard poked his Remington into Tommy Russo's side. "Not unless it's ta get the dynamite and go blow up the godforsaken mill. There be nothin' ta discuss. Either ya gonna do it willingly, or ya ain't. Say so, sonny," he poked Tommy again, "so's that we kin do what we got ta do. Then we kin all go home." He turned his head to the side and spit. "Iff'n we've still got one after this."

Russo silently cursed Sam for what seemed like the millionth time. *He* should be the one standing here with the business end of the old rummy's rifle in his gut.

Russo wasn't the only one wishing for Sam. Bertha leaned heavily on her cane. She had never felt so old, so useless. She looked anxiously at Charlie. Couldn't he see how tenuous her hold on the crowd was? Why couldn't he just do what they wanted? She had explained it to him, how they had to destroy the mill so that the Devil would go away.

330

"And the Devil is . . . ?" Charlie had asked.

"Adrian Blaise, that's who," Bertha had snapped, affronted by the calm tone meant to placate. There was no time to waste; the landslide had made it an imperative.

There was a rumbling in the ranks of the crowd. Outnumbered and unarmed, the crew nervously watched them.

"Settle down, folks," J. Norbert yelled. To his surprise, they did.

"Ma'am—" Charlie tried again.

"Stop stalling." Everett Hale elbowed his way forward. He had never wanted the complex, had fought it from the beginning; now he was delighted to be in on its destruction.

Dottie Cutter pushed him aside. Her eyes were wild with grief; her hair hung like wet hanks of wool. She screamed at Bertha. "We're wasting time. Make them do it. *Make them!*"

"Talking time's over," Art Bergstrom yelled, fed up both with the stalling tactics of the engineer and with the people. He craved action. In three long strides he was face-to-face with Russo. "Tell us where the dynamite is or I'll take your kneecap off."

"Now look here—" Amos spluttered, but Art shoved him out of his way.

Suddenly a voice rang out, loud enough to be heard over the crowd and the storm. "What the hell's going on here, Russo?" Sam demanded, ignoring the fact that Art was now pointing the rifle at him.

It was Bertha who answered, stomping through the mud to his side, giving a succinct explanation of why they were there and what they wanted.

Sam listened, nodded, then turned to Charlie. "Get the dynamite. We've got work to do."

For once the imperturbable engineer's calm was lost. His jaw dropped. "You can't mean it. Why, this business

331

about the Devil is just plain crazy. It's—"

The baying of the dandy dogs cut through the night. Eerie, unholy, terrifying.

The people drew together, looked about nervously as Dottie took a little bell out of her pocket and began to shake it.

"Don't argue, Charlie. Get enough dynamite for the mill and the boulder at the Devil's Dam." Sam turned his back on Art and the rifle, searched the area for Alison. She came immediately to his side when he held out his hand.

"You're going to destroy the mill?" she asked.

"It will probably go when the boulder does, but why take chances? We'll blow it first—"

"Sam, this is craziness," Charlie broke in. "If you destroy the boulder, then you're going to precipitate one hell of a landslide and most likely flood the notch. There'll be a lake here when you're done. A deep one." He looked about, lowered his voice. "What about all these people? At the very least, you're going to destroy their homes. Have you thought about that?"

"Yes." Sam squeezed Alison's hand. "I can't do anything about the houses, but I'm sending Russo and some men to blow a way out of here, right through the slide across the road. The people will have a way out."

Charlie stared at the muddy ground, then gazed off into the distance. "It'll be tricky," he warned.

"Work on it," Sam snapped, then took Alison's hand. "Come on, sweetheart, let's go."

Art didn't like being ignored; especially when he had the upper hand, the gun. He jerked his head in Alison's direction. "Not her. She stays here."

"She comes with me."

"No."

The two men glared at each other. The eerie howling filtered through the trees. Closer now. Art shoved the

332

rifle deep into Sam's side.

"She comes with me or I don't go."

"She stays here."

Impossible to tell if Art had a reason for his insistence or if he was merely flexing muscle because Sam patently ignored the threat of the gun. Alison broke free of Sam's grasp and quickly moved away. "It's all right, go with him. There are people here. I'll be safe."

Sam accepted her decision and immediately sought out Russo. "You're in charge here. You've got about an hour." He checked his watch. "Blow a hole through the slide and get everyone out. *Everyone,* do you understand?"

Russo understood that everyone meant Alison. "Yes."

"Good," Sam said, and with a last, long look at Alison, motioned to Charlie. Art and some of the men followed them and, after hesitating, Daniel Fortune did also. The others seemed only too anxious to get out with Russo.

Bertha touched Alison's hand. "You did the right thing."

Alison nodded, tears mixing with the rain on her face. She had a feeling that she would never see Sam again.

Less than ten minutes later the world jolted and the freight-train scream of moving earth again roared through the notch. Another jolt followed immediately. Sam and the men with him were thrown to the ground; shock waves sent trees crashing down. A man screamed, his agony so great it rose above the screeching of the tortured earth and the banshee howl of the wind.

Then, abruptly, an unnerving silence fell. Sam picked himself up and shouted to the prone figures still dazedly hugging the ground. "Who's hurt?"

"Over here," someone called.

When Sam got to the spot he found that Will Judson, one of the youngest of his crew, was pinned under a tree. The boy was unconscious. Sam found a faint, thready pulse.

In only a matter of moments Charlie had the men organized and working to lift the tree. Sam sent Jeff Whittaker running to the trailer for Henry Cutter. With a great deal of effort the tree finally was angled up and Will dragged clear. He looked dead; his pulse had weakened.

Art jammed the rifle into Sam's side while he knelt over the boy. "Let's go. We can't do anything for him."

Sam stiffened, then surged up, whirled, and grabbed the barrel, jerking the rifle out of Bergstrom's hands. With a roar of pure anger, he crashed his fist into Art's face. It made him feel better immediately. Art staggered backward, slammed into a tree, and slid down it into the mud.

Daniel Fortune picked up the rifle and handed it to Sam. "I'm sorry about Bergstrom."

Sam threw the rifle into the woods. As soon as Henry appeared he ran for the old mill. Time was an enemy.

36

The rush to leave started before Sam and the others disappeared from view; it escalated into a stampede after the two latest landslides. The mayor was in a near frenzy. Milly was at home. He had to get to her and get her out of Draconia, but J. Norbert was not about to abandon his civic duty. He struggled valiantly to bring some semblance of order to the scene, but most of the people ignored him.

Alison helped Bertha to her feet and tried to rake some of the viscous mud from her. The old lady, her eighty-three-year-old body swaying unsteadily, impatiently pushed her hands away. "A little of God's good dirt never hurt a body. Pick up my cane, there's a good girl." The wailing howl of the dandy dogs cut through the night, riding the voice of the wind. Their gazes locked when Alison handed Bertha the cane. Terror lurked deep in Bertha's faded eyes, but it wasn't for herself. "I tried . . ." Her voice trembled. "I fear I was too late."

Alison didn't know what to say, so she put her arm around Bertha's frail shoulders and gently squeezed.

Amos Hubbard rushed over and grabbed Bertha with the hand not clutching his rifle. "Come *on,* we gotta go!" He yanked her forward, then swiveled toward Alison. "I got room. You kin come with me."

But Alison was no longer there. She had seen Jeff Whittaker come running back, knew that something was very wrong, someone was badly injured and . . . *Not Sam! Please not Sam!* flashed through her mind.

It wasn't Sam, she quickly learned, and she wasn't the only one with a selfish thought. Dottie was hanging on Henry, begging him to leave with her, not to go to the aid of the wounded man. Conscious of Dottie's very real distress, Henry deftly disentangled himself and gently pushed her toward Alison.

"Come on, Dottie. Henry will be along in no time."

Dottie stared at Alison as if she had lost her mind. She rang the little bell vigorously. The wind greedily swallowed the tinkling musical voice. "There is no time," Dottie mumbled, and ran away before Alison could react.

"A silly superstition, that a bell will chase an evil spirit."

The voice was low and smooth and infinitely alluring. Alison's muscles clenched, then relaxed. Subconsciously she had been expecting this—him—all night. He stepped out of the gloom. The rain blew into her face, yet she could see his eyes glowed with fire, his lips curved in a lupine grin. He looked . . . *predatory.*

"No!" The wind swallowed her scream, then echoed it back to her in the keening howl of the pack. She had to run, try to . . .

He touched her, and as she had feared, she instantly was lost.

37

The two new landslides threw Tommy Russo into a panic. He forgot about everything except the need to get out of the notch before the whole thing was swallowed up by tons of dirt and rock. And him with it.

It didn't take long to gather the material and load the Jeep. Only when he was behind the wheel did he remember his promise to Sam. Swearing, he wiped the rain out of his eyes, smearing mud all over his face in the process. Alison was nowhere to be seen. He cursed and shouted at the others as they piled inside. "Where's the Fortune dame?"

The last man in slammed the door. "She left. Now let's get the hell out of here."

Russo was only too happy to comply.

"You sure you want to do this?"

Sam brushed by Charlie and put his hand on the plunger. "Take the men and get to the car. I'll be right behind you." His hand shook. One push and the old mill would be obliterated. Blown to hell.

"It's mine. My right." Daniel Fortune spoke quietly but

they had no trouble hearing him, or understanding him. Sam stepped back. Daniel didn't waste a second. With a bloodcurdling yell he pressed the plunger home. Then they all turned and ran for their lives.

38

Death was chilly and wet, puckering her skin, freezing fingers burrowing into the marrow of her bones. *I'm dead,* Alison thought, and shivered, then realized that she was lying on the cold ground, exposed to the fury of the storm. Not dead. Not yet. But . . .

An explosion sent a shock wave through the night. *Sam!* The old mill was gone and next was the Devil's Dam. She slowly rolled onto her hands and knees and struggled to her feet. She had to run . . . hide . . . She shuddered when she realized where she was, behind the cemetery . . .

Run!

Too late!

He materialized out of the mist that cloaked the base of the gate. Obscenely beautiful, evil . . . yet darkly intriguing. Even as she felt the tug on her senses, Alison resisted with every iota of her being.

Supremely confident, he advanced to within touching distance. Vulnerable, Alison refused to cower. "I'm defenseless. Is this what you want?" She laced her tone with scorn.

It amused him. He took another step, bringing him so close that he towered intimidatingly over her. "I want you." He scoured her with a hungry look.

She should be afraid—was afraid—but she also wanted answers. "Why? I wasn't privy to any deal. I have nothing to do with Dragon Meadow."

"I come when I am called."

"I didn't call you."

He laughed, the sound curling around her, smoky and intimate. It drew her into its vortex, dulling reality. "It matters not who called me. I take what I want, and I never refuse what is offered."

"I've offered you nothing," she managed to whisper.

"You will," he murmured silkily. "All I have to do is touch you. You won't resist."

It was true; it was her deepest fear. Alison struggled against his mesmerizing power, desperately trying to keep her mind clear. But the game was over . . . His breath fanned her cheek as his arms enfolded her. Her senses were inflamed by the onslaught of overpowering desire and she succumbed. Ecstasy swept reason and reality away. Dark desires, forbidden appetites, the promise of sweet fulfillment swept her to a painful arousal. She needed . . . *wanted* . . .

A tormented shout of rage ripped apart the fabric of fantasy. Adrian's arms were torn away. Alison's eyes snapped open and a cry of disbelief exploded from her throat as she looked down at herself, at her exposed breasts.

"Alison! Run! For the love of God, run!" Richard, his face swollen and discolored by bruises, grappled with Adrian nearby. Adrian laughed, the sound dark, soul-chilling. He tossed Richard aside as if he had no more substance than a puppet. Richard hit the hard ground with a jarring thud and lay still.

The wind keened through the graveyard trees, mating with Adrian's hideous laughter and with another sound, one that made Alison cringe in remembered fear. Like a swift-moving black river, the dandy dogs streamed out of the night, their target the motionless man.

"No! Stop them!" Half naked, trembling, hopelessly afraid, Alison only knew she couldn't allow Richard to be torn apart without trying . . . What?

Adrian raised his hand in silent command, granting the reprieve. He turned toward Alison, his eyes glittering with a dawning triumph.

She knew what he wanted, what she would have to give. She angled her chin upward. Her price was going to be steep.

Consciousness tugged at Richard, stealing him from oblivion. He lay with his face in the mud, listening, and knew one of the blackest moments of his life. That Alison was willing to fight for him . . .

Time.

Too late for him, but perhaps not for Alison; at least for her soul, if not her body. If only Sam would blow the Devil's Dam. Ignoring the dogs, although the ugly creatures eyed him rapaciously, he struggled to his feet. The manner of his death didn't matter.

Time. It was fast running out.

He looked around, but there was nothing he could use to delay the inevitable. The bargaining was almost over.

No weapon! Nothing! He trembled, defeated. A dog howled, inched closer to him. And then Richard realized he did have a weapon, his body, and if he used it well, he could take a long time dying. Time for Sam to blow the dam, for the waters to take Alison, to sweep her into a swift, pure death.

Poised for sacrifice, an alien sound immobilized him, a rasping screech that sliced through the air. Richard whirled around, stared . . . The gate was opening. A rush of hot air escaped and a thick mist swirled out, eddied up, twined sinuously around Alison's ankles, her knees . . . Something came through the mist, out of the gate. A hand touched her naked shoulder.

Aghast, Richard froze, his heart seizing in shock as Alison slowly swiveled around, saw what stood behind her, and silently crumpled to the ground. Then his eyes opened wide and his heart started to beat . . . too fast . . . too fast. He had to help her . . . save her. He took a step forward . . . another . . . another . . .

. . . and turned and fled.

He had recognized what came out of the gate.

39

The rain let up and the wind died as the men reached the parking lot of the Devil's Dam. Water flowed down from the mountain, over the saturated ground, spilling over the pavement. They quickly grabbed the equipment and ran for the trailhead. Sam hesitated, listening, at the edge of the woods.

"Hear something?" Charlie asked.

"It's what I don't hear. Russo should have blasted by now."

Daniel checked his watch. "We've made good time, perhaps . . ." His voice trailed off as a car careened into the lot at a dangerous speed. It took the final turn on two wheels, teetered at a steep angle, then tipped over onto its side. Daniel recognized it, and took off at a dead run.

It was Art Bergstrom who climbed up and wrenched open the door, reached in and pulled Richard out. Jerry's fists had done considerable damage; bruises stood out lividly on his face. His eyes were wild, as were the words that spilled from between his split and puffy lips.

Panic, overlaid with anger, speared through Sam. Russo had promised to see Alison to safety. With a great effort of will he damped down the anger. He would deal with it later. The panic wouldn't go away, so he ignored it. But when he looked at Richard he knew a new emotion, one that went beyond rage. He couldn't put a name to it, but for the first time in his life Sam felt the urge to kill. "You left her to die, you miserable maggot."

Trembling with shock, Richard pleaded for understanding. "Don't you see? She's doomed. She'll lose her immortal soul unless she dies before she makes the deal! You've got to destroy the dam. I only got away because that . . . that corpse—" Underneath the bruises his complexion turned a sickly green. He opened his arms in a supplicating gesture. "There's no time! *Don't you see?* Her only hope of salvation comes with a quick death."

Sam had to clench his hands into tight fists to keep them from going around Richard's neck. But his personal satisfaction would have to wait. "I'm going for her," he said to Charlie. "Give me half an hour, then blow the dam."

"But . . . the man's crazy. The things he said . . . it's impossible," Charlie sputtered.

"Wacko," Art sneered. "He's finally flipped." He shifted his feet uneasily. "Hey, how else could he see a dead man walking around? A ringer for his great-granddaddy, no less? Either he's crazy or he's stoned." He narrowed his gaze and stared at Richard appraisingly. "Maybe he and the old broad are on the same stuff. She's convinced the Devil's out to get her—and now this."

"Sam, maybe he's right. For all we know Alison might be safe with Russo and . . ." The look in Sam's eyes stopped Charlie cold.

"Half an hour, Charlie, whatever happens." Sam ran for the car. He would either be back with Alison or he would be dead.

Another explosion ripped through the notch just as Sam reached the cemetery. This time he didn't spare even a thought for Russo, for just as the reverberations died out he heard a scream and all he could think about was Alison—that she was still alive. He refused to think about what had made her scream.

The fastest way to the gate was through the cemetery.

He vaulted over the low stone wall and wove his way through the maze of tombstones to the back of the burying ground. Without the storm the night was still, eerily so. Something brushed by Sam . . . something made of mist and . . . A young woman . . . transparent . . . Others joined her. Four other women. Now they were five. Five women . . . made of mist and memory and . . .

Susannah. Patience. Rebecca. Dinah. Mary.

Sam knew them at once, said their names in his head, like a prayer. They were the victims. The righteous dead.

The gate loomed out of the dark. Sam saw the dandy dogs, bright-eyed, anxiously whining. He looked beyond them and his heart stopped. Alison . . . half naked . . . unconscious . . . held in the arms of . . .

Richard hadn't been hallucinating, had recognized his ancestor, although his body was grotesquely riddled by decay. Eleazar Fortune held out his arms to Sam, offering his precious burden.

Sam took Alison, brought her in close, held her tight to his chest. He looked squarely at the dead man, silently thanking him for the gift of her life.

Eleazar's ruined face took on the semblance of a smile. "She's mine!"

The words thundered through the air, instantly instilling a primitive fear deep within Sam. He tightened his hold possessively on Alison as Adrian Blaise stepped through the arch of the open gate. Gone was the urbane man, stripped of the polished veneer of civilization. The Beast had emerged; hate-filled, rapacious . . . supremely evil, exerting a mesmerizing power.

Although Sam willed himself to run for the sake of his life and his soul, he found it impossible to move. Adrian reached them in three long strides. Alison stirred to consciousness and gasped in fright at the surreal scene. Sam squeezed her close, trying to reassure her, wishing for her sake that she had stayed oblivious.

Adrian laughed and reached for her. He had almost touched her when a rotted arm knocked his hand away.

345

Adrian snarled his annoyance and whirled to dispose of the distraction. Eleazar grappled with him, momentarily breaking the Beast's concentration, his hold on Sam.

Sam didn't hesitate. He whirled and leaped for the stone wall, scrambling over it and only turning to look once he was on the other side. Adrian was all Beast now, growling his displeasure as a horde of the damned lumbered out of the gate and came to help one of their own. Instinctively Sam knew there were twenty-two of them; with Eleazar, twenty-three. Adrian struggled and bellowed his rage, but they held him fast. Reeking of corruption, they were impervious to his threats. Although confined, he signaled to the dandy dogs, sent the baying, yelping pack leaping through the air . . . over the wall.

The shades of the five women flowed in front of Sam, shielding him, letting him flee. The cemetery was thick with a churning haze. More shapes rose, took on substance, and interposed themselves between him and the pack of ravening animals.

Sam pushed Alison unceremoniously into the car and, once he was inside, made a squealing U-turn and sped toward the Devil's Dam. He had the accelerator jammed to the floor, only easing the speed to make the turn into the parking lot. At the trailhead he slammed the gearshift into park and ripped off his jacket, handing it to Alison. For a moment she just stared at it, then belatedly made a reflexive gesture to cover her breasts.

"Here, put it on." When she still didn't take it, he awkwardly stuffed her into it and then cupped her chin and angled her face up to look at him. "Did you make a deal with Adrian? Come to any understanding?" Alison gave a short bark of laughter, a harsh sound that made Sam's heart plunge into his stomach. "Did you?" he demanded.

"No! No, I didn't." She shuddered, then reached deep inside herself and once again tapped her reservoir of strength. She wanted Sam to understand. "I was trying to . . . to put an end to this insanity. There was no way out for me, so I thought that perhaps I could change things

346

for others—for you—but then that . . . he . . . it—"

"Eleazar. I'm sure it was Eleazar."

"Whoever. He interrupted."

"Thank God." Sam's heart resumed its rhythm. He helped Alison out of the car and stood listening for a second. The dandy dogs were close; he could hear them clearly. Without a backward glance he took Alison's hand and ran.

The woods were dripping and eerily silent. Neither spoke, needing their breath for the climb. They soon reached the basin, overflowing under the thundering cascade, swollen by the runoff from days of rain. From here the trail wound more steeply upward. Sam set a ruthless pace, sometimes dragging Alison, sometimes getting behind her and pushing.

A thin vapor filtered through the trees. Suddenly Alison stopped, the abrupt motion painfully jerking Sam's arm. He tugged at her, but she had her heels dug in. "What is it?"

"Lucy. I thought I saw Lucy!"

Sam had adjusted to the impossible. "You probably did. Come on, we're almost out of time."

At last they reached the point above the boulder where the men waited. The instant Charlie saw them he yelled to Daniel to set off the dynamite, but it was Richard who bore down on the plunger.

One second . . . two seconds . . . three . . . Alison glanced at Sam questioningly, became apprehensive when she saw the look on his face . . . five . . . ten . . .

Nothing happened.

Sam shouted in frustration, and when the echo of his shout died away the woods were again silent, although the stillness had a tenseness to it, a waiting . . .

"Goddamn fuse must have gotten wet. I'll go have a look," Charlie mumbled and disappeared in the direction of the gorge.

Moments passed and then laughter filled the silence. Dark . . . evil . . . Adrian Blaise walked out of the woods, a gleam of triumph lighting his lupine face. He was the Beast and he would not be denied. Immediately he sought Alison, but this time Sam could move. He got to her before Adrian and pushed her behind his back. "You've got to come through me!" he yelled. Like Jedediah with Susannah long ago, Sam didn't want to live without Alison. He would die protecting her.

Red flames leaped from deep in Adrian's dark eyes. A look of pleasure crossed his face, making Sam wonder if this wasn't what Adrian had wanted all along. All of a sudden a shrill howling rent the woods and the dandy dogs came running through the trees, jaws agape, salivating, intent on their helpless prey. They attacked the group at once, jumping up, their massive jaws clamping on flesh . . . gouging . . .

Adrian laughed and lunged for Sam.

The air filled with agonized screams, but all Sam could hear was Alison's, the sound tearing through him. But there was nothing he could do, for the fiend had him in his grip, and with his superior strength the contest was unequal. They grappled, a deadly dance of strange beauty, the fight taking them closer and closer to the edge of the gorge.

"No! No! You can't have him!" Alison cried, and launched herself at Adrian, pummeling his back with her fists and wildly kicking him wherever she could.

Taken by surprise, Adrian loosened his grip. Sam seized immediate advantage, swung around and pushed. Adrian was sent staggering back, snarling and hissing in incoherent rage.

Exhausted, Sam tried to gather his strength, knowing the reprieve was temporary. Dragging air deep into his lungs, he braced himself for the next assault, but Adrian took him out of the arena by going for Alison. Desperate, Sam shouted to her, but the warning came too late. As if in slow motion he saw the flame-eyed Beast reach out, hands now tipped by curving claws. Wide-eyed, Alison spun about and tried to escape. Adrian's arm snaked out, slashed deep.

"Nooooo!" The cry rose above the din of men and dogs. With determination gleaming from his eyes, Richard knocked Alison to one side and threw himself on Adrian. The Beast bucked wildly, swelled to a towering size. He threatened and cursed, then roared in fury, causing a hot wind to blow and the trees to quake. Richard hung on.

Charlie, just climbing over the edge, took one look and rolled out of the way.

Sam had just reached Alison, was pulling her away, when a shrill whistle pierced the air. The dandy dogs reacted as one; steel-trap jaws released sinew and bone, thickly muscled bodies pirouetted in air and tore toward the Beast.

No one moved, no one even breathed. Bloodied and battered, they watched the awesome attack. Fangs bared, dripping gore, the pack leaped straight for Richard.

Bruised face set stonily, Richard stood firm. His expression never wavered, not at the moment of impact, nor when the force pushed him back . . . over the edge . . . out into space. Perhaps, at the end, there was a hint of triumph, but it was hard to tell. Richard was gone, taking with him the Beast and the deadly dogs.

Alison fought down nausea at the sounds their bodies made, thudding against the rocks. Finally, the last frantic whine was abruptly cut off.

In the heavy silence that followed, she swayed weakly against Sam. "It's over," she whispered when he put his arm around her waist.

"Not quite yet. The rock has got to go."

"But . . . how?" Alison surveyed the group, torn, bleeding, not one without a wound.

"She's right, Sam. The fuse is wet, and we don't have another. There's no way to blow it." Charlie, his bleeding left arm held at an awkward angle, added his voice to Alison's.

"It's got to go," Sam reiterated stubbornly, "else the old pact remains. We've got to set aside the Devil's work.

We'll push, if nothing else."

"Let's go!"

The shout came from Art Bergstrom as he disappeared over the rim. He was followed by Daniel, then Charlie, then the others. Sam told Alison to stay where she was, and when she reluctantly agreed, only because loss of blood from her deep wound was making her feel faint, he, too, vanished over the edge. They made their careful way, inching down the gorge until they reached the rock. Using the last of their energy they pushed, shoved, and tried by every means they could to dislodge it.

"We need help," Charlie groaned. "We'll never do this on our own."

"There is no help," Daniel said.

Sam was staring up to the rim. "I wouldn't be too sure."

The others followed his gaze, up to where Alison stood . . . and to the twenty-three dead men who silently appeared by her side.

"Holy shit!" Charlie cried.

Led by Eleazar, the damned slipped over the edge and came to the rock where they pushed . . . and pushed . . .

A silent cry rippled through the trees. Alison quivered as an opaque whiteness flowed toward the gorge. Shadowy shapes coalesced, the righteous dead streamed to join the damned . . . and pushed . . .

The world shuddered and heaved as the mighty rock broke free. It began to tumble in a rending, screeching slide, taking dirt and rock and trees. Sam and the other men hastily scrambled out of the gorge as moisture-saturated soil gave way and slowly the mountain collapsed, burying Richard and Adrian and the dogs under tons of earth and rock.

At the top Sam grabbed Alison and pulled her up the trail, running for the crest and the ridge beyond where they could cross over to another mountain. The sun was rising, pinkening the air as a great cloud of dust arose from the wreckage of what had been Dragon Mountain.

When they were finally on safe ground, Alison turned into Sam's embrace. Over his shoulder she saw a hint of mist, a familiar figure, waving good-bye. "I love you," Alison whispered.

Lucy faded into the sunrise.

Sam smiled.

The Beginning . . . ?

From *The Albuquerque Journal,* Sunday, September 22:

DIABLO CANYON COMPLEX TO BE BUILT ON ROUTE 285

Ground was broken today for a new mall complex to be constructed north of Santa Fe off Route 285. The Diablo Canyon complex, named for the mysterious gate at the foot of Diablo Mountain, is on a 38-acre site and will contain condominium units, retail stores, restaurants, and a theater. A resort hotel is also planned.

The complex is being financed by the Mountain Venture group, which estimates completion in the spring of next year. The group developed the Dragon Meadow complex in Draconia, NH, but abandoned the project in June when a landslide deposited tons of earth and water into Draconia Notch. The area was deemed too unstable for development.

The principal, Adrian Blaise . . .